Breakfast at Stephanie's

Beth Thomas

Copyright © 2022 Beth Thomas
All rights reserved.
ISBN: **9798844583445**

DEDICATION

For Dad. Your turn!

CONTENTS

1	Married Man	Pg 1
2	Ex Man	Pg 26
3	Ladies Man	Pg 41
4	First Man	Pg 64
5	Nervous Man	Pg 89
6	Grumpy Man	Pg 119
7	Old Man	Pg 139
8	Young Man	Pg 160
9	Police Man	Pg 184
10	Surprise Man	Pg 205
11	Secret Man	Pg 223
12	Lonely Man	Pg 244
13	Superman	Pg 263
14	Old Man Again	Pg 281
15	Man's Man	Pg 305
16	Unmarried Man	Pg 327
17	Maybe Not-So-Old Man	Pg 348
18	Cave Man	Pg 365
19	Woman	Pg 382
20	Human	Pg 401

1
MARRIED MAN

Single at fifty. Balls.

I'm sitting in bed, it's nearly midnight, and my husband has just left me. The air in my ears is still vibrating with the sound of a door slamming. The water in the glass on his nightstand has just stopped rippling: it seems the T-Rex has gone. Ha. And soft strawberry cheesecake is silently sinking into the carpet. I should probably get up and sort it out, but for the moment I'm just going to sit.

I think marriages have a 'best before' date. I'd go as far as to say that there's probably a 'do not use after' date. And as we're now firmly in the 21st century, there should be a statement to that effect written into the vows. 'I promise to love, honour, cherish, in good times and in bad, in sickness and in health, until death do us part, and in any event not beyond the 25th anniversary, whichever is the sooner.' Twenty-five years validity on the marriage certificate, sorted.

Let's go back four hours – *four hours,* is that really all it takes to dissolve a life? – and find out what exactly happened here. Like, for example, how come I'm the one who's been left? How come it's his week to take the bins out? And why are there always *bristles in the en-suite sink?*

Four hours earlier. That's where it starts. Here I am, watching a dog with its head back, scratching its ear so vigorously and for such a long time that eventually it loses balance and falls over. It springs up and turns to look at the nasty lino, as if it was the floor's fault. I glance up to see if anyone else noticed, but there's a kerfuffle at the back of the room and everyone is staring over there. It seems Brian has 'disgraced himself', and someone is rushing over with a bottle of disinfectant and a small black plastic bag. I let out a long breath, and hope Brian is another dog and not someone's husband.

Whatever Brian has discarded on the floor by the tea cupboard was once, of course, an appealing bowl of beefy chunks that he valued and enjoyed. He devoured every last crumb, not wanting it ever to end, licking the bowl to savour any lingering hints of meaty deliciousness. Time passed; now it's a pile of shit.

Which is what got me thinking about my marriage.

My somewhat disenchanted expression is lit from above by unforgiving strip lights, which are casting a formless shadow around me on the nasty lino. My bum is going numb on a plastic chair, situated in a chilly church hall at eight-thirty on a Tuesday evening in November. This is not where I want to be. Half the occupants of the room are dogs. They're not who I want to be with. I have always had an image in my head of what my life would look like when I turned fifty and the kids were grown up, and this bleak scenario is definitely not it. I pictured myself standing on the deck of a giant white ship clothed in a tiny little strapless thing, laughing and drinking pretty cocktails while the sun turned the ocean flamingo pink. I saw hobbies and holidays and expensive handbags; jewellery and lunches and theatre trips; no mortgage, no money worries, and no more forty hour weeks. I look around me. My epiphany arrives at the same time as Brian's poo. I don't think this is coincidence.

I'm attending a dog-training class that Tim, my husband, booked us in for. 'Us' being me and the dog, Harry. Not me and Tim. He said Harry needed 'sorting out'. I'd had to agree, as I watched Harry lift his leg against the cuddle chair, but I wasn't sure why it was me that had to sort him.

'Because you're good at this stuff,' Tim had said, waving a casual hand before wandering away to do something else entirely.

At the front, Heidi is explaining in bright, spiky tones how we need to control our canines, while the owner of the offending mutt hastily enfolds the mess into a bag. Oh Christ, I forgot bags. I look down at Harry and send up a silent prayer – Oh Lord, in your mercy, please please please don't let Harry shit in here. Amen. Harry himself is completely oblivious to my assumed superiority, and is going to defecate wherever he likes. He generally does whatever he likes, toilet habits included. Right now, he's supposed to be sitting. All the other pooches are sitting, ears pricked, paying rapt attention to their owners, who are paying rapt attention to Heidi. Even the poo-producing pooch is the picture of propriety, pretending it never happened. Harry is resolutely standing. He is completely rapt in sniffing the end of my trainer.

'What breed is he?' the woman next to me says, looking at Harry.

'No idea,' I shrug. 'Lurcher mostly, I'd guess. With a bit of wolf hound, a dash of coyote and a touch of jackal thrown in. My husband brought him home from work last week.'

She lifts her eyebrows politely. 'Oh, really? Where does he work?'

'Korean restaurant.'

She blinks. Then frowns.

'Sorry, no, that was a bad joke. Terrible.' Note to self: grow up, eh? I smile. 'He doesn't work at the Korean. He's a surgoen.' She still looks like she might be going into shock, so I focus down at her furry pal. 'You have a sweet little dog.'

She beams. 'Ah, this is my little rescue, Daisy. She's been through some terrible times so far, but we're helping her live her best life now. Aren't we, Daisy-dog? Eh?' And she leans down and ruffles the dog's ears. The dog is, I note, wearing jewellery.

There's an expectant silence, and we both know it's there for me. I'm supposed to ask about the rescue at this point, but I'm disinclined to. Why does she have to refer to this dog as a 'rescue'? I know what she's done is a good thing. A kind and generous thing. She took on someone else's reject, an abandoned, homeless creature desperate for love, and gave it that love. Such an awesome thing to do. Except... Daisy-dog is not a rescue. She's a dog. The clue is in the name. 'Rescue' is what her owner did. So all this woman is doing now is drawing a little halo over her own head.

Eventually I manage an 'Aww,' then turn away to look at the microscopic dog on the other side. Tim will laugh, when I tell him. He will find that whole conversation hilarious. I experience a moment of excited anticipation of getting home, having a glass of wine together, and laughing in smug, self-congratulatory bliss that we feel no similar need to broadcast our good deeds because we know we are decent people and aren't shallow enough to crave approval.

The moment passes. Because that kind of intimacy doesn't really exist at home any more.

Heidi has instructed us to do something, and all the other dogs and owners are up now, walking nicely on the lead to the end of the room. Harry pushes between my chair and the next and goes off to sniff the floor in the corner. I let him. It's just easier.

Forty minutes later I'm home taking my coat off, and Harry pads, head down, into the living room. I've got a joke dog mask in my pocket that I bought at lunch time, so I unfold it and pull it over my head.

'*No*, Harry,' I hear through the open door, 'not on the furniture.'

I push the door and go in. Harry is circling on the armchair, then lies down with his back to the room. Tim doesn't even look up from his laptop screen. 'Did you teach him anything at all?'

'Oh come on, it was his first one, give him a chance.'

Tim shrugs, still not looking up, despite my muffled voice. 'This is exactly why I wanted him to go. To stop these bad habits.'

I plop down on the sofa next to him, and he looks at me at last. 'Oh for God's sake, Steph.'

'What?'

'You look ridiculous.'

'What do you mean?'

He goes wordlessly back to his laptop screen – looks like little Tim-Tim is thinking about getting a new car.

'Oh, you mean, this?' I point at my face. 'I was just trying to fit in. To make Harry less nervous.'

'Uh-huh.'

He used to laugh at my pranks. It's one of the things he's always loved about me. I pull the mask off and drop it on the sofa. 'If you want him trained so badly, why don't you take him?'

He doesn't answer.

'How can you know about his bad habits, anyway? We haven't even had him a week.'

'Aaron told me.'

'Right.' Aaron is Harry's previous owner, a colleague of Tim's. He's moving or something, can't take his dog with him. 'Did Aaron ever think about taking him to classes?'

'How should I know?'

'I dunno. He's told you about his bad habits, I thought he might have told you – '

'He didn't.'

'Right.'

Tim moves the mouse, then clicks.

'Why did we have to have him, anyway?'

He releases a long breath through his nose before answering. 'You know why, Steph. Aaron is moving in with his girlfriend and he can't take Harry because it's a rented place…'

'Yeah, I remember about that. What I meant was, why does it have to be us?'

He looks up at me at last, and shrugs. 'Why not us?'

'Oh, I don't know. Maybe because it's a tie, and expensive, and he needs a walk every day, and he can't be left on his own for long so someone has to pop back at lunch time – '

'These are all solvable, you know.'

' – and not to mention the fact that you didn't speak to me about it first. I mean, this is a big deal, Tim. You should have spoken to me about it before making the decision.'

He shrugs again. 'It was an emergency. You know that. Aaron was going to have him put down. I really didn't think you'd mind.'

'No, I don't mind. Of course I don't mind. If it saves him from being put down.'

'If I'd known you'd make such a fuss about it, I'd have let the damn dog be euthanised.'

'I'm not making a fuss. I just wish…'

'Yeah well. If wishes were money.'

I want to say more. It doesn't feel resolved. But it also feels like the end of the discussion. I clock the single glass of wine on the coffee table. 'Any wine for me?'

He glances at the wine, then goes back to his laptop. 'In the fridge.'

'Oh, OK.' I get up again and while I'm in the kitchen Tim calls out 'Top me up, would you?' so I bring the bottle back in. I top up both glasses and sit back down, picking up the telly remote. Then I remember I want to tell him about the super-woman at the class with the 'rescue' dog, and I want to laugh with him about how awful virtue-signalling is, and it might go on to a conversation about people using adjectives to refer to other belongings, like 'I'll give you a lift in the hybrid' or 'This is my Oxfam bargain,' and we'll laugh and drink wine and enjoy how much we both hate people.

But of course, our marriage isn't like that any more.

I look at him on the sofa next to me, his face lit white and pale by the laptop screen, and I try to remember the last time we shared a funny story. But that's OK, I can tell one now, and it will all be fine. I smile, formulating a way to begin.

'What?' he says, glancing at me.

'What, what?'

'You're gawping at me. Got something to say?'

'I'm not gawping.'

He shrugs. It's like a door slamming.

I point the remote at the telly and murmur 'Telly... *on!*', then wave it like a wand as I press the 'on' button. I've been doing this for years, decades, to make the kids laugh, and see no reason to stop just because they're not here. Tim used to smile too, but now I can practically hear his eyes rolling. He sighs, making sure it's loud enough for me to hear, closes his laptop and gets up; then reinstalls himself at the dining table, ten feet away. I don't look at him, and we both say nothing. My hand is still holding on the remote in my lap, so discreetly I increase the volume. Just a notch. Needling...*on.*

'I'm off to bed,' he says half an hour later, getting up. 'Can't concentrate with that thing blaring out.' He's got his laptop under his arm as he walks to the door. Silence is required for car browsing, apparently.

I glance at him as he goes past and make an exaggerated 'sorry' face, sticking out my bottom lip. 'Aw, if only the telly was portable somehow. Then I could have picked it up and left you in peace.'

'What?'

'I'm just saying, the telly is kind of stuck here, isn't it? In this room. Making noise.'

He frowns at me as if I'm making clucking noises instead of words. 'Night.'

I turn back to the film. Standard alien invasion, I think. I'm not really watching it, if I'm honest. But as soon as he moved to the dining table, I had to stay there until everyone was dead. I'm not being difficult; just sticking up for myself. Once he's upstairs, I turn it off and clear up the glasses and wine bottle. There's an empty Pringles tube on the coffee table too, along with some crumbs, so I scoop it all up and go to the kitchen. I stand by the sink for a few seconds and stare into the dark garden. Well, I stare in the direction of where I know the garden to be, but all I can see is my own face staring back at me in the black glass. I look tense, so I turn my mouth into a smile, and try to hold it there until I reach the bedroom.

Tim's in bed, the laptop open in front of him. I note he's brought a slice of cheesecake up for himself and it's sitting on the bed with a fork. Nothing on my side, of course. He glances up as I come in, then goes back to his laptop.

'Who were you expecting to appear?' I ask him.

'Eh?'

'Nothing.'

I do the night time routine – teeth, toilet, make up wipe – then back to the bedroom for the night cream. My mouth has gone all tight again, so I smooth it out with Nivea into another smile. Even I'm not convinced by it, but I leave it there anyway. At the very least it's stopping my top lip from getting wrinkled, and if I'm lucky it might manage to drag an endorphin or two out of me somewhere.

I pull back the duvet and get into bed, noting Tim grabbing the sides of the laptop as I do. I ignore it.

'At the dog class,' I start, but it feels weird. He doesn't alter in any way, doesn't even acknowledge that I've spoken. 'There was this woman.' At what point in my marriage did telling my husband a story about my day become so difficult? 'Tim?'

He grunts, 'Mm,' without moving. He's reading something. The cheesecake has reduced by one mouthful.

'I was just saying. There was a woman at the dog thingy.'

'Yeah?'

At least he's trying to sound interested. Even though so far my story isn't even slightly interesting. 'Yeah. She introduced her dog as her "rescue"…'

'Did she?'

'Yes. She did. And it kind of made me realise that…'

He closes his laptop and puts it on the night stand. 'I'm knackered, Steph. Can we chat tomorrow?' He shuffles himself down the bed, then turns back to rearrange his pillow. I watch the forgotten cheesecake wobble on its plate between us.

'Oh. Well it was only a quick thing…'

'Seriously. I need sleep. You can tell me tomorrow.' And he flops back onto the pillow and turns off the light.

'I was just going to point out,' I hear my voice say into the darkness, 'how we never tell each other funny stories any more.'

There's an irritated silence, then the light goes back on. 'Seriously?' he says, looking at me with disbelief in his eyebrows. 'You want to talk about this now? At half past eleven?'

I shake my head. I don't. I don't want to talk about it at all. Because talking about it will conjure it into existence, into a real problem that needs discussing and resolving, and if we don't talk about it we can just carry on as we are. 'No, no, forget it.'

He pulls himself up into a seated position and leans back on the headboard. 'No, come on, out with it. You've clearly got something on your mind, and I'm obviously not going to get any sleep until you've said it.'

I flinch. This is not what I want. Not at all. I just wanted… I want to…

'Oh Christ,' he says now. 'Are you crying?'
'No...'
'What the hell has got into you all of a sudden?'

I turn and look at my husband of twenty-four years, sitting there next to me in our marital bed, frowning, picking up his phone to read an email or Facebook rather than talk to me about how I'm suddenly feeling. Except as I think about it I know for sure that it isn't sudden. I've been feeling like this for weeks. Months. Possibly even years.

'When did we stop talking to each other?' I ask him, knowing *exactly* what he will say.

'We're talking now, aren't we?'

'I knew you would say that.'

'Bloody hell...'

I shake my head again. 'Oh my God. Tim, this is me, your wife of twenty-four years, telling you that I'm concerned that we're not communicating any more. That we haven't been for some months. And your reaction is to get irritated with me?'

He closes his eyes and inhales slowly through his nose. Then exhales, equally slowly. As he lets out this calming breath, he opens his eyes again and looks at me, infuriatingly cool. 'What *do* you want me to do, then?' He lifts his hands, palm up. 'Shall we have a massive deep conversation now, all about our *feelings* and our *hopes* for the future? Shall we blabber on until four a.m. and then end up with only three hours' sleep before we have to get up again? And then have a completely shitty day because we'll be crabby and headachey from lack of sleep?'

We lock eyes and stare at each other, his face a picture of annoyance, as if he's dealing with – well, with Harry.

'No. That's definitely not what I want.'

'At least we can be grateful for that.'

'What I want is a trial separation.'

Isn't it funny how one small thing can crystallise a situation, just like that? No, funny isn't really the right word. Shocking would be more appropriate. Surprising, maybe. Heart-breaking, definitely. It wasn't the woman with the rescue dog that made me say it. It was everything else.

'What?' Tim says, jutting his head forward at me. 'Seriously? Because I don't want to hear your hilarious little story in the middle of the night? Because I'm tired and have a huge horrible clinical meeting tomorrow and need to sleep? And suddenly you want a divorce? Jesus H fucking Christ on a pink bike and ribbons.'

'No, no, it's not that, it's…'

'Oh forget it,' he says, pulling clothes on. I watch him in panic. This is moving terrifyingly fast.

'No, Tim, I'm sorry, I didn't mean it…'

'I'll go to Howard's,' he says. 'Do what you want.'

The front door slams, there's the sound of the car, and fifteen minutes after going to bed, I'm separated.

The house is silent. I sit there, unmoving, wondering what the hell just happened to my life. Then Harry pads in and urinates against the dresser.

Tim Gibson and I met at a dance at the hospital where we were both working. It was a classic 20th century love story: married man meets girl in short skirt. I have had to persuade myself repeatedly over the following twenty-six years that I don't need to feel guilty, and I've just about managed it. I was very young, and single, and I had bloody good legs. I wanted to show them off, and why shouldn't I? Tim was thirty-one, a surgeon, which made him seem like a proper grown-up man, and very desirable. I can still remember the first time I watched him perform an appendectomy. His fingers were light and dextrous, more magical than any sleight of hand I'd seen. The fact that this proper grown-up, skilled, married man was showing interest in a little girl like me was spell-binding, so really I can't be blamed for what happened. I was pretty much hypnotised by the situation. He's the one who was married, he's the one who was supposedly more mature, he's the one who should feel guilty. I think his guilt lasted about twenty minutes.

'Married men never leave their wives,' WomanKind magazine told me sternly. 'End it, you're messing with more than one life here.' I didn't care, I was in love by then. And besides, I told myself, Tim was different. I wasn't just a bit on the side – he really loved me.

'Maybe you should get pregnant?' my colleague Lynne suggested. 'Then you'll always have him.'

'Getting pregnant to trap your guy will only end in heartbreak,' WomanKind magazine warned. 'DON'T DO IT.'

Don't worry, I didn't. It happened by accident. And remember, Tim was as much to blame for that as I was. So he left Karen and little Ben and we got a flat together.

'Good thing Ben's only two, actually,' Lynne said. 'He'll never remember any different.'

Tim was still married to Karen when the baby was born, but I was already using my mother's maiden name of Harkness by then, and was resolved to keep it, so it didn't matter. We made sure we were married before Amy came along though, more for my parents' sake than anything. Josh was the most adorable little page boy you'd ever seen, until he became possessed by an evil spirit in the evening when he got tired, and ripped the hired trousers.

'If he does it *with* you, he'll do it *to* you,' WomanKind shouted, in a last desperate bid to save face. I rolled my eyes and ignored it. It had lost all credibility at this point and wasn't to be trusted. And I can honestly say, twenty-four years later, there has never been any hint of even a possibility of Tim cheating on me.

'He's cheating on you,' my best and oldest friend Zoe texts me the following morning, after I've filled her in quickly on last night's events. Zoe and I met when I sat on her vol-au-vents at a university party. She was studying to be a lawyer, I was becoming a doctor, and we argued about which was more difficult and more valid. She won, of course. Lawyer, see.

I sit down heavily on the bed in my pants, staring at her message on my phone. Why the hell would she say that? Does she know something? Has she seen something? She sounds so certain, she must have some kind of proof. An ice-cold hard thing plunges through me: Oh my God, did he cheat with *her?* A grey bubble appears with the three dots in it, letting me know she's typing something, and my nerves start to shred themselves as I stare at that bubble. She's explaining. She's trying to come clean, apologise, tell me she never meant to hurt me. The bubble disappears, then reappears, and I imagine the struggle she is going through. She was drunk, it was a one-time-only thing, a huge mistake, she wishes she could turn back time and not do it, but now all she can do is ask for my forgiveness and hope that we can –

'Dramatic behaviour for an innocent man,' is what arrives.

Oh.

I'll be honest, she's right. Tim disappeared from the house at breakneck speed last night, not even giving me enough time to say, 'Get out.' He didn't argue, he didn't get upset – well, not in a good way. He simply left. And fast. What does that say about him? Did I just give him the excuse he needed to leave, without feeling any resultant guilt?

'No he isn't,' I eventually reply, and pull on my black trousers. Not what I had planned to wear today, but I don't have time for tights now. 'It was me who suggested separating remember.'

'True. I'm sure you'll sort it out. Xx'

I'm sure of that too, but Zoe being sure makes me irrationally annoyed. 'I don't know, we might not.'

'You will, trust me. Anyway can't really chat now. They've screwed up our reservation on the zip wire and we're going at ten instead of two.'

'Oh, no,' I reply, putting the kettle on. I never know whether what she's telling me is genuinely what she's doing, or if it's all been a giant forty-year-long joke. 'That's inconvenient.'

'It means we'll be having lunch at 2 instead of 1.'

I stare at the phone but can't work out what to say, so I leave it until I arrive at work, then send her a bland reply in the car park. After I've sent it, I sit in the car a bit longer, focusing on going through the door into the building with a failed marriage. I had to go in with a black eye once, and that was bad enough. Everyone nodding knowingly, touching my arm, reassuring me they were always there for me if I wanted to talk. Even the patients. I'd nodded, thanked them, reassured them right back that if I ever felt the need to offload about tins of potatoes falling from cupboards, they'd be the first to know.

The radio's on at reception when I finally do go in, and I hear it being hastily silenced. I wave a hand. 'It's all right Niamh, you can leave it on.'

Niamh looks from me to Steve and back. 'Oh, thanks Stephanie.' The music starts up again.

I pause at reception as I always do. 'Anyone else here yet?' I know what the answer will be.

Niamh shakes her head. 'You're first.'

Standard. I only work Mondays, Wednesdays and Fridays now, so on those days Ravi and Nina, the other two doctors who work here, generally walk in at one minute to nine, smiling beatifically at all the patients in the waiting room, as if everyone can relax now that they've arrived. By that time, of course, I am usually already in my consulting room, seeing my first patient. I nod. 'How's it looking today?' I ask Niamh. We're not open for business for thirty-five more minutes, but pinched faces are already pressing against the windows.

Niamh looks at the appointments screen. 'Pre-booked til about two. Mrs. Taylor is in at ten-fifteen. Nigel will probably drop by – not seen him this week yet. The rest are c's and c's I think.' C's and c's are coughs and colds – not literally, but it's code for standard minor ailments.

'OK.' I glance at the small battery operated radio next to the printer behind the desk. 'That thing sounds crappy. Why don't you get a decent one? Let me know how much and I'll reimburse you. It kind of cheers it up in here a bit, doesn't it?' I give her a smile and walk away into my consulting room, feeling their astonished expressions rippling through the air behind me. I just manage to stop myself performing a flourish and bow.

I didn't want to be a doctor growing up. I actually planned to be a magician from the age of seven, when my grandparents, the Harknesses, gave me a small children's magic set for Christmas. I was going to be Doctor Darkness – a play on Harkness – and had already looked into changing my name by deed poll as soon as I was old enough. It wasn't even expensive, and my real name – Stephanie Thripp – did not lend itself to breathtaking magical performances too well. That magic set changed my life. There was a plastic wand, which collapsed into two halves held together by string; three red plastic balls, two of which came apart smoothly into hemispheres; some double sided playing cards; some metal rings; a hat; a pair of white gloves; a small black and red nylon cape that was probably a fire hazard; and an instruction book. I was mesmerised. I had no interest in horse-riding or ballet or piano lessons or gymnastics; but that flowery cotton drawstring bag that Mum made to hold my kit filled every moment of my life, asleep and awake. The glamour of standing in front of a rapt audience, all focussed intently on me, while I made things move, change or disappear; watching the wonder on their faces at this seemingly impossible feat, as they turned to each other with wide, impressed eyes and whispered 'Wow!' and 'How did she…?' (And in the case of my sour-faced uncle Derek, 'Up her sleeve, you can see it.') It was like a drug, and I was instantly hooked. I practised and practised in every spare moment I had. I spent all my money on bigger, better kits, card decks, props, hats, cages and boxes. A better wand, made of porcelain, or rhino bone or something. A sleeker cape with red lining. A gorgeous velvet hat. A black waistcoat with red flowers on it. By the time I was fifteen, my kit was worth almost £75. Which was lot in the early 80's.

After wowing a crowd of slumped, drowsy ancients at Granny and Grandad Harkness's fortieth wedding anniversary party, I knew without a single doubt that this was what I would do. What I was born to do. Somehow, for some reason, I had been given a gift, and I owed it to myself and the world to exploit it. I was going to travel the planet performing stunning magical illusions, amazing audiences near and far, be written about, heralded, lauded and applauded. I was going to be the most successful magician the world had ever seen. So the dirty deed poll was done. Dirt cheap.

'Get your O levels first, love,' Mum said, spooning out potatoes. 'Give yourself something to fall back on.'

So I did. And with the change of one letter, I became Doctor Harkness, instead of Doctor Darkness. Which I know seems ridiculous because being a doctor is a vocation, right? You have to have really wanted to do it, ever since some aged relative gave you that little medical kit, and you first pressed your red plastic stethoscope onto Mummy's chest and heard that hypnotic sound. You have to be focused from that moment on – ready for the years of difficult and dedicated study, armed with determination, commitment, and a very strong stomach. But I wasn't. For me, it was more like completing levels in a game without knowing what the final goal was. I managed to get all A grades in my science 'O' levels, then all As at 'A' level too, and one day after that I looked down and found myself up to the knuckle in someone's uterus. I still think about that glamorous little drawstring bag, with the cups and the cards and the smooth, heavy wand. Mostly when a patient's tugging at a sock after graphically describing their foot fungus.

Mrs. Taylor is a regular. Her husband is dying, very slowly, and she comes in every week under some pretext to talk about him. Well, more about his terrible, slow progress, really. I need at least twenty minutes for her. Nigel is a homeless alcoholic who comes in most days at roughly the same time for a cup of tea. I know I shouldn't waste appointment time chatting to him, but I did it once, when I first started working here, and now I can't say no. I don't want to say no. But it does lengthen my day rather significantly.

I sit down at my desk and turn on my computer, catching sight of my face in the blank screen before it loads. The kids call this my 'resting bitch face', or RBF, which I think is very unfair. The fact that everything sags south when none of the muscles in my face are employed hardly makes me a bitch. I've looked at the effect closely in the mirror a few times (a day) since they said it and I'll admit, it does make me look quite pissed off. What I try to do when I remember is make the corners of my mouth turn up, just a tiny bit, when I'm not talking. It's not a smile; it's more a show of defiance. I'm hoping the exercise to my face will tighten it all up again in time. 'It takes more muscles to frown than it does to smile,' my mum used to say. I always thought that, by that argument, frowning is better for you.

Before I open my emails, I pull my mobile phone out of my handbag and set a reminder to go home at lunch time. Poor Harry will need to go out for a sniff, even if he's already peed on the sofa by then. Also I have no idea what other bad habits he might have. Urine will wash off, but I'm not sure I'll cope if he opens a brothel. I lay the phone down on my desk and stare at it. It does nothing. I pick it up again and click on the most recent conversation with Tim – 'Get dog food' 'Yep' That was four days ago, when we were still madly in love. Ha. Still the phone does nothing. I stare at it for a few more seconds, then press the sleep button and lay it back down again. I have no idea what to say to him anyway.

Nine hours later I'm pulling up outside my home for the second time today, only now, unlike at lunch time, it's dark. The absence of light on the street shows me very clearly what wasn't significant earlier: the curtains are still open, and the windows are black. The house is in darkness. Tim hasn't come back, then. He hasn't contacted me all day either, which I think is pretty harsh. All right, I also haven't contacted him, but he's the one who walked out. Yes, all right, he walked out after I said I wanted to separate, but I said 'trial separation' and surely it's down to him to get in touch? I mean, I still live here, he knows where to find me. I have no idea where he is. Yes, all right, he's probably at Howard's. But surely at the very least he'll want to arrange when he can collect some of his things?

When I get inside I realise why he hasn't. The hallway cupboard is mournfully empty, minus his coats and shoes, and a cursory inspection of the rest of the house tells me most of his other belongings are gone, too. At some point after I came back at lunch time, my husband popped by and cleared himself out. Except he's thoughtfully left a few beard bristles in the sink for me, as a kind of Harry-style memento of himself.

I stand in the living room and stare at the empty book and DVD shelves. He's even taken the Die Hard box set, which was a present from our daughter Amy for our 20th wedding anniversary. My eyes sweep the room, noting what he's considered to be his and worthy of taking, and what he hasn't. Absent photos, prints, ornaments and lamps leave blank incongruous spots on shelves and walls, like scars after a fight. My eyes land on the hideous red plaster bull his mother brought back from Spain 10 years ago, standing next to the fireplace because it's too large to go on a shelf. I've hated that malformed atrocity for a decade, like a malevolent presence squatting in our home, and Tim knew it; but he insisted we display it anyway, so as not to hurt his mum's feelings.

'Didn't fancy taking this with you then, bastard?' I ask the room, bending to heave the monster off the floor. 'You fucking *dick*!' I shout the final word and simultaneously lob the thing down onto the floor as hard as I can. It lands on the carpet with a dull thud.

In the kitchen, I discover – in the worst way – that he's left Harry, too.

2
EX-MAN

Of course, I'm the one who has to break it to Amy and Josh. Apparently that's fair, because it's all my fault.

'You're the one who wanted a separation,' Tim snaps at me nastily, over a delicious Christmas spiced latte in Costa the following Saturday. 'Walking in a Winter Wonderland' is tinkling gently over tinsel-clad speakers, and the café is stuffed with rosy-cheeked people and their giant carrier bags. 'It wasn't my fucking idea.'

'Just because I'm the one who called it, doesn't make the whole thing my fault.'

He juts his head forward and I'm reminded randomly of those two buzzards from the old Disney Jungle Book film. His bald head reflects the overhead fairy lights like a disco ball. 'Er, yeah, it does,' he says, taking a large bite of his chocolate tiffin. A crumb of chocolate gets stuck in the corner of his mouth and melts there.

'Us separating is only the point at which we acknowledge the relationship is over,' I say calmly, staring at the brown shiny blob. It calls to mind Harry's little gift on the kitchen floor on Wednesday. 'The relationship being over is down to both of us.' I think this is quite big of me, considering it's actually all his fault.

He shakes his head dismissively. 'Nuh-uh. The separation was your idea. Ergo, you have to tell them.'

There's little point arguing. I have no desire to stay here and talk to the blob any longer than I absolutely have to. Or the melted chocolate on his lip. Ha. I release a breath and agree, just so we can move on to the next subject. The house.

'You either have to buy me out, or we sell up and split the equity,' he says now.

'Why can't you buy me out?'

He juts again. The brown blob stretches. 'Er, duh, because you're living there.'

'You can live there.'

'I've already moved out.'

'You can move back in. I'm quite happy to find somewhere else.'

He stares at me malevolently for a moment, then looks away. 'I... I've already found somewhere else.'

I blink. 'Fuck me, Tim, that was quick!' I sit back in my chair. 'What, did you already have your name down on a place when I sprang this surprise separation on you on Tuesday?'

He's still not looking at me, but instead seems suddenly intensely interested in the abstract bronze wall art above us. Finally he dabs the brown blob away and it becomes a smear on the napkin, another casualty of our collapsing marriage. Then he sips his latte.

'Oh my God,' I say, leaning forward slowly. 'You did.'

'No I didn't, of course I didn't.' He wipes his fingers on the napkin, balls it up and dumps it on the table. 'It's not like that.'

I meet his eyes and don't look away, refusing to let him off. 'Then what is it like?'

I almost don't need to hear it. I know what's coming before he starts speaking, because I've known what was coming for twenty-six years. WomanKind tried to warn me, but I didn't listen. 'If he does it *with* you, he'll do it *to* you,' they said, but I was twenty-four and I knew better. I owe them a big apology now, but sadly they went under fifteen years ago.

'She's thirty-two, works in my office. Fiona Chapman. It started at the Christmas party, and –'

'Christmas!' I explode, and a few heads turn our way.

'Creeps up, doesn't it?' someone says, walking past.

'Are you saying this has been going on for nearly a *year*?'

Tim looks down. I think in shame, but actually he's brushing crumbs off his chinos. Then he looks up and meets my eyes. 'Nearly two years, actually.'

I narrow my eyes. 'You snake,' I whisper, as menacingly as I can manage while holding a blueberry muffin. I stand up. 'You know what,' I tell him, picking up my coat, 'I *will* tell the kids what's happened here. That way at least they'll get the truth.'

They won't. Of course they won't. I'm their mum and it's my job to protect them, no matter what the cost to me. So I will protect them from as much evil in the world as I possibly can, including finding out what a prick their dad is. But he doesn't know that.

And of course, if they should find out on their own, that's a different matter entirely.

I get home with an hour to spare before the estate agent is coming – I always planned to sell, regardless of what Tim was likely to say – so I decide to take Harry out for a walk. He's lying in his favourite spot in the armchair, his back to the room, curled into a circle. He has one paw over his nose.

'Come on then, boy,' I say to him from the living room doorway. 'Walkies.' He doesn't stir. 'Harry, come on.' His ears move a little when he hears his name. I walk over to him and crouch down by the chair. 'Come on, Harry,' I say, scratching his head. 'I know it's totally shit being rejected by someone you thought loved and wanted you, but in the end you are better off without him.' At the sound of my voice, he raises his head slowly and looks round at me. 'There's a good boy,' I tell him, using an excited tone to gear him up a bit. 'Come on, Aitch, let's go out, eh? Let's show this bloody world how well we can do on our own?' Harry doesn't move, then huffs and lays his head back down on his paws. He looks so unbelievably sad, and for some reason it brings tears to my eyes. 'Oh Harry,' I say, and lean over him, placing my face on his warm body and my arms across his back. 'I won't let you down, boy. I promise. We can look after each other now. This is our home and neither of us is going anywhere.'

Ninety minutes later, the house is up for sale.

I mean, obviously I'll take Harry with me. But as the agent said, it does restrict the sort of property I can buy.

'Flats are out,' she says matter-of-factly, her heavy tan foundation moving with the words. 'You'll be wanting somewhere with a reasonably sized garden, I imagine?'

I nod. Flats were out anyway. 'Three bedrooms, a garden, and a garage.'

She raises her laser-thin eyebrows. '*Three* bedrooms?' She makes a big show of looking around for the other two people. I catch a strong whiff of Elnett. 'A family, is it then?'

'Nope. Just little old me.'

She nods slowly, not in the traditional sense, but rather by moving her entire head and neck forward together. I'm fascinated by how her hair defies the laws of physics and doesn't react to the forward motion. 'I see. You know, when it's just us on our own, we really will save a lot of money by sticking to what we actually need. The difference between a two bed and a three is quite a significant amount, you know.'

'Understood. Because I'm not a moron.'

'Pardon?'

'I said, do you need to put anything more on? The advert?'

Luckily it has sailed over her perfectly coiffed and unbending hair. 'No, no, thank you. I think we've got everything we need.'

'Great.' I swing my arms, one of those meaningless gestures you do when you're waiting for the estate agent to leave, and wonder what Isaac Newton would have made of hairspray.

'OK, then. Well let me see what we've got on our books, and I'll get back to you.' She glances around her hungrily, like Elizabeth Bennett looking around Pemberley. It's cheesily exaggerated and it grates. 'You have a truly lovely home here, Stephanie,' she says, carelessly using my first name, which also grates. 'It'll be sold in no time, don't worry about that.'

'I'm not worried.'

'Absolutely. This place will be snapped up in no time.' She nods to herself. 'We have buyers waiting.'

She's over-egging, evidently reciting some spiel she has to get through. They're offering a full half a percent less commission on sale than the next place, so I calculate it's worth these minor irritations to stick with them.

'OK, great, thanks Angela.'

She reacts to the sound of her own name like Harry, jerking with pleasure. 'Okey dokey then Stephanie.' We're best mates now, apparently. 'We'll be in touch in no time with a queue of potential buyers. And in the meantime,' she says, and waves a Mary Poppins hand around, 'the less clutter, the better. OK?'

Bloody cheek. 'Yes, thank you Angela.'

By five o'clock it's dark, and the temptation to curl up on the sofa with a hot chocolate and a Christmas film is overwhelming. I put the kettle on and go into the living room while I wait for it to boil.

'Hey Harry.' I pat him gently as I walk past, but there's no reaction. 'Fancy watching a film with me? How about *Elf*?' I pick up the remote – telly *on* – and scroll through Netflix, but before I've finished searching I hear my phone buzzing on the kitchen table. Harry's ear twitches slightly, so I know he's still alive. 'Back in a mo,' I tell him. Then shake my head at myself.

It's a text from Josh. 'Wondering what your plans are for Xmas? Xxx'

My heart expands a bit. Josh is just about the most fantastic son anyone could wish for. A darling boy, always thinking about me, checking I'm ok, and now making sure I won't be spending Christmas all on my –

Oh shit. I close my eyes.

He's wondering what my *and Tim's* plans are for Xmas. Of course he is. I click reply and type 'Shagging 32-year-old Fiona Chapman under the Xmas tree will be on the cards for one of us.' Then I delete it and instead write, 'Not sure yet. Bit of upheaval here, lots to tell you. Can you come for dinner tomorrow? Xxx'

'Upheaval?' he replies. Not helpful.

'Yes. Dinner tomorrow? I'll explain then.'

'K. I'll check with Chloe but prob not a prob. Love you. Xxx'

While my phone is in my hand, I text Amy too, inviting her for dinner ostensibly to discuss Christmas. Amy's always been an anxious child, and I know she won't cope with this very well. My stomach starts churning as soon as I've done it.

I spend the rest of the day and most of the night worrying, and reminding myself that there's nothing to worry about. They're both adults, they had a fun childhood with married parents, they've both moved out and have their own lives, this need not affect them too much. Eventually I realise that the only way I'm going to get any sleep is if I write down the things going up and down on the carousel horses in my head, so at 2:34 a.m. I sit up and put the light on.

Maybe the best way to approach it, to upset Amy as little as possible, is to play it down. She will probably take her cue from my reaction, so I need to be calm, nonchalant and unruffled. Meh, I'm getting a divorce, whatever, anyone for seconds? In the end, it turns into a press release, mostly about love – or the lack of it, and goes something like this:

    I love them, they love me.

    Their dad loves them, they love their dad.

    Their dad no longer loves me. I want to eviscerate their dad with a spade.

It makes me feel much more on top of things. When they arrive we'll have a nice meal – a take-away, my treat, and I can order it in advance so it arrives exactly when they do – then we'll chat about what's been happening since we've last seen each other. Josh can fill me in on his work at the pharmaceutical company; Amy can tell me about how her counselling course is going; and there will be anecdotes about colleagues and mishaps. They'll be interested to see Harry and I will have them laughing by telling them about his endless gifts to me, and we will all say how happy we are that he's not dead, in spite of that. Eventually someone – probably Josh – will say, 'So, about Christmas…' and I'll say, 'Ah, yes, about that. Well, no biggie, but the thing is…' and then they will fall silent and serious and I will read out my pre-prepared statement, and they will nod and hug me and we might all have a bit of a cry and then we'll talk about how it will be perfectly fine going forward, while we do the washing up together. It's a flawless and comforting plan.

'Where's Dad?' Josh asks, as soon as he comes through the front door.

Crapshit buggerarse.

'Oh, look, there's Harry, you haven't met him yet have you,' I say desperately, pointing to the large brown dog on the arm chair. 'He's ever so sad, I think that's why he keeps leaving sh– '

'Mum.' Josh faces me. 'Has Dad moved out?'

My son is infuriatingly perceptive. I sigh, but don't answer. Amy arrives seconds later in synch with the Chinese food; eyes the warm, white carrier bag emitting aromatic steam and says, 'What's happened?'

'Dad's moved out,' Josh says obligingly, then we all sit in silence around a tray with the food cartons on it, picking at the odd bit of chicken.

'It won't affect you much – '

'*How* will it not affect us, Mum?' Amy practically shouts. 'Our parents are getting divorced. It's a fucking HUGE thing. Jesus Christ!'

'Amy,' Josh warns.

'Oh you can shut up too,' she bites. 'This actually *won't* affect you because we all know you're a robot and literally don't feel human emotions.' She stands up. 'This is bollocks.' Then she marches to the patio doors, yanks one open and stomps outside into the garden.

I stand up to go after her, but then decide that in fact I don't want to. It's freezing cold out there, and dark, and probably raining. She'll realise that in a minute.

'What happened?' Josh says.

I sit back down. 'Nothing really. We just kind of had an epiphany that we'd... fallen out of love with each other.'

He considers that a moment. 'Did this epiphany have anything to do with one of his colleagues?' he asks, startling me speechless. 'Come on Mum, I'm not an idiot. Or a child. I know what goes on.'

I swallow and blink a few times. 'What goes on? What do you mean, what goes on? You're making it sound like... I don't know. Like this, stuff, bad stuff, things, have been "going on". But they haven't. I mean...' I pause. '*Have* they?'

I give him 0.007 seconds to answer, then shake my head. 'Of course they haven't. Jesus, Josh, why would you let me think..? Why would you say..? I mean, it wouldn't...it doesn't... No, no. Ha ha. It's almost laughable.' I almost laugh.

Josh leans forward. 'Mum, I've known for a while. I was just hoping you wouldn't ever have to.'

There's a sudden stillness in the room. It just hangs there, like a huge glass bauble, while Josh and I look at each other.

'Oh shit,' Josh says, smashing it. 'You didn't know.' He closes his eyes and flings his head back.

'No, no, Josh, it's fine, I knew. It's fine.'

'Fine? It's *fine*? How can you say that? It most definitely is not fine, Mum.'

I shake my head. 'No, no, I didn't mean that. I mean, it's not fine. But... in fact it's not as bad as you'd think. Genuinely.'

He widens his eyes. 'Really?'

'Yes, really. No need to sound so incredulous. I can actually cope with things, you know.'

'I didn't mean that. It's just, you know, anyone would feel shit finding out stuff like that about their husband. I have been dreading this for years, ever since I saw him eating her face off in a taxi, and now that you know, "fine" is absolutely the last thing I expected you to be.' He huffs out a mirthless laugh. 'Christ, I've been worrying you'd have some kind of breakdown, or kill him, or go psycho and slash all his clothes or something... What?'

I'm staring at him. 'Years? You said years.' It sounds suspiciously like more than a couple. 'How many y*ears*?'

He nods. 'Well, yeah. I mean, I can't exactly remember, but – '

'How long?'

'I don't know. I thought you knew?'

'Rough guess, Josh. Just give me an idea.'

He looks worried now. 'Shit. Oh shitting shit. You didn't know, did you?'

'Yes. I did. I do. Her name is Fiona Chapman. Her surname is two versions of the word for "someone else's husband."'

But before I've even finished speaking his hand has come up in a 'stop' gesture, and he's shaking his head.

'What?' It comes out as a hoarse whisper, as if my body is reluctant to make the words. 'Is there more?'

He nods. 'You don't want to know.'

'Oh, yes I do.' I barely recognise my own voice. To my own ears I sound like someone with terrible tonsillitis, holding a meat cleaver. 'Dad told me it's been two years.' He closes his eyes. 'Was that a lie?' I pause. '*Another* lie?' He doesn't reply, so I press him. 'Josh? Was it a lie? Was it longer?' Eventually, reluctantly, he nods, and my stomach lurches like I've jumped out of an aeroplane. I grip the edge of the sofa, swaying.

'Mum, I said not to ask…'

'It's not right if you know more about my own marriage than I do. If you know something, at least allow me the dignity of knowing it too.'

He forms a word and I can see that it starts with 'B', so I shake my head. 'No 'buts', Josh. Please. Give me this small dignity.' He says nothing, but looks in genuine discomfort. 'Tell me the truth, please. When did you see them snogging? Was it going on while you were still living here?'

'Jesus, yes, all right. It was before I moved out.'

I flinch. 'Shit.'

'Oh Mum. I so didn't want to be the one to tell you. It's awful.'

'Well you're an adult. And clearly you knew this was going on, has been for more than five years, but didn't see fit to let me know then. Seems appropriate you should be the one now.'

'That's not fair.'

'Yeah, well, life's not fair, it seems. Get used to it.'

'Oh come on. You're my parents. It's been terrible knowing this all this time and not telling you. But how could I possibly? How could I be responsible for breaking up your marriage? Breaking up the family, my home, Amy's home?'

'Still, you should have...'

'No. I won't have that.' He stands up, and walks to the back door. Amy is still out there, upset and smoking, with no idea about all this. 'She was fourteen, Mum. She'd just done her options. For Christ's sake, how could I possibly have said anything?'

I don't answer. I'm thinking back to the parents' evenings at Amy's school, when we went round and met all the GCSE subject teachers, and discussed what she would do. She had a leaning towards English and the arts, which sat just fine with the magician in my heart. I made sure I smiled and hid my own feelings, wanting the decision to be just hers and not the result of any influencing by her parents. 'You choose whatever you think you'll enjoy, sweetheart...' 'Think carefully,' Tim the pragmatist butted in. 'Weigh everything up and maybe just speak to the science and maths people again?' I wonder now if he told Fiona about it afterwards. How his baby was making him proud, choosing all on her own, choosing applied sciences. It makes me slightly nauseous and I shudder. I look up at Josh, still staring out at the dark, stormy garden with my fragile daughter in it.

'I'm sorry, sausage.' He turns at my voice. 'You're right. This isn't yours to deal with. And I can't imagine how awful it must have been, to know about it all this time and keep it to yourself.' I get up and go over to him and I see he has tears in his eyes. 'Oh, Josh.' I put my arms round him and give him a smothering, mothering hug; and as he hugs me back I know he thinks he's the one giving comfort.

We separate and go back to the sofa. 'I really hoped you would never know,' he says quietly.

'Ah, it's OK, sweetheart,' I lie. 'We've decided to split now anyway, it doesn't make any difference in the end.' I smile at him. 'And, you know, if he fell in love with Fiona Chapman all that time ago, and has fought against it for years, for my sake, then I should be – What?' I frown. Josh is shaking his head, his expression pained. 'What's up?'

'Oh Mum, I'm so sorry. I'm so, so sorry.'

'What is it Josh? I mean, seriously. What now?'

He presses his lips together, and takes a deep breath. 'It wasn't Fiona Chapman.'

3
LADIES MAN

I stare at him. 'What?'

'It doesn't matter, though does it?' he says, almost pleadingly. 'I mean, like you said, you're splitting up anyway.'

'So... so he didn't...?' Questions are hatching and multiplying and seething through my head, like sped-up footage of maggots on roadkill. I put a hand up, to try and stop all the internal noise. 'He didn't fall in love...' I shake my head. 'She wasn't the only...'

Josh waits.

After a few seconds, I manage to discern one important question from the chatter. 'How do you know?' When he doesn't answer immediately, I press him. 'It's important. You might be wrong.'

'I'm not,' says the super-confident twenty-five-year-old man with his first job and first mortgage and zero life experience. 'And even if I am, it won't make any difference.'

I lean forward towards my wonderful, loving son and lower my voice. 'When you're fifty and find out that your entire twenty-four year marriage has been a lie, come back and tell me that it doesn't make any difference.'

He winces a little, surprised by my tone. 'I will if you're still alive.'

He's trying to make me laugh, and I love him for it. But I can't muster it up. I manage a weak smile, and close my eyes a second, then look at him earnestly. 'How do you know, Josh? Please just tell me.'

'Because I've met her.'

It's a kick in the stomach, while I'm already down. 'Who?'

'Fiona Chapman. I met her. Only once.' He raises his voice quickly over my instant reaction. 'I went to meet Dad for lunch, last summer. It was pre-arranged, I didn't surprise him or anything. But when he came down to reception to meet me – or so I thought – he had a woman with him. They were just laughing together, sharing a joke, and he kind of nudged her as they walked. Looked like they were going for lunch together.' Josh looks away. 'Then when he saw me, he looked kind of, I don't know, shocked. Embarrassed. Horrified.' He shakes his head. 'I don't know. Anyway, so he tried to hide it all by introducing us to each other. Fiona Chapman, his boss.'

'His boss…'

'Yeah.' He looks so sad for a moment. 'He'd forgotten we'd arranged to meet.'

I squeeze his hand. 'Oh Joshy, poor boy. At least you know it was nothing to do with you,' I say, smiling. 'Seems the man is a bit prone to forgetting his family all round.'

Now Josh gives me the same smile I was just giving him. He even squeezes my hand. The circle of life. 'I know, Mum. I'm sorry.'

'So, how do you know the woman you saw five years ago wasn't her? I mean, how close were you? Did you get a good look? Can you even remember? It's been a long time…'

'The woman I saw in the taxi was probably late twenties, early thirties maybe. Blond, tight dress, cliché in heels. You know.'

I do know. I've seen enough Hollyoaks to know. 'Well, yes, Dad says Fiona Chapman is thirty-two. How do you know it wasn't her?'

He rolls his head on his neck to face me properly. 'Fiona Chapman is not thirty-two. She's your age. Maybe older. She doesn't wear tight dresses or heels. She'd probably be more comfortable staying in with Netflix and her dogs than getting into a taxi at 10:30 at night. It wasn't the same woman. I'm certain.'

'*What*?' More shock. More upset. 'My age?'

Josh nods.

'Then why would he say she was thirty-two?'

He shrugs. 'I don't know, Mum. Maybe to spare your feelings?'

I shake my head. 'Doubt it. Probably embarrassed that the only woman he could find prepared to live with him is Camilla Parker-Bowles.'

Josh smiles, but it's a hard, bitter smile. 'Maybe.'

My head is swarming. Tim has decided he doesn't want to be with me any more and has replaced me with, basically, *me.* 'But why?' I whisper.

Josh shrugs, not realising what I'm asking. 'I guess he got bored of bimbos.'

So it transpires that my husband of nearly twenty-five years has been shagging a stream of different women for, at the very least, five years, when twenty-year-old Josh saw him getting into a taxi one night with a UOF (Unidentified Obvious Female, as he has been referring to them in his mind ever since), and possibly – probably – much longer.

Apparently you could tell just by looking at them that he had more than a professional relationship with Miss Cliché in Heels. Something about the way he was sucking her face, I think. I'm under no illusions, of course, that she was the first one. The chances of Josh spotting him on his very first foray into adultery are negligible to non-existent. And of course the laws of adultery state that the more you do it, the more likely you are to be spotted. Like fleas. Once you see a single flea in your home, you're already infested.

'Mum, please don't think about it any more,' Josh says, his voice becoming slightly petulant. 'God, I wish I'd never told you.'

'Never told her what?' Amy says, coming back in through the patio doors with a blast of smoke-polluted cold. She plonks down on the dog-less armchair and folds her arms. 'You two been discussing the divorce settlement?'

'No, no, nothing like that. Josh just told me what he's getting you for Christmas,' I say quickly, mustering up an excited grin. I hope it was excited. At this point it could have been homicidal.

Amy glances from me to Josh and back, deciding whether what I've said is actually likely. Josh rolls his eyes at her. 'You know what Mum's like,' he says wearily. 'She's already so excited she's likely to blurt it out to you at any point between now and Christmas.'

There's a pause while Josh and I hold our breath. Then Amy shrugs. 'Must be good, if you've felt the need to break the news to Mum already.' She arches her eyebrows at her brother. 'Splashing out this year?'

Josh and I release our breaths, and Josh smiles enigmatically. 'You'll have to wait and see, won't you?' And he winks theatrically at me.

'You're going to be blown away,' I tell her, getting carried away. 'It's incredible!'

'Yeah, all right Mum,' Josh warns. 'Don't get her all worked up or it will be a massive let down.'

'Now I am very intrigued,' Amy says, getting up and moving across to the other chair, where Harry is curled. 'Hello Harry,' she says, scratching behind his ears. 'He's lovely, Mum. I take it Dad's not keeping him?'

'No, it's not really practical for him at the moment.'

'Oh, right,' Josh joins in. 'So he's renting somewhere is he?'

'Or is he kipping on someone's sofa still?' Amy perches on the edge of Harry's chair and rests her hand on his body. He is characteristically unresponsive.

'Oh, yeah, good point, he's probably staying at Uncle Howard's, is he?' Josh asks. 'I mean, he won't have had time to sort out a lease or whatever yet, will he?'

Amy turns to him. 'Depends when this happened. I mean, there's literally no sign of him anywhere in the house. Either he's moved all his stuff out within a matter of days…'

'Or it happened weeks or months ago.'

They both turn to me expectantly.

'Oh come on, kids,' I say, rolling my eyes. 'You don't honestly think I would leave it that long before telling you?'

Amy shrugs. 'Maybe you thought it wasn't all that important. That we didn't really need to know. You did say it wouldn't affect us…'

'Amy, for God's sake. I only said that because you're both adults and neither of you lives here any more. Of course it's going to affect you less now than if you'd been little.'

'Yeah, whatever. When was it then? That you kicked him out?'

'I didn't kick him out. He left. After we'd had a discussion that we –'

'Right, yes fine. But when?'

'It was Tuesday night.'

Josh jerks. 'Tuesday? What, this week?'

'Yes.'

'Jesus, he's moved fast, hasn't he? To get all his belongings out already…'

I feel stung. 'Well, no, he hasn't taken absolutely everything…'

Josh walks around the room. 'His graduation photo, that Star Wars film cell I bought him, the 'World's Best Dad' trophy.' He turns to me. 'Seems to me he's taken pretty much everything.'

'No, I'm sure there's a bow tie of his upstairs somewhere…'

'OK, well anyway. It didn't take him long. So where is he, Mum? Uncle Howard's?'

I look at them helplessly. This has all gone so very wrong. 'Honestly, I don't know.'

'How can you not know?' Amy bites instantly.

'Because he hasn't told me.'

'Well have you asked him?'

'No…'

'Don't you think you should?'

'Well, I haven't really had time to – '

''Sake,' Amy mutters, and pulls her phone from her jeans pocket. She taps rapidly at the screen for a few moments. 'OK. I've text him. Hopefully he'll let us know.'

The room falls into silence as we all wait for Tim to reply. Even Harry uncurls himself from his customary circle a little.

'So… Christmas Day,' I begin, to break the silence. 'I'd love it if you'd all come here, as usual.'

'As usual?' Amy snaps. 'What's usual about this?'

'I know it's going to be weird, and different, but I'd really like to have our family Christmas here. Before I sell the house.'

'Oh Jesus!' Amy practically shouts. 'This gets worse and worse.'

'It's inevitable, Ames,' Josh says reasonably. 'Of course it will be sold. Mum won't want to stay in this big house on her own.'

The words 'on her own' just hang there for a few moments, then get sucked into the unknowable black hole of my future.

'We'll have to talk to Dad,' Amy says eventually, her tone softer. 'He'll be on his own too.'

'Well no,' Josh says, and I throw him a look. He stares at me pointedly and then says, 'He'll be with Uncle Howard and Auntie Lynn, won't he?'

'Maybe.'

'Well I still need to speak to him, to see what he wants to do,' Amy says. She glances at her watch, then stands up. 'I need to get back really. Sorry Mum, early start.'

I nod. 'Course. Don't worry.'

'I'll drop you,' Josh says, standing too.

'Great, thanks bro-seph.'

We all hug tightly in the hallway, Josh lingering a second while Amy gets her coat on. 'Now I'll have to find her something amazing,' he whispers by my car.

'Sorry!'

'It was you who made Christmas special every year anyway,' Amy says unexpectedly from the porch, and hugs me tightly. My eyes immediately fill with tears so I hurry them out, trying to avoid thinking about the four or five Christmases Tim missed over the years due to some 'emergency surgery' or other.

So that's the children told. Now for the rest of the family. I flop back down onto the sofa and pick up my phone. It dings with a text immediately. It's from Tim.

'Fuck me u couldnt wait to tell them cd u' He's ended his message with the eye-roll emoji.

Feeling a flare of injustice, I type back, 'You told me to tell them!!!' Then before I click 'send', I delete it and type 'Fuck u'. That's better.

It takes a few days to let everyone know about my new circumstances. If only you could wave a wand and it all be done in seconds. The closest thing to that is to change my Facebook status from 'married' to 'it's complicated,' but that wouldn't have been fair on Josh and Amy, so I resist. Oddly, it was easier informing friends and family than the bank, the council, HMRC, and my energy supplier. Friends and family didn't ask me for a form to be filled in and returned, signed, for the change to take effect within five working days.

Everyone's reactions are different of course.

My dad: Oh dear, love. I'm sorry. Has he met someone else, then?

Zoe: Shit bollocks, Steph. I have wine and Maltesers, be there in 10.

Steve at work: Oh, no. Um, I need to – oh, the phone's ringing.

Niamh at work: Don't worry Steph, you'll meet someone else. Let me have a think and I'll set you up with someone. My Justin knows loads of blokes…

Different, but all hideous, in their own way. I smile at them all and thank them for their kindness and wonder what kind of bloke Niamh's twenty-five-year-old mechanic boyfriend Justin will know who will suit a fifty year old GP. Then I read an email from the CQC about Diversity and Inclusion and I slap myself.

The weeks leading up to Christmas are dominated and ruined by a succession of strangers coming into my home to walk around it and tell me they don't like it. I hate every single one of them, but like waxing and smear tests they're a necessary evil. The first three offers I get are so low they actually make me angry.

'That's £30k off the asking price!'

'I know, my love,' Ange says, and she sounds like she's hanging her head. 'I almost didn't call you but it turns out I'm obliged to.'

I'm warming to her.

When I do eventually accept an offer, it's from a terrible woman whom I'd prefer to push over than allow to live in my home. Ange said the woman and her husband – Greg and Pam Dawlish – were in a good position, with nothing to sell, which made me dislike them quite a lot in advance. What kind of person buys a £500,000 house with cash? Probably an organised crime gang, or Russian mafia. Only explanation.

First appointment: they didn't show up. Thirty minutes past the appointment time, I rang the agent, thinking they'd probably been assassinated in a drive-by shooting. 'I'll give them a call, shall I?' says Ange.

Turns out they were in Bluewater. Apparently they were held up. At gunpoint, I was hoping.

'They want to make another appointment day after tomorrow?'

'Tell them they can stick their proceeds of crime right up into their most unreachable orifices.'

That's what I wanted to say. But you can't, can you? You lose your option to be rude when you're selling your house. 'Yes of course,' was what actually managed to squeeze itself out between my clenched teeth. 'What time would they like to come? Shall I bake a cake?'

When they finally crossed my threshold and walked into my home, they acted as if I wasn't even there. 'Not sure about these tiles,' he said to her. 'I hate this colour,' she said to him. 'We'd have to rip all this out,' they both agreed.

'You're aware this is still my family home at this point?' I wanted to say. But, again, you can't. You have to bend over and let them shove their rude opinions roughly up your backside in silence. Whilst smiling and offering to part your cheeks. Your future is quite literally in the palm of their bank balance.

'It's a good offer, my love,' Ange said when she rang, and I nodded wordlessly at my desk. I toyed with the idea of rejecting it, because I don't want to get involved with the mob. You can never get out once you're in, can you? But it was the best offer I'd received, so I said yes. Even though they'd opened my bedroom cupboard without asking. And turned the taps on in the kitchen. I mean, why? Did they really need to check they were working?

Now they're insisting on the boiler being serviced and the fence being repaired and the slightly drippy toilet being sorted. Ange's number has popped up on my phone almost every day for weeks. 'The Dawlishes aren't happy with the kitchen cupboards.' 'The Dawlishes aren't sure about the roof.' 'The Dawlishes want information about the neighbours.' If Ange had rung me and said 'The Dawlishes' one more time, I was planning to go round to their house in my rubber dog mask and stand in silence on the pavement opposite for a few hours, holding a bulky carrier bag. Staring at them through the eye holes. 'What's the problem, officer? I'm just standing here in a dog mask. It's not illegal, is it?'

'The Dawlishes want to move on the 18th,' is Ange's most outrageous request.

'That's a week before Christmas!'

'I know, my love,' she says. 'They really aren't very...' She pauses. '*Helpful* people, are they?'

'That's an understatement.'

'I know, my love.'

I sigh. 'Well I can't move before Christmas. It's impossible. Did they say why the urgency?' There's probably a hit out on one of them and they need to disappear.

'They did.'

I'm getting the feeling that Ange doesn't want to tell me. 'What is it?'

She takes a deep breath in, and says it very quickly on the exhale. 'They said, and I quote, "We've got Christmas."'

'What? What the hell does that mean? We've *all* got Christmas.'

There's another pause. 'I know, my love.'

Now all I have to do is send my signed contract back to my solicitor. It's on top of the bread bin. It's been there five days. My hand is still hovering over the red 'Abort' button.

I found a place to move into very quickly, and the old couple selling it have been lovely. Doug and Hilda. They're so ancient, they're still proud of their fitted kitchen. 'New kitchen,' Doug said to me, pushing open the kitchen door and stepping back to let me see. 'Had this all done up in '94. Cost a fortune, but you know it's going to last then, don't you?'

Pine doors. Cork floor tiles. White plastic sink. I nodded at him. 'It's beautiful, Doug.' I looked around, gently touching here, resting a hand there. 'Really lovely quality.'

'Thank you Stephanie.'

I closed my eyes and pictured it all on fire. The place was perfect.

So here we are, a few weeks later, and it's our final Christmas in the house. The house of Josh and Amy's childhood. The tree is up, the lights are twinkling, the third bedroom is floor to ceiling boxes. Amy is home and in a good mood, in spite of the 'Sold' sign outside. She wakes me up at 06:58 on Christmas morning by climbing into bed with me and snuggling up.

'Feliz navidad, Mumma,' she says, eyes closed again already. I turn my head and press my nose into her hair. It smells faintly of smoke, but after a few seconds I can just pick out the fresh shampoo-y baby head smell, and it brings instant heat to my eyes. She shifts her body slightly and I feel the size of her next to me. An adult woman. Where has my baby gone?

'Presents!' she yells, turning abruptly, grabbing my arm, flashing a grin. Ah, there she is. Then she's out of the bed and thudding downstairs so fast I feel that ancient panic that she will fall and twist and break.

There are no 'magic footprints' left by Father Christmas on the carpet this morning, and the Santa sacks are still in the loft. But there is a decent pile of wrapped gifts heaped around the tree, and when I come into the living room, Amy is kneeling there, sorting them into piles – an Amy pile, a Josh and Chloe pile, a Mum pile and – well, any under there for her dad have been left undisturbed. I stand and watch her for a few moments, wondering if it will really hurt all that much to have chocolate for Christmas Day breakfast one last time.

Josh and Chloe arrive at 11 with my dad. 'You didn't need to pick me up, Joshy my boy,' he's saying as he takes his coat off. Josh meets my eye wordlessly, then heads towards the Prosecco. Dad turns to me. 'He didn't need to pick me up.'

'I know Dad…'

'I'm perfectly capable of driving myself.'

'Yes, I know…'

'Or getting a bus, for that matter.'

'Not sure how many buses will actually be – '

'Anyone would think I've gone feeble.'

'No one thinks that…'

'Well I haven't. I'm as sharp as a snake. You need to lay off fussing so much.'

'Oh. OK.'

'I'd love a whisky and coke.'

'Coming up.'

'Oh, hello there Harry old boy…'

Josh and Chloe have bought me an Amazon echo, which I've heard of, but I'm not entirely sure what to do with it.

'It's amazing,' Chloe says, leaning forward in her seat. 'You can ask her to do anything.'

'Her?'

'Alexa,' Amy says, to be met by much shushing and hand waving from Josh.

'Sorry,' the heavy thing in my hand says, making me jump. 'I'm having a little trouble understanding right now. Please try again later.'

Amy, my little angel, has scraped together some money from her evening job cleaning offices and bought me a magic set.

'Oh, Amy.'

'I didn't know what to get you. And I remembered you used to like doing tricks for us when we were kids.'

'I did.'

'And I didn't have much money, so…'

My eyes fill up again. 'It's completely perfect. Thank you so much, baby girl.'

After dinner, Dad tries a few of the tricks, but fumbles them and feels foolish, so falls asleep in a huff.

Amy puts her new wireless earphones in ('OMG thanks Josh!') and climbs into her Ipad. Harry sneaks into the kitchen unnoticed and licks all the knives in the dishwasher.

'Harry!' I yell, just as he's running his enormous tongue along the blade of the electric carver. He doesn't even flinch, luckily. 'Get off that! Christ, you'll cut yourself!' I spot Josh and Amy exchanging glances and I can imagine their text conversation later. *Mum's turned into a dog lady. Yeah, she'll be buying him clothes next.*

Josh comes into the kitchen with me later and we spend some quality time together wondering how to get the last bit of turkey carcass off the roasting tin.

'Alexa, play 'Merry Christmas Everyone,' Josh says, and she does.

'I'm binning it,' I say in the end, and lob the tin out into the garden before I can change my mind. 'Got to down size anyway.'

'Good idea. Because that roasting tin would definitely not fit in the new place.'

'Oi, sarcastic!' We chuckle, looking at each other, and for just a second he's my cheeky little boy again. The fairy lights twinkle on the fogged-up windows, and through the connecting door I see the tree lights strobing gently through their colours, then flashing madly like something pissed them off. The smell of the wine and the gravy and the turkey all mingle with the steamy warmth from the oven, and for that perfect moment it really does feel like Christmas.

Then Josh draws in his eyebrows and the atmosphere changes. 'How are you doing, Mum?'

I hate it when he does this. He's talking to me in exactly the same way that I talk to my dad. The competent adult addressing the old fool who's not quite… *able* any more. I'm fifty! Fifty is the new forty. And I'm a bloody *doctor*, for crying out loud. A good one. I can spot meningitis in 8 seconds. Less, if there's a rash.

'I'm perfectly fine, thank you.' The plug hole is clogged with sprout leaves and other nameless lumps. Who scraped their plate into the bloody sink?

He half smiles. 'No, I mean, you know, *really*?'

'Yes, Josh. I am fine, you know, *really*.' Greasy, lumpy water sloshes over my arms and onto the side as I root around aggressively with my fingers. 'Christ's sake…'

'Ugh.' He turns away and grabs a plate from the draining board. 'You know what I mean. I'm not talking about your health. I'm talking about you, being single again. At fifty. It must be hard, to find yourself alone, after so many years of marriage, when virtually your entire adult life you've been in a couple. And now suddenly to be coming home to an empty house every day, being responsible for everything on your own, always being the one who – '

'Yeah, all right, thanks sweetheart.'

He hears the tone in my voice and turns to face me. 'What?'

'Well, you know. Ramming it down my throat, like it needed ramming. I'm very well aware that I'm single. At fifty. And it's Christmas.'

'I didn't mean...'

'With no prospects of ever finding anyone else.'

'I didn't say...'

'And eventually dying alone.'

'Christ, Mum, I wasn't...'

'And being eaten by badgers.'

Stunned silence.

'Yes, all right, I know you didn't mean that. But whatever you were saying, there's no need for you to brand it onto my forehead, is there?' I roll my eyes. 'Although I suppose an ambigram saying 'single' on my head would at least cut out any mind games, right?' I go back to the drying up. 'It could say 'miserable' the other way round. What?'

He stares at me. 'Wow.'

'Wow what?'

'Bit touchy, aren't we?'

'Fucking not.'

The rest of the day we take turns falling asleep on the sofa, interrupted by episodes of forcing down cold turkey and piccalilli sandwiches, soft French cheese, and mince pies. For one, or maybe two days, I put all my knowledge of heart disease and blood clots and cholesterol and diabetes to the back of my mind and focus on having fun with my family. Actually, that knowledge won't be silenced, especially when Dad starts on the Baileys, but I do my absolute best to ignore it. I want this last Christmas to be perfect.

'It's not our last Christmas,' Josh says, hugging me goodbye on Boxing Day. 'Don't be daft.'

I squeeze him and nod. 'You're right, it's just nostalgia. Pay no attention to me.'

He and Amy look at each other and make the 'head exploding' gesture they've always done, probably from the very first time I ever said that, years ago when they were still children.

'Why are you doing that?' I'd asked back then, tetchy.

'Duh, Mum,' Amy had rolled her eyes as if it was obvious. 'Because if you tell us to pay no attention to you, that will mean we'll pay no attention to you telling us to pay no attention to you, which means we'll have to pay attention to you, which means we'll pay attention to you telling us not to pay attention to you…' She gave up.

'It's a paradox,' Josh had finished for her. 'It makes our heads explode.'

Amy clings to me tightly before she leaves. 'I don't want to go back,' she whispers into my hair, her voice catching.

'Oh, baby girl.'

'Can't I just stay here? One more day? Please, Mum?'

'We talked about this. You know that won't help.'

'It will. It will help. I'll go back tomorrow, I promise. I'm just not ready…'

I step back a little so I can see her face, and smooth a strand of hair away from her cheek. 'My baby girl. I would love nothing more than to keep you here forever, and look after you, and make your life easy, and comfortable, and stress free. But that's selfish of me. It's what I want. You know it's not what you want.'

'No, no, it is what I want, Mum…'

'It isn't, Amy. Remember what the doctor said? This moment is always going to be difficult, but as soon as you get in the car, or as soon as you get back to your room, you'll be comfortable again. In your own life.' I look into her anxious face. 'Your adult life.'

Her eyes brim, and she bites her lip, but then nods, slowly. 'OK.'

'Good girl.' I lean in for another hug, and she grips me tighter than ever. 'Have you got your tablets?'

She nods, still holding on, then slowly, slowly, her grip loosens.

'I'll walk her in, Mum,' Josh says, just outside the door. 'I'll make sure she's settled.'

'I'm not a baby,' Amy snaps, pulling away from me. And she stomps out and up the path.

'Don't worry,' Josh says, squeezing my arm. 'She'll be fine.'

I nod. 'Thank you, darling.'

I stand there until I hear Josh's car pull away, and feel a deep drag of intense melancholy. It's crippling, numbing, and for a few moments I can't move. I need my babies here with me. I need to protect them, enrobe them with my love, keep them safe and make sure no harm comes to them. This is the worst part about being a parent – the part where you're still a parent but your children don't realise.

'Good parents make themselves redundant,' someone once said to me. Probably my mum, decades ago. 'If your kids still need you when they're adults, you're doing it wrong.'

I don't entirely agree with that, and clearly neither did my mum, still giving me advice after Josh was born. But I know if I cling to them, it's my need, not theirs, and that's selfish. My job is done; I am redundant.

Man, it hurts.

I close the door and go back into the living room, silent and empty. There's a massive load of clearing up to do, the remnants of the people who were here, evidence of enjoyment now ended. It can wait until tomorrow. If I stay down here any longer, I'm liable to start crying. Time for bed.

'Come on Harry,' I say, walking over to where he's lying in his favourite spot on the armchair, and I see his ears twitch. 'Come on, boy, time for bed.' I crouch down by the chair and scratch his ears. Josh's words come back to me as Harry huffs in his sleep, and I shake my head. 'We're not lonely, are we? Hmm? No we're not. We're absolutely and perfectly fine on our own.'

'Want to meet Justin's single uncle?' Niamh says to me two months later.

'Oh, God yes,' I tell her.

4
FIRST MAN

OK. I'm not desperate. I realise that does look a bit like it. But I'm really not. I was with Tim for 26 years, pretty much my entire adulthood, and letting another man into my life after such a monumental betrayal is going to take centuries. I am nowhere near even putting the post code of 'ready' into Google maps to consider whether it's too far, or too difficult to get to. I probably never will be. I'm fifty, intelligent, independent and strong. I'm done being a mum, I'm done being a wife. *Now* is time for me. And that time can start with a bit of trouser.

Can't believe I just said that. I stare at myself in the mirror, leaning forward, fixing a beady eye on myself. 'Who *are* you?'

My reflection is asking me the same thing. Neither of us knows the answer.

It's Wednesday, February 20th. Date night. Six days after my first solo Valentine's day in nearly thirty years. No, don't pity me. It was absolutely fine. I was perfectly happy watching *Love Actually* and drinking wine on my own, with Harry snoring on the chair as usual. I even bought myself a box of Roses chocolates and ate them on my own, too. There was no expectation, and thus no disappointment, and I ate all the purple ones. It was the perfect Valentine's Day. Pure coincidence that, when Niamh told me about Justin's single uncle the very next day, I snatched her phone from her hand and stared at the blurry photo of him as if he was Elvis.

All right, if I'm honest, two months of having to do absolutely everything haven't been great. Yes, yes, I'm an intelligent, independent and strong woman, blah blah, and this stuff isn't difficult. It's not difficult to clean the windows or clear out the gutters or cut the grass. It's not complicated changing the car insurance or inflating the tyres or booking the service. It's not beyond me to sell the house and pack everything into boxes and arrange removal men. No one has shown me or told me what to do, and I've still been able to do it. It's all very simple. It's just very tedious. And it's always bloody me putting the bins out. And I'm fed up. I don't need a man to look after me. I want someone to look *out* for me.

The house move was at the end of January. Is it childish of me to be gratified that it was over a month after the Dawlishes absolute final deadline of December

23rd? Gosh, it was most forgetful of me not to sign the contract when I sent it back, but they had to bear in mind that I did have Christmas, after all. Then I couldn't agree on the first week in January because it's a very busy time of year for me at work and I couldn't possibly get time off. In the end, they said they would pull out of the move if we didn't do it before the end of January, and as they have undoubtedly got billions of euros in cash stuffed into their sofa cushions and would probably take out a hit on me, I had to agree.

It wasn't easy, going from a spacious four-bedroomed, three-bathroomed, detached, in a sought after location, with conservatory, garage, shed, and large-ish garden mainly laid to lawn with decking area and attractive mature shrubbery borders; to a three-bedroomed semi-detached investment opportunity or ideal first time buy. After paying Tim his blood money – well, half the equity – I kept a huge chunk of capital back to get a new kitchen and bathroom put in, and have the entire place redecorated. I had my bedroom done the same week I moved in, complete with heavy thermal curtains and carpet to leave footprints in. It's my perfect sanctuary, and means I can retreat here when the awful pine kitchen gets too much. Consequently my urgency for arranging the kitchen and bathroom projects – on my own – has diminished somewhat. That hideous upheaval can wait just a little longer.

I glance at my watch – 19:52 already. Twenty minutes until I'm twelve minutes late. Can't leave yet. I flick the bedroom curtain back and glance outside. It's dark, of course, but a fierce wind is rushing in and out of the trees opposite, and the streetlight is showing me nicely just how biting that wind is, as trunks and branches bend and sway in its teeth. I drop the heavy curtain and instantly the roaring sound mutes. My gaze falls on my lovely warm bed, just waiting there, empty and smooth. The bedside light is on, casting a cosy orange glow around the room. Next to the bed the serial killer novel I'm reading is lying on the night stand. The killer has made a crucial mistake and cut himself on a broken wine glass. His blood has dripped onto the cheese board, and he didn't realise until he was already at his daughter's play and couldn't do anything about it. Now the detective has reached the crime scene and someone's put the cheeseboard in an evidence bag. It's pivotal. My entire body yearns towards the bed and the comfort zone it embodies and my anticipation for the date dissipates further.

I close my eyes. Why oh why did I agree to go in the first place? What the hell was I thinking? "Want to meet Mike?" Niamh says, and with one flash of a slightly blurry photo on her phone, I'm in. Oh God, Mike is six years younger than me, so he's technically still in his early forties. I, at fifty, am therefore in my early fifties, which makes him a decade younger. It's practically a generation. He's going to turn up on a motorbike, in a leather jacket and skinny jeans, and flash me a white smile before spotting my gilet and zooming away.

No, he won't. I'm not wearing a gilet. It's discarded on the bed, along with a tee shirt that says 'Think Happy Be Happy', some wide leg black velvet trousers, and a knee length peacock blue dress I bought in Monsoon last year and have never worn. Yet another bad decision, I think, eyeing it.

The trouble with being fifty is that it differs from being forty-nine quite massively, and I just don't know what I'm supposed to wear any more. Forty-niners can wear jeans with messy buns and leather boots. We fifty-ers are supposed to wear flowery nylon tops and slacks. With elasticated waists. On my fiftieth birthday I started getting emails about planning my funeral, and incontinence pads. The day before, I was still getting suggestions for live concert tickets and flights to Hawaii. The ticking over of that clock at midnight from the 7th to the 8th of September last year meant a whole world of change for me. And I'm not talking about hot flushes.

Although that is also something I could talk about.

But not now. Now I have to leave my softly humming, centrally heated home and my sleeping dog, and step willingly into an icy gale force blast (3 degrees below freezing, with the wind chill factor), drive eight miles to The Dog and Ball, and make difficult small talk with a much younger man who wants to be anywhere other than in The Dog and Ball talking to a woman in a long sleeved Marks and Spencer's top and a pair of jeans laughingly known as 'Girlfriend'. This is going to be so cringe, I wish I could fast forward two hours to the point where I'm home again.

I'm thirteen minutes late as I push open the door to the pub. I've made sure I'm late so there's no chance of sitting here on my own waiting for him. Can't bear walking into pubs on my own, and everyone turning to look. You end up being targeted. I walk two steps in, but needn't have worried. One or two people look round at the sound of the door, then turn away again when they clock a fifty-year-old wearing Marks and Spencer. I am fifty, and therefore invisible. I glance around, hoping to see the blurry photograph man walking confidently towards me with a welcoming smile and a quick wit, but he doesn't. It's a fairly small bar, and looking around I can see precisely zero men in their early forties sitting on their own. There are precisely zero men on their own of any age, in fact. Perhaps he's in a different part of the bar.

I walk up to the bar tender and order a gin and tonic, then carry it all the way around the bar to the end, then all the way back round again to the front. There is no different part of the bar. Blurry Photo Man is not here. He's either inconsiderately late, or I've been stood up. Which is the same thing, really. Relief floods my body, and I relax at last. I've bought a drink, so I'll stay and drink it, then head off.

'Are you Beverley?' a voice says near my ear and I start. Bugger. My g and t is already half drunk, and the prospect of going home to Harry and bed is tantalisingly close.

'No.' I turn, and get the first eyeful of my date for the evening. 'It's Stephanie. Are you Mike?'

He's skinny. I mean, *powerfully* skinny. Not just in an 'I keep myself fit' kind of way. This is skinny in an 'I only drink' kind of way. His hips are so narrow, he would go through a cat flap. To emphasise the narrowness of his frame, he's chosen quite possibly the skinniest jeans I've ever seen. I mean, I don't study his legs – these are so tight you can't look directly at them – but a peripheral idea of them is all I can take. There's no leather jacket or motorcycle helmet in evidence, but he is wearing Doc Marten boots. They look like clown feet at the bottom of his legs.

'Oh, ha ha,' he starts, but even some pretend laughing has brought on a fruity cough, and he puts a closed fist to his mouth and raises the other hand, presumably to stop me from saying anything. He's obviously got something else he wants to say. I hope it's riveting, as I have to wait a good fifteen seconds to hear it. 'Yeah, yeah,' he says at last. 'Stephanie, that's right.' He puts out the hand that was until recently a germ-catching fist. 'I'm Mike. Nice to meet you.'

I hesitate. I don't want to touch that virus-ridden hand, but how do you avoid it when someone puts it out towards you? 'Nice to meet you too, Mike,' I say, and with long-practised prestidigitation my right hand disappears into my handbag. 'Want a drink?'

He drops his hand, side-tracked by the offer of a treat, a tactic I've learned from Heidi at dog training. You can prevent 'undesirable' behaviour with distraction techniques. 'Oh, yeah, ta. Pint of bitter please.'

'Great. You get a table, I'll bring the drinks over.'

He wanders off, clearing his throat. I glance at the door to the car park. It's so tempting simply to leave at this point. I mean, I could buy the drink and ask the bar tender to take it to him. He'll never recognise me again, he's barely looked at me. And he probably already knows I'm not for him.

But when the drink arrives on the bar, I pick it up and dutifully carry it over to the table he's at. It's just too habitual to go against good manners and walk out on someone like that without any kind of explanation. I can't do it. I'll finish my gin, then make my excuses. And who knows, maybe he'll be interesting to talk to.

'Here you are,' I say, putting it down in front of him. He's unearthed a phone from the unfeasibly skinny jeans and is staring at it intently, probably on TikTok or something. 'Are you expecting a call?' I ask him sweetly as I sit down, and he looks up, almost surprised to see me.

'Nah,' he says. I raise my eyebrows and smile, and after a couple of seconds he lays the phone down on the table.

I sip my drink, then put it on the table and rest my hands in my lap. Then I pick it up again and take another sip. I wonder how many minutes have passed.

'So, er, Stephanie. D'you come 'ere often?'

'To the Dog and Ball?'

'Yeah.'

'No.'

'Ah.'

We sip in synch.

'How about you?'

'What?'

'Come here often?'

'Nah.'

'Right.'

The bar tender is staring at us, his chin on his hands. He catches my eye and grins, but it's not a friendly grin of comradeship, or sympathy, or even – heaven help me – attraction. It's a humorous grin. He's grinning at something he's finding amusing, and what he's finding amusing is us. This situation. This blatant blind date. He wants to see how it's going to end. I could go and tell him, but I think he'll find out just as quickly.

'So, um...' I begin. Mike looks up at me briefly, then goes back to contemplating the meaning of our existence. He's got quite long fingernails. 'What do you do?'

'Taxi driver.'

'Oh really? That must be interesting?'

'You wouldn't believe me if I told you.'

'Oh go on, try me.'

He stares at me a while. 'My ex-wife was like you. Always asking me things, wanting to know who I'd had in the back, you know.'

'Well, who have you had in the back? Anyone famous?'

He shakes his head. 'That's what she was always asking. Like, if I'd had someone famous, maybe my job would have been more interesting. Ha! Like her job was interesting.'

'Oh, well…'

'She's an accountant. You know? I mean, talk about dull.'

'Mm.'

'Which is weird because she wasn't really a dull person herself. You know?' He checks himself. 'I mean, *isn't* really a dull person. Ha! She is still alive!'

'Right.'

'I haven't murdered her!'

I have absolutely nothing left to say.

'Another one?' he says suddenly, then drains his pint and stands up.

I'm already shaking my head. 'Ah, no, sorry, I can't. I've got to get home, I'm afraid.'

'Oh?'

'Yeah, sorry. It's just, er, my grandmother is there, on her own.'

'Old lady, eh? She'll be asleep by now surely? What you having?' He's moving away, patting his pockets. If he produces a wallet from there, it'll be the best magic I've ever seen.

'Oh, er, no, she's, um, on medication. So, you know, I shouldn't…'

He stops. Turns. 'Hang on. You've left a frail old lady on her own to sort out her own tablets?'

Shit. I didn't think this through. 'Well, no, she's quite capable…'

'Oh. Right. Another drink then?'

Bollocks bollocks bollocks. 'Ah, well, no, because now I come to think about it, she's run out. And I've got the new bottle in my car…'

His mouth falls open. 'What? You're kidding me, right? I can't believe anyone would do that.' He looks at the barman, aghast. 'Did you hear that?'

The barman definitely heard. 'No, what?'

'She's left a little old lady at home without her tablets. Got the new bottle in the car. Old dear could be gasping by now.'

'Horrifying.'

Bloody hell, I only said it in the first place to spare Mike's feelings. I stand up now. 'Well, no, it's not really like that…'

'They make documentaries about people like you,' Mike is saying, shaking his head.

I blink. 'You know, I very much doubt that my life would be – '

'How you gonna feel if you get home and find her… you know.' He walks up to the bar and orders another pint of bitter. 'And you had the chance to save her.' he says loudly. People at nearby tables are starting to look round now.

'What's happened, mate?' someone asks him.

'Left an old lady at home without her tablets,' he replies, throwing a filthy look my way. 'Locked her in too,' he goes on, to my utter mortification.

'I think I'll just leave,' I mutter, making for the door.

'Yeah, you better,' someone behind Mike says. 'Get that poor woman her relief.'

'What's that?'

'Left an old lady without her life-saving medication.'

'Oh my God, I saw a thing about that on More Four…'

My car spits gravel as I speed away from the car park before the mob can get hold of any pitchforks. My heart is thudding and I'm glancing in the rear view mirror repeatedly, checking no convoy of headlights is following me. They aren't, but I take a circuitous route home anyway, just in case.

When I walk into the surgery two days later, there's a scramble of movement at the reception desk, and a sense of a conversation suddenly stopping. Niamh's and Steve's heads move sharply down, to focus ever so intently on the appointments diary and repeat prescription request log as I approach.

'Hey you two. How's everything this morning?'

Niamh looks up. 'Nothing,' she says, and fake starts, as if she's shocked I'm there. Not sure how she could be, I had to unlock and then re-lock the door to get in. I blink. 'Oh, I mean, hi Stephanie.'

'Hi Stephanie,' Steve joins in.

'Morning. Is everything OK?'

They both start nodding. 'Oh, yes, yes, all fine, nothing to report, everything's completely fine.'

I narrow my eyes. 'Are you sure?'

Still nodding. 'Yes, yes, absolutely sure. No problems at all. Nada. Zilch.' Pause. 'All fine.'

'Tickety boo,' says Steve, then widens his eyes and, unless I'm mistaken, receives a kick under the desk from Niamh.

'Well that's certainly very good to know,' I tell them both. 'I'm happy to hear we are all,' I pause briefly for effect, '"tickety boo."'

I ask them to email me the patient list, and as I open the door to my consulting room, I hear Niamh's voice stage whispering, 'Fuck's sake, Steve!' and Steve saying, 'I panicked, all right?'

Mrs. Taylor is my first patient of the morning, and she takes longer than usual due to her husband, Teddy, having taken a turn for the better over the weekend.

'I mean, he's up and about, Doctor,' she says, wringing her hands, the strain pulling at the lines on her old face. 'In the garden in his slippers, throwing bread around for the birds. When's it going to end?'

I see a chest infection, a baby with a rash, an ingrowing toe nail and a mysterious abdominal pain, all before ten. By now I'm supposed to be three patients further forward, and I've still got a home visit to do when surgery finishes, supposedly at 11. I put my head in my hands for a moment before I press the bell for the next patient, but the door opens anyway. Bloody Niamh... But when I look up, I see it's not the next patient, it's my colleague, Nina. Her presence makes me smile, even under the pressure, and I relax a little. I can give her 90 seconds.

'Ah, Doctor Dellis,' I say, steepling my fingers and rotating my chair to face her. 'I've been expecting you.'

'Forget that,' she says, plonking herself down on the other chair and leaning forward. 'Is that right, what I have now heard?'

I frown. 'I don't know. What was it?'

'Niamh and Steve have told me that you are keeping your very elderly grandmother captive and denying her the medication she needs.' She shakes her head. 'My friend. If you needed someone to prescribe for her, you only need to ask me.'

'Oh you're kidding?!' I stare at the door to reception, picturing them on the other side. I knew they were talking about me when I arrived. I'll have to have a word.

'No, I am honest, I would do that for you, if you got stuck.'

'I didn't mean – '

'I know, I know.' She puts up a hand. 'I'm pulling at your leg. But tell me, where did this silly story come from?'

Quickly I fill her in on the blind date with Mike on Wednesday, and my hastily made up excuse to get away from him. She starts laughing, in spite of my outraged face.

'I mean, for God's sake Nina, she only set me up with him because we're both single. That is literally the only thing we had in common.'

'I think you are right,' Nina sputters, wiping her eyes.

'It's as if all single people will automatically be interested in each other. Because they're all single. And being with anyone, no matter how unsuitable, is better than being alone.'

'Oh my, oh my,' she says, throwing up her hands in her dramatic Greek way. 'What is going to happen to you next, I wonder?' And she looks at me with those deep brown eyes crinkling with laughter.

My anger at the injustice of the accusation dissipates as I look at her, and her glee infects me. 'I don't know,' I tell her, laughing along. 'I'll probably be accused of soliciting or something next time.'

She nods, chuckling. 'Oh yes, no doubt. Be sure not to wear that sexy gilet of yours,' she says, holding her own face, 'you do look like a proper slut in that.'

Laughter bursts out of me, and I rest my head in my hands. 'Oh my God, Neen. I can't tell you. It was so awful.'

She wipes her eyes. 'Surely not *so* bad? How so?'

I shake my head. 'Well to start with, he was late.'

'*No*?!'

'Yes! By about twenty minutes.'

'Shocking.'

'I *know*. And when he finally turned up, he got my name wrong.'

'Good grief!'

I nod. 'And he was very... narrow.'

She frowns. 'No, you've lost me now. Narrow?'

I wave a hand. 'Doesn't matter. But, I mean, he had no conversation. I mean, he's a taxi driver, so I thought he might have some funny stories about that, you know? Weird goings on in the back, celebs or something. But...'

'Nothing?'

'Nothing.'

'Holy God.'

'I know. And then he asked me if I wanted another drink! Even though he hadn't said more than five words to me.'

'Oh no!'

'Yes! So I panicked and made up the story about dear old Granny. I mean, what was I thinking?'

She's laughing again, and puts her hand on my arm. 'I'm just so glad to hear that you are dating now,' she says. 'You are very eligible, Steph.'

I shake my head. 'Oh, no, no, no. You can forget that. I am never, *ever*, doing that again.'

Nina's face draws in, serious. 'Now Stephanie. You must not say that.'

'Oh yes I must. It was nothing but unpleasant, and has ruined my reputation with Niamh and Steve. It's not happening again, believe me.'

Nina shakes her head. 'The Thompson Twins out there will get over it. I can stop their silliness, that's no problem. But you are an attractive woman with a lot to offer. Do you want to be alone for your life?'

'Yes, absolutely I do.'

She smiles. 'I don't believe you, Doctor Harkness. You are a human being. We are social creatures. We crave company.'

I pout. 'I have company. I have Harry.'

Nina presses her full lips together. 'Harry is the dog, right?'

I shrug.

'So I think yes, the dog. Who is lovely, I am sure. But he can't keep you warm at night.'

'Yes he can.' I'd caved a few weeks earlier to letting H sleep on my bed at night. I really don't know why I'd left it so long – we're both happier now.

'OK, maybe. But he can't cheer you up when you're sad.'

'He does that too.'

'But he can't comfort you…'

I'm already nodding. 'Yep.'

'Ugh, all right. So dog Harry is the best. But he can't take out the rubbish. Can he? Hm? He's not some circus dog, is he? Walking on his two back legs to push the bin down the path? Is he?'

I grin at the image, then shake my head. 'No.'

'No. I thought so. So. He will comfort and cuddle you and love you. But he is not a man. He will not share life's burden with you. He will not bring you water when you have a headache. He will not hold your hair when you vomit…'

'I never vomit.'

'…he will not take you dancing. Or listen to your problems. Or hold your hand when you feel sad. Will he?'

I take a deep breath and release it slowly. 'All right, I get your point. Maybe another human would be nice, too.'

Nina nods once. 'Yes. Nice. That's it. So.' She pulls her phone out of her cardigan pocket and swipes on the screen. 'You have to try this app.' And she turns the phone to face me. 'It's called *Butterflies*.'

I end up so far behind with my appointments that I have to postpone the home visit until the end of the day, and call in on my way home. Freya Gerburg is a lovely lady with cerebral palsy, wheelchair-bound and prone to sores. She's also a very successful web-designer, writer, and lecturer, which never fails to impress me. I'm exhausted by the time I reach her, but the way she smiles as she pulls herself in and out of her chair to show me the sore patch on her back lifts my spirits. Really, what do I have to complain about?

'Ooh yes, that looks painful, Freya. I'll send you some antiseptic and pain relief.'

'Thanks Doc.' She pulls down her top and settles back into her seat with a wince.

'How did it happen, do you think? Have you been using that cushion?'

She looks away, and clears her throat. 'Yes?'

'Oh Freya.'

'I'm sorry, Doctor. But it hampers my work.'

'How does it?'

She shrugs. 'It puts my body at the wrong angle.' I frown, so she elaborates. 'When I'm at the computer. It just affects the angle I'm sitting at and makes my legs ache.'

'Ah, I see. I'm sorry to hear that. But we won't give up. I'll see what else is out there, and we'll keep trying until you're comfortable.'

'Thanks doctor. I appreciate that.'

When I get home later, Harry raises his head off the arm chair and waves his tail at me twice. It's taken a few months, but he seems to have finally realised I'm here and I'm not going to let him down.

'Hello boy.' I perch on the edge of the chair and scratch his ears. He doesn't move away. 'Wanna go out? Huh? Do you wanna go out?'

It's almost the last thing I feel like doing when I get in from work in the evenings, particularly in February, but Harry has been so patient all day waiting for me without laying waste to the living room, so I owe it to him. As I get his lead from the drawer in the kitchen he does the Harry version of jumping up and down and barking in excitement: climbs down from the arm chair and strolls into the kitchen to find me. His demeanour is improving slowly, and he no longer walks around with his head hanging and his tail tucked under. He's not exactly jumping for joy – or for anything – but his tail is a little looser and his head is a little higher.

We walk to the Leas, which is a gorgeous promenade along the cliff top, with views across the Channel to France. It runs from Folkestone town centre by the Memorial Arch; past the top end of an old, out of service funicular railway that used to operate a five minute whoosh and rumble to get you from the Leas down the cliffside to the beach; passes the Leas Cliff Hall; and ends at the top of Sandgate hill. The footpath is bordered by grass and flowers on both sides, and there's a bandstand where music and events are played in the summer. With the railway not working, you have to use one of several different paths and steps to get down the cliff to the beach. Or back up.

The Leas is about half a mile from my house and takes almost forty minutes to get to, as Harry has to stop at every lamp post, fence post, hedge and car to identify which dog last peed there. I watch him investigate, nostrils twitching as he runs his nose around about a tenth of a millimetre away from the concrete and categorises each urine scent – yep, Yorkshire terrier; uh-huh, labradoodle; wtf, human??

When we eventually arrive I let him off the lead as it's quiet. There's a strict 'dogs on leads' policy along here, but there are also strict 'no cycling' and 'no roller-skating' policies, and they are flouted constantly.

Yes, yes, I know, they're mostly kids.

I usually walk from the top, Sandgate hill end of the footpath where I join it, all the way down to the other end, by McDonald's, and back, while Harry ambles behind, stopping and smelling any – well, it's not flowers – at every possible opportunity, before jogging gently to catch up with me. It's dark, of course, being six o'clock and February, but there are plenty of people around and the street lights keep me feeling safe.

'Evening,' a woman says to me cheerfully, and we both stop while our dogs greet each other in a completely different way.

'Hiya.' I smile at her. 'Cold tonight.'

'Oh, yes, it is. Bitter.'

'Roll on the spring!'

'Absolutely.'

And we walk on. 'Come on Harry, time to go.'

'So glad we don't have to meet people like that!' she says, indicating our sniffing dogs as we pass each other.

'I'd have no friends at all!' I quip, then immediately wish I hadn't. Now she's going to think there's something unpleasant about my nethers. 'No, I only meant...' But she's gone, and her little terrier along with her. I look down at Harry. 'For God's sake, why did I say that?' He makes eye contact with me briefly and his tail swishes once. It always has the power to make me grin, and I bend to scratch his ears. 'You're a lovely boy, aren't you?'

There's a series of benches at intervals along the footpath, and tonight one has a single occupant. As I come closer I realise it is an old man, hunched into his coat, muffled up in a thick scarf, hat, and gloves. His hands are folded over the end of a walking cane, which is clamped between his knees. He looks like a quintessential Englishman, surveying his grounds.

'Evening,' I say, giving him a smile as I go past.

'Nnng,' he kind of grunts, barely looking at me. Rude.

Up ahead Harry is doing the poo dance, walking quickly backwards and forwards over the same stretch of path, keenly sniffing, then turning again, so I march quickly over to him, unfolding a bag as I go. I send up a silent prayer of thanks to the Me who thought to load all my coat pockets with bags, so I'm never without one.

There are plenty of bins along here so I can get rid of it quite quickly, and forty minutes later I'm unlocking the front door with numb fingers. The central heating makes my entire body tingle with pleasure as we come inside, and I close the door behind me, bolt it, and put the chain across. Such a cosy feeling. Harry jumps immediately onto his chair – now adorned with a grey blanket patterned with little black paw prints that I bought just after Christmas. Why bother fighting it? No one else is going to sit there, are they? He circles a few seconds, then settles down with a 'huff' and falls instantly to sleep. Typical. I, on the other hand, am now assailed by an appalling and torrential tsunami of heat that begins in my face and then attempts to explode the rest of me in fiery rivers. I fling off my jacket and fleece as if they, not I, were on fire, and flop onto the sofa, arms outstretched. This is absolutely no use to me whatsoever now. Where are all the hot flushes when you're outside in the chilly park at six-thirty on a February night?

The old man on the bench pops into my thoughts suddenly. I do hope he's got back to his own home by now and is padding about in his slippers, humming to himself as he puts on the kettle and makes toast. But, it occurs to me to wonder, why was he on that bench at all, at this time of night, at this time of year? I so wish I'd stopped to talk to him.

I dial for food, which is quite satisfying when you live on your own. You can just do it, no one raises any eyebrows or makes any comments. Apart from Harry, who raises not only an eyebrow but the entire rest of his head when it arrives.

'Did you see me coming after you for some of yours?' I ask him, and he flops his head back down onto his paws.

This is great, I tell myself, stuffing in pizza to *Holby City*. I do what I want, when I want, and there's no one to answer to, or explain to, or apologise to. I'm just doing whatever the hell I choose.

Twenty-five minutes into the episode and the elderly couple we met at the beginning, walking their dog and holding hands, are mown down on the pavement by a runaway tractor. Standard daily incident in Holby, not worthy of even one person shouting 'Sorry, did you say, a *tractor*?' Despite the careful ministrations of a sexy male doctor with designer stubble, both die. It's a dreadful shock. We all thought they would pull through. They were on adjacent beds, chatting, worrying, reassuring. Making jokes and being generally cheerful and in love, even after seventy-odd years. How wonderful and unlikely. All the doctors loved them, the nurses loved them, the audience loved them. But Florence suffered a massive haemorrhage and just stopped, right in the middle of a sentence.

'Oh, Brian,' she said, 'we must remember to post the –'

'What was that, my dear?' Brian said, trying to look over at her. But he never heard the end of that sentence, as Florence's head lolled and her hand flopped out of the side of the bed. 'Oh, Florence my girl,' he said. 'Where did you go? Have you left me?' He waited a moment before concluding that Flo had indeed left him, and then he smiled. 'Don't you be frightened, my girl. I'll be right there.' He wrung every last drop out of us before reaching for her hand, putting his head back down, and peacefully slipping away.

Before the crash team rushed in with a trolley and jumped on him.

Harry raises his head when he hears me sobbing, so I change channels.

I start watching a horror film where an evil spirit spends centuries luring children to their violent and grisly deaths, but it does nothing to cheer me up. It's no good, the old couple are in my head, and for the first time since I was eighteen, I feel my age. What if it were me in that accident – or probably one not involving farm machinery? Who would be there to hold my hand and reassure me?

Quick flashback to the sexy, stubbly doctor.

No, that's not what I meant. With any luck I'll be 104 when I go, and he won't look twice at me anyway. But I don't want to spend the next fifty-four years on my own. And worse, I don't want to die on my own. So it's with sickening trepidation that I pick up my phone, click to the app store, and conduct a search for something called *Butterflies*.

5
NERVOUS MAN

Being fifty must have some advantages, I think to myself as I'm warming my feet up with the hairdryer a few weeks later. Yes, it has its drawbacks, there's no doubt about that. Club 18-30 holidays are out. You can't enter the Radio Two short story competition. The lad on the till doesn't ask for ID before speedily clicking the 'clearly at least two decades over twenty-five' button when you're buying super glue. And now it seems you have to endure 14 dull and pointless conversations on an app before finding one that you might even consider thinking about meeting.

But there are definitely some advantages, too. I point the hairdryer under the duvet for a few seconds, then drop it and jump into bed before it gets cold again. Ahh, bliss. The advantage for me right now is being in bed at 9 p.m. and knowing that nothing and no one will disturb me until I wake up naturally around 7 a.m. tomorrow. My kids are adults and don't need me, my husband is gone, my dog is silent. I have nowhere to be and no one counting on me. It's a liberating feeling and I fall asleep almost instantly.

I'm awoken at 2:13 by my phone ringing. I'm instantly alert, the adrenalin flooding through me, preparing my muscles, my heart, and my lungs, for whatever horror I am about to face. The screen shows me that it's Amy, and I release a breath, my heart rate slowing slightly. I settle a bit and put the bedside light on. If some horror has occurred, it's not likely to be delivered to me by my teenage daughter. If it had been Josh, I might have felt differently; but I'm positive this is not a horror or disaster for anyone but Amy. Her mental health has not been great through her teens, and she still calls me at unspeakable times of night occasionally.

'You ok, darling? Did something wake you up?'

There's a pause and I hear her rapid breathing. She's not hyperventilating, but she's getting close. 'I can't sleep.' Her voice is dry and hoarse.

'Oh no.' I press the phone closer to my ear, as if that will bring me closer to her. 'Something on your mind?'

When she was about ten, Amy had a dream featuring our neighbour's cat, Mrs. Violet McTibbles (named by their 7-year-old daughter Grace). Amy said she dreamed she saw it lying on the road, all bloody and broken. It was very upsetting for her and caused Tim and me a lot of – well, just me, come to think of it – a lot of problems with getting her to go to sleep. And then, about a week later, just when I thought she was starting to get over it, the cat disappeared. Poor old Mrs. McTibbles was never seen again. To be fair, she probably got fed up of being bullied by the other cats, and ran away.

Amy, of course, has never forgotten this incident, and tends to dwell on her thoughts a bit too much, worrying that she's having another premonition. Thus far, Violet's demise has been the only one, but I can't simply dismiss it. Amy's self-esteem struggles a bit, but this ability to predict the future has helped her find herself, find what it is about herself, that's special. She clings to it in her darkest moments. 'I may have just fallen out with my best friend / got a bad grade on an essay / lost my job, but at least I can predict death.' I don't want to take that away from her, but I also want her to have a good sleep and not be awake night after night.

'I'm just so worried that...' She stops, but her breathing is still heavy.

'Worried about what, sweetheart?' Although I know, from past experience, what the answer is going to be.

'I'm too scared to go to sleep.' She swallows, takes a shaky breath. 'In case I don't wake up again.'

'Oh sweetheart. How awful to feel like that.'

'I know. It sucks.'

'Has something triggered it, do you think? Scary film? Depressing conversation?'

'No, nothing specific. Just a… feeling. You know?'

I can honestly say that in all my fifty years, I have never suspected that I wouldn't wake up in the morning. Apart from a school trip to Paris when Sonia Halston threatened to smother me in my sleep. But I just asked to be moved to a different dormitory. We all did, actually.

'I'm not surprised you can't sleep. Can you read for a bit?'

A pause. 'What shall I read, though?'

'How about some Harry Potter?'

Pause. 'Which one?'

'Your favourite one – Goblet of Fire, isn't it?'

Pause. 'Could do.'

I know what she's aiming for, and luckily I've got all the Harry Potter books lined up in my underbed drawer. 'Would you like me to read it to you, sweetheart?'

Pause. 'Would that be OK?'

My eyes accidentally spot the time – 02:24 – and dart away again. 'Of course, darling.' I drag the covers back and scuttle round to the other side of the bed. Harry lifts his head up, sees it's only me doing something inexplicable, and drops it back down again with a sigh. I pull out the drawer, grab the book, then scuttle back to my side. 'Shall I start from the usual place?'

It's the part where Harry has to retrieve a golden egg from a fire-breathing dragon. I read all the books to her when she was little and still felt safe, and now this process swaddles her again in that intense feeling of childhood security. The sound of Harry's terrifying race to grab the egg without being incinerated alive very quickly soothes her off to sleep, and before long I hear her breathing deeply and evenly. Thank you, J.K.

I of course am completely unable to get back to sleep until 05:55. Then the bin men arrive with a lot of clattering and shouting at 07:30, and Harry wakes up needing the garden.

Luckily, it's a day off, so at least I haven't got to dispense any medical advice with a marshmallow where my brain used to be. I make a strong coffee and ponder over the fact that Amy never wants her dad to help her with that kind of thing. I start frowning, but then very quickly realise that I'd rather be the parent she calls than the one she doesn't call. Even at two o'clock in the morning. I yawn widely, enjoying the sensation, then decide that fresh air will help to wake me up, so I clip on Harry's lead and go out.

I don't have the energy to walk all the way up to the Leas with Harry today, and come instead to the local 'rec', which is much nearer home. But doing laps around this huge field is brain-foggingly dull for those of us unable to smell the previous comings and goings of all other animals in the vicinity, especially when my brain is already quite foggy. After half an hour I'm considering heading home, even though I know poor Harry wants to stay, so when my old friend Zoe joins me on the walk, he gets a reprieve. Oh, God, no, she doesn't join me physically. She's joined me on Facetime. She's not a dog fan. Or a winter fan. Or a walking fan. Zoe's idea of a walk is putting the bins out. So she's at home in bed on her Ipad while I trudge round and round, throwing a ball for Harry, then retrieving it myself. It's not completely pointless: he watches it fly semi-enthusiastically, but then loses interest and wanders off to sniff something.

Zoe called me to have a rant about her step-son, Nathan, which is quite diverting, and makes these dull circuits more bearable. On the downside, though, her face is filling my screen and preventing me from reading the four texts from a certain person that have arrived since I've been out. My fingers are twitching.

'He's nine,' Zoe keeps repeating. 'What kind of nine-year-old behaves like that?'

Thankfully she's not looking for a response. 'None,' I say, just in case.

'Exactly. It's ridiculous. It's obviously his mother, indulging him all the time. She literally lets him get away with murder…'

Another message notification pops up at the top of the screen. That makes five messages now, and if I don't read them soon my phone is likely to melt. I feel a little grin spreading as I imagine what the messages might say, and a champagne bottle pops its cork inside me, fizzing and bubbling. There's a little squeal in there somewhere, bouncing around like a toddler on orange smarties, but it can't get past the wall of fatigue. Plus Zoe's having a tough time at the moment. She won't want to hear my exciting news.

I've only been texting this man for a bit over two weeks, but it's been going so well I feel like I've struck gold already. It's less than a month since I downloaded the *Butterflies* app, and it's been nothing but brilliant. I researched online dating a bit before I filled in my profile, and read so many horror stories of married men, and men just looking for quick hook-ups, and men who send anatomical photos, and men who ask for them, but my own experience has been fantastic. That first evening, after I'd spent half an hour filling in all my details and uploading a photo, the messages started flooding in. It did actually recommend uploading a selection of photos, each one showing you doing something different – on holiday, out with friends, flying a plane, that sort of thing. This would apparently give any potential matches a great insight into your personality and see how exciting a relationship with you might be, but I didn't think me in my pyjamas eating a chocolate orange would put me in a very good light. In the end I went with a candid photo that Josh took at Christmas, where the warm, muted light from the tree and the fire place makes my skin look very glowy and youthful, and my hair is in charming disarray from the turkey. I'm smiling and I look thin so on it went. And it went down a storm.

'Beautiful lady,' was the first message. Literally the very first one! I actually flushed with pleasure. 'Thank you Shawn,' I replied. 'What do you do?'

'Make ladys happy 😀😀😀 xxx,' he replied, so I left it there. But he was only one of about 9 responses I got that very first evening, all of them quite flattering. After 26 years with the same man, it conjured up images of the discos of my teens, when you couldn't move for a hormonal lad trying to touch your bum, while *Tainted Love* played in the background.

To be honest, most of them were inappropriate. Wanting to meet up immediately, suggesting things they'd like to do to me, or that I could do to them. Of the nine, I ended up blocking Shawn ('Make ladys happy'), Nick (just his abs), Douglas ('Wasssuuuuuuuup??'), Brendan ('Where do you live?'), Tony ('I'm a professional tennis player and tennis coach, I play tennis every day, do you like tennis?'), Kevin (shirtless in bed), and Marc-Jean (cowboy hat). But that was OK because I was left with Stuart and Paul, who both seemed very nice. Stuart's photo featured him in a tux, pouring champagne into a glass, laughing; and Paul looked a bit like Kevin Bacon. Stuart had a great write-up too – humorous, interesting, grammatically correct – and definitely looked like an intelligent man with lots going on in his life. Paul's just said 'Looking for that special someone', but, you know, Kevin Bacon.

So I chatted to them both for the evening, which felt very risqué. Obviously I didn't mention to either of them that I was talking to someone else at the same time, but it got a bit tricky once or twice when I forgot what I'd said to each one.

Me: So your job sounds very interesting – set designer. Is that in theatre or television?

Paul: Im in insurance lol where did you get set designer from lol

But I think I got away with it. Stuart became more and more interesting as the evening went on, and I ended up pausing my *Game of Thrones* DVD so I could concentrate properly on the conversation. He had a fifteen-year-old daughter and a twenty-year-old son, both of whom lived with their calm and friendly mum, fifteen miles away. He and their mum had split amicably – 'a mutual decision' – just over two years ago, and he was comfortably settled in an open-plan and light-filled warehouse conversion apartment on the south-east outskirts of London. I could picture it – very chic and modern, all white walls and chrome appliances, cream rugs and an accent colour of burnt orange or teal picked out in an occasional glass vase or wall print. I could even see myself walking around the place barefoot, holding a glass of sparkling wine, my perfectly smooth and pedicured feet sinking into the deep carpet. I'd be in cream linen trousers and blush silk chemise. 'It's great living in an old warehouse,' he said. 'Whenever I need a wooden pallet or some cable ties, I can just pop downstairs.'

'I can understand the pallet, but I'm a tad concerned about your need for cable ties.'

'Oh, don't worry, it's not for tying anyone to a leaky pipe in my basement for seventeen days.'

It made me chuckle, although it was an odd choice of topic to joke about, given our circumstances.

He worked as a designer, mostly for theatre but occasionally got one-off jobs for new office buildings or hotels. 'The lobby is the most important part of any building,' he said. 'It's where everyone gets their first impression of the company, whatever it may be. So it has to be tarted up to a standard probably higher than any of the internal rooms or corridors. To tempt people in. Like one of those awful photos you ladies love to use with the bunny ears or the sparkles.'

'You mean you create a fake first impression, then?'

'No, that's not what I meant.'

'That fails to deliver when you see it up close?'

'Bit harsh!'

'Leaving everyone with a lingering sense of disappointment?'

'I need to rethink my strategy.'

He was charming, and I was charmed. It felt like we had clicked with each other immediately. And his photo was very attractive too. In fact it got more and more attractive as the evening went on.

'You're a very attractive woman, Steph,' he said, instantly moving up another forty steps on his own attractiveness ladder. 'How would you feel about meeting up for coffee or a stroll? No pressure, we can chat more first if you like?'

It's a no-brainer. 'I'd love to, Stuart.' At this point I was astonished to notice that it was after midnight. I'd been chatting to him for over three hours. 'I need to sleep – work in the morning. Shall we chat tomorrow to make the arrangements?'

'Yes, I'd like that. What an amazing evening it's been.'

'It really has, hasn't it?'

'Definitely. I don't know about you, but I feel like we've got a real connection here, and that's the first time it's happened for me online. You're great to talk to, and we are so on the same wavelength. Sleep well, beautiful Stephanie. Looking forward to chatting some more tomorrow xx'

I never heard from him again.

Next day there were a couple of messages in my inbox and I opened them eagerly as soon as I woke up, but they were just from Paul. 'Morning Stephanie hows u' He hadn't even made the effort to use a question mark. I ignored it and went about my day, periodically checking the app to see if Stuart had been in touch. By lunch time there was still nothing.

'What's the protocol?' I asked Nina, over my meal deal. 'The last message last night was from me, and I was the one who suggested chatting again today, so it feels like it should be him getting in touch today. Would you say?'

She shrugged. 'How would I know?'

'But you're the expert! You're the one who told me about the app!'

She rolled her eyes round a mouthful of date loaf. 'I know about the app, Steph. I don't know about the fragile and incomprehensible delicacies of all human interactions.'

'Fuck's sake.'

'Excuse me Doctors,' Niamh said at this point, putting her head round the door of Nina's consulting room. 'I've got someone on the phone who says she needs to speak to a doctor urgently. Would one of you mind…?'

Nina put her hand up. 'I'll take it.' She widened her eyes at me, then rolled them pointedly towards Niamh. 'Put it through, Niamh.'

I lifted my hands in a 'What?' gesture.

'Go and ask *her*,' Nina stage-whispered, as her phone started ringing. 'She's young, she's probably more in the know about these things than we are. Good afternoon, Doctor Dellis speaking.'

I stared at her in horror, then wordlessly vanished from the room. Speaking to Niamh about my love life was right up there with do-it-yourself brain surgery on my list of things to try.

In the end I decided that I'm fifty, I don't need to play stupid teenage 'don't come across too keen' games, and sent Stuart a text. 'Hiya, how are you today? When shall we meet for our coffee then? I have an hour this evening, between six and seven if you're free?'

He didn't reply. And then, in a blink, our messages all disappeared. One second I was re-reading them for the third time, next second they were gone. Before my very eyes. I stared at my phone, closed and re-opened the app, turned the phone off and on again, re-opened the app. Nothing. Not so much as a full stop.

'He's blocked you,' Nina said at the end of surgery.

I blinked. 'What? *Why*?'

She shrugged, shutting down her computer. 'Who knows, Steph? That's the male psyche for you. Completely unintelligible.'

'But... I didn't do anything. We had a connection. He wanted to meet me. He was looking forward to chatting today.' I pause. 'He said I was beautiful.'

Nina shrugged. 'Like I said, incomprehensible.'

'Ooh, maybe he died? It could happen – people die all the time.'

'What, so you think maybe someone in the hospital, or a family member, took the trouble to log onto his *Butterflies* account and block you, right before they are calling the funeral home?' She peered at me over the top of her glasses.

'I don't know, maybe?' I stuck out my bottom lip. 'It's not fair!'

Nina shrugged. 'No, my darling. It is not.' She squeezed my arm. 'See you tomorrow.'

I stood there immobile a few moments, clenching and unclenching my fists. An explosive feeling was building inside me, but it had nothing to explode at. Stuart was so utterly inaccessible and invisible, the anger roaring through me was akin to the rage you feel when you stub your toe – intensely powerful; immensely powerless. I wanted to understand. I *needed* an explanation, I felt I was owed that. But I couldn't get one. I would never get one. I just had to swallow this rejection, this feeling of being used and dropped like an apple core, and get on with my life

'New love sweeps away the old,' my mum said to me once, when I was sobbing over Martin Cook in the fifth year. I snogged Steve Goldsack a day or two later, and found out that Mum was right. So when I got home that evening, after being blocked by Stuart, I replied to all of Paul's dull but pleasingly persistent messages.

That was over two weeks ago, and in that time I've come to see that Paul is actually quite a sweet chap. I'm not sure his sense of humour is exactly on my wavelength – 'Check out this video, it's so funny!' Cue video of a dog walking around on its hind legs in a Santa hat – but he's quite intelligent, easy to chat to, looks like Kevin Bacon, and, crucially, hasn't blocked me. After a week or so of exchanging messages on the app, I finally felt confident that he wasn't suddenly and inexplicably going to disappear, so I gave him my number and we started texting more regularly. The past few days he's become a bit more playful, and now we're arranging to meet up. Which is undoubtedly what the five texts on my phone are about.

'I don't know how much more I can take,' Zoe is saying, whilst peering intently at the screen and dabbing at a flaw in her foundation. 'I'm at breaking point, Steph.'

'Oh, Zo, it must be hard – '

'Hang on,' she says, and looks over her shoulder. I glance behind me at the same time, but all I can see is Harry cocking his leg against someone's bike. I walk away quickly, and fortunately he follows. Zoe comes back. 'Sorry, Waitrose are here. Chat later.' And she's gone.

Sure enough all of the texts are from Paul. He's suggested a time and a place tomorrow, Saturday, to meet for lunch. 'Bar Gigi,' he says, 'right on the seafront, in a place called Sandgate. Do you know it?'

Of course I know it, I flipping live here. Sandgate is a five minute drive from my house. I go there all the time.

His next text says, 'It has a lovely little terrace.'

Yes, I know all about the terrace, thanks. I flipping live here. In the summer, it's exactly like a beach bar in Greece or somewhere in the Med. In March it will probably be deserted and bleak.

'Their menu looks good,' Paul says next. 'Lots of fish dishes.'

Yes, Paul. It's a seafront bar, in a seaside town. I've been there about seventy times.

'Do you like fish dishes?' is the next one.

If I'm honest, it feels a little bit... insistent. These messages are about a minute or two apart. I didn't answer because I was face-timing someone else, but it feels as if Paul might have been expecting an instant response.

'Well I do,' his final message says. 'If you're still alive I hope I'll see you there tomorrow, at 1pm xx'

If I'm still alive. It's been twenty-five minutes since his first message! I decide to leave it until I get home to reply because I'm feeling some kind of sarcasm coming on and have to wait for it to pass.

I walk home and give Harry his post-walk treat (that's a thing, right?) then have my post-walk-treat – a long pee while scrolling through Facebook and falling into the trap of watching dog rescue videos, followed by bear rescue videos, only brought to a conclusion by my legs going numb. I make a coffee, sit down on the sofa, and am immediately assaulted by a flood of drenching heat again. I've heard that when you're suffering with hypothermia, you get so cold that you eventually feel terribly hot and start stripping off your clothes. That's when you die of course. As I strip off layers down to a vest, I feel like I know what that must feel like. When it's over and I've descended gracefully back from my brief sojourn on the surface of the sun, I turn to my text messages. I re-read the five from Paul, and wonder what on earth I was so angry about earlier. Completely irrational. He's interested, not insistent. Attentive, not manipulative. Considerate, not certifiable. He's made a phenomenal effort to research my home town, and has even looked at the menu and made sure I'm going to like it. What a sweetheart.

'That sounds great,' I text him. 'You sure you're happy to drive all this way?' He's in Surrey somewhere, apparently.

'Of course I have a lovely car I will enjoy it'

'OK then. See you tomorrow at 1.'

'Tomorrow at 1 cant wait x'

Sandgate isn't really a town. It's more of a road that leads along the seafront from Folkestone to Hythe. I'm sure the residents would disagree, but I've lived here all my life and I've never worked out where the residents actually are. The main street is lined with endless antique shops and cafés, with the occasional additional antique shop, clothes boutique, charity shop, yet more antique shops, and extra cafés. I say the main street – there is only that one road. Then it opens out to the seafront and you can see across the channel to France on a clear day. Sometimes you spot the squat power station at Dungeness and think it's France. Sometimes the view of France is obstructed by the diesel fumes of cross-channel ferries, or fishing vessels. But on a warm, sunny day the sea looks tantalisingly blue and sparkly, seagulls are swooping and screeching after the fishing trawlers, the waves drag and push on the shoreline, and the salty scent of spray and seaweed reminds you of your seaside childhood days.

It's nothing like that today. Today it is raining and grey, and blustery March winds are hurling raindrops at my windscreen, obscuring the view of the ferries and trawlers. I am looking for a parking space as near to Bar Gigi as I can possibly get, and am actually considering turning the car round and going home. Paul seems like a genuinely nice chap from his messages, but I feel no excitement about this meeting. Yet again my mind goes back to the gorgeous but elusive Stuart, and I imagine how I would be feeling driving here in the rain to meet him, with all the excitement and promise it would have held. I shake my head, to rearrange the contents, and keep driving, forcing myself forward when I want to go back. It reminds me of the feeling you get before walking into an MOT service centre.

Sensibly, people are staying away from the seafront in their masses today, so I manage to find a spot almost directly opposite the wet and windswept terrace of Bar Gigi. As I walk away from my car towards the bar I see a solitary, eager-looking man just standing up under the battered plastic awning that looks so chic in the summer. He's wearing a grey crew neck, charcoal grey jacket and jeans. OK so far. Maybe this will be worth it.

'Stephanie?' he says, coming towards me.

The only thing even slightly resembling Kevin Bacon at this point is the hair. And it's 1984 fluffy Footloose Kevin, not modern day, hot older man Kevin.

Now I think about it, the fluffy 1984 Bacon hair is probably what tricked me into thinking Paul looked like him. Doesn't matter because he's already a million points up on Mike from last month, and not just because he remembered my name. He was also on time, and has more girth than a giraffe's neck.

I smile, 'Hi Paul,' and put out my hand, while Paul keeps on coming, making my arm bend and squashing my hand between our two tummies as he embraces me clumsily.

'Oh,' he says, realising where, and why, my hand is. 'Sorry, I thought we were going to...' He presses his lips together and swallows.

'Never mind, doesn't matter. How are you? How was the drive?'

'Not too bad,' he says, and as he's talking about the traffic I start to notice something odd about his lips. '...solid from junction ten all the way to Clackett Lane,' he's saying, and now that I've noticed it I can't look away. His top lip is actually *trembling*. It's distorting out of shape and clearly not behaving properly, as he keeps rubbing his mouth with his fingers to try and make both lips stay still. I blink. His voice is shaking too. '...left just after 8 o'clock this morning.'

'Well I'm glad you made it,' I say, and look away to give him a moment to recover himself. 'Let's sit inside, shall we?'

'Oh, yes, yes, that's a good idea, sorry,' he says, picking his keys, wallet and phone up off a sodden table nearby.

While we're looking at the menus, I can't help but see that his hands are trembling, making the menu pages flicker and shake in the air. Eventually he lays it flat on the table and peers down at it, but now I can see that his head is shaking too. He looks up suddenly and catches me staring.

'Ready to order?' I ask him.

'Oh, er, sorry, not quite, sorry. But, you know, you go ahead, don't mind me.'

I'm not sure what he means by this, as neither of us can order anything until the waiter comes back. 'No, it's OK, I don't mind waiting.'

He glances up at me and swallows again. 'Sorry, sorry, won't be a mo.'

I avoid watching him frantically trying to read the words in front of him as his panic grows out of control. Instead I take my phone out and quickly write a text to Zoe 'Call me in forty minutes with an emergency.' Then I delete it without sending it, and send the same message to Nina instead. Not sure how many people I want knowing about this mortifying process.

Paul is now dabbing his forehead with his napkin.

He manages to make it through the main course without choking, although he doesn't eat much. It's a wonder he manages to move any of the fish from his plate to his mouth successfully, considering how much everything is vibrating. We eat in absolute silence. I do have some small talk questions lined up, but I decide to let him concentrate on one thing.

Eventually he pushes away all the food left on his plate and his cutlery hits the china with a careless clatter. I wonder how much time is left before Nina rings me. I wonder if she'll do it. I wonder if she even got the message.

'That was delicious,' I say, laying down my knife and fork silently. 'How was the Dover sole?'

He nods. 'Oh, yes, yes, very nice, very tasty. Very very nice indeed.'

'Good.'

'So, er, Stephanie, what do you do?'

We've been texting each other for two weeks. We went over this on day two. 'I'm a G.P., remember?' Paul closes his eyes and screws up his face, as if in pain. 'Are you OK?' I ask him, leaning forward.

He nods, and opens his eyes, a pained expression lingering on his face. 'I'm so sorry, I'm such an idiot, of course I remember you saying you were a G.P. Sorry, sorry, sorry. I remember I made that joke about – '

'Checking you out, yes, I remember that too.' It's an occupational hazard in my job, but it doesn't make it any easier to deal with. And everyone thinks for that insane second that they're the first person to say it. 'And you're in insurance. I remember that.'

'Ah, well, yes, sorry, that's not quite true.'

'Oh?'

'No. I should have been completely honest with you, Stephanie. So sorry. But actually I'm between jobs at the moment.'

'Oh dear. Sorry to hear that.'

'Nothing for you to be sorry about,' he says. 'It's not your fault, is it?'

'No.'

'No. But, er, the fact is, I had to leave my old job three months ago because I, er…'

He's struggling to say it. His top lip is going mad with anxiety. Please don't let it be a sexual harassment charge.

'…I had a heart attack,' he says, then pulls a weird face, as if he's just made a joke. 'Bet you're surprised to hear that?'

'Well,' I say, not even slightly surprised. Of course he had a bloody heart attack. The man is practically paralysed with fear at the prospect of selecting something from a menu, how was he ever going to cope with sales targets and appraisals? 'That's terrible,' I finish with, and at this moment, mercifully, my phone rings. I grab my bag and stand up, producing my phone like a rabbit. 'Sorry,' I mouth to Paul, then walk a few steps away from the table. 'Hello?'

'Plumbing or medical?' Nina asks me. It takes me a second to work out she's asking me what sort of emergency I need.

'Oh, hi Amy, how are you feeling?'

'You're on a bad date aren't you? Because if it was going well, you would have told me go away by now.'

'Oh, no, love, that's not good. Do you want me to come and get you?'

'Ah yes, it is what I thought.'

'Of course, darling.' I glance overtly at my watch. 'I can probably get to you in about half an hour, is that OK?'

'I hope you have made the volume on your phone not so loud,' she says quietly, sending me into a sudden panic. 'It is completely possible that he can hear every word I'm saying to you.'

'Oh no, don't be daft, you can't get the bus if you're feeling poorly. Stay where you are, I'll be there as soon as I can.'

'You're a terrible person.'

'Love you too. Bye.'

I slide the phone smoothly into my pocket and look at Paul. He's fiddling with the cuffs of his jumper. His face is red and covered with sweat and he looks as if he really should take the jumper off. He's probably having the same thought, but hasn't quite got the courage to do it.

To his credit, he doesn't make it awkward or difficult. He says simply 'Emergency?' when I arrive back at the table, and looks sort of knowing when I nod. We split the bill and leave, pausing briefly on the pavement.

'So, er, would you...? Do you think you'd want to...?' he begins, and I don't think he's going to ask me if I want to switch my insurance provider.

'I'm sorry, Paul. It was great to meet you and I had a lovely time, but I don't think we're a match.' His face falls and he looks suddenly much older. *Please don't have a heart attack.*

'OK,' he says. 'That's a shame.'

'It is, but, you know, we can't be attractive to everyone, can we?' I do the farewell smile and head tilt, touch his arm and start to turn away. 'All the best, Paul.'

'I'm not surprised, though.'

I stop and turn back. He's gone quite grey and his top lip, now strong and fixed, is dotted with beads of sweat. 'What do you mean?'

He shrugs. 'Why would someone like you be interested in someone like me? I mean, look at us. You're an attractive doctor, probably pretty well off, nice car, big house. Perfect life.' He glances down at his grey jumper. 'I'm an ex-insurance salesman with no job, no home, no car and no life. My wife left me, I've just had a heart attack and am currently sleeping on my sister's sofa. Complete loser.'

It's difficult to know what to say this. I mean, he's right, isn't he?

No, no, he isn't. There no such thing as a loser, I sincerely believe that. I was being flippant. There are just people going through tough times. I take a step forward. 'What are you talking about? You're not a loser, Paul. You're going through a very difficult part of your life right now, that's all. I mean, Jesus, you had a heart attack and survived. You lost your job, and you survived. Your wife left you, and you survived.' I smile at him, and genuinely mean it this time. 'You're not a loser, you're a survivor.'

'Ha. One way to look at it, I suppose.'

'The only way to look at it. It's actually very impressive that in spite of those three quite massive setbacks all happening at once, you've still managed to get out of bed, get washed and dressed and get here to meet me.'

He lets out a small laugh. 'Now you're taking the piss.'

I shake my head. 'I'm absolutely not. I promise you.'

'Doesn't feel like it. I mean, I've been getting myself dressed since I was about four. Plenty of practice runs before I arrived at this natty ensemble.'

I grin. 'You're not giving yourself enough credit. You didn't have a three times broken heart when you were four.'

He smiles and I think he genuinely means it too. 'But that date was terrible, wasn't it? Be honest.'

'All right, I'll be completely honest.' At this moment, someone walks past us on the pavement, ears blatantly flapping. 'Tell you what, let's go back inside and have a proper chat. Over a coffee.'

He nods. 'I'd like that.' But then suddenly his brows knit together and I've practically started chest compressions when he says, 'But what about the emergency?'

I blink. What's he talking about? And then I remember. 'Ah. Yes. Well…'

'Fake?'

'Sorry.'

He shrugs. 'It's OK. It was a terrible date.'

We go back inside, much to the astonishment of our waiter, who freezes in the act of clearing our table and stares at us. 'Could we have two coffees, please,' I ask him. 'Decaf.'

It turns out Paul's wife left him two months ago.

'Helen – that's my sister – she says I need to get back on the horse straight away. You know, start dating again.'

'How long were you married?'

'Nearly 16 years.'

'Did you feel ready to start dating again?'

He shrugs. 'I don't know, to be honest. I don't really know what I feel.'

'So our date today was the first one you've been on since you met your wife, 16 years ago?'

'Well, yes. Except it was eighteen years ago.'

'You're still grieving, then. On top of having recently had a very close shave with death, which has probably left you a bit traumatised.'

'S'pose so.'

'So you asked me to be honest. About our date.'

He nods, closing his eyes. 'Go on then. Hit me with it.'

'OK.' I hesitate briefly, working out how best to word this, conducting a dynamic risk assessment of the effect my words might have. I glance at the entrance to make sure there's a clear pathway for paramedics. He's regained some colour now, but he's still a serious risk of stress cardiomyopathy. I meet his eyes. 'It wasn't great,' I say, as gently as I can. 'But I genuinely think it's because you didn't really want to be here.'

'Oh, no, no, Steph, I did, I was really looking forward to it…'

'No, I know, I don't mean that. What I'm trying to say is that I don't think you are anywhere near ready to start dating yet. I think you thought this is the thing you need to do to feel better. Get back on the horse, get your life back on track, get yourself sorted.' I hesitate. 'It's as if you have a wife-shaped hole in your life, and you feel you need to fill it.' I pause. 'The sooner the better. And then everything can carry on as before. Would you say that was right?'

His eyes dampen and he looks down, rubbing his nose. 'I just miss her so much,' he says quietly. 'I think it was her leaving that brought on the heart attack.' He shakes his head and laughs. 'Sounds ridiculous, I know, but it's like she literally broke my heart.' He glances up and gives a half smile. 'And I mean literally literally.'

I nod. 'It's not ridiculous. There is a thing called Takotsubo Cardiomyopathy, also known as – '

'Broken heart syndrome, yeah I know. I googled it.'

I nod. 'Course you did. How long after her leaving was your heart attack?'

He breathes in and out slowly a couple of times before answering, which makes me instantly go back to amber alert. His lips and fingertips still have good colour, and the greyness has subsided. There's no more apparent sweating. He doesn't seem unwell. He raises his hand and in a horrible moment I think he's going to rub his jaw or arm, perhaps to ease pain there. I'm almost out of my seat. But he doesn't. He picks up the little sugar biscuit that came with the coffee and crushes it into crumbs on the table. Thank God.

'Two days later,' he says. 'We'd just had a horrible argument on the phone and I suddenly felt, you know, really unwell.'

I nod. 'And have you felt unwell like that since then?'

He laughs without mirth. 'Don't go all GP on me please.'

'Oh, God, I was wasn't I? Sorry. Force of habit.'

'Understandable. But anyway, I know exactly the symptoms to look out for, and exactly what to do if I get any. So you don't need to worry.'

'No, of course.'

He smiles again. 'It's nice that you did, though.'

'Well, still annoying.'

'Maybe a bit.'

'Sorry.'

'It's fine. Anyway, does that mean that you think she could have caused my heart attack then? Because Helen tells me I'm a stupid idiot for thinking that and that I just need to eat more healthily and get more exercise.'

'Well, without going all GP on you again, Helen is right about diet and exercise, but wrong about the break up not causing it.'

'I knew it!'

'I mean, obviously there's no concrete proof that that definitely was the cause. But it's possible. There is a correlation.'

'Ha. My wife tried to murder me by heart attack.' He widens his eyes. 'It's the perfect crime!'

'Mm, yeah. Bit hit and miss though, wouldn't you say? I mean, not as guaranteed as the old 'reverse the car over him' technique.'

His smile drops suddenly and his face darkens. 'That's how my brother died.'

I smack myself in the face. 'Oh shit, Paul, I'm so sorry. I don't know what the matter is with me today…' But now I see that he's grinning and shaking his head and I realise that he's actually having a joke with me, and I laugh with relief.

'Can I text you now and then?' he says on the pavement a few minutes later. 'I don't mean as a GP. Or as a… date. Just as a friend?'

'I'd really like that. We can swap murder stories.'

He nods, smiling. He looks a million times better than when we arrived earlier. 'We can. If anyone ever tries to get me with organ failure, I'll let you know.'

That wasn't the outcome I was looking for, I think to myself as I drive home. But it certainly doesn't feel like a complete disaster. I'm smiling, and I've made a new friend at the very least.

6
GRUMPY MAN

March's fierce winds and rain eventually give way to April's blustery rain and sleet. I'm standing at my front door again, coat on, hood up, head down, trying to drag a reluctant princess Harry out of the house in the evening. He keeps putting one paw out then looking at me as if to say, 'You're kidding, right?'

'Oh come *on*, Harry. For God's sake, I'm not out here for my benefit you know.' I say it out loud, but not quite loud enough for anyone passing to realise I've started talking to my dog. 'You've been snoozing, I've been working. I so do not want to be out here right now.' I'd had to blue-light a six-month old baby girl to hospital with what looked like bacterial meningitis, and her mum had gone completely to pieces. 'All I want to do is get my pjs on and watch Netflix and chill.' I hesitate. Amy told me a few months ago that that actually doesn't mean what it sounds like. 'Come on, boy. There's a bag of Thai Sweet Chilli crisps in there with my name on them.' Harry inches forward, notices yet again that it's not very nice out, and retreats. I close my eyes.

'Hey,' says a gravelly voice behind me. 'Stephanie is it?'

It's my elderly neighbour, who has suddenly and silently cracked open his front window.

I smile through the rain. 'Yes, that's right. Hi... er –' Oh God. I've forgotten his name. I was just about to say it and in response it immediately blinked out of existence in my mind. In fairness, we have only met once since I moved in. Plus at this age my short term memory is like wet soap. Hi,' I say again, trying to hide the tone in my voice making it obvious I've just forgotten his name.

'Graham,' he says now, dead pan.

'Oh, yes,' I smile. 'Filthy weather.'

'Do you think you could close your front door a bit more quietly, Stephanie? It makes the entire house shake.'

I blink. That certainly was not what I was expecting. 'Oh. Does it? When exactly has that happened?'

'When you leave or enter the house, when do you think?' And he bangs the window closed, aggressively yanking the handle down to lock it. The curtain falls back into place and I'm alone again. I look at Harry's bum, the only part of him I can see as he has now done a complete one-eighty in the hallway to face the kitchen, and feel my jaw clench.

'That wasn't very nice, was it Harry?' I whisper. Harry doesn't turn round, and as my already thin enthusiasm for this miserable jaunt has now been completely obliterated I give in and go back inside. I snatch the front door and jerk it roughly towards me; then at the last minute slow it right down and close it as carefully and quietly as I can. I'm fifty, not fifteen.

Then I stick my middle finger up at the adjoining wall.

'What a horrible, miserable old git,' I say, pretending I'm talking to Harry. 'Absolutely no need to be so bloody rude about it. Slamming my front door, for God's sake.'

'Either make a positive impact on the world,' my mum's voice says in my head, 'or make no impact.' Or, wait. Is that actually my own voice, talking to Josh and Amy?

Ten minutes later, I'm back outside, knocking on Graham's door. I've got a small box of Roses that I was going to have on Saturday evening, but this is a better use for them. I can buy another box, anyway.

The door opens a crack, the chain on. 'What is it?' Graham asks me, as a greeting.

'Graham, I didn't get the chance earlier to apologise for the door thing.' I hold out the chocolates. 'I'm so sorry if I've been disturbing you.'

He stares at the chocolates, then up at me. I wonder for a hideous moment if he's got dementia and is now looking at a complete stranger offering him chocolates at his door.

'Don't like choclit,' he says. But interestingly doesn't close the door.

'Oh.' I lower the box. 'I'd like to get you something to make up for it though. Is there anything you do like?'

'No,' he says. And slams the door.

Well that's just fan-fucking-tastic, isn't it? I stomp back over to my own door and let myself back in. No one can say I haven't tried, because I bloody have. I fling my wet coat and shoes on the floor in the hall and march back into the living room. I was out there in the pouring bloody rain, getting wetter and colder, sacrificing my chocolates and my evening, trying to be nice. Trying to make amends for perhaps, possibly, on rare occasions, maybe once, being a bit thoughtless with closing the front door. And what happens? More bloody rudeness. I flop down onto the sofa in my damp pyjamas and wet hair, feeling uncomfortable and unrelaxed. Not the kind of start to my evening I was hoping for. Bloody great. Luckily there's an unopened box of Roses in my hand.

The next day is Thursday so I'm not working, and I take the opportunity of a temporary lull in the downpour to go out with H for a super long walk. It's about twenty-five minutes at a brisk pace down to the Sunny Sands (that's a misnomer for any beach located in the UK), so it takes Harry and me forty-five. Our enthusiastic brisk pace lasts about seven seconds, before we screech to a halt so that Harry can sniff something. He does this roughly every 15 seconds. 'Harry if you'd get a move on, we can spend more time at the beach before the heavens open.'

When we get there, the tide is out so the whole beach is a monochromatic scene of dark, hunched two-legged figures, stark on the expanse of pale sand, battling against the elements in hoods and hats; and their speedy little four-legged companions galloping around having an absolute riot. I unclip Harry's lead so he can bound towards the shoreline at top speed and plunge joyously into the waves. He never does that though. He simply stands and looks at his surroundings, then walks behind me when I move.

Grumpy Graham next door is still playing on my mind, so I send a quick text to Paul. Maybe he'll be able to give me a man's perspective on it all. 'Free for a chat? Something weird happened.'

'Can't talk now,' he says. 'Working.'

'Ooh, good news. What's the job?'

There's a long pause, giving me time to speculate. Obviously it's the sort of workplace where you're not allowed your phone out, hence the delay. Which means it must be one where people's personal information is stored. Probably an office job then. Also, why didn't he tell me about this? We were texting only a couple of days ago.

'Soz not that kind of job, working on 3D computer model of mums old dog Mothers day coming lol'.

Oh yes, the blight that is Mothers' Day. It tortures us when our kids are little – because bad behaviour is so much more depressing on Mothers' Day – and it taunts us when they're adults, because our own mothers are gone.

'OK, maybe chat later xxx'

I shove my phone back in my pocket and hunch my shoulders against the wind. God, I really need to offload to someone about Grumpy Graham. It's just so bloody unfair that he gets to be as rude as that to me, just because I may have accidentally closed the front door too loudly. And the key word here is 'accidentally.' Now he's been far more unpleasant to me, and upset me far more as a result, deliberately. How is that OK?

'Morning,' a cheery voice says, and for one mad millisecond I think Grumpy Graham has transported himself here to apologise. I look up and find an elderly lady wearing a scarf like the Queen in front of me. 'Isn't this lovely?'

I look around at the uninviting, windswept beach. The sky is an unremitting grey, giving no hint at all as to where the sun might be; the sea is relentlessly churning, made restless and moody by the fierce wind; and sand is being whipped into all the dogs' faces. I imagine the surface of Mars would probably look like this, except less bleak.

'I wouldn't say lovely exactly…'

She smiles and I can see that she is quite beautiful. 'Oh, forget the weather,' she says, with a flap of a gloved hand. 'Can't do anything about that. I mean this beach, here in the town where we live. Being able to walk here. Not everyone can.'

'Oh. Er, no, I suppose not.'

'And look at our dogs!' She turns, and behind her I see two little grey things, probably a quarter of Harry's size, zooming around the sand together like bullets. Harry has actually left the bit of beach directly behind me and has moved nearer, presumably so he can watch their antics. 'That's what it looks like to truly enjoy life,' she says, turning back to me.

'You're right,' I say, nodding. 'Look at those two. Getting so much out of just running around.'

'It gladdens my heart to watch them,' she says, and clasps her hands together. 'I wouldn't want to be anywhere else, wind or no wind.'

She must be late seventies, at least. Probably has all sorts of aches and pains by now so the simplest things, like getting out of bed or making a meal, are an unpleasant chore. I'm a good twenty or twenty-five years younger and my own knees hurt on the stairs. But here she is, cheerful and grateful and making the absolute most of every minute. She looks back at me one more time, then takes a step towards her little dogs. Suddenly I feel like I don't want to stop talking to her.

'I wish my dog would enjoy himself a bit more,' I say, walking with her. 'Look at him, just standing there.'

She glances at Harry. 'Is he sad?'

'I think so. His owner decided one day last year that he didn't want him any more. I've had him about five months now, and he's been quite miserable ever since.'

'Oh what a shame,' she says. 'I don't understand how anyone could do that.' She looks at me. 'They're like children, aren't they?'

I nod, although I'm not sure whether she's talking about the owner or the dog. 'I'm Steph,' I say, on impulse. 'It's lovely to meet you.'

'Hannah,' she replies, but doesn't hold out a hand. I guess that gesture is strictly for men in her generation.

'What are your dogs called?'

She grins and faces her two little fluff balls. 'They're called Ginger and Freddy. My absolute darlings.'

'What lovely names.'

'Thank you. Not particularly clever or original, but I was such a fan. What's your chap called?'

'Harry. I wouldn't say he's my darling, but I like having him around. He keeps me company.'

'Ah, on your own, are you?' I nod. 'I'm sorry to hear that. Divorce or death?'

I'm a bit taken aback by her directness. But then again, at… whatever age she is, I bet she's decided there's not enough time left to waste on niceties. And it makes me smile that the possibility of me never having been married hasn't even occurred to her. Must be another generational thing. 'Divorce.' I glance at her. 'A messy one.'

She nods, slowly. 'Death for me. But I had more than fifty years of marriage to quite a decent man, so I can't complain.'

By the end of twenty minutes chatting, I've learned that she brings Freddy and Ginger here most mornings, so I resolve to try and find her again on Saturday morning. Harry is the most interested I've ever seen him, as he watches Ginger and Freddy running about, and Hannah is like a sudden patch of sunlight falling on me on an otherwise dull day. I don't think I've ever met anyone quite as positive.

I decide to go home via The Leas, as it's such a lovely place to walk. You can actually see the white cliffs of Calais, and French street lights, on a clear day; and there are flower beds all the way along the footpath, lovingly tended year round by the council. During the London Olympics in 2012, one of the beds was planted so that the flowers came out in the shape of the Olympic rings. The town was astonished. I have to slog up the zig-zag path to get to the top, but even that is enjoyable today. My legs ache as I come round the final switchback, and I'm hot and out of breath, but when I finally reach the top with a surge of exultation, my body says, 'Think you're hot now? I'll show you hot,' and I erupt into drenching sweat. I claw at my coat and hoodie, frantically trying to get the layers off before I supernova. Fortunately for me, and the rest of planet earth, the wind up there is cold enough to douse the flames within a minute.

I've been texting an accountant called Justin for a few days, and when I get home forty minutes later I check my phone to catch up on all the messages he's sent me while I was out. There's a grand total of one. And it's 'Hey, how's your day going?' I drop the phone onto the kitchen side and put the kettle on.

I don't know what I'm expecting from these men on *Butterflies*. No, that's not true. I know exactly what I'm expecting. It's just that my expectations are clearly very out of synch with what I'm actually going to get. Maybe I need to lower my expectations. When the kettle boils I pick my phone up again, open Justin's message and reply with, 'Great so far. Lovely walk along the windy beach, met a charming old lady called Hannah. How's yours?'

'Great, just working,' he replies, the lack of acknowledgement of my answer irking me. 'Are you free tonight?'

Then I screen shot our interaction and send the picture to Nina.

'What's wrong with that?' she texts back.

'Bit dull?' I suggest.

'Yes but men are not good at text are they, darling? You know this. Don't judge him on his texting ineptitude.'

She's right, of course. I remember texting Tim eight years ago from my mum's bedside as I waited for her to exhale for the final time. I'd wanted to express the depth of my feelings, watching someone I loved having to suffer so much; knowing that the only way this nightmare could end was with her death. I wrote about all the years gone by, all the years to come, her suffering, my pain, and her final, terrible release from hers. He'd sent a sad face emoji, and the words 'At least it's over.' Then had suggested a take-away for dinner.

'OK,' I send back to Nina. 'I'll meet him. But when he turns out to be an inarticulate dullard, I'm blaming you.'

'Fine,' comes the reply. 'But perhaps he won't be.'

The rest of the day I'm restless and tense. My mind wastes minutes on concocting believable excuses not to go, ranging from mown down by a runaway tractor to an outbreak of rabies, but they all sound like excuses. If Justin said any of them to me, I'd know. Luckily his texts are nothing like as interesting. Our conversation throughout the day consists of a series of extraordinarily dull statements on both sides. 'Just been to Sainsbury's.' 'Forgot the milk.' 'I'm having soup.' And so on.

I text Nina and Paul and Amy and Zoe, but they all continue to tell me I should go and what have I got to lose and I'll never meet anyone if I don't. Well, Nina, Paul and Amy say that. Zoe says 'Sorry, can't talk, feeding an elephant.'

So I get ready and say goodbye to Harry. 'I won't be long,' I tell him. 'I'll probably only stay for one drink. Two hours, tops.' Then I force my feet to move me out to the car and take me there.

Justin is pleasant enough, actually. At the beginning. He's on time, dressed nicely, standard human-width hips, confident enough to kiss my cheek lightly when I arrive. He's already bought me a glass of white wine – 'I took the liberty' – so we sit down and the date begins.

'This is a nice pub,' he says, as an opener. 'Good choice.'

'Thanks.'

'There are some total dives around, these days, aren't there?'

'Oh, God, yes, there are. So what do you – ?'

'Folkestone's gone right downhill since I was a kid.'

'Oh, did you grow up round here?'

'Yes,' he says, nodding. 'My parents moved here from south London. I think they'd had enough, do you know what I mean?'

'Oh, really? What, the crime and pollution? Congestion charge? Extortionate cost of parking?'

He grins, but I'm not sure anything I said was particularly funny. 'If you like,' he says.

I nod slowly, frowning. 'Sorry, I'm afraid I don't really get what you mean. What didn't they like about it?'

'Come on. Work it out. South London, yeah?'

I shake my head. 'Nope, sorry, not getting it.'

He rolls his eyes. 'Oh, here we go. Are you a bloody "remainer"?'

I blink. 'Um, you mean Brexit? What does that have to do with it?'

'You are, aren't you? Knew it. Typical middle class liberal, living in your cosy little bubble.'

'Hang on...'

'Believe me, if you'd lived where my parents lived, you'd have voted out, too.'

I'm shaking my head. 'What? How does where you live affect how you voted?'

He flicks his eyebrows up, then makes me jump by bursting out laughing, throwing his head back, rocking in his seat, holding his tummy, and 'whoo'-ing. It dies down eventually, and he wipes his eyes, shaking his head and chucking out the odd giggle; then he looks at me and it all starts up again.

I push my sleeve back and look at my watch; the hilarity dies down remarkably quickly.

'You really are priceless, Steph,' he says, wiping his eyes again, although I can see quite clearly that they're not watering. 'Absolutely priceless.'

I think I know where this is going, but I want to draw it out of him, like a handkerchief. I want to make him say it. I smile sweetly. 'What's so funny?'

He jerks his head back, as if in surprise, but it's so exaggerated it's clearly fake. 'You're not even kidding?'

'No. I'm not even kidding.'

He picks up his pint and takes a long swig. 'You must have been to south London, surely? At least once?'

'I believe so.'

'So you've seen what it's like.'

'Yes.'

'So.'

I shrug. 'You've lost me. Please, Justin. You're going to have to spell it out.'

He presses his lips together, takes a quick glance around, then leans so far forward that three quarters of his body are on my side of the table, and whispers, 'Pakis.'

I immediately stand up. It's the adrenalin, bubbling me up with anger. Now I'm up here I feel a bit silly, but I have principles. He catches my eye, a bit startled. 'Everything all right?'

'Not really, no.' I pick up my bag and swing it onto my shoulder. 'I think I'll leave you to it at that point.' And I do it. I actually leave. Just like that.

There's a roaring in my ears and a wide grin on my face as I march out to my car, and I feel like my insides have all leapt to their feet and are cheering and whooping and clapping and shouting; and even though I'm shaking a little bit and my face is burning, I feel right at this moment that I will never sit through another terrible date again, because now I have the strength to –

'Oh, Steph?'

Everything skids to a stop. I turn and find Justin standing there, probably about to ask what my problem is, or try and persuade me to stay. I raise my eyebrows and throw a completely disinterested look at him, just to let him know he's already blown it and nothing on this earth will persuade me to go back. 'Yes?'

'You left your keys.'

OK, so that was the one thing on this earth that could persuade me to go back. But I didn't speak to him, just grabbed them, spun on the spot, wobbled a bit, and marched off.

There's a carnival atmosphere in the surgery when I get in the next morning. The little stereo Niamh and Steve procured is playing '*Happy Birthday To You,*' by Stevie Wonder; three balloons have been Sellotaped – somewhat recklessly, I feel, as everyone knows that balloons and Sellotape are not friends – along the front edge of the reception desk; and Niamh is wearing a little plastic silver tiara, and bright red lipstick.

'Wow, what's this all about?' I ask.

'It's Niamh's birthday,' Steve says, at exactly the same time as Niamh says, 'It's my birthday.'

I nod. 'Yes, sorry, I did guess. I was being...' I wave a hand. 'Doesn't matter. Happy birthday Niamh.' I walk towards my consulting room door. 'I wish I'd known, I'd have made a cake.'

'Oh, no, don't worry, Nina brought one in.'

I stop, my hand on the door handle. 'Did she? Wow. That was nice of her, wasn't it? Where is it?'

'Over here.' Niamh points behind her to the table with the printer on it, and I go back to have a peer. Nina's done well – it's a gorgeous, tall, pink thing, at least four layers, dusted with silver, sugar balls and fondant roses. There's even a ribbon round it at the bottom.

I nod appreciatively. 'That's beautiful.'

'I know, right! She made it herself!'

'She did not!' I burst out, then spot Niamh's face. 'Um, stay up all night again, did she?' I add hastily. 'Bless her, what an amazing thing to do.'

'Yeah. It's sick,' Steve joins in, which is perhaps not the best urban slang to use while standing in a doctor's surgery.

I dump my bag and coat in my consulting room, then come out again and along the corridor to Nina's, knock once, and burst in. She jumps guiltily and looks up from her phone, then places it lightning fast face down on the desk. 'Oh, good morning, Steph, how are – '

'How did you know it was Niamh's birthday?' I ask, sitting on the other chair. 'I mean, how? *How*?'

'Calm down please,' she says, letting a satisfied half-smile appear on her face. 'I thought everyone all knew it was today?'

'Well I bloody didn't. Why didn't you tell me? I thought we were friends?'

'We are friends…'

'Oh, and no bloody way did you make that amazing cake yourself, you great big fraud.'

'Yes I did.'

'No. You did not.'

She stares at me a few seconds, then caves. 'All right, OK. I didn't. But I could have.'

'No you couldn't. No one puts ribbon round cakes apart from professionals. What's going on? Why the sudden interest in Niamh and her birthday?'

'Don't be so silly, Steph, it's not sudden interest. I am always taking a keen interest in all of our staff, as should you.'

I stare at her and frown. It makes no sense. Just as I'm about to say something else, the door opens and Ravi puts his head round. 'You've outdone yourself with that amazing cake, Nina,' he says, fixing his gaze on her. 'What a lovely thing to do for Niamh.' There's a super-charged electric moment as they lock eyes, then Ravi blinks as he realises that I'm sitting right there. 'Oh, hello Steph. Um, so, don't forget to keep to the seven minutes per patient today, yeah?' And with one more lingering look at Nina, the head disappears and the door closes.

I turn back to her, my mouth open. She doesn't look at me, focused as she is on logging onto her computer. I'm sure she must have already done this when she arrived. I lean forward, and put my elbow on her desk, but she continues tapping her password in.

'Either you're avoiding looking at me, or that's the longest password in the history of all passwords including the Barclays online banking app.'

Finally she turns. 'Hmm? Sorry, what?'

'Oh come on Nina! Ravi? Seriously?' I shake my head. 'I mean, *Ravi*?'

'What about him?'

'You're shagging him!'

She closes her eyes, as if the very thought offends her. 'Please, Stephanie. That's ridiculous.'

'Oh, thank God.'

'It's not just a shag. It's a meaningful connection.'

'You're not serious?! Oh my God, that's even worse!'

'Why would I not be serious?'

'Well, because you said he's a misogynistic fuckwit, for a start.'

'I have not ever said that.'

'Yes you have! It was in a text, hang on, I'll prove it to you.' I pull my phone out of my pocket and click onto my conversation with Nina, then start scrolling back. 'It wasn't even that long ago…'

'OK, OK, you can stop. Steph, you can stop now.' I stop. 'I know I didn't think much of him before. But he's not so bad, really, when you get to know him.'

'We *do* know him. He's the one who thinks he's superior because he has a penis, remember? Constantly giving us instructions? Avoiding any of the gritty jobs…?'

'No, I mean, know him properly, outside of work. In a casual place. He's all right. You know? Nice. Friendly.'

'Maybe when he has an ulterior motive.'

'Pardon?'

'Is 'nice and friendly' what you lie awake dreaming of, then?'

'Oh, stop being so mean about it. Holy Christ, you've seen what's out there. Single men of our age are just not...' She shrugs. 'Not particularly...attractive. Ravi is a pretty good catch, if you want my opinion.'

There's more I want to say, like the fact that she's compromising. That I'd rather be on my own than be in a relationship with someone who calls all women 'girls'. That she's convinced herself that she can't do any better. But it's almost nine o'clock and we both have patient lists as long as the Dead Sea scrolls. Which means no one really knows how long they are.

I stand up and pocket my phone. 'I'd better get going.' She doesn't look at me, her eyes and mouth cast down. I take a tiny step towards her. 'Neen, I'm sorry I was... negative about it. Honestly.'

'That's OK.'

'No, I really mean it. I'm sorry. I was surprised, that's all. If he makes you happy, then who am I to judge?'

She looks up and beams. 'Thank you, my old friend. That means a lot.'

I walk back to my own consulting room, past Ravi talking to Niamh in reception. I form a smile, trying to see him more favourably, and he turns to me and winks. As I pass, I hear him saying, '...discreetly, yeah? A little tap will do, after about six and a half minutes, just to hurry them along a bit, remind them that other people are waiting and to stop being so inconsiderate.' Niamh is nodding but I can see the panic in her face: how the hell is she supposed to keep track of how long each of Ravi's patients is in there for? I feel a bubble of anger. Appointment management is part of his job, not Niamh's. If his patients are rambling on, it's up to him to cut through to the nub of the problem, and keep appointment times down. Yes, it's a nigh on impossible job, to offer a good service while rushing people out as fast as you can, and I generally fail. But to put that onus on to the receptionist is despicable.

As I open the door to my own room, I vow to myself that I am definitely not *ever* going to compromise what I want. Being single has its good points, and I would definitely rather stay that way than end up with someone like Ravi.

Also I'm going to find a decent, intelligent and attractive man. I mean, just to prove Nina wrong.

7
OLD MAN

Niamh is having a birthday party the following day, and everyone from the surgery is invited.

'See you tomorrow night!' she calls from the doorway as she's leaving at the end of the day. We've let her go a bit early today, as it's her birthday, so Steve is tidying the reception area on his own, while Nina and I tidy up the waiting room. No sign of Ravi, of course.

'Yes, definitely,' I call back with a wave.

Nina glances at me, then goes back to straightening the leaflet rack. 'Are you going to the party then?' she says, uber-casually.

'Oh *Christ*, no.' I can't say any more for a moment as I'm reaching under a seat for an empty coke can and my head feels like it's going to burst. I grab the can and straighten up, pushing my hands on my thighs for leverage, and a little 'oomph' sound comes out of me. I never used to make that noise when I stood up in my forties. I turn to Nina. 'Spend an evening in a bleak sports hall with loud, shouty music, migraine-inducing lighting and a massive crowd of twenty-one year olds? Hmm, let's think about it a moment, shall we?'

She shrugs and turns away. 'I'm going.'

'Going where?' Steve says, coming round from reception.

'Niamh's party.'

'Cool,' he says, nodding. He pulls the hood on his sweatshirt up, thrusts his hands into the pockets on the front, and walks to the door. 'Seeya tomorrow,' he says, and slouches away.

'You've changed,' I say to Nina, narrowing my eyes. 'Is this Ravi's idea?'

'Come,' she says, after the door closes behind Steve. 'It might be fun. Ravi and I will be there. And Niamh's family are probably about our age.' She raises her eyebrows. 'You must say yes to opportunities like this. That is how your life can change.'

'I don't want my life to change,' I mutter.

'Oh, am I too late?' Ravi announces, coming out of his consulting room and looking at us. I'm holding an empty carrier bag, a doll's head, a couple of old magazines, and a small plastic cow. 'Sorry girls, was just finishing off some paperwork.'

'That's OK,' Nina says, smiling at him, at exactly the same time as I say, 'Immaculately timed, as always.'

'Well unlike you girls, I pride myself on my timing.' He puts his head back. 'Got through all my appointments with three minutes to spare today.'

'Oh, well done you,' Nina says, at exactly the same time as I say, 'Did you make anyone well, though?'

'Are you ready?' he says, flicking his head towards the door.

Nina nods. 'Two minutes,' she says, and turns to me. Behind her, Ravi takes an exaggerated look at his gigantic watch. Nina's looking at me and doesn't see it, which makes my day. 'We're going out for dinner,' she says. 'Why don't you come with us? I hate to think of you going home to an empty house every day.'

There are few things I'd less rather do than spend yet more time with Ravi, as much as I love Nina. But I have no ready excuse. I experience about 0.02 seconds of undiluted panic, and then, 'Oh, sorry, I can't, I have a date,' comes out. With Ravi right there listening. I cringe inwardly. I think I'd rather have said I was having a personal wax.

'A date?' he says, dropping his sleeve back over his arm and sidling up to me. 'Well, well.' He pats my arm, and flashes his too-white smile. 'Nicely done, Steph. I've been thinking to myself for ages that a lovely girl like you would be snapped up in no time. And I was right. Eh? Look at her – she's got it all, hasn't she, Noonoo?' He turns to Nina and sadly misses the expression on my face.

'Well, yes, she has,' Nina starts, but I want to do this myself.

'It's not just about me being chosen, though, is it, Ravi? I mean, I'm not, I don't know, sweets. Waiting to be selected, with no say over who selects me. I have some part to play in the choosing too.'

'Oh, yeah, right, course,' he says, looking at his frankly stupid watch again. I'm surprised he can raise his arm at all. 'We need to leave, Noons. Table's in half an hour.'

'Oh, yes, you are right,' Nina says, and grabs my arm. 'Have a good time,' she says, holding my gaze. 'Relax, be yourself. He won't know what's hit him.'

'But it's not just about me impressing *him*,' I say to myself, as the door closes behind them.

Of course, there is no date tonight, other than with Harry, so I've no one to impress, or be impressed by. We take our usual forty-five minute traipse to the park and back, and as we pass the bench I think about the old man that I saw sitting here a few weeks ago. It was February, and bitter that night, I remember. Now, for April, it's actually quite a pleasant evening – at least a couple of degrees above freezing – and dry, so I sit for a few moments on the bench and enjoy the gardens. Harry is having a lovely sniff around the base of the bin that's next to me – no doubt recognising several different varieties of food crumbs.

'What is it, boy?' I ask him. 'Cheese? Chocolate? Chips?' He doesn't acknowledge that I've spoken, let alone respond, so I sit back on the bench and make myself comfy. At this point I notice the rectangular bronze plaque, on the top most horizontal slat.

For my beloved wife, Maureen, who loved to sit here.

The gardens are less beautiful without you, my darling.

Until we meet again, your husband, Bernie. Xxx

And suddenly I get a strong feeling that the old man on that February night, hunched on this bench on his own in the cold and dark, was Bernie. Still sitting here, only now without Maureen, holding onto a memory of a happy time, yearning to be back there with someone he can never see. And unwilling to go home to a house empty of meaning. My throat aches and my eyes fill with heat, thinking about him being so alone, with no one to comfort or console him, and I let out a small sound. I clutch my tummy and lay my head on the top of the backrest, and just see Harry stop sniffing and raise his head to look at me. He takes a step nearer to me, sniffs the air near my knees, then gently presses his head into my lap and rests it there.

'Oh, Harry!' I lean over him, rubbing his ears, and press my lips onto the top of his head as a tear spills over. 'Oh you lovely boy! You are, aren't you? You're such a lovely boy, you'll never leave me alone, will you? Eh? You'll make sure I'm not left alone.'

Of course it's a ridiculous thing for Harry to promise, and we both know it, so after a few more moments I get up and walk briskly back home. I feed Harry, feed myself, get Alexa to play 'Calm My Dog' (a series of very well-known pieces of relaxing classical music – whether or not they're known by dogs, who can say?) and log onto *Butterflies*. I haven't been on for several weeks, so naturally I have an avalanche of six 'flutters' to respond to. I wonder, as I scroll through their profiles, whether I've got enough time to line one of them up for a date for Niamh's party tomorrow night.

Grant, 60, hasn't written anything on his profile at all, choosing instead to rely on a smiley windswept photo. Grant's lucky still to be able to look windswept at 60 – most men of that age don't have enough hair for it. He's not bad but... 60. I don't know. I'm struggling with finding *50*-year-old men attractive, let alone a decade older.

Lee, 47, has written 'Well where do i start just ask.' Lee seems to think that the women are lining up to ask him questions about himself. Why would they? What is interesting about you, Lee?

Mark has chosen a picture of himself in an anorak, kneeling by a body of water somewhere, holding a huge fish. So has Stephen.

Vince looks OK. He's forty-eight, likes eating cinema and has a dog looking for a long-term relationship. Vince needs to learn how to use a comma.

The last one who's sent me a smile is John. He's put 'World thumb-wrestling champion 2001 (disputed)' which instantly makes me smile, so I click on 'send message'.

'What did the VAR say?' I type, then click 'send.'

A grey bubble appears immediately, telling me he's replying. By spectacular coincidence, I must have just caught him when he was also online. Is this an omen, I wonder, watching that grey bubble flicker. He's already made me smile, with those few words, and now we've coincided. I'm a scientist, so I don't believe in fate. But I'm also a magician, and anything is possible (until proved otherwise). Maybe now, after a few false starts, John will be someone who thinks the way I do, and his message, when it arrives, will make me laugh again, and I will know straight away.

Ooh, here it is.

'Hi Sexy lady xxx'

My eyes roll so far back in my head I see my brain. Then I fling the phone down onto the sofa and put the telly on. *Ocean's Eleven* is on again, so I lie back and think of Clooney.

Next morning Harry and I are up and dressed early, ready to get to the beach and – with luck and precise *Ocean's Eleven* style timing – bump into Happy Hannah, and Ginger and Freddy again. I've checked the beach forecast online and the low tides are at 10:13 and 19:20 today, so I'm planning to arrive at 10:15. My logic is that I'm guessing Hannah will choose the morning one.

Admittedly, George and Brad had a lot more at stake than I do.

'You're going to see your new friends,' I tell Harry, grinning and putting a lot of emphasis in my voice to get him excited. 'Yes you are, you're gonna see them, Freddy and Ginger, your friends.' I bend over and rub both his ears roughly as I'm talking, building up the drama. I'm rewarded with a single swish of his tail as he looks at me, which pretty much makes me explode with affection. I play it cool though. Don't want to smother the poor thing. 'Oh! Oh, good boy, Harry! You're such a good boy. Aren't you? Shall we go walkies then?' I get nothing this time, which brings me back down with a jolt.

It's much less windy on the sands this morning, and consequently quite a bit warmer. The usual suspects are here – retrievers and labs galloping gracefully; Jack Russells zooming; springers…well, springing – all bounding around after balls, frisbees, and each other. There is something so pure and joyous about watching a dog running, and it brings a big smile to my face. I turn to Harry. 'Fancy a bit of bounding today?' He stares resolutely ahead. Well. One step at a time.

After fifteen minutes or so of walking about with Harry trudging silently behind, he suddenly trots round in front of me and stops, ears pricked. Sure enough, I spot the two little grey bullets that are Freddy and Ginger, maniacally circling the elegant figure of Hannah. I pick up my pace and catch up with her, Harry still slightly ahead. As we reach them, Freddy and Ginger spot him and zoom over to greet him, sniffing and wagging excitedly. Harry's tail swishes again, more than once this time, and I feel my heart expand a little.

'Oh, hello again,' Hannah says, when she notices us. 'Your chap looks happier today.'

'Hello, nice to see you again. He does, doesn't he? He's definitely taken a liking to Ginger and Freddy. It's wonderful to see him getting even slightly enthusiastic about something!'

Hannah smiles. 'There's something about dogs, isn't there?' she says. 'There's a kind of simple purity to them. No nastiness or deceit or meanness.' She gazes at the three dogs, all wagging tails and sniffy noses. 'Just pure joy.'

'Absolutely.'

'How's the dating going?' she asks me, and I'm so pleased and flattered that she's remembered me, and everything I told her on Thursday.

I shake my head. 'Terrible. You?'

She bursts out laughing. 'Oh, goodness me, what a question! I don't date, my dear. What would be the point of that?'

'Do you mean what's the point because of your age? Or because you've already had the perfect marriage?'

'Good heavens, our marriage wasn't perfect. We had our difficulties, believe me. He… had the occasional affair, you know.' She looks down briefly and I feel like it still pains her to refer to it. 'More than one. But, you know,' she shrugs, 'he was my life partner. He made a few mistakes. So did I. We muddled through it together.'

I'm startled by this revelation, and it makes me think about Tim, of course. Could I have forgiven him for Fiona Chapman, and all the other unknown vaginas he visited? Do I have the same fortitude as Hannah? Could I move past it?

Fuck no. He's a prick and I wanted out even before I knew about Fiona and her… peers.

'My husband did that too,' I tell Hannah, who simply nods without comment. 'But our marriage was already in its death throes when I found out about it, so it was a mercy killing, really.'

She smiles. 'That's the spirit!'

We're interrupted by what appears to be a gigantic, soaking wet, woolly mammoth lolloping up to where we're standing, and shaking itself vigorously all over us. Hannah gets the worst of it, and covers her eyes with her forearm, squealing. In seconds her smart navy coat is covered with slobber, sand, and sea water, before the culprit lopes away, back to the ice age.

'You're caked!' I tell her, trying to brush it off.

'I know! Look at me!' she laughs, not caring at all. 'What an enormous dog that was! Do you think it was quite real?'

We laugh a moment and try to clean her up but it's all so wet and sloppy, it's hopeless.

'Oh, it doesn't matter,' she says, flapping a hand. 'It's a coat. I'll brush it when it's dry, or take it to the dry cleaners.'

I'm a bit in awe of her by now. The revolting mess that came my way is prickling at me, demanding to be cleaned instantly, even though it's on the outside of my clothing. I have to work hard not to carry on scrubbing and brushing at it and try to look unbothered by it, like Hannah.

'You're an inspiration, you know,' I say to her, stopping for a moment.

She stops too and turns to me. 'Gosh, I've never been called that before.'

'Sorry if it's a bit weird. I know we barely know each other, but I don't think I've ever met anyone with quite such a positive outlook. It's inspirational.'

'Well, thank you Stephanie. What a lovely thing to say.'

And for some inexplicable reason, that is maybe to do with fate, or magic, or both, at this moment I think about my dad, and a germ of an idea starts to sprout.

'Would you like to bring Freddy and Ginger round for tea one day?' I ask, before I decide it's easier not to.

She smiles broadly and looks genuinely thrilled. 'How wonderful. Thank you, Stephanie. I'd like that very much.'

I grin. It almost feels like Her Maj has just agreed to drop by for a Digestive. We make an arrangement for a week's time, after our respective dog walks. It also feels as though I've arranged a play date for Harry, who is still a-quiver with interest over Freddy and Ginger's antics. He's not actually joining in, but at least he's present.

Which reminds me suddenly of Niamh's party tonight.

'Why the big sigh?' Hannah says, glancing at me as we walk. 'Something troubling you?'

I'm a bit taken aback. I didn't even realise I'd made a sound. 'Oh, no, nothing serious. But thank you for asking. That's so nice of you.'

'Well it may not seem serious but it's obviously on your mind. A problem shared and all that.'

I catch a glimpse of her lovely, open face looking at me before she turns back to focus ahead, and she seems genuinely interested. It's the kind of face that I can imagine confiding deeply in. She'd be the one I'd tell if I was having a secret affair, or had accidentally killed someone. 'It's so trivial, honestly. It's just a party I've been invited to…'

'Ooh, a party, how wonderful!' She clasps her hands together and beams. 'Now why ever would a party invitation make you sigh, Stephanie? A beautiful young woman like you should always be seen at a party if she possibly can. Ah, I wish I was still young enough to go to parties. I'm usually asleep before they start, though!' And she chuckles to herself.

'It's not as simple as that,' I say, still smiling at being called a "beautiful young woman." 'This is the birthday party of someone who's around my children's age. It will be full of other twenty-somethings in crop tops with flat pierced belly buttons. And I'll have to wear slacks.' I think about the slacks. 'And a long floaty blouse.'

'What are you talking about? Slacks? Why will you have to wear slacks? Slacks aren't party wear at all.' She pinches the fabric of her own navy trousers. 'These are slacks, Stephanie. They are for dog-walking. They are not for wearing to a party. You need to wear a gorgeous cocktail dress and wow everyone when you walk in.'

Now I'm laughing. 'I'm fifty years old, Hannah! I'm officially invisible. The only way I'd be noticed walking into a room, let alone wow anyone, is if I were on fire.' I pause. 'Actually, I think even then I'd need to be playing the bagpipes…'

She stops walking and turns to me, leaning in as if confiding a secret. 'Well then, lovely lady, you have obviously been walking into the wrong rooms.'

We part company soon after, and walking home I think about what she said. What rooms could possibly be walked into where a tired fifty-year-old menopausal woman would wow anyone? A mortuary, maybe? No, probably not. The people in there would be unlikely to be wowed by anything.

Harry and I pass – and sniff in Harry's case – several other benches, virtually identical to Maureen and Bernie's as we head home. Two of them have solitary souls sitting on them, just staring. It's funny, I've been aware of them along here, but never really noticed them before. I check them all for plaques, and most of them have one. 'Darling Mary,' 'Wonderful Robin,' 'Our dear friend Frances,' and so on. My throat aches as I pass, thinking about the person left behind, feeling that pain of loss, deciding to erect a bench, then busying themselves with the process. Selecting a plaque, writing the words, sorting the funds, the location, the installation, maybe getting the friends and family to be present when it's placed. As if somehow getting that done, that complicated sequence of events that will no doubt involve paperwork and licences and permission of some kind, allows them to keep hold of the last wisp of the person who's gone, even as it's disappearing from their fingers. And it strikes me – not for the first time – what a complete bastard grief can be.

When Mum died, I think Dad decided to die too. He stopped eating and talking and would have stayed in bed all day if someone hadn't gone round and got him up. It was the point at which he started to look frail. As if an important organ had been removed from his body and his system couldn't function properly without it. He got grey and thin and lost all his lustre. He's got a bit back now, but he's not who he used to be.

Harry goes straight to the armchair when we get home, which is a little annoying because he's gradually ruining it, but it's far too late to prevent that now. My idea is rumbling around in my brain and I want to discuss it with someone, but who? Nina will probably be doing something with Ravi (I shudder a little bit at the thought), and Zoe will no doubt be paragliding or ice-sculpting or making sugar flowers or something. So I text Paul.

'Are you busy? Free for a chat?'

He replies by calling me, so I turn sideways on the sofa and put my feet up. 'I'm free,' he says, in an *Are You Being Served* kind of way.

'Oh my God, I haven't heard that for about forty years!'

'And yet it's still so apt.'

'Hmm, not sure it quite fits in with this millennium's greater acceptance of a more diverse culture.'

'Well it's better than Mrs. Slocombe's pussy, anyway.'

I laugh. 'Yeah, that's true.'

'Anyway, what can I do for you?'

'OK, so before I go on, have you been back on *Butterflies* recently?'

There's a short pause and I wonder if he's considering lying to me. I advised him to leave it for now, until he was feeling more recovered from his three major setbacks, but of course I'm not his doctor, or his mum, or even a particularly close friend as we've known each other such a short time, so I wouldn't be at all surprised if he ignored my advice.

'I haven't,' he says finally, and I believe him. 'I think you're right – nothing good will come of that until I've sorted my head out a bit better. Why do you ask?'

'Right. Well I just wanted to make sure you hadn't met the love of your life on the app and were going to extol its virtues to the heavens and piss me off. Because I think meeting people that way is a terrible idea.'

'Do you? Why?'

'Lots of reasons, really. Sometimes you can't tell if someone's attractive or not until you meet them. A static photo doesn't really show what someone looks like.'

'No but it's not just about appearances, is it?'

'No, no, you're right. I'm coming to that!'

'Oh, sorry.'

'But yeah. Appearances aren't the only thing that can make someone attractive. It's about their way of speaking, sense of humour, intelligence, ability to hold a conversation etc etc. It all has to be done in a few texts, doesn't it? And, to be brutally honest, men are shit at texting.'

'Oh, are they? You mean, as an entire group? Like, fifty percent of the world's population can't do it?'

'No, I don't mean that…'

'That's what you said, Stephanie.'

'Did I?'

'Yeah.' I can hear the smile in his voice. 'It could be considered a little bit sexist, you know.'

'Well...'

'Have you had a text conversation with every man in the world?'

'No, of course not...'

'Every man in England?'

'No...'

'In Kent? In Folkestone?'

'No...'

'OK, so how many text conversations have you actually had with men, then? And I'm talking about since you've been single. Text conversations where you're both looking for a partner.'

'That's not the point...'

'How many?'

'OK, it's about four, but...'

'Right. So on the basis of four bad conversations, you're assuming the other three and a half billion men in the world are exactly as bad?'

'No, but I do think it's relevant that I haven't had any good ones. That's four out of four that have been bad. One hundred percent.'

There's a pause. 'OK. I suppose that even out of a low number like four, one of them might be OK at it. So maybe it's not such a leap after all.'

'Thanks for that oh-so-gracious climb down. Anyway, my point is that meeting people in person is, generally speaking, more effective. Do you agree?'

'Well obviously. I mean, if you want a relationship with someone, you do have to meet them eventually, don't you?'

'Course. But I mean, you know, an initial meeting. The old fashioned way. Meeting in the office, or bumping into someone on the street, or both reaching for the last pair of gloves in a shop…'

'Wait – aren't these all film plots?'

'Oh maybe, it doesn't matter. I've just had this idea and I wanted to see what you thought.'

'You mean the innovative and clever idea of people actually meeting in person? Oh, yes, it's brilliant. And yet so simple…'

'You can be quite annoying sometimes, you know.'

He doesn't say anything straight away. Then, 'That's what my wife said.'

'Oh, Paul, I'm sorry. Putting my foot in it again.'

'Nah, forget it. You're both right. I'm working on it. So what was this idea of yours then?'

'Well, it's weird but since Tim and I split up, I've seen so many people on their own. Round the town, you know. I think when we were still together I just didn't notice them. Which makes me feel – I don't know, a bit bad.'

'Don't feel bad, that's standard,' he says. 'It's like when you get a new car, and suddenly you start seeing that type of car everywhere.'

'My singledom is not like a new car.'

'That's not what I meant…'

'No, I know. I'm messing around.'

'Aha.' He manages to say it sarcastically. 'So. You've seen a lot of people on their own?'

'Well, yes. Out on walks with Harry, mostly. There's this one guy who sits on a bench we go past, and this morning I noticed it has a plaque on it dedicated to his dead wife. It's so sad.'

'That is sad. How do you know it's his wife that's croaked, though? Maybe he was just sitting there?'

'I thought you we were working on not being annoying!'

'Sorry.'

'Anyway, in fact it doesn't really matter whether it's his wife's bench or someone else's wife's, the point is he was sitting there on his own, in the freezing cold. Could have just been having a rest, but...'

'But why would he sit on that particular bench, in the freezing cold?'

'Exactly.'

'And, I'm guessing, also dark.'

'Yep. And windy.'

'OK, I got it. It's definitely his wife's bench.'

'Yes, that's what I thought. And then I met Hannah.'

'Is that the bench wife?'

'Well no, Paul, that would be very creepy because the bench wife is dead.'

'God, of course she is. Stupid me. So who's Hannah?'

I tell him quickly about Happy Hannah, and then Grumpy Graham next door, and I throw in my own dad, and eventually come round to explaining my idea.

'Instead of all these people sitting on benches on their own, why aren't they sitting on benches together?'

He thinks for a moment. 'The same bench, you mean?'

'Yes. Well, no. Kind of. Maybe not an actual bench. You know. More of a metaphorical bench.'

'A metaphorical bench? Would this be in a metaphorical park somewhere?' He stops himself. 'No, sorry, forget that. Being annoying again.'

'Actually that wasn't annoying. My metaphorical park is a bit of a sticking point. With a small number of people like four, I could easily have everyone round here. But what if it became fifteen, or twenty?'

'You could rent out a community centre, or village hall somewhere?'

'That's an idea.'

'But don't they already do coffee mornings for – what's the P.C. thing to say these days? Senior Citizens? Retired people? Some community centres have craft activities and dancing or book clubs. It's kind of already catered for.'

He's right. My idea balloon, previously inflating and stretching and lifting me off my feet with excitement, suddenly deflates with a loud raspberry. 'Crap.' I sigh. 'I thought I was onto something.'

'Maybe you are,' he says. 'Just because coffee mornings and craft things and dancing already exist, doesn't necessarily mean it caters for everyone. What if someone just wants someone to sit on a bench with?'

'Hmm. Maybe.' I'm still deflated. 'Anyway, I've got a party to go to so I'd better get going.'

'Don't be downhearted,' he says. 'I still think you've got something.'

'Thanks Paul. Chat soon.'

8
YOUNG MAN

On my top ten chart of things I least want to do tonight, in order of reluctance, 'Attending Niamh's Party' is surprisingly only at the number two position, pipped to the number one slot by 'Trimming Harry's Claws'. But the bench plaques, and Nina, and Dr. Stubbly in Holby, have all persuaded me that maybe I would like my life to change. I don't want to go on endless terrible dates any more. Ha, I never did, of course. Who does? But even if all the dates had been amazing, it's definitely not what I want. What I really want is to meet someone meaningful. Someone to sit on a bench with, or laugh about Harry with. And ultimately to have breakfast with. It's a potentially small, but very significant, change, and whether significant or insignificant, it won't happen in front of the telly with Harry, even with beautifully short, tidy claws. Unless there's a house fire and a male fire fighter has to carry me to safety.

Nah, that guy would be far too young for me anyway. They probably make the fifty-year-old fire fighters stay in the office and do admin.

So I have a riffle through my clothes and realise I don't have any devastating cocktail dresses amongst them. Honestly, what have I been doing? There's nothing for it but to nip into town and pick something up. My first thought is Sainsbury's – the TU stuff is quite nice, as long as you're careful, and there's no faffing around with parallel parking or pay and display. But then I suddenly remember that I'm single, my money is all my own, and I have no one to please but myself. To hell with shopping in supermarkets! I'm fifty and fabulous and I will spend £200 on a dress in a boutique in the town centre if I want to, and no one can tut or raise their eyebrows or tell me I look a bit silly in a dress like that at my age. I shove my foot down on the accelerator and speed gleefully past the Sainsbury's turn off, flicking vees towards the giant orange sign as I do. Then I clock the petrol price and realise that £1.23 a litre is 2p less than Tesco and actually it makes sense if I pop in and fill up while I'm here. I go round the roundabout and come back, keeping my revs down, indicating carefully, letting one car onto the roundabout in front of me. I fill up, pay-at-pump, and *then* drive gleefully away towards daring expenditure and glamorous extravagance, flicking the vees again as I go.

'Sorry, sorry, no, not you,' I mouth at the shocked woman walking along the pavement.

Parking in town is a nightmare on a Saturday, of course. If you want to get near the shops, you have to pay £5,000 per hour; but for £1 you can park in the underground car park and walk eighteen miles. I've opted for the latter, and am circling the first level looking for a space near the ticket machine *and* the exit before the thought suddenly occurs to me, NO! To hell with economy! and I plunge my foot down, screeching back round the car park on two wheels, engine roaring, tyres squealing on the smooth concrete surface. I have to stop and wait nicely for the barrier to raise and let me out; then I speed off recklessly towards the town centre.

After going three times round the one way system, I finally see someone click their remote central locking on the pavement, and the car parked just ahead of me flashes its hazards once. I do the 'Are you going?' mime to the man on the pavement, pointing at his car, then at him, then at the road, and he nods, so I indicate and prepare to wait. Eventually, after apparently having a three course meal in the driver's seat, he moves off, and I manage to squeeze my car into the gap on only the fourth attempt.

There aren't many boutique places in Folkestone; it's not really that kind of town. You're more likely to find designer knitting emporiums, or independent pet clothes boutiques. But I know of a couple. The first one I go into is somewhere I've walked past hundreds of times on my way to the vegan ice cream place, but I've never been inside. It has a window display made up entirely of black and white items. Even the woman busying herself with something behind the counter is in a black and white geometric off the shoulder jumpsuit. I eye her surreptitiously as I go in. She looks like she's stepped out of an A-Ha video. She's far too young to know that, of course.

I browse inside for a few seconds, then turn to face her, to ask for advice. She looks up briefly, clocks me (I note that she has continued the black and white theme with her eye make-up) then goes back to moving black and white socks around a display case. It's a small shop, I'm the only customer, and she's apparently too busy to serve me.

'Do you have any party wear?' I ask eventually.

'No,' she says immediately, raising her head for two seconds, but not quite enough for her eyes to draw level with mine. I give her five more seconds then turn and walk out, calling out 'Thanks, bye!' as I leave. Pretentious bloody monochromatic window display.

My enthusiasm for this expedition decreases the further I get from the car park. I wanted to nip in, grab something expensive and sensational, and nip home again. Now I've got to trudge all the way to the Old High Street to find another boutique.

It's hard to believe that The Old High Street was ever a high street at all. It's narrow, steep and cobbled, and miles away from the centre of town. Luckily for me, it's recently had a cash injection from somewhere and is now quite an arty and chic place to shop. I go into a tiny little place called *Pretty Petals*, and a bell rings over the door as I go in. I half expect Ronnie Barker to make an appearance.

'Help you love?' the woman behind the counter asks, giving good eye contact and making me feel welcome. No affected artistry here. I tell her I'm looking for something for a party and she selects several skirt and top combos and ushers me into the tiny curtained cubicle that serves as a changing room. With the first ensemble on, I stare at myself in the mirror for a few seconds, then text Amy a photo.

'Really good,' she texts back.

'Ames. Look again.'

There's a pause from Amy, during which a woman's voice suddenly says into my ear 'What do you think, love?' I jump and put my hand on my chest as my heart goes into double time. Then I realise it's just the woman in the shop, separated from me by a thin sheet of material. Not the restless spirit of an old Saturday girl, destined forever more to ask if anyone needs the next size up.

'Just getting a second opinion,' I tell her.

'Fancy dress, right?' Amy texts now. 'You're going as Nanny McPhee?'

'I'm looking for something a bit… younger,' I tell the assistant, handing her back the outfits a few moments later.

She nods. 'Two doors down, love.'

Two doors down is called *Trendz* and this is most definitely not the right room to be walking into. Here there are sequins and off-the-shoulder and short skirts and hot pants. Where on earth does a fifty-year-old fit in? *What* on earth does a fifty-year-old fit in, come to that? I'm not old enough for *Pretty Petals* and I'm too old for *Trendz*. Maybe I should just go back to Sainsbury's…

'Party wear?' the (male this time) assistant echoes back to me. He looks me up and down once, then holds up a finger. 'One second.'

He comes back with a gorgeous fitted white silk shirt covered in large dark pink flowers, and some white skinny jeans. I gaze at myself in the mirror, feeling a little bubble of excitement. Maybe I'm not 'Woman at TU' any more.

'How about this?' I text to Amy.

'That looks lovely, Mum.'

'Thank you baby. Ok for a birthday party?'

A few seconds of silence. 'What age?'

I shrug, even though she can't see me. 'Twenty-one. Niamh, from the surgery.'

'Oh how is she? Ask her what the Pink concert was like.'

'I can't, she's not in this cubicle with me.'

'No need for a sarcastithon.'

'Sorry. Just need your opinion.' An unseen hand rattles the cubicle door from the other side, and I stare at it in alarm. 'Won't be a minute!' I call out. 'Please hurry, Ames.'

'Aren't there any dresses?'

'Can't wear a dress, I've got lumpy legs. And a muffin top.'

'You have not don't be silly. You're a very young fifty. Hattie couldn't believe how old you are. She thought you were, like, forty.'

I don't allow myself to say that fifty actually *is* like forty, but simply enjoy the compliment. 'That's nice of her.'

'Yeah she's nice. You need heels.'

'I am not wearing heels.'

'Come on, Mum. Just some low ones.'

She's right. The pretty pink kitten heels finish it off perfectly.

'Two hundred and seventy-five, ninety-seven please.'

I've never spent so much on a single outfit before. Not even for my wedding. But it's much prettier than my wedding dress, and I don't have to tie myself for the next twenty-four years to an oaf while I wear it. Win-win.

On my way back to the car, I can't help but pop into the pretentious place with the monochromatic theme and walk straight up to Ziggy Stardust at the counter.

'Remember me?' I ask her. 'I was in here about an hour ago, but you ignored me.' I hold up my beautiful multi-coloured paper bag with the *Trendz* logo on it, and smile sweetly. 'Big mistake,' I say, grinning. Then I walk out, with Roy Orbison playing in my head. I've always wanted to do that.

Niamh's party is inside the Leas Cliff Hall, three storeys down from street level in the Channel Suite, which is distressingly (because I can't not go), yet reassuringly (because I can leave easily), close to home. The Leas Cliff Hall is perched right on the Leas cliff edge (clue's in the name) and has function rooms at the bottom, so you can get a sea view even three levels down. When I come to be standing outside the double doors of the Channel Suite, I turn and catch a glimpse of myself in the shiny lift door after I've stepped out of it. Heavy music is hammering out of the suite making my ossicles rattle, and there's the tell-tale bright purple light of a migraine-inducing laser show coming under the doors. I turn sideways-on to the lift door, then the other side, then put my hand on my tummy and lean back. Probably look about five months gone. I add the other hand into the small of my back and it goes up to six months. What in God's name am I doing here? I glance back to the double doors into the suite and picture myself going through them. I will push them both at the same time, in the middle, and walk purposely forward, then let them swing shut behind me and stand still for a moment to take in my surroundings; and allow my surroundings to take in me.

Except, of course, no one will notice.

And at this moment my body produces a flush of wicked heat. Sweat pushes up through my carefully applied make-up, ruining it before I've even entered the bloody room.

OK. I'm not going in. No way. Nope.

'You coming in then, Mum?' a male voice says behind me, and I spin, expecting Josh. Except in the split second that I wonder why on earth Josh is here, I also realise it's definitely not Josh's voice, and then it sinks in that whoever it is was definitely not talking to me.

But when I stop spinning, I can see there's no one else here. Just me.

And Him.

I'm rendered momentarily speechless by his appearance. I think a small piece of my soul might have left me and floated dreamily upward. This is quite probably the most beautiful man I have ever encountered. I take a few moments to drink in the vision before me.

White shirt – tight, but not that unpleasant outlining-every-ab tight. Just a beautifully-close-fit tight. Black jeans, also tight, but not put-you-off-your-meat-and-veg tight. A suggestion of their contents rather than a stark outline. Hair – salt and pepper, thick enough to run your hands through, but not so much that it gets in the way. Chin – heavy dusting of stubble that's so close to being a beard you couldn't tell the difference. Beautiful pale lips, currently turned up into a suggestive little smile. And those blue/green eyes… Actually his eye colour is pretty standard, but right now they're focused on me and the effect is extraordinary.

'Oh, I'm not preg – ' is my instant response. But I shudder a bit with mortification that he thought I was. 'I mean, I was pushing my...' I shake my head. 'I was just... reminiscing.'

He smiles. 'Coming in, then? Or not sure?' He glances back towards the double doors behind which Niamh's party roars, then turns to me again. 'It's a good party. You might have fun.'

I smile back. 'I think I probably won't.'

'But how can you know unless you try?'

'I can make an educated guess. You know, from years of party experience.' I incline my head at the doors. 'This music is so awful. No discernible tune, meaningless words. You can't dance, you can't chat, you can't listen. It's unuseable.'

He nods. 'And it's your years of party experience that have brought you to this conclusion?'

'Well, not that many years.' I give him a sideways smile.

Now he's chuckling. 'Well, if you change your mind, come and find me. I'm the one doing the music.' And he walks off to the stairs, turns and winks at me ever so coolly, then bounds up them two at a time.

I close my eyes. Shit shit shit. Of all the people to moan about the music to, I pick the flipping DJ. I glance up the stairs and wonder if I go straight into the lift now and shoot back up to street level, will I encounter him again at the top? Then I wonder if I want to time it so that I don't, or so that I do.

It's 'don't'. Obviously. I take a step towards the lift, my giant red reflected face showing me exactly how much I *don't* want to bump into him again, and just before I push the 'up' button, two things happen: the double doors behind me bang open and someone shouts, '*Steph!*'; and my phone rings in my bag.

I turn, whilst simultaneously reaching into my bag to retrieve my phone, and am disappointed to find a grinning Ravi lurching towards me. And he's coming in fast and low. I step back deftly and bring my bag around to my front as I rummage inside it, as a kind of shield. Ravi looks like he's had one too many Babychams and now thinks he is irresistible to all women. Come to think of it, that is his general belief anyway. I notice at this point that he's wearing rather too skinny jeans. I back up some more, and click on my phone.

'Hello?'

'Steph,' Ravi drawls, at the same time as the person on the other end of the phone shouts, '*Steph!*' It's a female voice.

'Yes, it's me,' I reply, nimbly moving away from Ravi's trajectory.

'Are you coming to the party or what?' She's struggling to make herself heard over the multiple plane crash that's apparently happening next to where she's standing.

Ravi has stopped moving, thankfully, but is still looking at me, the frankly repulsive smile on his face indicating the frankly repulsive thoughts lurching through the wasteland of his mind. 'Stephanie,' he drawls, as if he's finally acknowledging some long-held secret attraction between us.

'Oh Christ,' I mutter, eyeing him. 'Never gonna happen.'

'It's not that bad!' the person on the phone yells, and I've realised by now that it's Nina. 'Niamh is here, she's got a bit of a surprise for you! You gotta come!'

'Aw, Steph, we make a great team, don't we? You're single, I'm single, we should get together.'

'You're delusional!' I tell him, forgetting that I'm still holding my phone.

'Aw come on,' Nina shouts. She sounds like she's moved to a slightly quieter corner of the room now, next to a multiple train pile-up. 'You don't have to stay so long. But Niamh really, *really*, wants you here. And I do also. You will not regret it, I promise you.'

'Think you're too good for me, then, do you?' Ravi is asking me now. 'Think you're a bit special?' His tone sharpens unexpectedly, and it fills me with apprehension, making the situation seem suddenly so much worse than an offensive proposal. 'Reckon you can do better? Is that it?'

'I'm already here,' I tell Nina, and start planning a way to get past Ravi and through the double doors. He's swaying slightly, and as irritating and misogynistic as he is, I'm pretty sure this is just his own arrogance fuelled by alcohol. He's not interested in me as a person; he's interested in himself as a woman-magnet. Ugh. A little bit of bile rises in my throat, making my eyes water.

'You wouldn't know what had hit you,' he slurs now, looking away from me and around the tiny vestibule, seeking out his next target. 'Ladies love a bit of the sexy Sankaran.' He appears to be addressing a skinny floor lamp in the corner.

I leave the lamp to look after itself, and start moving towards the double doors. At this moment the DJ from earlier bounces down the stairs to my right and takes in the scene in one glance.

'You still here?' he asks the vestibule in general. 'Thought you were going in.'

Ravi turns away from the lamp towards DJ and stumbles a bit. 'Who are you?'

DJ puts his palms outward, in a peace gesture. 'I'm the DJ, mate. You all right?'

''Course I'm all right,' Ravi says, turning back to the lamp. 'Nothing wrong with having a conversation, is there?'

DJ glances at me, then jerks his head towards Ravi. 'Nothing whatsoever my friend.' He winks at me and it makes me giggle, as we watch Ravi make his move on a seductive piece of furnishing. 'You coming in, or what?'

I nod and step around Ravi towards DJ. It's ridiculous, I'm walking away from my colleague whom I've known for over fifteen years, towards a complete stranger I met moments ago, but I feel very comfortable to be doing so.

'I wonder how long it'll take him to realise why she's so quiet,' I say, as we go through the double doors into the Suite. As we enter we are slammed in the face by a sound that feels like being slammed in the face by a dustbin lid, and my words are instantly smothered.

'WHAT?' DJ shouts, moving his ear close to my mouth.

'I SAID I WONDER HOW LONG BEFORE HE WORKS OUT WHY SHE'S SO QUIET!'

DJ stops, so I do too. 'HAHA! I'D LIKE TO BE A FLY ON THAT WALL!' he shouts.

And at this point Nina jumps on me from the side like Bill Beaumont in a boob tube.

'*Steph!*' she yells, grabbing my arm and squeezing it. 'I'm so happy you are here! Come on, we are going to find Niamh.' And she pulls me away. I just have time to make a brief eye contact with Delicious DJ and mouth 'Thanks!' before we are separated forever by the heat and the dark and the infernal laser show.

'It's a man,' Nina shouts towards my ear as she pulls me.

'What is?'

She makes a huge show of rolling her eyes, to make sure I see it. 'Niamh's surprise! She has someone for you to meet.'

'Oh God no. Please, Nina. I absolutely do *not* want to meet any more of Niamh's suggestions.'

'Don't be silly,' she says, not even looking at me, concentrating on navigating a safe path through hazardous chairs and tables in dangerous lighting. 'You won't know until you meet him.' She stops abruptly and turns to me. 'He's very fuckable,' she says, with wide eyes .

'Jesus…'

But there is no resisting her, and a few seconds later brings us to the bar, where Niamh is leaning, holding a Corona bottle. Her face breaks out in a huge grin the second she sees me.

'Steph!' she shouts, and grabs me in a slightly damp embrace. She's never greeted me like this before, so I conclude that she, also, is pissed. 'I'm well glad you came.'

'OK.' I glance around. 'No Steve?'

'Oh I think he's outside having a shag,' she says, way too casually. Then nudges me when she sees the horror on my face. 'Sorry, *fag*. Outside having a fag.' But she dissolves into giggles and I don't know what to believe.

'So, Niamh,' Nina says, pushing forward, 'tell Stephanie about your surprise. Yeah?'

'Oh, yeah, right.' Niamh starts, but Nina can't wait.

'It's her dad!' she exclaims, and claps her hands together.

I look from Nina to Niamh. Nina is nodding happily, but Niamh is frowning at Nina and looks like she's going to say something. Probably annoyed with her for spoiling the surprise. 'Her dad?' I manage eventually. Since when did surprises stop being huge fun? 'You mean, Niamh's dad? You're setting me up with Niamh's dad?'

But before they can confirm or deny this, a familiarly devastating white shirt-clad arm reaches around Niamh and picks up a pint glass that's standing on the bar. The rest of the godly torso follows, including the rather fine head, and Niamh turns towards it and flings her arms around the smooth caramel neck, pressing her young, unlined lips to the stubbly cheek. And stupidly, as I stare, I feel utterly bereft that this god, this Adonis, the beautiful man from the lobby earlier, is clearly Niamh's boyfriend, Justin. Who is probably about 30, and with whom I wouldn't have a hairdo in a hurricane's chance. Even if I was twenty years younger. I feel my face flushing with embarrassment, and for the first time am grateful for the insufferable blinding laser show.

'Everyone,' Niamh says, her arm still looped loosely around Justin's neck, 'this is Ed. My dad.'

There's a chorus of 'Hi Ed's from the people standing around me, but I feel momentarily side-swiped. I can sense Nina looking at me, grinning and jerking her head towards Ed, but I don't look at her. Ed is greeting everyone in our group, including Steve who's just turned up (not smelling of smoke, interestingly) and when he reaches me, he blinks in surprise and smiles.

'Ah, it's you,' he says, sounding a bit like Rupert Holmes. 'I didn't realise you knew my daughter.'

How could he? He's only seen me once in a hallway for about twenty seconds. 'Yes, she works for me.' His eyebrows go up. 'Oh, I mean, she works at my practice. My surgery. Er, I mean, our surgery.' I incline my head in Nina's rough direction. 'Hers and mine.'

Realisation breaks across his face. 'So you must be…' He looks from Nina to me and back, then again, then presses his lips together. 'You know what, I'd rather not guess. I know that one of you is Nina, one of you is Ravi and one of you is Stephanie, but it feels risky to chance it. Which one are you?' He chuckles. 'I mean, I think I'm safe in guessing you're not Ravi?'

'Ha, no, you're right. That was Ravi, doing the Dick Emery with me in the lobby just now.' I look round for Nina, but she's safely chatting to Steve a few feet along the bar and in this ear-numbing racket has no chance of overhearing us.

He turns his head a little, and frowns. 'In the lobby? Oh, you mean that drunken twat chatting up the floor lamp?'

'Oh, do you know him?'

'No?' His eyebrows flick together in momentary puzzlement. 'What makes you think I know him?'

I laugh once through my nose. 'Oh, just that you managed to sum him up so succinctly just then.'

He frowns again. 'Sorry, I'm not sure what you mean.'

'Doesn't matter.'

'Oh. OK.' He leans in. 'What's a dickummery?' He sniggers. 'Is it what I think it is?'

I have no time to wonder what on earth he thinks it is, because at this moment Nina butts her head in. 'So, Steph, you are talking to Niamh's dad here.' She flicks her eyebrows up and down a couple of times. 'What a funny thing.'

'Ah,' says Ed. 'You're Steph, then.' He looks at Nina. 'Which means you must be Nina.'

Nina giggles and puts a hand over her mouth. 'Goodness, you're so funny. Isn't he funny, Steph?'

Ed is doing an uncertain half-smile, and looks like he thinks he's missing something.

'Oh, er, yes, he is.' I look at Ed and smile, then turn back to Nina. 'So, where's Ravi gone?'

She shrugs. 'Oh, he will be here some place, I'm sure. Probably buying some more drinks, or maybe chatting to the waitress, yeah?'

'When we saw him, he was chatting up a floor lamp,' Ed says, grinning.

'Chatting up who?' Nina says, looking from me to Ed.

'No, no one,' I tell her. 'He's just a bit worse for wear I think. Bumped into a lamp.'

'Ah.' She nods slowly. 'Well, he will find me in the end, I'm sure. Now, what are you two discussing?' She immediately shakes her head and puts both hands out. 'No, don't worry, you just carry on. I am going to move myself away.' She waves from literally three feet away, then does a complete one-eighty and walks approximately four steps. Then she levers herself onto a bar stool, keeping her back to us, and sits there, ramrod straight.

Ed and I watch her, then look at each other.

'Well that was weird,' he says.

'She's probably pissed.'

'Being pissed is no excuse,' he says, winking at me.

'Ed!' someone shouts, interrupting my train of thought. Ed jerks and looks up. A short, grey-haired man in a cardigan is walking briskly towards us, waving as he comes.

'Oh shit,' Ed says, pushing himself away from the bar. He turns back to me as he walks backwards towards Cardigan Man. 'I was just about to buy you a drink.'

I lift my shoulders. 'Oh, well. Never mind.'

'Only a soft one, though.'

'Oh? Why? Watching the pennies?'

He frowns again. 'What? I don't think so. Anyway, you shouldn't have alcohol, should you? In your condition.' And he turns and walks off to meet up with Cardigan Man, and they walk away together.

If only Ed hadn't seen me posing in front of the shiny lift doors, pretending to be six months pregnant.

Apparently he's going to go on about it relentlessly, even though I tried to explain it. I close my eyes as I remember. He told Ravi I was 'delicate'. Oh God. It's going to be all round the surgery by Monday. And everyone will be speculating who the father is and how long I've been seeing him and Wow she moves fast, her marriage only ended five minutes ago. How mortifying. And worse: Ed genuinely thought I was pregnant, when he saw me. And possibly still does. Which means I must look it. I glance down at my new top. I need to get out of here.

I stand up but in the same instant the noise and light of the party change dramatically, making me look round. That godawful laser show has finally stopped, the house lights have come up, and the sound is aggressively familiar. I say aggressively because it instantly affects me, like a punch. It's a drum and bass intro, with occasional random synth sounds, which are quickly joined by intensely familiar musical notes, going up for two, up one more, then down one. Oh my God, what *is* that?

'BILLY JEAN!' Nina shouts, running back to me. 'BILLY FUCKING JEAN!'

She's right. Someone is singing the opening lyrics now, and I find myself jerking my body and bopping my head. I turn to Nina and we grab each other, grinning. 'WHO IS THIS?'

She leans in and shouts, 'It's Niamh's dad! Look!'

And sure enough there's Ed at the other end of the room in a cleared area that I hadn't noticed before, holding the mic and singing like MJ with his eyes closed and legs planted wide. One of his knees is going up and down in time to the music, and every so often he's doing a little MJ shrug. He's even wearing a white trilby, low over his eyes. I don't think I've ever seen anything more alluring than that. I stare, all thoughts of my pregnant humiliation and getting the hell out of there completely gone.

The electronic sounds of the music are being made by Cardigan Man, who is standing next to Ed, pounding on a huge electric keyboard. Someone really should have advised him against the cardigan.

'This is amazing,' I shout to Nina, who is dancing enthusiastically next to me. She nods, but doesn't say anything. She doesn't need to.

Billy Jean ends, to riotous applause and whistles, and after a few seconds while Ed turns and picks up a guitar that's lying behind him, the next track starts. It's another very familiar and simple drum rhythm, coming from the keyboard and broadcast through two huge speakers placed either side of the set. Then Ed comes in with the bassline and it's *Footloose* and produces an instant requirement to start bopping from foot to foot. Nina and I catch each other's eyes and laugh, throwing our heads back as we wave our arms around, Kevin Bacon style.

Track after track follow – *Take on Me, I Think We're Alone Now, Je Suis un Rockstar, Call Me*. It doesn't stop. For those intense forty-five minutes, I feel like I'm sixteen again, doing all the silly 80s dance moves, singing along, pushing the sleeves up on my jacket – except I'm not wearing one, but I mime it anyway. Nina and I put our handbags on the floor and dance round them, and before long Niamh and another couple of young women (who weren't born when these songs first came out) come and join us. It's the best fun I've had for months. Probably years.

'Thank you very much, everyone,' Ed finally says into the mic, when *Happy Birthday* (the Altered Images version) has finished. 'Happy birthday to my baby girl, Niamh! Happy birthday, darling!' And he blows a kiss into the mic. Niamh screams and waves back at him, but I'm feeling a little stirring feeling and wishing he was blowing that kiss towards me.

A quick trip to the ladies' is required to mop my face, which is red from the exertion rather than the hormones. Needless to say, though, the extra heat generated from dancing brings on a heat explosion, and I'm very grateful to be safely in a cubicle when it goes off.

When I get back to the bar, that terrible laser show is on again, and the recorded music is back, thumping out its meaningless shouted words and heavy obscuring drums. Ed is back in the same spot, so I go over to him.

'That was amazing,' I tell him. 'Really, really good.'

He nods and grins, pleased with the praise. 'Thanks. Oldies but goodies, right?'

'Well, you know, not *that* old…'

'Oh, Steph, there you are,' Niamh says behind me and I turn. 'Hi dad,' she adds. 'Great set.'

'Thanks baby girl.'

'You didn't tell me your dad was so talented,' I say to her, and she looks a bit uncomfortable for some reason.

'Well, no. You only met him tonight.'

'Yes, but… you know… you never said at work…'

'I need a comfort break,' Ed says, straightening up. 'Be right back.'

Niamh looks relieved that he's gone, and seems to relax a bit. 'Steph,' she says, and it sounds a bit odd. Like a child about to tell her mum she's smashed the priceless Wedgwood vase.

'Yes?'

She smiles, then looks away, then focuses on me again and draws together all her resolve. 'There's someone I'd like you to meet.'

I blink. 'Oh. Well, thank you, yes, Nina told me. I've already met him. Your dad, right? He's lovely.'

But even before I've finished speaking I see that she is shaking her head. 'No, um, that's the problem. Nina got it wrong. It's a bit embarrassing, really. My dad's only thirty-nine.'

'Oh.' I feel an internal shrivel that starts in my belly and spreads right up to my scalp. She thinks I'm too old for him. What am I saying? I *am* too old for him. Thirty-nine? Oh my God, he's so *young.* No wonder he thought those were oldies. 'OK, well, you know, that's only... a few years difference....'

'Yeah. So. I didn't really think... Yeah, it's not my dad I want you to meet.'

'Right. Of course not.'

'Yeah.' And at this point I notice that there is someone with her, another man, just behind her, looking out at the dancers. And as she turns to him, he faces me and she says those three terrible, terrible little words.

'It's my grandad.'

9
POLICE MAN

'Oh, wow,' I say. 'That's great.' I hold up my index finger. 'Hold that thought, sorry, I think I've left my phone in the ladies. Be right back.'

I throw down a handful of salt petre, sugar, and match heads, and disappear in a puff of smoke.

I don't think about what I'll say to Niamh on Monday. I don't think about the sweat running down the side of Ed's lip-lickingly sexy face as he belted out the lyrics to *Sweet Child of Mine*. I don't think about anything except escaping from Niamh and her ancient arthritic grandad. Oh my God, I am fifty! *Fifty*! I am not ready for the retirement home and Saturday night bingo quite yet. I want to watch live music, it turns out. I want to dance round my handbag and scream when *Wet Wet*

Wet come on and carry my shoes home. I am not old enough to be dating someone's grandad. No no no!

As I drive home to Harry and my bed, I realise that Ed thought – even for a moment – that I was pregnant, which means he's probably ruled me out straight away anyway. Can't blame him really. Who wants to take on another man's child, right from the beginning? He's probably thinking about all the ante-natal appointments he'd have to go to. Me moaning about my swollen feet. Timing contractions at two in the morning. It's quite an awful prospect even from my point of view, and I'm the one that's pregnant. Or, well, you know, in his head. Still, at least he thinks my ovaries are still working. Life in the old girl yet.

All of which ultimately brings me to the cinema with Gavin the following Friday night. We spotted each other across a crowded chat room on *Butterflies* on Sunday, and it was 'Like' at first site.

Nope, doesn't matter how you say it, this online auction is not romantic.

I glance at him shovelling popcorn into his mouth, and smile, even as another three or four pieces fall onto his shirt and lap. One tiny crumb is stuck on his chin, which at least implies his chin isn't womanly smooth. He smiles back, and offers me the bag, but I shake my head. His licked fingers have been in there so it's a 'No' from me. He shrugs and goes back to happy snacking.

Frankly, I blame Steve Wright for this. I was listening to his Sunday Love Songs on Radio 2 when

Gavin and I started chatting, and I came over all optimistic. All those people writing in about the loves of their lives, their best friends and soul mates, loving them more now than ever before, thirty perfect years, blah blah blah. Don't get me wrong, I'm not naïve. I know it's all a trick, played on us singletons by the smoke and mirrors of media. I know that Donald and Lilith will have paused for two seconds and smiled at each other while Steve read out Donald's message, and Lilith will have given him a peck on the cheek and squeezed his arm with a 'Thanks, love.' And half an hour later she's gritting her teeth in the armchair while he slumps in front of the Grand Prix eating Doritos. 'For *God's sake,* Don, get a tooth pick.' I know all this, just like I know the dinosaurs in Jurassic Park aren't real, but my adrenalin still surges when the T-Rex appears in the rear-view mirror. Our instincts override our sense. Enter Gavin stage left, who likes walks in the countryside, live music and a DVD with a bottle of wine and a take away.

Oh, and popcorn, it seems.

Gavin is also a Policeman. He says it with a capital P. I don't think Gavin is going to be anyone I'll be prepared to have breakfast with eventually, but he managed to keep a conversation going for three days, which is quite unusual for the app-users. It made him stand out. I mean, having enough wits to keep a conversation going shouldn't be a stand-out feature, but sadly in the online world it's right up there with 'knighthood' and 'own yacht'.

To be fair to the other app-users, Gavin's conversation was almost entirely about being a Policeman.

'What do you like to do in your free time, then, Steph? Not getting into trouble, I hope? I'd have to come and arrest you.'

'You're right, this online dating lark is awful. At least you know you'd be safe with me. I'd protect you, never fear. And if I couldn't, I could always radio for back-up!'

'Oh you have a dog? I used to work with the dog section. Brought down an escaping drug dealer once, just with the dog.'

But then, of course, we arranged to meet up, and like all the others Gavin took that as his cue to stop messaging.

'Why don't they want to keep chatting after they've arranged a date?' I complained to Nina on Wednesday.

She shrugged. 'Maybe because the object for them being on the site is to arrange a date.'

'Objective.'

'What?'

'Nothing.'

'Oh, I see, you are correcting me again.'

'Helping you, Nina. I'm helping you.'

'It's not helping, you know. I don't need help.' She took a bite of falafel wrap. 'But you do, so you need to keep me on your good side.'

'That's true.'

There was a tentative knock on the door at this point, followed by 'Nina?' in Niamh's voice. I looked at Nina in horror, and shook my head. She rolled her eyes. 'You can't avoid her forever you know,' she stage-whispered.

'Yes I can!'

'One second,' Nina called out to Niamh. 'I am coming out. For my lunch. A coffee. Can you put the kettle on, Niamh?'

'OK,' Niamh's voice said, and we heard her moving away.

'So what did this grandpops look like, anyway?' Nina said then, turning to me. 'I mean, did you take a look? Niamh is a pretty girl, maybe he was handsome and fit?'

'I am *not* going out with a grandad,' I told her, then left quickly and scuttled back to my own consulting room before the kettle finished boiling.

By Friday, I still hadn't had anything more from Gavin.

'That's just yet more difference between the men and women,' Nina said, taking on the role of mum in response to my complaining. 'It's a normal thing, that the men are not so good at texting. Don't you agree? They don't like to talk on the phone either. Or reply to emails, or Facebook messages.' Her lips got a bit thin at this point. 'It's all the same to them, they just don't like it.'

I leaned forward. 'Everything OK with you and Ravi?'

She flapped a hand. 'Oh of course, everything is fine. I'm just being a super-demanding typically needy girlfriend, that's all.'

'Nina, it's not needy or super-demanding to expect a reply to a message.'

She smiled weakly. 'Oh but you don't know what the message was, darling. It's all fine, everything is fine.' She shifted in her seat, uncrossing her legs and re-crossing them the other way round. It was a signal that that part of our conversation was over. 'Have you spoken to Niamh about her grandpa yet?'

I glanced at the door. I had actually come face to face with Niamh when I arrived that morning, and she'd had that look on her face that said 'I want to set you up with my wrinkly old grandad Bert,' or whatever the old man's name was. I hadn't given her the chance.

'Hi Niamh, sorry, terrible hurry, loads to do before the horde arrives,' and dashed into my consulting room.

'You are going to have to talk to her about it eventually,' Nina said. 'You can make something up, if you like. Tell her you've met someone. But at least speak to her.' She took a bite of her wrap. 'It's rude, you know,' she said, as a small piece of cauliflower flew towards me. 'You've said the same thing about your men.'

I nodded. She had a point. 'I know, I know, I will. That's a good idea, actually, telling her I've met someone.' In fact, I was thinking, my man Gavin might fit the bill nicely, even if I never heard from him again.

Oh, The Bill, haha haha!

'Yes, it is.' She chewed thoughtfully. 'Or you could meet him? You know, just to see…'

'Oh shut up,' I said, standing up.

'She's only twenty-one, you know,' Nina said, as I pulled open the door and stepped through it. 'Her father must be maybe forty-something…'

'Thirty-nine.'

'Ah, thirty-nine, yes? So then, you know, Grandpa might only be – '

I slammed the door.

By the time I got to my final patient for the day, I was running forty-five minutes late. Whatever Ravi may like to think, it is just not possible to give someone the care and attention they need in just seven minutes, so I generally don't fever finish on time. I was exhausted and hungry and just wanted to stop thinking for a moment, but then Mrs. Taylor came in and I managed to give her a smile. Whatever my day was like, I was pretty sure hers had been worse. She was in with a sore throat, but it didn't stop her talking.

'I don't know how much longer I can keep going,' she said, while I waited with the tongue depressor.

'It's a terribly difficult time for you, Mrs. E,' I said. 'Shall I take a look at..?'

'He's asleep most of the time now. But, you know, still has…' She pursed her lips. 'You know. *Functions.*'

'Well, yes, sadly the body does continue to try to keep going, long after it – '

'The things I have to do for him. Breaks my heart, to see him like that. My big, strong Teddy.' She shook her head. 'No dignity in death, is there, Doctor?'

'There absolutely is not.'

'I mean, he hasn't eaten a thing for about four days.'

'Ah. I'd say that's a fairly sure sign that – '

'But then his stomach squeaks and growls all the time with hunger.' She dropped her head onto her hand. 'It's so difficult, doctor. I just don't know what to do.'

I put my hand on her arm. I know we're not supposed to touch patients apart from in the course of an examination, but Mrs. Taylor needed some strength right now, and useless platitudes wouldn't do. 'Audrey, I can only guess how awful this is for you. But I can tell, from what you've said, that it's finally coming to an end. You are being incredible for Teddy, and if he could, he'd be saying "Thank you."'

'Do you think so?'

'I really do. His death will happen, probably soon, and he'll be so thankful you were there with him to help him with this final part of his life. Just as you were for the rest of it.'

Her eyes filled with tears, and she forced a smile, then patted my hand. 'Thank you.'

'And you mustn't worry about getting it right for him. Because you are. Whatever you do, it's right. You are his dignity now.'

She lowered her head to search in her handbag, and nodded as she rummaged. Then she pulled out a tissue and dabbed delicately at her nose, and looked up to meet my eyes frankly. She looked so tired. 'I want this to be over,' she said. 'But I also want him to stay with me forever.'

Her throat was inflamed and clearly very sore today, and I worry about how much care she's taking of herself. I want to suggest moving Teddy to a hospice, but I know she won't allow that. She will want to be the one with him in his final moment, not an unknown nurse or doctor, no matter how kind they are. And she wants him to feel safe, at home in his own bed. These drawn-out deaths really do make a mockery of the Hippocratic Oath – even all the various so-called 'modern' versions. The harm that's being done to poor Audrey Taylor by the pointless prolonging of her husband's useless life doesn't seem to count for anything. It may be a controversial viewpoint for a doctor, but for cases like Teddy Taylor, there is a very strong argument for euthanasia.

Don't tell anyone I said that.

Gavin and I have gone for a spy thriller – a nice, generic film that no one could be revolted, scared, offended, or bored by, regardless of taste. A few bland, bloodless deaths; at least one car chase; a twisty plot. Everyone's happy. We're only half way through the ads at the moment.

I spent the evening getting anxious about the date. It was a beautiful spring evening and Harry and I had a lovely wander along the Leas. Flowers were blooming, fragrances were wafting, birds were chirping. I was oblivious to all of it, gripped as I was in the now familiar claws of dark dread that comes with blind dates. With low sun on my face and a warm breeze stirring my hair, my thoughts were dragged down by reluctance, and preoccupied with excuses. It would be be awkward; we would have nothing to say to each other; we would both struggle to keep the conversation going; there would be countless interminable silences. Surely now that I'm fifty I can decide not to put myself through these uncomfortable experiences? I'm only answerable to myself, after all. Surely one advantage of being single is that I'm only pleasing myself now? And the prospect of this encounter does not please me.

Yeah, but I also don't want to die alone.

All the benches along the Leas were occupied this evening, mostly with parents. I knew they were parents because their charges were either running after the seagulls, or screaming *like* a seagull. I looked for the old man, but there was no sign of him anywhere. Bernie and Maureen's bench had a thin girl in headphones and eyeliner on it. She was daring anyone to try and sit next to her by wearing a gigantic black tunnel in her ear lobe. She clearly wasn't appreciating the beautiful view across the Channel that Maureen so loved, engrossed as she was in staring at her phone, so I stopped a few feet away and stared out to sea, sighing loudly. 'Isn't that beautiful?' I asked Harry, who was sniffing the bench leg behind me. He didn't respond. Neither did Ear-Tunnel Girl, probably because of the headphones.

I figured that jeans and boots were good enough for a cinema date, so didn't bother changing when I got back. I left my hair down and put a bit of mascara on. That would do. We arranged to meet inside by the popcorn, and as I was eight minutes late Gavin was already here when I wandered over. He blatantly looked me up and down, then smiled.

''Ello, 'ello, 'ello, Stephanie.' Mentally I paid the bet I'd made with myself that he would say that. 'You look exactly like your photo, I'm pleased to say.'

'Hi Gavin.' He looked like only one of his photos. Not the good one. 'Nice to meet you. Are you having popcorn?'

'Hell yeah,' he said, in what was to become a very familiar way. 'Not a crime, I'm pleased to inform you. Not yet, anyway. One of the main reasons I love the cinema.'

He bought one of those gigantic sacks of popcorn that would probably feed a family of four for a week (although they would need a vitamin C supplement) and we headed off into screen three to find our seats.

'I wonder why no one eats popcorn outside the cinema,' he says now, as we wait for the trailers to finish. 'I mean, this stuff is delicious.' He turns to me and grins. 'Isn't it?' And he shoves a handful of popcorn roughly into his mouth. 'Mmmm.'

The endearing boyish gesture makes me smile. OK, so maybe he's not too bad. 'You're right. Imagine what it would be like to eat it every day.'

He's nodding. 'Hell yeah, it would be fantastic. You could have salted for main course, and sweet for pudding.' And he pushes another handful in.

'Or you could sprinkle it on salad.'

'Hell yeah! Or use it as a cheesecake base.'

'Or pour chilli over it.'

'Or curry?'

'You could probably make a lovely popcorn sauce.'

'There must be practical applications too.'

'Undoubtedly. It's universal.'

'Like maybe put perfume on it and use it as pot pourri.'

'Ha! Yes. Or throw it at weddings!'

And suddenly, his face drops. He breaks eye contact and shakes his head. 'Definitely not. That's littering.' He rotates slowly to face the screen. 'Irresponsible.'

'Well, it's organic, so if the birds didn't – '

'Shhh. Film's starting.'

'It's got a few seconds yet – '

'SHHH.'

I stare at his profile, slack-jawed, which he absolutely must be aware of in his peripherals, but he continues to focus dead ahead and moves not one muscle. I don't think I've ever met anyone who feels this strongly about littering. I want to poke him, to make him look at me, but of course I can't do that. So I am forced to sit there in utter mystification as the opening sequence starts. Waves of frigid air are emanating from him, and he puts his elbow on the arm rest between us then puts his chin on that hand. It creates a very effective barrier, but from what, I have no idea. He needn't have any worries about me trying to sneak a part of me over to his side. At this point, I'd rather hack my own arm off (and then dispose of it properly in a litter bin). I'm inclined to leave but why should I? I want to see this film. I resolve to think of myself as being in the cinema alone, with a total stranger next to me, and I start to relax.

On the screen someone in a white robe is pushing their way through a busy market place, in what could be a village somewhere in North Africa. Someone else is in pursuit. The person in front glances back repeatedly, sweat beads clear on his forehead. The man in pursuit is gaining, and the market sounds and background music are getting louder. Suddenly a motorbike roars onto the screen and in one smooth move the rider pulls out what I think of as an automatic gun and begins shooting. It's incredibly loud and the effect in the cinema is some kind of surround-sound. It feels like the shooter is right behind us. And in the seat beside me, Gavin flinches dramatically, and shouts 'Oh hell no!'

I turn to look at him, but the loud shooting has stopped now. The man in white is running, and the man pursuing him is on the ground, bleeding. 'That's not good,' Gavin says to no one in particular, and I notice other heads turn briefly to look over at him. 'He needs first aid or he's gonna bleed out.' He mimes pressing some kind of dressing onto an imaginary wound on his leg and then raises it off the seat. 'R.E.D.,' he says, loudly. 'Rest, elevate, direct pressure.' Again, he doesn't look at me, in spite of my insistent staring.

The film continues; the story unfolds. The man in the white robe is on the bad side of a drug deal gone wrong. Motorbike Man is working for the drug lord and trying to recoup their losses. When Motorbike Man comes around a corner, White Robe Man (now wearing chinos and a khaki shirt) trips the bike up with some kind of scaffolding pole, and the bike goes over. Motorbike rushes towards Khaki, and there is a violent fist fight, dubbed with a lot of loud and unrealistic clattery knuckle noises. It sounds more like someone hitting a cauliflower with a wet fish. First Khaki is on top, then it's Motorbike, then Khaki again; either way, throughout the fight Gavin makes repeated little comments, like 'Oho, got you there!' or 'Nice one!' without bothering to lower his voice at all. I start to hear tutting, and 'shh'-ing from elsewhere in the darkness, and hostility seeps down from the people sitting behind us, but I'm not going to apologise to them. I'm starting to want to be completely disassociated from Gavin.

'Oh! Whoa! Ah!' He makes a multitude of appreciative sounds as the fight progresses, and eventually starts slapping the arm rest and punching the air. Every time I look at him, not quite believing what I'm hearing, he's got a face like an excited child.

'Are you OK?' I whisper in the end, just in case he's actually having some kind of seizure.

'All good,' he whispers back, apparently deciding a quiet voice is important. 'It's a white knuckle job, isn't it?'

'Do you want to leave?'

'Hell no! Why would I want to leave?'

'Well I wasn't sure if you were… enjoying it.'

'Don't be daft! I love this kind of thing!' He focuses on me for a few moments. 'You can leave if you want.' He faces back to the screen. 'I won't mind.'

I blink. I want to see the end. 'No, I'm enjoying it.'

It's one of the strangest dates I've been on, but not the worst. The film has a nice twist at the end when it turns out that Khaki and Motorbike are both working for the same King Pin all along. How they could not have realised I don't know, but I manage to suspend my disbelief for long enough.

'Didn't see that coming,' I say conversationally to the couple coming down, as I wait to join the traffic on the stairs.

They stare at me wordlessly as they go past, then as they descend I hear her say, 'Who the *fuck* was that?'

Gavin and I shake hands in the lobby. 'Good film.'

'Hell yeah!'

'Bye, Gavin.' It's the last time I'll be seeing him. I think he knows.

The next day is Saturday and I've got Happy Hannah coming for tea after lunch. I'm looking forward to that. I walk with Harry down to the beach and together we watch the other dogs run around on the sand. Harry stands just in front of me, not moving more than a couple of feet away, and it feels wonderful to know that he feels safe near me. A ball flies across Harry's eyeline, followed immediately by a tall, gangly Dalmatian, stretching out its body and legs to their fullest extent; then instantly pulling them back in, and repeating the action – out, in. It's very fast. Harry tenses, the front part of his body dipping slightly as his rump lifts a little, and I recognise a playful stance, just for a moment.

'Oh Harry!' I exclaim, bending down to him. He turns immediately to look at me, and his tail wags. 'Did you want to play, Harry? Is that what you want?' I rub his head, wishing I'd thought to bring a couple of tennis balls for him. 'Oh, I don't have one, boy. I'm so sorry. I promise I'll bring one next time.'

'I've got a spare, if you'd like it,' a voice says behind me, and Harry and I look up. He's wearing a grey hoodie and jeans, and looks around my age, maybe a bit older. Nice open face, even teeth. Broad smile making his eyes crinkle. He's holding out what looks like a brand new tennis ball. Unbidden, my eyes zoom to his ring finger and find it delightfully bare.

'Oh, wow, thank you.' I take the ball. 'Are you sure?'

He pulls his wallet from his jeans back pocket and flicks it open. 'Yes, absolutely. I'll just need a small deposit…'

I hand the ball back. 'Oh, sorry, I don't have any – ' I catch his eye. 'You're joking, aren't you?'

'Of course I am! You can keep that one. For nothing.'

'Oh thank you so much.' I turn to find Harry looking up at me expectantly. 'Do you want to play fetch, Harry? Do you?' I pull my arm back and throw the ball as hard as I can, which is about fifteen feet, and yell '*Fetch it*!'

Harry's head whips round to follow the path of the flying ball, but he doesn't move.

'Go on Harry. Get it!'

Harry looks back at me, uncomprehending.

'Looks like he doesn't want to after all,' the man says behind me.

'Yeah, I think you're right.' I turn to face him. 'He's never fetched a ball before, as far as I know. But when he saw that Dalmatian sprinting off, he looked like he might want to.'

'He's probably excited by it, but just doesn't know what to do. Maybe you could show him?'

I widen my eyes. 'You think I should run over there and pick it up in my teeth?'

He laughs. 'No, no, that's not what I meant. You can pick it up normally, and then put it in your mouth.'

'Oh, yuck! I don't think it would make any difference whether...' I catch his eye a second time. 'You're joking again, aren't you?'

He flicks his eyebrows up. 'Well, it is rather an amusing image. But yes, I'm having you on. Sorry. It's a bad habit I've picked up from children.'

'Ah, yes, the influence of children on the parents. No one warns you about that in Parent School do they?'

'No they don't. Honestly, I used to be a calm and quite serious financial adviser. Now I'm often to be found leaping about the place pretending to be a gorilla.'

Ah, so his children are quite young, then. 'How old are they?'

'Who?'

'The gorilla aficionados.'

'Oh. Well, Lola is twenty-seven and James is thirty...' He tails off and looks down. 'I'm so sorry, I'm doing it again. I just can't seem to help myself. Lola is actually four, and James is seven.'

'Wonderful ages. Interested in everything, and very easy to please, as I remember.'

'Their parents would probably disagree with you there!'

Now I'm confused. But I can't just blurt out, "Sorry, I thought you meant you were their dad?"

'You thought I meant I was the dad, didn't you?'

'Pardon? Oh, no, I didn't... I mean, I wasn't really, you know, thinking about it.' I focus on Harry, who is sniffing a small patch of sand in front of him. It must smell exactly the same as all the other sand, but he's paying it very close attention.

'I'm their grandad,' the man says now. 'Jack.' And he holds out his hand. I only know this when he says, 'Don't leave me hanging,' and I look round to find his hand outstretched towards me.

'Oh, God, I'm so sorry, I didn't notice. I'm Stephanie.' In my embarrassment I grab it far too quickly and there's a crack as his middle finger is bent back too far.

'Ouch!' He snatches his hand back and rubs the finger.

'Oh my god, I'm so sorry. Is it OK?'

He stares down at his hand and shakes his head sadly. 'I think it will have to come off.'

'Now I know you better, I am going to assume that's a joke.'

He looks up and grins. 'That's some handshake you've got there, Stephanie.'

'Um, Steph. Sorry, should have said that, really. Sorry about the freak handshake injury.'

'It's absolutely fine. I gave up my curling career many moons ago.'

I look at him and find myself smiling. 'I just don't know what to believe.'

'And with that, I must dash, I'm afraid.'

'Oh.'

'It was a pleasure to meet you, Steph. And Harry over there.' He stands in front of me for a moment. 'You could just let him get used to the ball to start with. You know, leave it in his basket, let him find it and mouth it a bit. Then once he knows he's the owner, try rolling it a short distance. See what happens.' He touches his fingertips to his forehead, shouts, '*Arnie!*', and exits stage left, followed by a galloping Dalmatian.

On the walk home I ponder the improbability of meeting a rather delicious grandad, just a week after failing to meet one. Jack was by no means an old man, so maybe Niamh's grandad would be worth meeting after all. I sigh. Nina is going to be impossible about this.

No, no, she won't, because I'm not going to tell her. There's a vast difference between being the grandad of Lola and James, ages four and seven; and grandad of Niamh, age twenty-one. One is a perfectly reasonable, pleasant, nice-looking and distinguished, definitely fanciable chap. And one is an old man.

Just as I'm walking up to my front gate, I receive a text from an unknown number that says,

'Hi mutual friend give me your number she dont know why I hope its ok wondered if you fancied coffee soon?'

I stare at it for a moment, and blink. Now what in God's name does that mean? What's wrong with using a bit of punctuation? I'm not being pedantic, whatever Amy may think, but I do struggle to understand text without punctuation. I often have to ask her to translate comments I read on Facebook where there aren't any commas or semi-colons. Is this person a mutual friend with someone I know? Are they asking me to give them my number? Or are they saying they got my number from a mutual friend whom 'she' doesn't know? And where does the coffee fit in to it all?

My phone beeps again, and the next text arrives.

'Ed xx'

10
SURPRISE MAN

I actually stop walking for a moment, and stare at the message. Ed. Ed, Ed, Ed. Which one of the terrible dates I've recently been on was Ed?

The name rings a very strong bell, but just as I feel I'm about to remember, a voice nearby interrupts my thoughts.

'Heads up, lady.'

I look up and realise I've blindly started walking again whilst staring down at my phone and am about to crash. The voice belongs to Grumpy Graham, from next door, who is on his knees on his front lawn; and to my utter mortification I've over shot my own front path and am about to stumble into his. Right now, I have a faceful of his lobelia. From his kneeling position, so does he.

'Oh, God, sorry,' I stammer, backing up. 'Wasn't looking where I was going.'

'Is that right?' he says, enunciating every word very slowly.

I decide not to react. 'How are you today? Enjoying the weather?'

He's already focussed back on whatever mind-numbing activity he's doing down there, and just grunts as a reply.

'Good, good,' I say, and walk back to my own front door. 'Come on Harry.' Harry is already standing with his nose against the door, but Graham doesn't know that.

The mysterious text from mysterious Ed goes out of my head as I shower and change, and then try to make the house chic and elegant enough to receive Hannah later. The terrible pine kitchen makes this impossible of course, so instead I sit down and google a few kitchen fitters. It gives me a little thrill of excitement, which forces the absolute realisation on me that I am indeed firmly in my fifties now. It also insists that I wonder why I haven't organised this already. My original plan was to get this done within a month of moving in, and being fifty and finally a proper grown-up means I should have galvanised myself more promptly. I had valid reasons to put things off in every other decade so far: twenties due to babies; thirties due to babies and debts; forties due to, well, still babies and debts, although much bigger ones. Plus fear, of course. Even after forty. But now at fifty I have the means and the time – and the confidence – to ring any number of tradespeople whenever necessary. As soon as I want to.

And I can sound authoritative and in charge, and not a useless, stammering idiot who wouldn't have a clue if she needed a 900 mil carcass, or if the dimensions were external or internal. There are definitely pros and cons to this age.

I ring four, and leave four voicemail messages. I'm quite proud of myself for it and award myself a small slice of Jamaican ginger cake from the plate I've prepared for Hannah's visit. It's no effort at all to move the other slices around to fill the gap. And I'm pretty sure that a statuesque and elegant woman like Hannah won't eat a single one anyway.

When Hannah finally arrives for tea she's four minutes late. Yes, yes, I know, that's not late in the true sense of the word, we need to allow it. But when you've been glancing out of your front window every minute for the past twenty, even four extra minutes feels like a lot.

I offer to take her coat, then do a really weird thing of trying to pull it off her shoulders for her, like some ridiculous maitre d' in a bad American rom-com. 'Oh, sorry, sorry, I'll just let you do that…' She manages to disrobe without aid, and hands me the coat, which feels like a creamy white cloud in my hands.

'Would it be too much to ask you to hang it up, please?' she asks me, as I follow her into the living room, still cradling the coat. 'I hate to make a fuss but it is cashmere, and you know what that's like.'

'Oh, God, yes, of course, silly me.' I go back to the hall and hang it up, not quite resisting the urge to put my face lightly against it for a second. Oh dear God. I just manage to stop myself shouting 'Alexa, add cashmere coat to my shopping list.'

'What an ugly man you have living next door,' Hannah says, turning to me with a smile when I go back in.

'Oh, er – ' I glance to the front window where I can still see Graham's brown-top bin. An unpleasant man, yes. But I wouldn't have said 'ugly.' And I don't know Hannah very well, but she doesn't strike me as someone to comment negatively about a person's appearance. Unless…wait. Of course. She means *on the inside*. 'Well, yes, I have certainly found him quite difficult to deal with…'

She lifts her eyebrows. 'Have you? That's odd, isn't it? I found him completely lovely.'

And realisation hits me that she didn't say 'ugly', she said '*lovely*'. Which is even odder. I blink.

Hannah pauses for a second with her back to the armchair, and indicates the seat with her hand. 'May I?'

'Oh, yes, of course. Please do.'

'Thank you.' And she lowers herself down onto the chair. Harry is curled up as usual in the other armchair, but instead of having his back to the room, he's curled the other way and has lifted his head to watch what's going on. Hannah smiles at him across the room. 'Hello there, Harry boy,' she says, and, to my amazement, Harry's tail lifts off the seat and drops back. 'How lovely to see you again.'

'Where are Ginger and Freddie?'

'Oh, goodness, I didn't want to bring them onto Harry's territory straight away. He can get used to our smell first of all, and then perhaps I could bring them for a short visit next time?'

Delight bursts in me like sped-up footage of a flower opening. *Next time.* 'Oh yes, yes, definitely. By all means.'

'That's terribly presumptuous of me, Stephanie,' Hannah says. 'I'm so sorry. But I do like you and am sure we can be friends. I hope that's all right?'

'Yes, yes, of course. Me too!'

'Oh, wonderful.' She drops her hands into her lap and looks around at the brown carpet and orange stripey wallpaper. 'What a lovely room.'

'It's not, though, is it? I can tell you're being nice and there's really no need. But I'm going to get decorators in very soon.'

She's nodding, and gives me a knowing smile. 'It has sweet dimensions though.'

'Oh yes, I know what you mean. Sixteen feet by twenty are my absolute favourites.'

Hannah turns her head a little. 'Are you teasing me?'

'Oh, I'm sorry, yes I am a bit. But you don't need to find something lovely to say about this room. It's terrible! I know it, and the dimensions don't really change anything. But I see potential, and I've only been here four months so I've not really got round to doing it yet.'

'Tease away, my dear, I can take it. I can see that the décor needs updating, but that potential you see – that's down to the dimensions. I meant it when I said it's a lovely shape. Some rooms are a little too narrow and long, aren't they, so you feel like you're sitting in someone's hallway. But yours – ' she glances around again ' – is wide and light. The width is very similar to the length, so it doesn't feel cramped. Do you see?'

All of which makes me feel completely shitty. 'You're right. Thank you. And I'm sorry, I was only messing around.'

She puts up a beautifully manicured hand. 'None taken, lovely girl. Now, tell me what colours you're thinking of.'

I make some tea and bring it through on a tray (that I bought in Asda yesterday) with the Jamaican ginger cake. Hannah surprises me by eating two slices. 'Life is for living,' she says, as she's helping herself to the second piece. 'And that most definitely includes ginger cake.' We chat about colours and themes and she gives me the name of a decorator she's used and it's all I can do not to ring them immediately.

'Thank you so much for the recommendation. It's been on my mind to ring someone but…' I shrug. 'I just haven't got round to it.'

She eyes me closely. 'Are you anxious about it?'

'No, no, not anxious, of course not, I'm a fifty-year-old woman, why would I be anxious about that? Ha ha.'

She tilts her head forward with a smile. 'Oh, I don't know. I just wondered if maybe your anxiety levels have been increasing lately, for various reasons. You know, along with several other things going on. Like, perhaps, hot flushes? Sleeplessness? Lack of recall?'

My instinct is never to talk about menopause. No one wants to hear about it, just get on with it and stop your whining, so this feels like a shaft of sunlight breaking through heavy cloud. 'Oh, er, yes, I suppose you're right.'

'It will get better. Believe me. You'll feel like you again eventually. Just go easy on yourself.'

I nod. I must look like eight-year-old Josh staring up at his karate instructor years ago.

'And don't forget to ask for help, my dear. When you need it.'

After an hour or so, there's a lull in the conversation and I wonder if she's thinking it's time to go. But she doesn't move, or even look at her watch. She makes firm eye contact with me and dips her head slightly, a slight smile on her lips.

'Now Steph. You have to tell me. I've been dying to ask you since I got here. What do you know about Graham?'

'Graham? You mean, Grumpy Graham, next door?'

She glances towards the front window. 'Grumpy? Oh, I wouldn't exactly have said 'grumpy'...'

'I think that's more testament to you as a person than his personality, to be frank. He's always been perfectly foul to me.'

She turns to me. 'I'm truly shocked. He was nothing but wonderful when I spoke to him earlier.'

'Again, that says more about you than him.'

'You have to admit he's handsome, though? Surely you can see that, at least?'

What I could see was a curmudgeonly old codger who thought the world owed him something for reaching the ripe old age of 124. I'd never even looked at his features. 'Yes I can definitely see something... *striking* about him.'

'Yes,' Hannah says, widening her eyes. 'Striking. That's it. He's commanding, isn't he? He has a presence.'

'You're really quite taken with him, aren't you?'

'You know what, Stephanie? I am. I don't mind telling you.'

I think for a moment. 'Would you like me to invite him in?' I don't relish the idea of Graham sniffing round my home, but if Hannah has seen something in him, I should look again. Anyway, he won't accept, fingers crossed, but at least I'm trying.

Hannah's hands go to her head. 'What, now? Heavens!' She pats her hair a bit, but of course it's already immaculate. 'How do I look?'

She's wearing slim dark blue jeans with black ankle boots, a cream blouse and a coral coloured cardigan. Her hair – pure white and short – is bouffant back over her head, like Jane Fonda, and is just about the most glamorous hairstyle it's possible to have over the age of sixty. I look again and finger my own hair. Well, at any age, really.

'You look gorgeous,' I tell her. 'Honestly. You always do.'

'Goodness, I do not. You should see me after I've been up all night drinking vodka.'

My eyes widen.

'Joke,' she says, winking.

Two minutes later I'm outside Graham's door, waiting for him to 'spruce up' as he called it when I invited him round.

'That foxy lady still there?' he'd asked me.

'If you mean my lovely friend Hannah, then yes, she is.'

'Two minutes,' he said. 'Need to spruce up.'

He emerges now in a cloud of Blue Stratos, hair smoothed down with what I can only hope is water, and probably combed. He's still in jeans and a shirt, but he's added a red bow tie and beige cardigan to the ensemble. By the angle of his head, it's clear these two items have made him feel like quite the man about town. He pulls the door, and just as it's about to close he thrusts his arm back in and yanks a tatty brown fedora back through the gap. He puts it on, adjusts it minutely on his head, then turns to look at me, smirking.

'No,' I say quietly, shaking my head.

'No?' He touches the hat again, adjusting its position like a cowboy, checking his reflection in the glass of the door.

'Indiana Jones you are not.'

He locks eyes with me and curls his lip slightly, then removes the hat and throws it back through the door. 'I think you're wrong, but who am I to know?'

'Wear it then, I don't care.' I don't say this, but I have to rub my hand across my mouth to stop myself.

After I've introduced Graham to Hannah and Hannah to Graham, I go out to the kitchen to let them chat, ostensibly to make tea. I sit at the table and click onto Facebook on my phone as I sadly acknowledge to myself that I'd had an idea at the back of my mind to introduce beautiful Hannah to my dad. Maybe bring some life back to his life, get my old dad back. But I see now that he would not have suited her, or she him. He's a pipe and slippers man, and I have a faint suspicion that she and Graham might go out dancing later.

I scroll through the self-indulgent and terrifyingly narcissistic drivel that clogs Facebook now, barely reading it. These young people are the future custodians of the planet. We will be handing the care of it over to people who take selfies instead of panoramas. The daughter of someone I used to go to school with got married last year, and she's still posting photos and updates about the wedding. Wedding update a year later, Helen: it's over, love. Someone else is at the gym. A third person really and truly loves her husband so much, he's her rock.

I'm on the verge of clicking off and opening up the Butterflies app when I see a post from Amy. She hasn't posted in a while, so it's nice to see. It's something generic about the awful service she's had in Costa Coffee this morning, and it makes me smile. The comments are mostly from her uni friends, berating her for being impatient as the baristas in Costa are all students, but one of them catches my eye because it's so long. I realise as soon as I start reading that it's from Tim's mum, Marie, who has no idea at all how Facebook works.

'Dear Amy, it's Granny here. How are you sweetheart? Your Grandad and I haven't heard from you in a while and wondered if you had any ideas for your birthday this year? Or maybe you would prefer some cash, to help you out? Any sign of a boyfriend yet? I can't believe you don't have one, a pretty girl like you. Poor Grandad has been at the doctor with his feet again. He's been told to change his diet but he's a stubborn old fool so I suppose he deserves everything he gets. It would be lovely to see you at some point over your birthday. Are you going to visit your father? Perhaps we could see you there? All our love, Granny and Grandad. Xxxx'

I immediately come out of Facebook and text Amy, 'OMG Granny and Grandad on FB lol!' and I'm chuckling the entire time. She replies instantaneously with a red-faced embarrassed emoji, followed by one crying with laughter. Thank goodness she's laughing about it – it could have been so much more mortifying than it is. Honestly, how can Tim's mum not know by now that things written on someone's wall can be read by all their friends? Maybe people of advancing years should be given a basic half-day training in Social Media usage. Just to understand how very un-private it is. Second thoughts, maybe people of advancing years should be given a full three week intensive course on the internet in general. Social media is the least of their worries, if news reports about banking scams are to be believed. I had an email this morning purporting to be from my bank, asking me to click on the link below and input all my online banking details immediately, "to stop my acount be suspending." How can anyone with even a quarter of a brain fall for that? Surely getting older doesn't mean you lose the ability to be discerning? Or is it simply panic, brought on by not understanding how online banking really works, and not knowing how easy it is to hack into someone's account and send a fake email?

It's concerning really. People not willing or able to use the internet must be feeling horribly left behind these days. And frightened. Still getting the bus to the bank to pay a water bill; still walking round Waitrose with a trolley; still writing cheques to the window cleaner. My dad has a mobile phone at least, but it's an ancient Nokia thing that you have to wind up. He can't access the internet on it, and I don't think he's ever even turned on the laptop I bought him. He still keeps records of his finances in a hard-back ledger, writing down all his ins and outs religiously before he goes to bed. I've mentioned the ease of online banking, shown him the app on my smart phone, demonstrated the fingerprint security, but he's adamant. 'I want to be in control of my finances,' he'd said, his lips a thin line.

'You will be, though, Dad. As long as you're careful, and stay alert, no one could – '

'Precisely,' he'd said, putting up a hand. Conversation closed.

And now, of course, even meeting a new partner is mostly done online. My mind flashes back to Bernie on the bench, alone on The Leas, staring out to sea. I just can't imagine him, or my dad, or Graham next door, staring instead at a screen full of elegant faces, spending an hour scrolling and swiping. 'Nope, nope, nope, ooh yes, nope.' Of course there are some silver surfers out there, eagerly logging on every day to watch the wrestling, but they must be a minority.

My phone pings at this point, and I see I have a message on Butterflies from someone called Darren. I don't even remember matching with him, but I must have done for him to be able to message me. With similar expectations to what I get when I open my dad's fridge, I open his message, and see immediately that he's sent me a photo. That's a first. I squint and look more closely, as it's difficult to make out what I'm looking at. I can see what appears to be a man's jaw and neck, blurry and small in the background; but my view of Darren's face is rather obscured by the long, pinkish balloon, huge in the foreground….

Oh.

I slam my phone face down on the counter. What the hell?! How dare he? How dare he assume that I am happy to have *that* on my phone? Surely that kind of behaviour must be illegal, akin to the dirty old men in long macs and no trousers who populated my childhood nightmares? Ugh. I eye my phone, lying there on the counter in my kitchen, my haven, and it feels tainted now. Besmirched. I can't leave that monstrosity on there, polluting my life. With my lip curling I pick the phone up again in my fingertips, find the 'delete' button without properly looking at the screen, then unmatch with Darren. Then I drop the phone again and walk away from it.

Of course, I'm a GP, I've seen my fair share of flaccid, wrinkly members in my time, so unlike those organs I'm hardened to it. But what if Happy Hannah – beautiful, graceful Hannah – set up her own Butterflies account, then received a picture like that? I walk over to the sink and catch sight of my ghostly reflection in the window. My nose is crinkled in disgust. I'm fairly sure Hannah would not let many things faze her, and I feel like she could give someone quite a telling off if she needed to. But why should her digital life be similarly polluted? I glance at the door to the living room. They seem to be getting on well anyway, so I'm sure Butterflies is off the agenda. For Hannah, even if not for Graham. But there must be thousands of lovely lavender-scented elderlies out there who are craving some companionship. Likewise some decent old gents who don't want to be on a bench on their own any more. But how to get these people together, when they don't or can't use the internet? I think about the chap on the bench, and my dad, and Graham. Maybe I could help them, if they wanted it? Could I?

How on earth did this happen? Am I matchmaking for Silver Surfers now? The idea brings on a smile. Silver Surfers. Although in fact I'd be looking at a mostly non-surfing demographic of course. And for grumpy anti-socialites like Graham, the pre-existing coffee mornings and knitting circles would definitely not suit. But that doesn't mean there isn't someone out there for him.

Turns out there is.

There's a tentative tap on the door and it opens slowly to reveal Hannah. Beaming, beautiful Hannah, with a grumpy git by her side.

Except – my jaw drops – Graham is smiling. I look again to make sure he's not having a stroke, but no, his mouth is turned up on both sides. His eyes are twinkling. There's an energy about him that can't be down to just

Jamaican ginger cake. I realise for the first time that he has cheekbones, and a good head of hair, and quite a strong chin, actually. He's taken his cardigan off and I notice that it's now draped around Hannah's shoulders. It's quite unnecessary as the heating has been on and the house is toasty, and actually Hannah looks a bit flushed with warmth. But she's taken it and put it on anyway. Her arms are crossed over her chest at the wrists, and she's holding each edge of the cardigan around her. My chest expands a little.

'Hello Stephanie,' she says, and her voice sounds different. She has a classy voice, smooth and shiny like glass. But now it sounds effervescent, as if it wants to fizz and she's trying to contain it.

'Hello Hannah.' I'm smiling broadly. 'Everything all right?'

'Yes, thank you so much.' She glances over her shoulder at grinning Graham, then looks back at me. 'Well, now. Graham and I have found that we have quite a lot in common, so we're going to…er…'

'Go,' he cuts in, gallantly. 'This fascinating lady has agreed to have dinner with me.' He huffs once. 'Me!' he says again, and he and I share a look.

'Yes,' says Hannah. 'So, thank you very much for the tea and cake, Stephanie.'

'Yes, thank you,' Graham says, then adds, 'I'm not a big fan of ginger cake, though.' Just in case I mistakenly thought aliens had been in and switched him with a decent human.

'Oh, right, sorry Graham. I'll remember that next time.'

'Appreciated,' he says, and nods his head at me. There's a lot implied in that nod, so I nod back, with a half-smile.

'You're welcome.'

They turn as one and walk slowly back to the front door.

'Have a lovely evening,' I tell them, but they don't need it.

'Bye!'

Well that was not what I was expecting from today. I wander back into the living room where Harry is wide awake on the armchair. When he sees me, his tail bangs twice on the cushion, so I kneel down and put my arms round his neck.

'Maybe you're the one for me, boy,' I tell him, nuzzling his neck. 'Maybe I don't need a boyfriend at all.'

And for some reason I'm reminded suddenly of the text from mysterious Ed earlier, and in that moment I remember that it was Ed I met at Niamh's party. And Ed is Niamh's dad.

Following on swiftly from that recollection comes the memory of Ed singing and playing guitar, and I picture him laying down his instrument so he can text me.

I jump up and retrieve my cleansed phone from the kitchen side, then open Ed's message again.

'Hi mutual friend give me your number she dont know why I hope its ok wondered if you fancied coffee soon?'

It is a little tricky to follow, but I can at least work out that he's asking if I fancy a coffee, so with my success with Hannah and Graham still sparkling in my head, I send a text back.

'That sounds great.' I pause. Am I really going to do this? My stomach flips and part of my brain tries to tell me to stop; but the 'what the hell, you're fifty now' part keeps on going. 'How about now? My place?'

'On my way,' he replies almost instantly. 'whats your address'

Oh, come on, don't judge me. You're only young once, and it was ages ago.

11
SECRET MAN

Well, maybe not that long ago. Turns out I still got it.

Ed is just as sexy as I remember him from Niamh's party, and he's not bothered at all about the fact that I'm a doctor.

Ha ha, joke. He doesn't care that I'm a doctor of course. What I meant was, he's not bothered at all about the fact that I'm a decade older than him. To be fair, he also doesn't *know* that I'm a decade older. Neither do I, for that matter, but we both make private guesses. I've gone 'worst case scenario', which is 36 (I'm thinking he would have to be at the very least fifteen when Niamh was born). I have a very vague half-memory that someone has actually told me how old he is at some point, but I can't quite access it, so I make a guess at around 40, give or take twelve to eighteen months. I have no idea what he thinks my age is because we don't do much talking when he arrives. I mean, he could look around the place and see photos of my adult children, but he doesn't. I mean, *at all.*

'Wow,' he says, forty minutes later, echoing my own thoughts.

'Yeah!'

He looks at me and widens his eyes. 'Who knew?'

'Mm.' I frown. 'Who knew what?' He'd better not say 'that a fifty year old woman could still pull those kinds of moves,' or something.

He just shrugs. 'I don't know, really. I'm just surprised. Overwhelmed. Delighted, I suppose.'

'Right.' I look around for my clothes. I'm still wearing the top half, but trouserless and prone on the living room floor is not where I want to be. Call me prudish but I would not be comfortable with Graham tapping on the window right now. 'I need to…' I say, and heave myself upright, biting down on the usual 'oomph's and 'uh's that accompany any getting up procedure. Ed glances up at me and I'm immediately self-conscious. If I was sitting behind a news desk, I'd be completely fine; but standing here in my top half and no bottoms feels ridiculous. From my viewpoint, my thighs are looking every minute of their fifty years. 'Could you pass me my…?'

'Oh, yeah sure. Is this the…?'

'Yeah, but there's also the…'

'Oh, yep, here it is. Here you go.'

'Thanks.'

'No probs.'

I leave him on the floor to sort himself out and walk briskly out to the kitchen where I turn one of the taps on full and start washing up the cake and tea things from earlier.

'Ooh, Jamaican ginger cake,' Ed says behind me suddenly, making me jump.

'Help yourself, it's only going in the bin.'

'Whaaaat? Why would you do that?'

'I don't really eat cake.' I turn and face him. 'Fat and sugar – worst things for you after smoking and alcohol.'

He pauses in the act of pushing an entire slice into his mouth.

'Oh, don't let me stop you, Ed. I'm not your – ' I'm not even sure if I was going to say 'doctor' or 'mum'.

'Ha, manks.'

I finish the washing up in silence while he munches noisily through two more slices. Then I turn round and smile as I dry my hands. 'What are your plans for this evening then?'

He flicks his eyebrows up a couple of times. 'Oh, now you're asking. How about some dinner?'

'Oh, um. I didn't...'

He shrugs and turns, starting to move back to the living room. 'Hey, that's fine. I mean, I will be eating more food at some point today, it would be great if you were there to monitor it.' He puts his hands up. 'Joke! That was a joke.'

'Hah. Funny.'

'Sorry. Not meant as a dig.'

'It's fine. Honestly.'

He nods and grins. 'So. Shall we eat together? I don't mind either way.'

My mind hurtles through my options for this evening. I've got a portion of chilli defrosting in the microwave which I was planning on having on the sofa in my pyjamas later with a glass of wine and Harry exuding odour from the armchair. It's certainly a draw.

'Where are you thinking of going? I mean, I definitely don't want to bump into my neighbour and his new lady friend, if we can avoid it.'

'Well then let's go where they aren't?'

'Great idea. Shall we have a coffee, and decide?'

While the kettle is boiling he wanders round the pine kitchen, nodding and stroking. 'Wow, this is vintage.'

'Oh, God, I know. The previous owners were so proud of it. I don't think they'd noticed that forty years have passed.'

'Want a quote?'

I turn to look at him. 'What?'

'Yeah. I'm a kitchen fitter.' He winks. 'Among other things.'

'Oh.' I turn back to the kettle feeling the mystical, magical power of serendipity at work. Only today I was berating myself for not sorting this out already; and now here I am, getting someone in. I wonder briefly about 'mates rates', then dismiss it as a form of prostitution. Then un-dismiss as surely it's not prostitution if you're both enjoying it?

He spends an hour measuring up and we discuss appliances, door types and worktop options. Neither of us feels it necessary to bring up the living room's recent activities. We celebrate afterwards with a hearty tagliatelle at the pizza and pasta place on The Leas.

'We should do this again,' he says in a low voice in my car later. Then he kisses my cheek and is slamming the door and waving before I can say 'I'm free Tuesday.' I mean, literally before I can say it.

The following Monday is a day full of horrors. The first thing that happens is an encounter with Niamh. She's outside the surgery on her phone and ends the call just as I walk up.

'Morning,' she says, smiling at me, and my stomach lurches as I immediately spot the resemblance between her and Ed. Same colour eyes; same shape mouth; same cute smile.

Oh God, that smile.

I take it all in in a kind of fascinated horror, seeing things about Niamh that I've never noticed before. When she's looking at you, she doesn't directly face you but stands at a half turned away angle. There's a light dusting of freckles across her nose. Her eyes are quite widely spaced. Of course, these are the only things about her I can take in right now, and I'm preoccupied with the thought that on Ed the overall effect is very appealing.

'Steph?'

'Oh, God, sorry Niamh, didn't see you there. Morning.'

'You were looking right at me.'

'No, er, sorry, I know. Sorry. Miles away.' I flash her a smile, then try to get past without talking to her any more. I don't want her to mention her grandad again. Or her dad. In fact, I want to hear nothing from Niamh about any members of her family.

'I'd rather Niamh didn't know about this,' Ed had said, over dinner on Saturday.

'My granite worktops?' I said, raising my eyebrows, lips twitching.

He'd frowned. 'No. Why would I care whether she knows about them?'

'No, I was… I mean, it was…'

'I mean about us. You know.' He flicked his eyes towards my general genital area. 'What happened.'

'No, I completely agree. Less she knows, the better, as far as I'm concerned.' I'd nodded. 'Don't want her or Steve to start thinking she's going to get special treatment.'

'No, me neither. And I don't want her to know I've been down on her boss's floor – down on her boss.' My skin shrivelled onto the bones, but he was grinning at his own cleverness. 'Could be a bit cringe.'

'Hmm.' I'd nodded slowly, unable to look at him. 'Quite.'

'Steph, wait,' Niamh says now, just as my hand brushes the handle of the door. I close my eyes, then turn back.

'Yes?'

She presses her lips together. 'I just want to... Shit. I want to say... I'm sorry about, you know, trying to set you up with my grandad.' She looks down, to the side, up at the sky, then the other side. 'I can see now it's a bit cringe.'

I blink. 'A bit – '

'Cringe, yeah. Can we forget it? Soz.'

I give her a beatific smile. 'Course we can, angel. No harm done.'

She releases a long held breath and her face smoothes out. 'Oh God, thanks. 'I've been kind of avoiding bumping into you since my party.'

'Oh, have you, lovely?' Another big smile, and I gently touch her upper arm. 'Oh sweetheart. There's really no need.' My relief is making me generous. 'I'm sure he's a lovely guy.' Too generous. 'I was quite flattered, actually.' Niamh's eyebrows shoot up, and suddenly her face is all expectancy and hope. Oh bloody hell. I put up a hand. 'But as luck would have it, I've just started seeing someone, so...'

She deflates in front of me. 'Oh. Ok.'

'Sorry, my lovely.'

'No, please don't be sorry Steph. *I*'m sorry. I wish I'd never...' She kind of shakes her shoulders, then turns and smiles at me. 'So? Who's this new fella, then? Tell me everything.'

'God no. I mean, no, nothing to tell. You know? No one you know. No one you'd ever know. I mean, you wouldn't like him, I expect. Not your type at all. In any way.'

'Oh, right.'

The day gets worse from there. When Nigel the homeless alcoholic comes in for his 11 o'clock appointment, I look up as the door opens and my jaw drops. He's almost unrecognisable. His left eye is bruised blue and almost closed with swelling, but it's still possible to see that the white part beneath is blood red. His right eye is bloodshot and sorry looking, clearly feeling guilty for getting off so lightly. There's a large gash on his forehead, held together by some grubby, peeling steri-strips, and his chin and jaw are wincingly pink with a large shiny abrasion. He looks like he's been dragged along the road on his face.

'Good God, Nigel, what on earth happened?'

He saunters in, trying to look like it's not bothering him, but he's clearly limping too. 'Got beaten up, doc.'

I stand up and go round the desk. 'Come and sit down, come on.'

'Cheers.'

'Do you want a cuppa?'

'That'd be great, cheers.'

I use the kettle and tea bags on the windowsill behind me to knock up two mugs of tea, then empty three packets of sugar into Nigel's. He takes it and wraps both hands around it, pulling it in close. I notice at this point that the knuckles on both hands are also missing skin and dotted with dried blood.

He sees me notice and looks down. 'Had to defend myself, didn't I?'

I nod slowly. 'So what happened?'

He stares into the mug and breathes deeply. 'Four or five blokes, big blokes, like, boxers or summing. Like, huge. Built like brick sh- ' He glances at me. 'Like brick outhouses. Woke me up night before last, kicking me. Dragged me out my sleeping bag. Beat me up. Nicked all my stuff.' He takes a long slurp of the scalding tea, but barely winces.

'Oh Nigel. You went to hospital?'

He nods. 'Yeah. Someone called an ambulance. Slept in a proper bed. Didn't like it. Came out yesterday morning.'

'Well did you have x-rays? What did they say?'

He shrugs. 'S'ok. M'ok. Just wish I had me bag. You know?'

I close my eyes. As if homeless people don't have enough to cope with without arseholes stealing the paltry few possessions they do have. 'I'll get you one,' I tell him. 'What else do you need?'

He shrugs. 'Just a bag, doc. That's all I need.'

I go out to reception and send Steve out into town in search of a sleeping bag. 'Get a good one,' I tell him. 'Warm and waterproof.' He turns, but I stop him. 'Get him some food too. A Subway meal or something. Something hot, and big.'

'Ok boss.'

'So did you speak to the police?' I ask Nigel when I come back in.

He shrugs again. 'What for? Another homeless getting rolled over? Nah, no point. Kids'll do it again anyway.'

I lean forward. 'I thought you said it was four or five gigantic boxing types built like brick shithouses?'

Nigel chuckles and turns his head sideways. 'Nah. 'S kids, innit. Didn't wanna say. Pulled around by a bunch of snot noses. Embarrassing.'

I get rid of the filthy steri-strips on his head, then clean the wound and glue the edges together. He remains utterly still and silent throughout the process, even though I'm sure it must have been hurting him. 'Now go and wash your hands over there. Fill the sink up, Nigel. There's hot water and soap. I want to see those hands sparkling.'

Several heads turn to stare at him when he goes back to the waiting room, so I let him wait for Steve in one of the examination rooms.

'Thanks Doc. Really 'preciate it.' He sits demurely on the chair.

'Get up there,' I tell him, jerking my head towards the trolley. 'Go on. Have a lie down. I'll make sure no one comes in.'

He looks at me, nods once, then bends to remove his shoes. I leave and close the door, turning the DO NOT ENTER sign round on the door as I leave.

'You're soft with that man,' Ravi says later, while we're all eating our lunch together in Nina's room. 'That alcoholic. You do know it's his own choice to live like that, right?'

'Oh shut up, Ravi,' Nina says, before I can. I turn and look at her in surprise.

'Don't tell me to shut up,' Ravi says. 'It's true. No one forced him to start drinking alcohol. No one forced him to use all his rent money on booze. No one forced him to make himself unfit for employment.' He shakes his head and forks in another meatball.

'You have no idea what caused it,' Nina says. 'You think you know, but you don't know.'

'I don't have to know. I know all I need, and that is that he chose to start drinking alcohol in vast quantities every day. Ipso facto. You know?'

'Ugh,' Nina says. She gets up, collects up her lunch remnants, and marches out of the room. There's a moment's silence while Ravi and I stare at the door, then she comes back in. 'This is my room, *you* leave.'

Ravi looks at me with his fork in his mouth.

'No, Ravi, I mean you,' Nina says, not looking at either of us. 'Please leave.'

'Oh come on Nina, you're over-reacting again…'

'And *don't* tell me I'm over-reacting.'

I pull my phone out of my pocket and open up Facebook. Ooh, Roman Originals has 20% off everything.

'Nina,' Ravi whines, spreading his hands out. 'Come on.'

'Just go away please.'

Something in her voice makes me glance up at her. She doesn't sound angry, she just sounds…defeated. After a few more seconds of utter disbelief, Ravi gathers up his lunch and leaves the room. Nina flops down and closes her eyes.

'You OK?' I ask her, leaning towards her.

She opens her eyes and looks at me. Then she rolls them and a smile plays around her lips. 'Do *not* say I told you so.'

I smile back. 'I wasn't going to.'

'Good.'

She eats another mouthful of her wrap.

'I'm bloody relieved though!'

I have one more horror to endure at work before the day staggers to an end. An appointment in the afternoon with Mrs. Taylor. She looks grey and drawn as she sits down, and turns tired, red-rimmed eyes on me.

'Good to see you, Audrey. How are you doing?'

'He's gone, Doctor. My Teddy has gone.'

'Oh, no. Oh Audrey. I'm so sorry.' I lean over my desk towards her but this time don't touch her. She sniffs and extracts a tissue from her handbag. 'When?'

She waves a hand. 'I don't know.'

'You..?'

'Oh, gosh, no, that sounds worse than I meant it to. Goodness, of course I know. I was with him. Thank God

I was with him.' She sniffs and dabs her nose. 'It's just, you know, the days all blend together, don't they? What day it is or what time it is or what to wear or have for dinner all seem so trivial now.'

'Of course.'

'It must have been… what day is it today? Is it Tuesday?'

'It's Monday today.'

'Ah. Well, it was four days ago. When was that?'

'Probably Thursday. Was it Thursday? The ninth?'

She shrugs. 'I suppose so.'

'How was it?'

She sniffs again and presses the tissue to her nose, shaking her head. Her eyes, already red-rimmed, fill up. 'It was peaceful. He'd been asleep all the time for a couple of days. Only opened his eyes briefly now and then to look at me, you know. Give me a little smile. Squeeze my hand…'

'He knew you were with him, then. That's important, Audrey. He didn't feel like he was doing it on his own.'

'Of course he wasn't doing it on his own. That big fool couldn't do anything on his own, always needed me there to put him right.'

I smile, in spite of my own eyes feeling hot and my throat aching. 'You were such a great team, you two.'

'We were, Doctor. We were partners. He was everything to me. Everything.' She drops her hands into her lap. 'Do you know, we have been together for fifty-eight years?'

'Wow. That's impressive.'

'We met when I was sixteen. Married at twenty-three. I've never had another boyfriend. I knew right away that I'd marry him. It was meant to be. When you know, you know, don't you?'

I disagree with this sentiment in every way possible. 'Oh yes, definitely. And that was obvious to anyone that knew you, Audrey. Meant to be.'

Her eyes unfocus as she gazes back into some past memory – dancing with Teddy when she was sixteen possibly, or one of a million other happy moments they shared along the way. Eventually she raises her eyes to me again. 'Trouble is, Doctor, I don't know how to be without him.'

I nod. 'It's a very daunting prospect at the moment. A huge change. Try not to think about the future too much, just focus on getting through one day at a time...'

She's shaking her head. 'No, no, I'm sorry but that won't do.'

'Oh.'

'I don't mean to be rude, dear. I know you're trying to help. And I appreciate that, I really do. I just mean that I can't be on my own. I never have, you see. I've always had Teddy there, my whole life. Everywhere I went, everything I did, Teddy was there. I haven't ever experienced anything without him. Oh, apart from the little personal things, you know, like child birth and so on. While Teddy was poorly I didn't really go out, only to the supermarkets. I just can't do it without him.' She presses her lips together. 'It's like asking the sky to carry on without the sun.'

'Audrey, it's understandable to feel like that now…'

'No, I don't mean "now". This is how I feel. My 'self', my life, don't exist without Teddy. I don't exist without him.'

An alarm bell goes off faintly in my head. 'What exactly are you saying, Audrey? Do you mean you want to end your life?'

She blinks. 'Good heavens no, dear. I'm 73, my life will be over soon enough, without any help from me.' She smiles. 'I suppose I'm after advice, really. How to continue without him. How one goes on, being on one's own.' She tilts her head up towards me and raises her eyebrows. Not for the first time in my career, I've been mistaken for someone with all the answers.

I think for a moment. Like Audrey, I've found myself single again later in life, although for a different reason. Not something I anticipated when I married Tim twenty-four years ago. Not something anyone anticipates I suppose, unless they choose to be alone. Poor Audrey didn't. And I didn't. But that doesn't mean we can't choose again. I think about all the terrible dates I've been on recently in my blinded, single-minded quest to get my life back after Tim's betrayal. The rudeness, the racism, the careless crassness, the self-absorbed insensitivity, the casual discarding. On and on it's gone, one after another after another, until I've been left feeling like nothing more than a gleaming new car in a showroom, waiting to be picked. What about me, I've wanted to shout, what about *my* choice? Don't I get a say? And if that's the conclusion I've come to, why have I continued the search? Why am I continuing? I acknowledge to myself that Ed, as sweet as he is, is not a long term attachment. So what am I doing? Trying to replace Tim? Find another man to fill the man-shaped hole that has formed beside me? Any man? I shake my head a little, confused by my own behaviour. It's exactly what Paul was doing after splitting from his wife, and I advised him against it. Looking at Audrey delicately dabbing her nose and eyes, I realise I need to follow my own advice. And I'm suddenly not entirely sure I need to fill that man-shaped hole. In fact, I'm no longer even sure there's a hole at all.

I smile and lean towards her. 'I think you just have to tread water for a while,' I tell her, and myself, 'until you're ready to start swimming again.'

She looks at me. 'But swimming where? And who with?'

'That's up to you. But you don't have to decide now.'

She shakes her head and her face drops into one of almost unbearable sadness. 'But… I can't swim without Ted. Without… someone. I need…' she looks up and tilts her head, '…I need water wings.'

I nod. 'Support? Of course you do. There is plenty of it, Audrey. There's an organisation called Cruse…'

'No, no, I don't mean that. I understand about grief, I know what to expect. I've been through it before, when my sister died.'

'I get that. But each time will be – '

'I mean I need another person by my side.'

I blink. Her voice went a bit strident then and I wasn't expecting it. It has the effect of breaking through my self-absorption and really understanding at last what Audrey is trying to say.

'You want a companion.'

She smiles and closes her eyes, letting out a breath with a little nod. 'That's it.'

'You're not talking about… dating? I mean, romance…'

'Good lord no! Teddy was my man. He was for me, there won't be another. I'm going to need a friend. Company. Someone to shop with, laugh with, go for dinner with.' She looks at me. 'Sit on a bench with.'

My eyes widen. 'Sit on a bench with.'

'Yes.' She frowns. 'Why are you looking at me like that?'

When I get home, Harry greets me at the door, his tail swishing so hard, the entire back half of his body is swaying side to side. I bend and scratch him behind the ears, feeling so grateful to have him there, pleased to see me when I come home.

'Hello Harry, hello my lovely boy, who's my lovely boy? Are you? Are you my lovely boy? Huh? Are you?'

Harry confirms that he is, then walks briskly to the kitchen and stares at the cupboard under the sink where his food is kept.

'All right, H, I know you're hungry, just give me a minute to get in, eh?'

Fed and watered, I clip his lead on and get out into the weak evening sunshine, eager for the walk and the peace it affords me. It feels as though Audrey Taylor may have sparked an epiphany in me and I need to think about what it means. She said she wants a companion, someone to "sit on a bench with", exactly the same idea that I had when I saw that old man on a bench on his own weeks ago, in the freezing cold. I wonder if I could make something happen for him, and for Audrey, and for my dad and people like Graham next door and happy Hannah, and I feel on the brink of working something out when my phone dings in my pocket and it's a text from Josh.

'Have you heard from Grandad today?'

Worry ignites in my chest and I abandon texting a reply and ring Josh straight back.

'Why are you asking about Grandad? Has something happened?'

'Oh, hi Mum, lovely to hear from you. I'm fine, Chloe's fine, the job's fine, we're all fine, thanks.'

'Oh stop it Josh. I'm guessing if all that hadn't been fine, your text would have been about that rather than about Grandad. So why are you asking if I've heard from him?'

'Fair. OK, well I've had a bit of a weird WhatsApp message from him. Wondered if you'd had it too?'

'About what?'

'OK, hold on, I'll read it to you.' There's a brief pause, then, 'Hi Joshy my boy, bit of advice I'm after. What would you do if you were asked to go somewhere you very much didn't want to go?'

I frown. Harry looks up at me and I realise that I've stopped walking. 'Sorry Harry.' I start again, and Harry resumes his intense nose exploration of the ground. 'What the hell does that mean?'

'I have no idea. I thought you might.'

I'm shaking my head, even though he can't see me. 'Nope. Not a clue.' A dozen scenarios instantly flash through my mind – a summons to hospital; a summons to court; a sickening bank cash point scam; a Nigerian prince with false financial promises. 'Have you answered?'

'Not yet. Texted you first.'

'OK. Good. Great. Thank you. Ask him what it is.'

Pause. 'I don't know. Maybe he doesn't want me to know.'

'I don't care, Josh. You bloody ask him.'

He lets out a breath. 'All right. I'll ask.'

'Great.' Pause. 'Are you doing it?'

'Mum...'

'This could be serious. It could be a hospital appointment or something. The sooner we act, the more chance he has of…'

'OK, OK, I get it. I'll do it now.'

'Right. I'll wait.'

'You literally want me to do it right now? While you're on the phone?'

'Yep.'

'Right. OK. Hang on.'

I wait while he texts back, watching Harry sniffing something on the ground. 'No, no, don't eat that, that's not food.'

'What?'

'Nothing. Have you done it?'

'Yep. Oh, he's typing.'

'Oh God.'

'Try not to worry, Mum. If he's just had the hospital appointment come through, it's still early days. They've probably caught it in time.'

'Maybe.'

'And don't forget, if it was something life threatening, they'd ring rather than send a letter.'

'We don't know it was a letter.'

Pause. 'No. That's true.'

'Anything yet?'

'Hang on… No, still typing.'

I can picture my dad, hunched over his phone on the edge of the tatty old grey sofa that he won't replace because it still has a dent in it where Mum used to sit.

He'll be peering through his glasses at the screen, scrunching his face up, typing out words with one finger. Probably telling Mum all about it.

'Anything?'

'Still typing. I'll let you know when it comes through.'

'Jesus, what's he writing, War and Peace?'

'Give him a chance, you know he's slow at texting.'

'Yes, yes, you're right.' Something's got Harry's attention and he lifts his head and pricks his ears, staring intensely ahead. 'What can you smell? Eh? Can you smell a squirrel?'

'*Pardon*?'

'Nothing.'

'Oh, here it is. It's – '

'Wait.' Suddenly I don't want to hear it.

'What?'

'Just…give me a minute. I want… I want this world to carry on a bit longer.'

'What do you mean, this world?'

'This existence. This life, my life, where my dad is OK. Before we have to plunge into the horror of whatever is coming.' I look around me and focus on the sunshine flickering through the tree branches, the warm breeze carrying the scent of the flower beds, Harry's quivering nose, the sound of the traffic on the road. This wonderful, peaceful world where I've got no worries. I let out a breath. 'All right. Go on then. What is it?'

'Mum. It's a wedding.'

12
LONELY MAN

A wedding.

The thing my dad doesn't want to go to, and is so anxious about he's actually taken to the dreaded and incomprehensible WhatsApp ('What's what? What does that mean? There's a word missing, surely?') to ask my son for advice on how to avoid it. The thing that filled my heart with a sick dread as soon as I was aware of it, the thing that made me think my world was about to change. Not a biopsy, not chest pain and nausea, not even a series of unpaid speeding tickets. A flipping wedding – one of the most joyful and pleasurable experiences a lonely old man could possibly be invited to.

'Whose wedding?'
'I don't know. D'you want me to ask him?'

I think for a moment. Josh interrogating him about the details will definitely make him suspicious. 'No, don't do that. I'll give him a ring later.'

'Maybe not too soon? It will look like I've immediately rung you.'

'He won't notice, Josh. And if he does, so what if you rang me?'

'I don't know. I s'pose I was just worried that he might think we don't spontaneously think about him. That we only contact him when one of us rings one of the others and lets them know he's been in touch about something weird, which then prompts us to contact him.' He pauses. 'Instead of, you know, contacting him instinctively. Out of love.'

I stop again, frowning, and Harry looks round at me. 'You're over-thinking it. I'll speak to you later.'

I don't ring straight away but wait the forty minutes it takes Harry to be contented with his outing and point himself towards home again. I love the fact that he does this. It makes me feel that he knows where his home is, where he belongs.

It's dark by the time we get home, so I close the curtains and put a frozen portion of chilli in the microwave, then pour myself a small glass of wine. Then I keep pouring until it becomes a large glass of wine. It's already mostly gone by the time the chilli is ready to eat.

While I eat, I flick open the Butterflies app and scroll through a few grim mug shots. It's more out of habit now than anything else, an alternative to scrolling through Facebook. Mike's profile says "No loonies, no bunny-boilers, no saddo wanabe sugar babes need apply!" which makes me fume. I wonder how many women think to themselves, 'Oh, I'm a bit of a bunny boiler, better not message him.' I instantly match with him so that I can tell him what I think of him. It seems Mike believes his classy and erudite profile is just the job, so I need to craft the perfect message to disabuse him of that. Before I get the chance to write anything, though, a message arrives from him.

"Nice mouth xx"

Funnily enough, those words cause my mouth to become rather unpleasant for a few seconds. I might have felt differently if it had said 'Nice smile', but the use of the word 'mouth' seems to include the interior aswell. I spend a few minutes typing a satisfyingly savage reply. Does he think that his revolting message commenting on my mouth is a good way to, presumably, get to know me? Is he aware that if we were required to repopulate the earth after a devastating plague, the human race would die out before my "nice mouth" was coming anywhere near him? I click send, but don't block him straight away as I know that blocking him will erase it. I need to be sure he's read it before I do that, so I wait for the little grey bubble to appear, letting me know he's replying. I'm not quick enough though, and the message arrives. 'Lol,' he says.

'Think u need to see a doctor, u sound like care in the community isn't working for u.'

I type back, 'I am a doctor, you creature,' then I delete it and block him as planned. Why do I even bother?

I come out of the app before I get sucked into the spiralling vortex of misogyny, and end up saying something I won't regret. I need to call Dad, so will get my fix of casual everyday sexism then.

So Dad has been invited to a wedding, and apparently doesn't want to go. Well of course he doesn't want to go, he's an 84-year-old widower who hasn't been out of the house to socialise for years. I think about it. I don't think he's been out to socialise since Mum died. He doesn't even socialise online. I bought him a laptop a few months after she died, so that he could maybe connect to people that way, but he's never used it. Not even to shop for books on fly fishing.

In spite of what I said to Josh, there is the chance that Dad will get angry if he thinks he's being checked up on. Being eighty-four does *not* mean he's old, or less fit and mentally able than he was at thirty-four. Unlike the rest of God's living creation, advancing years will have no effect on my dad whatsoever. He's probably the world's first and only immortal.

'Oh, hello Steph, love,' he says, his voice not exactly welcoming.

'Hi Dad, how are you?'

'Well, yes, I'm perfectly fine of course, as you know.' I don't bother telling him that, as time has passed since we last spoke, I absolutely don't know. It's an exercise in futility. 'How are you?'

'I'm fine, thanks. Nothing to report.'

'Ah, good. And how are the kids?'

'They're well, thanks, but you know that, you speak to them more often than I do.' I'm fairly sure that he does this not so much to ask after Josh and Amy but more to show an interest in my interests. It reminds me of when I was a little girl and he'd ask me what Barbie had been up to. 'You know Josh is thinking about a new car…'

'Ah yes, the Vauxhall. Tell him it's a good car. I looked into it.'

'Did you? That was nice of you. Where did you look?'

'Well I spoke to Andrzej down at the garage where I get my MOT done and he said they weren't a bad car. And I've been doing some reading, you know.'

'What reading?'

There's a slight pause. He knows what I'm getting at.

'I went to the library,' he says now. 'Looked up a few handbooks on Vauxhall.'

'You know there's masses of stuff online you could have looked at.'

'Oh, well, you know, I would have, but Andrzej at the garage was quite helpful, told me everything I needed to know.'

I take a deep breath and hold it for a second. 'Dad, I can come and show you how to use the laptop again if you want? There's so much on the internet you'd enjoy…'

'Ah I'm sure there is, Stephanie, and when I need to look at it, rest assured I will.'

'What does that mean? No one *needs* to look at it. Well, I mean, some people run businesses on it and stuff, but I'm not… What I mean is, I'm talking about the things you can do for pleasure. The films and books that you'd – '

'I am *not* going to have anything to do with any of that, thank you very much. And if you've got nothing better to suggest, then I'd – '

' – suggest I say nothing,' I finish for him. 'Yes, I get it. But you're incorrectly assuming I was talking about a certain type of film, but actually – '

'I'll hear no more about it, thank you.'

'OK, OK, I yield.'

'Thank you.'

There's an awkward silence while I try to think of a way to bring up the conversation with Josh. Dad's probably trying to think of something to say.

'So you've spoken to Josh recently, then?' I eventually come up with.

'You know I have. That's why you're calling, isn't it?'

I blink. Apparently his determination not to let the years touch him is working. 'Well, partly, but I also wanted to have a chat…'

He makes a Trump expression. I can't see it, but I know it's there. He does the "pshaw" sound, like he's just heard something completely ludicrous to which he is unarguably superior.

'OK, OK, you got me. I did speak to Josh. He tells me you've been invited to a wedding.'

And at this moment I get one of those incredible, brilliant flashes of inspiration that feels like some shimmery, otherworldly arm has broken through the sky to the spine-tingling sound of choruses and harps in harmony, then reached down and touched my head with one dainty golden finger. My brain lights up, neurons explode across synapses and I almost, *almost* believe in angels.

'Yes,' drones Dad. 'Remember Marcus's daughter Julia? It's her wedding. Some head teacher she met on her computer. Her second marriage, actually, but that's neither here nor there.'

'Oh that's lovely. Congratulations Julia. When is it?' And what app was she using?

'Lovely it may be. For Julia. Not for Marcus, of course, as he'll no doubt be footing the bill. Second time around too. I wonder how many more times he'll have to put his hand in his pocket…'

Julia is a fifty-three year old solicitor, probably earning the entirety of Marcus's pension in one afternoon, and will undoubtedly be paying for the wedding herself. I bite my tongue. Another exercise in futility to point this out.

'So, Josh said you don't want to go?'

'Of course I don't want to go. Who wants to see their friend of fifty years showing off how much money he's got? "Oh, Phil, won't you come over here and admire the ice sculpture?" "Oh, Phil, what do you think of this wonderful champagne tower?" Not blooming likely.'

'Oh Dad, I'm sure you'd have a fabulous time.'

'I'd say that was very unlikely.'

'Why? You've known Marcus forever. And Julia. They're lovely.' This is a lie. They're awful, awful people. Marcus is a restaurant complainer. Always finds something wrong with the food and belittles the wait staff. Then argues with the manager until he gets a free meal. And Julia is worse, if that's possible. She's spectacularly selfish. I have actually witnessed her leave a room and come back in again while a blind relative was telling her an admittedly dull story about returning something to Debenhams. She even put her finger to her lips to me, to make sure I didn't give her away, then crept into the next room and ordered Chinese. Vile people.

'Hmm, well, maybe. But they won't want to be bothered with me, will they? They'll be very busy, getting married and giving a speech and so on.'

'Oh that's a great shame.'

'No it isn't. I'll be perfectly happy staying indoors.'

I picture him on his sofa, his thin, white hair smoothed carefully over his bald crown, surrounded by decades of mementos from long ago holidays and laughter-soaked salad days, all muffled in the depth of quiet that only comes after a bereavement. My eyes heat up and I wish I was with him so I could give him a hug.

'I know, but I was going to ask you a huge favour. It's something quite important and I really need your help.'

This is the key moment, the shimmering angel-arm idea. I've dangled the bait. Will he take it?

'You know I'll do anything for you, love. Of course I will. What's up?'

'It's to do with the wedding.'

There's a pause this time. 'Well, if it's something I can help you with, you know I will.'

'Thanks, Dad. Thing is, a patient of mine just lost her husband, and she's feeling a bit, you know, lost at the moment.'

'I do know.'

'Yes. So I've been thinking that what she could really do with is a day out somewhere. I was going to take her out for lunch myself, but I'm not sure I should, seeing as she's my patient.'

'You want me to take her to Julia's wedding.'

I blink. Why did I ever assume getting old would lessen him? 'Oh Dad that would be amazing. Would you? She just needs a bit of fun, you know? Something good to happen. And as soon as Josh told me about this invitation, I thought it would be perfect. She's a lovely lady, very articulate. I'm sure you'll get on. And you're the ideal person to talk to her as you know exactly how she feels, and you're such a good listener.'

It's in just over two weeks, on the fourth of May, so I need to let Audrey know as soon as possible. 'I'll speak to her on Wednesday, Dad. She'll be so excited.' It's very meddlesome of me, to set her up on a blind date without even asking her if she wants one, but I feel confident she won't say no. And even if she does say no, it's no harm done as Dad will be just as happy to stay at home.

On Tuesday afternoon, Ed comes over and takes a final look round my sides. My kitchen sides, I mean, and that's not a euphemism.

'I can start the kitchen on Monday,' he says, later, pulling his trousers back on. Ok maybe it was a euphemism. I'm doing the hunched over walk of clothes-retrieval behind him. 'Should take about a fortnight. Can you manage without your kitchen for two weeks?'

'Ah, no, I can't.' My bra is still on my wrist. Life hack – will have to remember that.

Ed's chuckling. When he turns round I'm in jeans and a bra, which I don't mind being seen in. 'I'm sure you'll work something out.'

What? Oh, the kitchen. I panic. No kitchen for two weeks? 'No, Ed, I'm serious. I can't.'

He laughs some more. 'You're funny.'

'I'm really not.' This is when being a doctor is truly not helpful. I'm sure most people would simply live on takeaway for two weeks, but I can't stop seeing the damage done by all that saturated fat and salt. 'Is there any way you could do it in less than two weeks? Do you think?'

He stares at me as he zips up his hoodie, then looks in the direction of the kitchen. 'Um, yeah, OK. How long would you like it to take?'

'Really? I wasn't expecting that.'

He shrugs. 'I can be flexible.'

'Great! What's the minimum amount of time you can do it in?'

'Well, that depends. Are you talking about completely finished, or just useable again? Like, all the tiles finished and grouted, everything painted, completely finished? Or just workable, with the tarting up to be finished as and when?'

'Oh, just workable. The tarting up can be done whenever, I just need to be able to cook food again.'

'Well that's two weeks then.'

I blink. He lifts his eyebrows. Waggles them. 'Ohhhh. You're being funny.'

He grins at this point, and tips two fingers to an imaginary hat.

'Great.'

'You're welcome.' He finishes tying his shoe laces and heads towards the front door. 'Do you want to give me a door key?' Panic knifes through me again, and Ed puts a hand up. 'Hey, there's no need to look so terrified, I'm not moving in.'

'I wasn't…'

He shakes his head. 'It's fine. I just thought I could crack on while you're not here.'

I release a breath. 'Oh God. Yes. Of course.' I lift down the spare key from the hook by the door and give it to him.

'I'll give it back when I've finished,' he says. 'Don't worry.'

'Don't be daft, I'm not worried.'

He lifts his eyebrows. 'OK. Well, that was great, thanks Steph,' he says, which makes me feel weird. Have I just given him something, other than the key?

'Ed, you're not doing "mates rates" for the kitchen are you?'

He turns at the door, frowning. 'I've given you a bloody good price, Steph, I can't drop it any more, else it wouldn't be worth my time…'

I've already got my hands up. 'No no no! That's not what I meant. I'm not after mates rates. In fact, I can't emphasise enough just exactly how much I don't want mates rates.'

He jerks his head. 'OK…'

'I mean, if anything I'd like to pay you more.'

'As tempting as that is, let's leave it at the price I quoted, shall we?'

'Knock knock?' comes a very familiar man's voice from just outside the front door we're standing at. 'It's only me, Stephanie. Dad.'

Oh god. My dad just heard me trying to pay my kitchen fitter more than the quote. He's going to be impossible about this. I'm fifty, but in his head I'm an incompetent child, just starting out in the world. 'Oh, hi Dad! Just coming!' I give Ed's arm a quick squeeze. 'OK, Ed, well thanks so much for coming,' I say loudly. 'I'll send you over the first payment now, as a deposit.'

Ed's nodding. 'Yeah, all right. See you Monday.'

'Yep, first thing Monday.'

I reach past him and open the door, to find Dad standing there with a bunch of flowers.

'Hi Dad, lovely to see you. Bye Ed.'

Ed's just stepping over the threshold when he turns to me with a wink. 'When I'm done, we'll make a start in the bedroom, shall we?'

I stare at him. Dad blinks, then pretends he can't see him by picking at the rot around the door frame. 'Right, yes, well, I'll think about redecorating when the kitchen's finished.'

Ed grins and tips his invisible hat again. 'Righty-oh.' And finally, thankfully, he's gone.

'Dad, hi.' I lean forward and we hug. 'Come in, come in. Cup of tea?'

'Ooh yes, lovely. Thank you.'

I walk ahead of him down the hall, glancing quickly into the living room, and nearly faint with horror. 'Come through to the kitchen,' I tell him quickly, glancing at him as I pull the living room door closed. 'I'll tell you about what I'm having done.'

He watches me pulling the living room door shut, and nods. 'All right.'

I get him seated at the kitchen table and give him Ed's plans to look through, then put the kettle on.

'Just need to…' I tell him, vaguely gesturing over my shoulder.

He nods again without looking up. 'OK love.'

I walk casually to the door, pull it closed behind me then sprint noiselessly back up the hallway to the living room. It's the work of about 30 seconds to stand the coffee table back up and put the cushions back on the sofa neatly. There's an empty wine glass on the floor, apparently from when the table went over, so I hide it behind the sofa. One last look, then I go back to the kitchen.

'This looks nice,' Dad says, tapping the kitchen plan. 'Although I'm not entirely sure why you'd be paying out to have it changed.' He glances around. 'It's lovely as it is.'

'Oh it's hideous Dad!' I say, at exactly the same time as he says, 'It's very similar to mine and your mum's.' I bite my lip. 'I mean, it does have some redeeming – '

He shrugs. 'Well, your mum loved it. She chose it all, and if she loved it, it's good enough for me.' He looks sideways towards the garden. 'Even if it's not good enough for you.'

'No, I'm not saying – '

'Are you sure you've got the best quote, love?' he says now, meeting my eyes directly. Here it comes. 'Tell me to mind my own business,' he says, but I know from past experience he absolutely does not want me to do that, 'but I wouldn't advise telling your builder that you want to pay him more than he's quoted.'

Knew it. I assume an air of distracted indifference by crouching down and opening the cupboard under the sink. 'Ah, no, it's fine, Dad. That was just a joke between me and him.' I stick my head in the cupboard and rummage around in the back, then re-emerge holding a new J-cloth.

Dad shrugs and casually looks down to examine the plan again. 'Oh, well, you know, just in my experience, once you've said you're prepared to pay more, they'll always find more to be paid for.'

I spin on my tiptoes and my knees make their delightful gravel-in-a-sieve sound. 'Yes, I know that. This is not my first rodeo.' I grab hold of the work top and haul myself carefully to my feet again, then close the cupboard. 'Ed and I are good friends and I was just making a joke, that's all.'

He presses his lips together. 'Hmm. Well in my opinion you can't be friends with your kitchen fitter.'

'Oh come on…'

He puts up a hand. 'Just my opinion.'

'And why is that?'

'You may disagree, Stephanie, but I personally believe that someone doing work for a friend will always find a way to exploit that friendship to get more money out of you.'

'Christ, no wonder you're not keen to see Marcus.'

'What?'

'Nothing. I just think that real friends don't do that. Real friends want to make sure you get the best deal possible.'

He nods slowly and smiles. 'You're very naïve, Stephanie.'

I close my eyes and breathe deeply, then turn to the kettle and make us both a mug of Earl Grey.

'Shall we go through?'

He nods, so I open the double doors we walk through to the living room. As we go in I spot one of Ed's socks dangling off the mantelpiece and grab it quickly. 'It's nice to come in here. I don't often.'

'Apparently not,' Dad says, handing me Ed's other sock.

'Oh. Thank you.' There's never a hole in the ground around when you need one, is there? While Dad installs himself on the sofa, I vanish the socks behind the armchair when he's not looking. Honestly, I'm fifty now, and I still don't want my dad to know I'm not a virgin.

'Anyway,' he says finally. 'I wanted to talk to you about this woman you were telling me about yesterday.'

'Dad, she's not "this woman." She's called Audrey and she's lovely.'

He nods and take a loud slurp of tea. 'Ooh, Earl Grey. Delicious.'

'You're welcome. So what do you want to know about Audrey?'

'Oh. Um. Well. Let's see.' He does an exaggerated stare at the ceiling, as if he's searching the far reaches of his mind. 'Is she coloured?'

'Dad, for God's sake! You can't say "coloured", it's racist. You have to say black or minority ethnic now.'

'That sounds a lot worse.'

'It most certainly doesn't. The word 'coloured' implies that the default is… Actually, no, I'm not having this conversation with you now. Audrey is not black, or minority ethnic. I honestly don't know why it even matters.'

He shrugs. 'It's culture, isn't it? We don't want to be too different.'

'Why not? I think it would be very interesting, learning all about a completely different – What?'

He's shaking his head, looking pained. 'I'm eighty-four, Steph. I can't be bothered with learning anything now. I don't have time.'

I put my hands up. 'All right, fair enough. A shame, but if that's your view…'

'It is.'

'…then we'll leave it. Audrey is white.'

'Good.'

'Ugh.' I take a breath. It's a generational thing, I suppose. My grandparents wouldn't have known any better. 'Anything else?'

'No, that's about it.'

'You're kidding? That's literally the *only* thing you want to know about her?'

He looks a bit shame-faced. 'Well, I kind of wondered if we might meet. You know, before the wedding. Get to know each other a bit.'

'Oh, yes, that's a good idea. Then you can relax a bit when…'

'So Marcus doesn't think we're on a blind date.'

Turns out Marcus himself got remarried a couple of years ago – to some 'bimbo' according to Dad – and Dad thinks he's going to be very full of himself for it. It's clearly had a part in persuading Dad to agree to go and take Audrey, so I'm thankful for it. I tell him I'll speak to Audrey tomorrow, and ring him afterwards.

'Is Graham in next door?' he asks me as he's leaving.

I blink. 'How the hell do you know Graham?'

Dad opens the front door. 'Don't know really. Known him for ages.'

'But how did you know he lives here?'

'Well obviously because I've seen him here, Stephanie. Honestly.'

'Right. You just never said, that's all.'

'Why would I?'

'Right. You sure you don't want a lift home?'

'No, it's fine. Might as well put this silly bus pass to use, now I've got it.'

He's had it for twenty-four years. 'OK. If you're sure…?'

'Yes, absolutely. Thanks anyway, love. Think I'll just give Graham a knock…' And he steps over the little hedge that separates our front paths, and knocks on Graham's door.

'Right. Bye then, Dad. Speak to you tomorrow.'

'Yes, that's right. Bye love.'

13
SUPERMAN

It occurs to me the following day that if my dad is going to take Audrey on a day out, she probably shouldn't be my patient any more. I can't see her as my "Step-Mom" any time soon, but it could get weird.

'What would happen if she forgets to pick up a prescription?' Nina says when I tell her. 'And then asks your dad, oh Phillip darling, would you please ask Stephanie to write me a prescription on Sunday?'

'Yes, you're right.'

'Or maybe it's Christmas. Hello, Stephanie, Merry Christmas, did my faeces result come back yet?'

'Yep, got it.'

'Or perhaps the whole family is out in some fancy place for your birthday dinner, and she asks you – '

'Yes, Nina, thanks, I got it.'

She looks at me. 'Are you OK, Stephanie?'

'Course I'm OK. Why?'

She shrugs with her entire body, in that giant, dramatic Greek way that she does. 'No reason.'

'Right.' There's definitely a reason.

'You just seem a little bit stressed out today.'

'I'm not.'

'And on Monday.'

I frown. 'I wasn't stressed on Monday.'

'Aha!' She points at me. 'So you are stressed today.'

'Oh for God's... Ok. Maybe I am a bit. But it's so pathetic, I don't even want to talk about it.'

'I am here to listen, my friend.'

'Well, I'm having a new kitchen fitted and it means I have no access to my kitchen for two weeks.'

'My dad's a kitchen fitter,' Niamh says, leaning over the reception counter.

'Er, yeah, I know. Actually, he's the one fitting it for me.'

'Oh?' Her eyebrows go up, and she stares at me.

'Starts on Monday.'

'Right.'

'Well, as gripping as it is here,' Nina says, picking up her handbag, 'I don't have the time to stay and listen and watch. I have people to heal.' And she goes into her consulting room. Then she comes out again. 'So you want me to take Audrey Taylor then?'

'Oh, yes please.' I turn to Niamh. 'Can you change Mrs. Taylor's record that she's now Nina's patient?'

'Sure. Why's that?'

'Actually, don't do it just yet. I need to call her first.' I turn back to Nina. 'No need to switch her if she doesn't go.'

Nina nods. 'It is true.'

While I wait for my patient list for the day to print off, I look up Audrey Taylor's record and get her phone number. Unusually there's no landline number, just a mobile. When she answers it's clear that she's somewhere outside.

'Oh, hello Doctor,' she says, wearily. 'How lovely of you to call. That's good customer service, that is. You don't get that from Dunelm.'

'No, well, you know.' Instantly I feel guilty because I haven't rung her to see how she's doing at all. 'How are you doing, Audrey?'

'I honestly don't know, Doctor. One day I'm fine. Next day it hits me like a ten ton truck and I'm flattened. Can't even move. It feels like finding out he's gone all over again.'

'It's perfectly normal to feel like that. Your brain has to adjust to the very strange fact that Teddy is gone.'

'Yes, that's it. He's been around such a long time, though.' She chuckles. 'So have I, of course. But it's absurdly difficult fully comprehending that I'll never see his stupid, dear face again.'

'Of course. Your brain is in the habit of him being around and now has to lose that habit. It's not easy.'

'That's it.'

'But you're outside?' I can hear birdsong, and a breeze blowing across the mic.

There's a rustling sound which I assume is Audrey nodding. 'Watering his roses. I hate the blooming things, always have. Why did he have to grow the ones that have tiny little spears all over them? I'm forever stabbing myself on them.' She sighs. 'They're all I've got.'

'How are you feeling mentally? I mean, are you feeling depressed?'

'Oh, I don't wash with all of that nonsense. I'm sad because my husband has died. Of course I am, I'd be a very strange and unpleasant person not to be. But depressed? I've no time for that, Doctor.'

'Well, it is a real thing, Audrey…'

'Nonsense. My mother lived through the blitz. Didn't see her moping around sniffling into a hanky. She just got her head down and got on with things. Brought us four kids up, kept a house, home-cooked dinner on the table every day. Taught us the proper meaning of discipline and respect. None of this namby-pamby pandering.'

Of course depression and anxiety existed back then. Probably more then than now, given what everyone was going through. They simply went undiagnosed, and generations of mentally ill people got no help and took it out on their loved ones. Or themselves. I'm not going to say any of this to Audrey Taylor, though.

'That's amazing. I'm glad you're coping.'

'I am, Doctor. It's a comfort to know I won't have to wait long before I'm with my Teddy again.'

'You mean, because of your age? Or are you planning to – ?'

'Honestly Doctor, you've got a real bee in your bonnet about that, haven't you? Of course I'm not planning anything. I'm seventy-three, remember? It's all going to happen quite naturally.'

'OK, good. I have to ask, you know.' It's gone nine o'clock and Julie Carter is due in now. I need to get to the point. 'Listen Audrey, there's something I wanted to ask you. I wonder if you wouldn't mind doing me a huge favour?'

So Audrey Taylor agrees to help me out by going with my elderly old father to a wedding. And my healthy and vigorous dad agrees to help me out by taking an elderly widow. Now all I have to do is arrange for them to meet each other before the wedding in two weeks. It feels a bit like Shakespeare.

At the end of the call, Audrey tells me that Teddy's funeral is on this coming Saturday, and invites me to go. And I shock myself by immediately thinking, Aha, I'll bring Dad along, and it can be the perfect chance for them to meet.

'Thank you Audrey. Of course I will be there.'

Weirdly, Dad jumps at the chance.

'Hmm, yes, OK.' A cloud passes over his face and I'm sure he's thinking about Mum's funeral, eight years ago.

'Are you sure, Dad?'

He looks at me. 'Bit of a weird place to meet someone for the first time, I grant you.'

'Yes.'

'But it takes away the need for that awful awkward small talk.'

'I suppose so.'

'And everyone will be dressed up nicely.'

'Are you being sarcastic?'

'Oddly enough, no. Any silences will be perfectly natural. And I can ask her about her ex-husband, if we struggle to converse.'

'He's not her ex-husband, Dad. He died, they're not divorced.'

'You think death doesn't make him an ex? I'd say he's more of an ex now than any divorced man I've ever met.'

We agree that I'll pick him up on Saturday for the funeral and maybe have some lunch afterwards, depending on whether or not there's a wake.

'I am partial to a prawn vol-au-vent.'

'Dad!'

As in all the best, and worst, Hollywood blockbusters and BBC dramas, it's raining on the morning of the funeral. The sky is sad and heavy with no break in the dark grey all the way over the trees and roofs to the visible horizon. I stand at my bedroom window and stare at the depressing sight, thinking of Audrey waking up this morning and looking out of her own window. I can't decide if it would be worse if it were a beautiful sunny day, set to the sound of a million birds, and lawn mowers, and children riding bikes and screaming. Maybe it would feel wrong. Disrespectful to Teddy that people are out enjoying themselves, getting on with living their lives, making the most of lovely weekend weather, on the day his life draws quietly to a close.

A sudden squall gusting against the window startles me as it hurls rain fiercely at the glass in a clatter, and I watch as the drops run down it like tears. In Graham's garden next door, one of his patio chairs is transported on a brief but thrilling journey across the lawn and into the hedge, where it comes to rest with its legs in the air, its final repose. This awful weather will be very uncomfortable at the crematorium later, but that's a small inconvenience as it feels entirely right. Tears are on the window, and dripping off every gutter, every roof tile, every leaf and branch. Even the flowers are crying. The world is sad for Teddy, and for Audrey left behind. Which makes me wonder, are the movies right? Does it rain at every funeral? It makes me almost, *almost* believe there's a God, or some kind of higher power, orchestrating everything, making sure Teddy has the proper respect for his final day.

Then I blink and shake myself. Nope. No deity with that much power would allow childhood leukaemia.

A sudden bright flash and simultaneous deafening bang of thunder make me jump, and stop me where I stand. Hairs rise on the back of my neck. I turn to face the window again, eyes wide, and examine the sky with a frown. *Could it...?*

Nah. I drop the curtain and go into the bathroom.

Nina has agreed to come along to the funeral too, to show support for her new patient, for which I'm grateful. I haven't spoken to Audrey yet about Nina taking over as her GP, but there's plenty of time for that. Nina's presence there will make Audrey pre-disposed to like her, or at least respect her, and that's all it will need. Audrey herself, at the moment, is a very fit seventy-three, with not even so much as elevated blood pressure, so I don't anticipate her needing Nina's ministrations much. Certainly not for a good few years, anyway.

I pick Nina up first, and she gets in the back, knowing that my dad is also coming with us.

'Hi, Steph,' she says, shaking her open umbrella through the door before closing them both. She settles on the seat, then notices the large scruffy brown dog sitting next to her. 'Oh, hello there Harry. Did you know Teddy well?'

'Do you think it's weird that I brought him?' I delay pulling away and turn round in my seat to face her. We have to raise our voices to be heard over the rain clattering on the roof.

'Hmm, I don't know,' Nina says, scratching Harry under the chin. 'You don't see so many dogs going to funerals, do you?' She leans down to Harry's face. 'No you don't. Do you? Eh? No. Not so much for you, I think.' She looks back at me. 'Dogs are more wedding-goers, I think.'

'Oh God, you're right. It's just, he'll be on his own for such a long time if I leave him. Shall I take him home?'

She's taken Harry's head between her hands now and is rubbing his ears. 'No, I don't think so. He can sit in the car, can he? For the service? And then come into the house afterwards. I'd think Audrey won't mind, anyway. And he's a lovely old fellow, isn't he?'

Harry responds by hitting the seat once with his tail.

'Yes, that's a good idea. Probably shouldn't take him into the church.'

'It's a crematorium, Steph. Poor Teddy is being incinerated. It won't be a problem for him to sit in the car.'

'OK. Well let's hope not.' I put the car into gear and pull away from the kerb. 'By the way, it's 'cremated.''

'What is?'

'What's happening to Teddy. You don't say 'incinerated.''

'Oh? But it means burned, right?'

'Yes, it does. But when it's a person, you say 'cremated.''

'Ah. Is there a different word for each thing you burn?'

We have to go in the wrong direction, away from the crematorium, to collect Dad in Hythe, but I'd rather go 10 miles out of my way to collect him than have him drive himself, or get on a bus, in this weather. At this point, the rain is tropical, falling vertically in dense, heavy drops, and I ring Dad from the car rather than getting out to knock on his door.

'Oh, OK,' he says, when I've told him we've arrived. 'Where's the service?'

'Dad, come and get in the car, we can chat then.'

'Where's the service?' he says again a few minutes later, slamming the car door quickly, but not quickly enough for the seat and carpet not to get soaked.

'Hawkinge crem.'

'Ah.' He nods once. 'We'll be inside then.'

'You'd be inside if it was a church service.'

He says nothing, just stares steadfastly through the windscreen.

'Hi Phil,' Nina says from the back seat. Dad half turns and clocks Harry, who is staring at him.

'Hi Harry,' he says, uncertainly, then looks at me.

'That was Nina,' I tell him. 'She's sitting behind you. Harry doesn't talk.'

Dad rolls his eyes. 'I knew that. You take life far too seriously, Stephanie.' He twists right round to see Nina. 'Hello Nina. Lovely to see you.'

'You too. You look well.'

'Well, thank you, but I'm sure I look like a tatty old piece of furniture by now.'

'Ah, do you mean a priceless antique then?'

Dad humphs and shakes his head with a smile, but I can tell he liked that.

There's a line of cars queuing to get into the car park when we get to the crematorium. Two people dressed all in black are standing by the door holding black umbrellas, shaking hands with people as they arrive. One of them is wearing a black top hat, so it's either a very stylish relative, or they're the funeral directors. Everyone else is sensibly inside. I find a space not too far away from the building, and after telling Harry to stay (he's got no choice) and that I won't be long (he doesn't understand), we all cross the car park using the head-down hunched run designed to get us not too wet in torrential rain.

We make our way to an empty area fairly near the back, behind some tall hair. It seems like the right thing to do, as we're not family.

'Is the beehive a suitable hairdo for a sad occasion, do you think?' Nina whispers. A fat snigger explodes out of me and I put my hand over my mouth, converting it nimbly into a cough.

'Maybe it's designed to cheer everyone up,' I whisper, and am rewarded with seeing her equally uncomfortable as she covers her own mouth.

'Stop it you two,' Dad hisses, giving us both a stern look, before resuming reading the order of service. Nina and I glance at each other and press our lips together. What is it about funerals that makes you almost incapable of not laughing?

The service itself is fairly standard. Mostly about Teddy's life, of course, with a fair bit of God, and where Teddy is now. I can't deny it must be comforting for those left behind to believe their loved one is still around somewhere. I manage to find Audrey down in the front, and she is sitting very elegantly upright in an unexpected fuchsia hat. She is flanked by people in their thirties and forties, sniffing quietly and dabbing their eyes, presumably her children. Audrey herself is stoic.

'Which one is she?' Dad asks me during 'All Things Bright and Beautiful'.

I incline my head towards Audrey. 'Front row, pink hat.'

He lifts his eyebrows. 'That's an interesting shade.'

'Hmm.'

The service, and the discreet little curtains, draw to a close, and we all shuffle out. I look around me at the number of people attending and it seems that Teddy was a popular man. Nearly all of them are of a similar age to Teddy and Audrey. Many of them seem to be alone.

Outside, the rain has stopped, but there's still no sun. It's dull and miserable, but it's not crying any more.

When he was about twelve Josh launched a theory that all old people know each other, like it's some kind of club. He put this theory together based on what he'd observed getting the bus to and from school every day – how each elderly person getting onto the bus would always, without fail, greet another elderly person already seated.

'Hello there, Jeff, how are you then? How's that boat of yours?'

'Oh, hello Lilian, you're looking well.'

'Morning Ray, lovely one again, isn't it?'

'It is that, Frank, it is that.'

Standing outside the crematorium waiting to speak to Audrey, I finally see what he meant. Everyone there, and there are probably close to fifty people, knows someone. Not just one person either, for the majority. I watch in fascination as they all shamble through the door out into the dullness, and almost instantly start recognising people and greeting them. The men shake shaky hands, while the ladies raise powder clouds gently embracing. Some of them clearly saw each other days ago; some of them act like long lost brothers, and delight brightens the grey day where the sun failed.

I turn to Dad. 'Look at that,' I whisper, leaning in close. 'Everyone knows each other!'

'What?'

'I said, everyone knows each other. Like Josh says.' I look around me in wonder at all the people greeting each other and chatting. 'It's like a miracle.'

'What the bloomin' heck are you going on about?'

'This!' I sweep my arm out at the small crowd. 'Look!' I look from the crowd to Dad and back again. 'All the people – '

'Yes? What about them? There's a lot here, aren't there? Must have been a popular bloke.'

'Well, yes, but...' I look back at the people around me and see them starting to drift away, some in twos, most in small groups of one. The miracle I just witnessed is over. Dad missed it.

'Oh Doctor, thank you so much for coming,' a familiar voice says behind me and I turn to see Audrey, except twenty years younger. I smile at her, thinking 'daughter', but then it strikes me that I've never met the daughter, so how does she know I'm a doctor? And as a liver-spotted hand falls lightly onto my arm like an autumn leaf, I realise it's not Audrey's daughter at all.

'Audrey!' It bursts out of me, but it's not surprise, I knew she was here. It's amazement. 'You – ' She looks incredible, but I just manage to stop myself saying it. No one needs to hear that they look fantastic at their husband's funeral. I search frantically for a sentence to finish my exclamation, but nothing comes.

Audrey's eyes shift to the side and she fingers her fuchsia pink hat. 'My Teddy hates black,' she says to the floor. 'And, well, so do I.'

'It's a beautiful outfit.'

'Oh, goodness. Thank you. I bought it specially.' She takes a small step closer to me and lifts her head. 'I didn't want to feel dull today, Doctor. Not today.'

She has on a beautifully tailored long charcoal coat with a fuchsia satin lining, and tiny piping around the pockets and collar exactly matching her hat. She's evidently had her hair done, as it's much shorter than it was, and cut closer to her head, and there are multiple colours threaded through it – red, blonde, brown, even a dark purple. She's wearing make-up – smoky eyes, matt pink lips, even some blusher – which instantly takes years off her; but the single most rejuvenating thing about her, the thing that takes my breath away, is her smile. It reaches all the way to her eyes, which are sparkling like I've never seen before. Her husband's death seems to have breathed new life into her.

I put my hand over hers, and squeeze it. 'I bet Teddy is falling in love with you all over again, wherever he is.'

'Oh, Doctor. My gosh.' She touches her hair, then smoothes down the front of her coat. 'This is the most expensive thing I've ever bought. Is it all right? I had to choose it all on my own.'

'It's absolutely perfect.'

'That it is.'

We both turn and I remember that I've brought my father along. 'Oh, Dad, there you are.'

'I've been standing here the entire time.'

'Right, yes, well, anyway. Audrey, this is my dad, Philip Thripp.'

She looks up at him. 'Philip Thripp?'

'Yes.' Dad nods. 'Sorry.'

I blink. Why is he apologising?

Audrey shakes her head, smiling. 'Goodness, no. No need to apologise. It's a wonderful name.'

'It's a mouthful.'

'Yes, it is. That's what makes it so wonderful.'

'You think so?'

'Gosh yes. It's like Philip Pirrip, isn't it? From *Great Expectations.*'

'*Great Expectations*!' He says, at exactly the same moment she does, and they both stop, wide-eyed and surprised.

'Oh, I think I'll just let Harry out onto the grass,' I say, looking at my car where a canine face is peering over the steering wheel. I turn to Nina. 'You coming?'

She shakes her head. 'No, it's OK thank you, I don't need the grass right now.'

'I'd like you to come.'

Nina looks at my face, then follows my eye-flick to Dad. Luckily she's quite clever. 'Oh, yes, of course, you are right after all.'

Dad looks at her briefly with a strange expression, but he can't be drawn away from Audrey for long.

There is a wake back at Audrey and Teddy's bungalow in Dover. As we drive there, Dad questions me relentlessly about Audrey's health.

'Dad, for God's sake, I'm not going to tell you anything,' I snap at him as we pull up outside. 'I can't, and I wouldn't anyway, even if I wasn't her GP.'

'Just a yes or no, then? If she's got anything serious?'

'No, seriously Phil,' Nina says, touching his arm as we all get out of the car. 'Stephanie can't tell you. Not even one small thing.' She puts her hand up as Dad opens his mouth. 'And I can't tell you it either.' She squeezes his arm. 'So please don't ask.'

Nina, Harry and I walk up the front path, and after ringing the bell I step back a little from the door and look round for Dad. He's still on the pavement, fifteen feet away. I give Harry's lead to Nina. 'Would you mind taking him for a moment, please?'

'Oh, yes, of course but what...?' She looks around, sees Dad, then looks back at me. 'What's happening?'

'I'll just be a minute.'

At this moment the front door is opened and a young man in his twenties is there. 'Hi, I'm Jason, Teddy's secret grandson. Would you like a profiterole?'

Back on the pavement, Dad is fretting. He's moving from foot to foot, rotating, looking at the car, then back to look at the house. When I arrive at his side, he turns an anxious face to me. 'Can you take me home, love?'

'What? Why?'

He shakes his head. 'I've changed my mind.'

'What, about the vol-au-vents?'

He tuts and sighs and throws a 'Trump' at me.

'Joke, Dad.'

'Hilarious. Can we just...?' He gestures towards the car.

'But why? You seemed to be getting on really well with – '

He shakes his head again, looking down. 'I can't do it again.'

Realisation drops like a hammer, and I hit myself several times on the shins with it. 'Oh Dad. I'm so sorry for being insensitive. It's reminding you of Mum's funeral, isn't it?'

He turns sad eyes to me. 'What? No, no, that was eight years ago. I have been to other funerals in that time, you know. People my age croak all the time. That's not it.' He wrings his hands. 'That's not it at all. Oh bloody hell.'

I step forward and take his hands. 'What is it, then? You're worrying me a bit. Are you feeling unwell?'

He shakes his head and shakes my hands away. 'Are you taking my temperature?'

'No…?'

'Oh stop fussing. I'm absolutely fine.' He tuts and steps away from me, looking at the house again.

'Then what?'

He stares at the house, his brows drawn tightly together, his mouth sagging with worry. Then as he stares, suddenly he jerks his head back, as if he's spotted something, and his brow smoothes. He steps forward, close to Audrey's front garden, and leans over the low wall. Then glances back at me, pointing down. 'Look at this!'

'What?'

'Just, quick, look. Come *on,* will you.'

I go, and look, and see a neat, well-tended lawn with crisp cake-slice edges. I nod. 'Nice lawn.'

Dad does his Trump thing again, and I have to pretend I've seen someone in the house and wave to them, so I don't have to look at him.

'Yes, well done. It's a nice lawn. That much is obvious.' He straightens up and moves his hands over his hair, then tidies his tie and brushes down his coat. His expression now is back to how he'd looked the moment he'd said 'Great Expectations' at the crematorium.

'Please tell me what's going on?'

He turns to me at last and looks into my eyes. His are sparkling and creased and more alive than I've seen for years. 'Don't you get it? The lawn. It's tidy, well-tended. And Teddy has been frail for months.' He nods and grins, waiting for me to join the dots. I can't.

'Which means…?'

Dad's rolling his eyes, but luckily my phantom friend appears at the window again, frantic for my attention, so I'm far too busy waving back to notice.

'Good God, Steph,' he says, forced to vocalise his irritation, 'you'd think a doctor would get it. It means that Audrey must have done it. Audrey has been tending the garden.'

I nod slowly. 'Uh-huh.'

He stares at me with impatient eyebrows, rolling one hand over and over.

And suddenly, Hey Presto! I see it. Finally I know what is going on. 'Oh Dad.' And I step in and give him a tight, tight squeeze.

'Yes, yes, I love you too. Now, can we please go in?'

14
OLD MAN AGAIN

Inside, Nina is holding Harry's lead in one hand and a profiterole in the other. She's staring at the thick brown sauce spreading over her cherry red nails. As soon as Harry sees me he raises his head and swishes his tail a few times; as soon as Nina sees me she shoves the lead into my hand and grabs a plastic cup of wine standing on an occasional table next to her. 'Ugh, thank God.' She takes a long slug. 'What was that all about?' In goes the profiterole, to wash down the wine.

'Hang on two secs.' I make my way through the stuffy little room with the antimacassars and the horse and carriage ornaments and the shiny china figurines, Harry silently weaving behind me through the legs, and find what must be the dining room. There's a dark red-brown oval dining table with a white cloth and curved feet pushed to one side, and its chair children are behaving nicely around the edges of the room. Each one is occupied by a still and silent person holding a paper plate layered with sandwiches, sausage rolls, chicken fingers and French fancies, but no one is eating. There is also a stack of plastic cups, and, hurrah! a small crowd of open wine bottles on the table. I pour one, recklessly mixing the last dregs of a Zinfandel with the end of a Liebfraumilch to make a full cup, then hand a cocktail sausage to Harry before making my way back to Nina. She has a tell-tale dot of cream on her chin.

'Is Phil OK then?'

I nod, gratefully sucking down the sickly wine combination. 'Yeah, he's fine. Silly old sod.'

'What was it about, do you think?' She reaches forward and takes the wine from my hand, then ticks her forefinger backwards and forwards at me.

'Right. You're right. Driving.'

'Uh-huh. So, Phil?'

I smile. 'I think he's worried about getting his heart broken again.'

'Really?'

'Yeah.' I note that Nina has shelved her empty cup and is now tucking into mine. She winces at the sweetness. 'That's why he was asking about Audrey's health.'

Nina's face lights up with understanding. 'Ah, to make sure she doesn't die on him like your mum did.'

'Well, yes, not to put too fine a point on it.'

'Did you tell him she's as fit as a fidget?'

'Fiddle. And of course I didn't, Nina. What do you take me for?'

She shrugs. 'So what made him come in then?'

'Audrey's garden.'

A slightly squiffy smirk appears on Nina's face. 'Her – ?'

'No, Nina, not that, and don't be gross. I mean her actual garden, outside.' I tell her quickly about the crisp lawn edges, and how Dad used them to draw the conclusion that Audrey must be healthy.

'You mean, he's decided that she can't be ill, if she is physically capable of keeping them neat?'

'Exactly.'

She thinks a moment. 'But, you know, Audrey might have been paying someone to –'

'We won't mention that, Nina.'

'Okey dokey.'

'My, what a beautiful dog you have!' a nearby voice says suddenly, and we both turn to find no-one there. It's the work of a nanosecond to notice that the speaker is now crouching down, vigorously ruffling Harry's ears. Harry is immobile.

'Thank you.'

'It's Harry, isn't it?' the man says, standing up.

'No, Stephanie actually.' I recognise him, but God knows where from.

He grins and in that moment I realise it's the nice man from the beach who lent me – *gave* me – a tennis ball for Harry.

'Hello again Stephanie. It's Jack – we met on the beach, remember?'

'Yes, yes, I remember. How nice to see you again, Jack. Albeit in – '

'Such awful circumstances, yes. How have you been?'

'What's that Harry?' Nina says suddenly, leaning in slightly. 'You need the grass again?' She looks at me. 'I'll take him, it's no problem.' And she takes the lead from my hand and disappears.

Jack and I look at each other and smile. 'Harry seems chatty,' Jack says.

'Yes, well, he's a diva, gets his needs met instantly. Where's… Arnie, wasn't it?'

He nods, grinning. 'It was indeed. He's probably at the gym.'

I giggle. 'Oh. Treadmill?'

'No, oddly enough he prefers the free weights.

'That is…' I laugh as I'm speaking, '…odd.'

Jack shrugs. 'He looks after himself. What can I say?'

'Hmm.' We both smile, then in synch look around the sombre room at the nodding grey heads. What did Dad say? If it gets awkward, you can just talk about the dead person.

'Wasn't it a lovely service?' I start.

'Oh yes, very moving. Teddy was obviously well-loved.'

'Yes, he must have been. Lots of people.'

'Did you know him well?'

'Er, no, not really. I used to be his GP.'

He sucks air in over his teeth. 'Ooh.'

'Sorry?'

'That's a bit awkward, isn't it? You being the, er... And Teddy being... you know...' He puts both his hands around his own throat and pokes his tongue out a fraction of an inch.

I glance around, hoping no one saw that. 'You're suggesting questions might get asked...'

'Now I'm not saying blame will be apportioned, but...'

'Fingers might get pointed.'

He shrugs. 'The crowd could turn ugly.'

I look out at a room full of comfy shoes and beige cardigans. 'That does seem quite likely.'

'Maybe we should make our escape?'

'While we still can?'

'I noticed an exit this way.' He jabs his thumb over his shoulder, looking behind him.

I laugh, but ultimately neither of us moves. Obviously we're both over 13 and sneaking out of funerals is frowned on after that age.

'Guess we'll have to risk it,' he says, glancing around.

'I guess we will.' Something occurs to me. 'So how did you know Teddy?'

'Oh, we were on the same curling team.'

I narrow my eyes. 'You told me you'd given up curling.'

'Aha! You have a good memory!'

I don't tell him that in fact the opposite is true and I've remembered him exceptionally. 'Well, it's not every day you meet a curling team member.'

'It is if you're on the team…'

'Of course it is.'

We smile at each other, feeling a bit silly. Well, I'm feeling silly. No, not silly. What is that feeling? It's familiar, but I haven't had it for a very long time.

'In fact, I knew Teddy from work. We worked at the same place a long time ago. He was my boss, back in the day.'

'Wow. You've known him a long time then? What was he, nearly eighty?'

'Eighty-one.'

'So would have retired…'

'…Sixteen years ago.'

'And you've managed to keep in touch all that time.'

Jack shrugs. 'He's a great guy.' He checks himself. '*Was* a great guy.'

I nod. 'He was. I mean, as a patient I never really got to know him, but Audrey has told me a lot. And there was a huge turn out today, wasn't there?'

He nods. 'He was very popular at the bank.'

'Wait – are you saying all these people are ex-colleagues of his? From the same place?'

Jack looks around, nodding. 'Yeah, pretty much. Teddy worked there for nearly fifty years, started at seventeen, I think. The most junior role. Then worked his way up. So he saw a lot of people in that time, coming and going. Yes, I recognise most of these people from there.'

And just like that Josh's theory about all old people knowing each other is blown out of the water. I can't wait to tell him.

'What's that little smile all about?'

'Hm? Oh, no, nothing. You've just cleared something up for me, that's all.'

'Ah.'

At the other end of the room, Audrey comes in and asks if everyone is ok for food, and would anyone like another drink. A man in his forties comes and gives her a hug, and guides her to a chair, then leaves through the same door, presumably to get her some food and drink.

'It's Audrey I'm worrying about now,' Jack says, watching her. People are standing around her, bending to talk to her, and she's looking up at them, making fake smiles with her lips. She looks tiny, sat there. 'She's got no idea what to do on her own.'

'In fairness, Teddy hasn't been much company for her for quite a while, has he?'

'No, he hasn't, but he gave her drive. A reason to get up and get on with things.' He turns to me. 'What's going to motivate her now?'

'Does she have any friends?'

He shakes his head. 'I don't know. I don't think so. She was happy with just Teddy.'

I wonder about telling him about my dad, and the 'companion' plan I've got in mind. And it occurs to me that I haven't seen Dad for a while.

'I don't suppose you've seen an old man in a shirt and bow tie, with a brown jacket over the top and a big old mac, have you?'

'Oh, yes, yes, I have, actually.'

I turn to Jack. 'Oh! Where?'

He looks around the room, and then slowly back to me. 'Everywhere.'

Dad's in the kitchen, standing by the sink holding a cup of water. He doesn't look too comfy there.

'Oh, Dad, there you are! Are you all right? I didn't know where you'd got to.'

'Yes, yes, here I am.'

I lean in and lower my voice. 'Have you spoken to Audrey?'

'No I haven't.' He sounds sulky, like a kid who didn't get the toy he wanted. 'She's been talking to everyone but I don't know anyone and frankly I'd like to go home now.'

'Did you try to talk to her?'

'Anything I can do?' Jack says, walking in behind me.

'Oh, no, nothing, thanks Jack.'

'Who's this then?' Dad asks.

'Oh, hello, I'm Jack Warner, a friend of Stephanie's. It's nice to meet you, Mr...' He holds out his hand to Dad.

'Thripp,' Dad says, shaking it. 'Philip Thripp.'

'Oh, like in – '

'*Great Expectations,* yes, yes, that's it.'

'Except it's Pirrip, not Thripp,' says a small voice by the fridge, and we turn as one to find Audrey standing there.

'Oh, hey Aud,' Jack says, stepping forward and kissing her cheek. 'How are you holding up?'

'Hello Jack. I'm holding up fine, I think. How about you? Bearing it?'

'Oh, Audrey, that's so typical of you, always thinking about others.'

'Nonsense,' she says, pushing his arm gently. Then she turns to me. 'Hello again, Doctor. It's so nice of you to come, I do appreciate it.'

'It's my pleasure, Audrey, honestly. I liked Teddy a lot.'

She smiles and looks just over my shoulder. 'So did I.'

'Have you had something to eat?' Dad says suddenly. 'Will you let me bring you something? You must be shattered.'

Audrey puts up a hand. 'Oh, no, no, honestly, I don't think I could eat a thing.'

'You should try,' Dad says, moving nearer. 'This is very stressful, your system probably needs more nourishment, not less. Isn't that right, Stephanie?'

Everyone turns to look at me. 'Um, well, it's not a terrible idea...'

'See?' Dad says. 'I'll get you a plate, why don't you sit down somewhere?'

He guides her back out of the kitchen, leaving Jack and me to watch them go.

'Wasn't she just sitting down?' Jack says.

'Let's not tell him.'

He turns to me. 'You know, hearing Audrey calling you doctor makes me think of something. Which surgery are you at?'

I tell him the name. 'Why?'

'Well it's only just occurred to me – you're a doctor and you're called Stephanie. And now I know which surgery you're at, I know for sure. My grand-daughter works for you.'

I blink, wheels and cogs creaking round in my brain, working much more slowly than they used to. 'Your grand-daughter? You mean…Niamh?'

'Niamh, yes,' he says at the same time, and in that hideous yet amazing moment all the pieces thunk heavily into place. The shadowy unidentified man in the background at Niamh's birthday party, the man she was trying to introduce me to before I legged it home, was Jack, now standing in front of me. Grandfather to an adult woman.

'Oh wow.' I smile. 'You're a grandad.'

'Ha, I've never had that reaction before!'

'Oh, sorry...'

'No, it's fine. But you already knew I was a grandad. I told you the day we met on the beach – remember?'

Of course I don't remember. That was way more than fifteen minutes ago. 'Oh, yes, of course you did. I was picturing... little grandkids. Toddlers. Not... an adult woman. With a job.'

'Well, Niamh is my eldest. The others are still quite little...'

'Ah, right. Wow, what a small world it is. I think we nearly met a third time, aswell. On a different occasion.'

'We did?'

'Yes. At Niamh's party – did she try to introduce you to someone?'

He looks to the side, his eyes crinkling as he dredges up his ancient grandad memory. 'Yes, she did. Wait, was that you?'

I nod. 'I believe so.'

'Oh ha! What a coincidence.'

'Isn't it though?' I smile at him and look through the door to the living room to see if I can see Nina. We need to make a move now. We've been here long enough, Audrey has seen me, Dad has talked to Audrey, Jack is someone's grandad. Time to go.

'So how do your dad and Audrey know each other?'

His voice is in the background. Where the hell is Nina? 'Hmm?'

'Audrey and your dad. Have they been friends for long?'

I drag my gaze back to Jack's face. 'Sorry? Oh, no, no. They just met today.'

'Today? What, you mean… they were introduced for the first time at a funeral?'

I think I catch sight of a shoulder that could be Nina's, moving away towards the front of the house, but then it's gone again. 'Um, yes. Yes, they met today, at the crematorium.'

His eyebrows draw together while he smiles. 'What was it then, some kind of blind funeral date?'

I look at him properly at last. 'Oh, God. No, no, that wasn't what I was… I just brought Dad along because I thought... I suppose I thought he and Audrey might… be… you know, good companions for each other.'

He stares at me until I have to look away. 'You set Audrey up on a blind date, at her own husband's funeral.'

'No, it's not a blind date. Obviously.' I frown. 'That would be incredibly insensitive. The idea was that as they've both found themselves in – '

Geriatric Jack puts his hands up. 'Hey, no, I think it's a great idea. Nothing weird about it at all. I mean, what better way to help someone get over the loss of the person they've loved most in the world for the past half-century than to usher in a new one.' He winks. 'Putting the 'fun' into 'funeral.''

He's ridiculing me, or my idea, or Audrey and my dad, or something, and it's making me feel horrible. I give him one more decisive head shake. 'You've got it wrong. But I can't make you understand.' The shoulder appears again, so I incline my head towards it. 'I see Nina. Sorry, I have to go.'

I dive through the door into the living room, while Jack is still saying 'Oh, really? That's a shame. I was hoping to...' The shoulder had better be Nina's, as I make the split second decision to plunge through the sparse crowd and grab it.

'Oh, I'm so sorry,' she says, spinning round. 'Oh, it's you.'

'Ready to go?'

Nina blinks. 'What's your fire? I'm just chatting to Charles here.'

For the first time I notice the young man to Nina's left, holding a paper plate bearing a single sausage roll. 'Charlie,' he says amiably, holding out a hand. 'Teddy's secret son.'

'Secret son?' I take his hand, noticing that he's probably not exactly young, but also probably not quite fifty either. 'That sounds intriguing.'

Charlie pushes out his lips. 'Not really. Standard extra-marital nonsense.' He leans in close. 'Bit awkward, actually. No one wants to speak to me, but Mum made me come.'

'Ah. So Audrey...?'

'Only found out about me – and Mum – a few days ago.'

'Jesus.' I think back to Audrey at the crematorium, with her make-up and new hairdo and chic, expensive coat. Is this the reason for it all, standing in front of me in a grey jumper? 'Has she spoken to you?'

Charlie nods. 'She's a lovely lady. Considering who we are, she was very welcoming.'

I nod. 'She is a remarkable person.'

Weirdly I have a sudden flashback to Happy Hannah, talking about her own husband having done something similar to Teddy, and how she simply forgave him. Well, it probably wasn't simple, or easy. But she managed it, and so, it seems, did Audrey. She's a clever woman, and I have no doubt whatsoever that her first knowledge of Charlie and his mum was not just a few days ago. That woman, like so many others, will have damn well known *what* was going on, even if she didn't know *who* was going on. And she made the decision to stay married to him anyway.

At this point, Tim pops into my head. Tim, my husband of twenty-four years, ex-husband of less than one. Father to my children, partner in my life. Have I made a hasty decision? Should *I* have forgi–

Jesus God *no*!

'Come on Charlie,' Nina says now, hooking her arm through his. 'Let's go, should we?'

Charlie looks down at this tiny Greek woman holding his arm and smiles, then puts his other hand over hers. 'Definitely. I don't think I should really be here.' He glances around. 'My boy is here somewhere...'

A bell tings in my mind, as, miraculously, I remember something from earlier. 'Jason? The secret grandson?'

Charlie nods. 'That's him. You seen him?'

'Yes, a while ago, by the front door.'

'Let's look for him there,' Nina says, and the pair wriggle away in that direction.

I look around for my dad and track him down a minute later in the garden, leaning casually against Audrey's pebble dash, chatting to another ancient old man. I note they are both holding plastic cups.

'Ah, Steph, there you are,' he says, as if he's been hunting for me for ages. 'Come and meet Ivan...'

'Nice to meet you Ivan. Dad, we have – '

'You too.'

' – to go.'

'Do we? Why? What have you done?'

'God. Nothing. But Nina is ready to go, and so am I.' I have a strong sense of urgency, like I need to escape *right now* before the fuse runs out. I look behind me, dreading seeing Jack's milky grandad eyes seeking me out across the room, but luckily there's no sign.

Dad pushes himself away from the wall, and drains his cup. He's going to regret that later.

'Well, it was great to meet you, Ivan. Maybe I'll – '

'You too.'

' – see you again one day.'

I take Dad's arm, and try not to compare this with Nina taking Charlie's. 'Good to meet you Ivan. Have a – '

'You too.'

' – good rest of the day.'

We pause at Audrey and I give her a hug and she thanks me for coming, she really appreciates it, and I tell her it's absolutely no problem, it's been my pleasure because I thought a lot of Teddy (slightly less now) and wanted to give him a good send-off.

'He wasn't a saint,' she says simply, 'but he was mine.'

By the time I've dropped off Dad and Nina, my disappointment over Teddy being a cliché and Jack being a grandad has started to wane, and I feel like nothing more than pouring some wine into a glass and then my throat, and dropping into a chair to watch The Red Wedding again. But as I open the front door, I'm greeted by the delectable sight of Ed's bare tummy, and I change my plans instantly. He's up a step ladder in my kitchen, arms above his head measuring cabinets, the resulting gap between his low-slung jeans waistband and the rising edge of his navy blue polo shirt clearly visible. The knowledge that I've just been talking to his dad darts through my mind, but luckily my reduced ability to concentrate means it's not there long. Every cloud. Harry trots straight into the living room and climbs into his usual armchair for a mid-afternoon nap;

and I head straight into the kitchen for some mid-afternoon delight.

'Hiya,' Ed says, a pencil in his mouth, 'dust caking sun neasurenents. 'Ow was de funeral?' He descends the two steps to the floor and leans in for a kiss.

'Come upstairs and I'll tell you.'

'Ooh, that good, eh? I do love a sexy funeral.' He drops the pencil and the tape measure and follows me upstairs.

A couple of hours later Ed's gone and I'm feeling much more myself. I've got red wine and a red wedding and am definitely not so old as to be attracted to someone's grandad. Good God, no. I'm only fifty, and as fifty is the new forty and forty is the new thirty, in real terms I'm a spring chicken. At this moment, Harry raises his head and peers at me for a few seconds. He's got one ear inside out and one eye slightly more closed than the other, which is giving him the appearance of intense scepticism.

Or maybe that's just me.

The following Monday, Ed turns up at 7:30 and marches past me into my kitchen, where I had been standing drinking coffee in my pink Pingu pyjamas.

'Wahey!' he says, slapping my bottom as he passes. 'That's a sexy look you've got going there, Mrs. Harkness!'

'I'm not Mrs. Harkness,' I tell his back, rubbing my buttock. 'I'm – '

'*Doctor* Harkness, yes I know. Sorry.' He dumps a lot of tools roughly down on the kitchen side and turns to me as I come back into the kitchen. 'You're going to have to get all this stuff cleared out, Steph.'

I eye the tools, and can't help noticing that one of them has left a mark. 'What stuff?'

He raises his eyebrows and looks around the kitchen without saying anything. It's one of those gestures that is designed to make the other person feel fucking stupid. It works.

'Oh, you mean…?'

He nods. 'Yep. Unless you don't want to keep your…' He picks up the nearest thing to him – my Nespresso machine. I nearly cry out, and reach to grab it, but he yanks it away and steps back. '…Nez Prezo thingummy. Whatever that is.'

I take a step and seize the machine, then pull it in close. 'I definitely do want to keep it.'

Ed shrugs. 'No probs. Just get everything you want to keep cleared out and stored somewhere, and I will dispose of anything else.'

It takes me half an hour, and makes me late for work. Well, I still arrive before surgery opens, but only just. Why the hell didn't I do that the evening before?

Nina bursts into my room as soon as she hears me arrive, tapping her watch. 'Why the hell did you not do that the evening before?' she asks, after I've explained.

I shake my head. 'I know, I know, stupid.'

'Well anyway,' she says, pulling up my patient chair. 'We only have a few minutes now so I will tell it quick. I am in love.'

'What?'

'I know. It's fast. But it's right. And, you know, I am not so much young as I was now.'

'Not as young as you were.'

'Yes, that's what I said. So no time to waste. No?'

I sit back in my chair. 'Who with?'

Nina smiles at me knowingly and dips her head. 'Stephanie. *With whom.*'

'Oh, God, all right, with whom?'

'Well, you remember at the funeral, there was Teddy's secret son?'

'Oh, yes, Charlie. I remember. He seemed very nice...'

'No, no, it's not him. It's his next door neighbour! Lucian.' And she places both hands over her heart and sighs like a Pink Lady.

'His *neighbour*?'

'Yes. You know, the person who lives in the next house? My Lucian. His house is next to Charlie, and he lives all alone with his cat called Martin.' She's smiling like Doris Day, but then she looks at me and her smile drops. 'Oh, what's the matter?'

'What?'

'Your face. You have some problem?'

'Oh, Nina, I'm sorry, I don't mean to be negative, but you only met Charlie a few days ago, so when did you meet Lucian? Can you really be in love with someone you've known for such a short time?'

She stands up, frowning. But then the frown smoothes out and she beams again. 'No, I won't let you spoil it. You don't know about love.' She turns and opens the door. 'How is it going with Niamh's dad, then?'

Niamh's face is twenty feet away, behind the reception desk, and looking this way at the sound of her own name. 'He's making a start this morning,' I say smoothly. 'Reckons it will only take about ten days max, including decorating.'

'Wonderful,' Nina says, then goes out into reception and shuts the door. She doesn't slam it as that would be childish. But it makes a bang nonetheless.

She avoids me for the rest of the day, but I see her, swanning around with a beaming smile on her face. I fight against my impulse to think of it as ridiculous and try to reverse the direction of my thoughts. Maybe you do know what you want more quickly at this age. Maybe you can settle on someone, if they're the right person, in a short time.

When I get home that evening, there's no sign of Ed, other than a note on the stairs that says, ominously,

'It's not as bad as it looks xxx'

I carry on through into the kitchen and behold the wreckage. It looks like a ruin, like something that's just been discovered by archaeologists. The only thing left of my kitchen, weirdly, is the washing machine. I stand paralysed in the doorway for a few moments, my thoughts scattered amongst the debris, until eventually one of them nudges against the back of my leg and I turn to find Harry standing there, acknowledging the devastation along with me.

'I know,' I tell him. 'It's definitely as bad as it looks. Worse, actually.'

As we stand there together, a tiny movement amongst the wreckage catches my eye, and I look to see a gigantic spider picking its way through the rubble like a scavenger. Harry spots it too, and we both contemplate it in silence. Eventually, like me, it finds the washing machine and scuttles beneath it, thinking it might have found some sanctuary there. What it will no doubt actually find is a dozen other spider bodies, dead and desiccated, entombed by the need to perpetually spin their webs in places where flies never go. Bizarrely it makes me think of Paul, and me, and all the other people hopelessly looking for love on *Butterflies*. Spinning our webs where we'll never get a catch.

'Let's go out,' I tell Harry, and a minute later we're outside again.

During the walk I manage to construct a plan for the evening involving a delivery of dinner, which leaves my brain free to devote the rest of the time to thinking about the spider under the washing machine. Something about it is snagging my brain, pulling a rope and ringing a chord, but I can't extract the thought out of the miasma that is my fifty-year-old brain. God, I used to be sharper than this, I used to be able to make connections and draw conclusions in a tenth of a nanosecond. The spider, and Nina, and Butterflies, and my dad all swirl around together like some cliché nightmare sequence in a terrible film. I can't work out what my brain is trying to tell me, but when I get back home an hour later, I order the food, and then call the one person who understands about the hopelessness of online dating versus the perils of coupledom, and might be able to make some sense of everything.

'Hi Steph,' he says, and straight away I detect something hesitant in his voice.

'Hi Paul. How's things?'

He pauses for a tenth of a nanosecond too long. 'All fine with me. How about you? Met the man of your dreams yet?'

'Yes, I have actually. He'll be here in thirty-five to fifty minutes with a chicken korma and a peshwari naan.'

Paul laughs. 'That's good.' But it doesn't sound right. He's definitely holding something back. 'I was planning on calling you, actually.'

'Oh?'

'Yes. Been meaning to for a while but, you know.'

'No?'

'Right. Well. I've got some news.'

'I bloody knew it! I could tell the minute you answered the phone that something was up.'

'Could you?'

'Have you been back on *Butterflies*, Paul?'

'Kind of...'

'Oh my God, you've definitely met someone, haven't you? Tell me all about her! How many times have you seen her? What's she like? How did the first date go? Has she said she likes you too?'

The entire time I'm speaking I get the sense that he's trying to cut in. I can hear little 'Uh' and 'Er' sounds, but for some reason I don't let him interrupt. If I'd stopped for two seconds to analyse this conversation, I'd have realised that his voice was nothing like happy enough for the outcome I wanted. So I bluster over him, on and on, filibustering to stop him from spoiling everything.

Eventually I pause, and there's a strained silence.

'It's not quite that simple,' he says.

'Oh, what's not simple? Come on, if you like each other, what's to stop you?' Then a thought plunges through the silence like a knife through the dark. 'Oh shit. Oh no, Paul. She's married, isn't she?'

There's another strained silence. Then he says, 'No.'

'Oh. Well what, then? Is she engaged? In a relationship? Moving abroad? Oh my God, *dying*?'

'Jesus, Steph, will you shut up a minute?'

It's like that old film, where the man slaps the hysterical woman. I'm stunned into silence and all I can hear is the echo of my own relentless questioning in the preceding few minutes. 'Sorry, sorry, sorry. I don't know what's wrong with me. Tell me about her.'

He clears his throat. 'Well, ahem. The first thing you should know is…' He takes a deep breath, and releases it slowly. I bite my tongue to stop myself from hurrying him up. 'The first thing is…His name is Jacob.'

15
MAN'S MAN

The name is unfamiliar in his mouth. You can hear it, the way he elongates the 'J' sound. He's not entirely comfortable saying it.

'Bloody hell, Paul, that's a turn up!'

'Mm, yeah. Bit of a surprise, isn't it?'

'How did it happen, then? I mean, I'm assuming you weren't catfished, but thought ah what the hell and decided to go along with it anyway?'

He laughs. It sounds slightly less strained now. 'Are you busy?'

He arrives thirty minutes later in a polo neck and a haircut. He looks more confident, and fit, and – well, quite bloody attractive now. He's completely transformed. He kisses me on the cheek and goes straight along the hall towards the kitchen, then stops at the threshold and turns to me, holding up the bottle he's brought.

'Oh, sorry, I'm having the kitchen done.'

'Ah, that explains it,' he says, grinning. 'I thought for a moment you'd tried baking a cake.'

'Hey, just because you're gay now, doesn't suddenly make you a baking expert.'

He nods once. 'Fair enough.'

'OK, glasses are on the TV stand – here, let me.'

Fortunately the bottle is a screw cap, as I have absolutely no idea where a corkscrew might be. I pour us a glass each and we settle down for a long chat. Harry lifts his head to see what's going on – his version of guard dog duty – then resumes the 'at ease' position.

I look at Paul with wide eyes, waiting to hear what on earth happened to bring about this dramatic change in him. And as I watch him licking his lips from the wine and smoothing his hair from the wind, I wonder how I could have missed it.

'So?' I prompt him. 'What happened?'

'OK. So. You remember *Raiders of the Lost Ark*? That old Harrison Ford film?'

'Course I do. It was my favourite film for years.'

'Well remember when the Nazis are looking for the lost Ark of the Covenant?'

'Yes, because of its power or something.'

'Exactly.'

'But Indiana Jones finds it first.'

'Yes, that's it. Because the Nazis are digging in the wrong place.'

'They're digging in the wrong place!' I say it at exactly the same time as him, then he stares at me with his eyebrows up, waiting for me to catch on.

'Oh my God! You're the Nazis!'

'I am, as you say, the Nazis.' He nods once, a grave expression on his face. 'Well, maybe, not Nazis, exactly, given that I'm ...' He gestures down at himself, a sweeping motion with both hands.

'No, yeah, maybe not the best analogy...'

'No. But yeah, I was digging in the wrong place, with a staff that was too long.'

'Is that a euphemism?'

'No, ew, shut up! It's a metaphor.'

'I know that. So all this time you've been looking amongst the women, when you should have been looking amongst the men. Is that what you're saying?'

'Pretty much. I mean, I was never completely happy with Joanne. I missed her when she left, as you know...'

'Heart attack.'

He nods. 'Heart attack. I mean, I think her leaving probably did cause the stress that caused that. But I don't think it was her, per se. It wasn't Joanne Hunt herself, her personality, her face, her presence in my life specifically. I think it was companionship. Someone there all the time; that feeling of togetherness, sharing my life with someone important. I didn't want to be alone, that's what scared me.'

Companionship. There it is again. It's what we all want, isn't it? Not necessarily romance.

'I definitely didn't fancy her, anyway.'

'Wow. That must have been some amazing realisation?'

'Not really. I'd known I didn't fancy her for quite a while.'

'Oh. But you still…?'

'Had sex? Nooo, not for years. But we stayed together anyway. We – well, I – enjoyed the companionship of being married. I loved her. But not in a romantic way. We were more friends, really.'

'So why did she leave?'

'Met someone else.'

'She wanted more, I presume?'

'I guess so.'

'I get it.' I sip my wine. 'So you were always gay, probably realised this in some way but didn't acknowledge it, and only did something about it after your relationship with a woman had failed. Is that it?'

'Bloody hell, that's twenty years of my life gone very quickly isn't it?'

'So then what happened?'

He grins. 'What happened was,' he says, balancing his glass on a skinny jeans-clad knee, 'I made myself go to a school reunion a few weeks ago.'

It turns out that, unbeknownst to Paul, Jacob – Jake – had a crush on him for thirty years. Used to follow him around at school, turned up wherever Paul was, made a nuisance of himself, stalked him at his home, a window was broken, police were called, and so on. It's a classic story about the excruciating pain of unrequited love.

'Little twat,' Paul says, smiling fondly.

I take a sip of wine. 'So when...? No, I mean, how...?'

'Difficult to say. Jake and I had a long conversation at the reunion about what happened back in the day, and at the end of the evening he came back to my place and...' He shrugs. 'It just felt right.' He looks down. 'I'll be honest, I was a bit worried about telling you.'

'Really?'

'Yeah. Well, not just you. Anyone. Everyone. It's such... Such a strange thing to tell.'

'Oh Paul. It sucks that you were worried. Telling people who care about you that you've found true love should be a happy thing, not an anxious thing.'

'Yeah, well, tell that to my ex-wife.'

'What did she say?'

He closes his eyes. 'She was quite...nasty about it. Made it all about herself. In a very personal kind of way.'

'Oh God, what an unpleasant person she sounds.'

He smiles. 'You're right, that's exactly what she is.' He leans back and lets out a long breath. 'I don't know why I've avoided telling you. This has been easy. Lovely.'

'You've actually avoided telling me? Why, did you think I was going to be all horrid and homophobic about it, or something?'

'Sorry, Steph. No offence. But sadly homophobes do still exist.'

'Not in here they don't.'

'Mmm, I don't know. Didn't you say you've got an old man living next door?'

'What, Grumpy Graham? Are you assuming he's homophobic just because he's old? Bit ageist of you, isn't it?'

'No, no, I'm not assuming he is homophobic. I'm just saying that, statistically speaking, his age group are more likely to be homophobic than, for example, someone of your kids' age.' He lifts his shoulders. 'It's a generational thing. The unconscious bias in that particular demographic is –'

'Yeah, all right, I get it.' I remember my dad asking me about Audrey's skin colour and cringe all over again. 'That generation were subjected to appalling prejudice in every direction while they were growing up.'

'That's what I'm saying,' Paul says. 'They can't even help it.'

We hug at the door and promise to meet up again soon. 'And bring Jake next time,' I call, as he walks away. 'I can't wait to meet him.'

Ed turns up at 8 o'clock the following morning, and he's brought Ralph with him.

'Morning missus,' Ralph says, and goes past me towards the ex-kitchen.

'Morning gorgeous,' Ed says, slapping my bum again.

'Ed, can I have a quick word?'

He stops and turns back. 'Everything all right?'

'Can you come in here a minute please?' I glance at the living room door.

He takes a step nearer to me and lowers his voice. 'No, Steph, not now. Ralph is here, we're going to crack on. Maybe a bit later, eh?' And he winks at me.

'No, you misunderstand. I need to speak to you.'

'Oh.' He glances behind him, then comes back up the hall and goes into the living room. 'What's up?'

I close the door behind me. 'Can you please stop slapping me on the bottom? I don't like it.'

He flinches backwards. 'Oh. Wow. Didn't see that coming.'

'Didn't you? Really? I mean, you seriously think women like that?'

He shrugs. 'Never really thought about it.'

I stare at him for a few moments. 'You've never…? You mean you routinely inflict pain on…' I stop myself. 'You know what, never mind. I think we've reached the end of… whatever we were doing here. Sorry.'

'No, we've only just ripped out the old cabinets, there's loads still to do.'

'I'm talking about our relationship, Ed. Or whatever you want to call it.'

He nods and looks at the floor. 'Yeah, I knew that. I was messing around.'

'Oh. Right.' Odd time to be messing around.

'I'll finish the kitchen, don't worry. I won't make it awkward.'

'Thanks Ed. I appreciate that.'

We turn and move towards the door, and he puts his hand out towards my bottom. 'Can I give it one more go, for luck?'

'No you bloody can't!'

'I'm *kidding*!' He puts his hands up palms out. 'Jesus, you need to lighten up a bit.'

Thankfully it's Tuesday, so no work for me. I grab Harry's lead from the hook by the front door, prompting the sound of four feet lightly hitting the floor from the chair in the living room. Harry's face noses around the door to see what all the commotion is, and when he spots the lead in my hand, his ears lift about half an inch. 'All right Harry, calm down a bit, will you?' He comes fully into the hall and swishes his tail. 'Shall we get out of here?' I say to him, and he agrees it's a good idea, so I clip his harness on, call out to Ed and Ralph that I'm going out, and leave for the beach. Looks like I'll be spending most of my free time there for the next ten working days.

As I'm closing the front door behind me, Grumpy Graham's front door opens and a figure emerges. I glance across, ready to say 'hello' to Graham, and find myself looking into the lovely face of Happy Hannah. I blink. Is she… doing the walk of shame?

'Hi Hannah,' I say, even though it seems likely she'd rather not have been spotted leaving a man's house at – I check my watch – eight-thirty in the morning.

'Good morning Stephanie,' she beams, pulling Graham's door closed. 'Harry taking you off for a walk?'

I glance down at Harry to find him nose to nose with a slug. 'Yes, as you can see he's raring to go!' Hannah directs one of her sunshine smiles towards Harry, who remains oblivious. I take a step nearer to her and see her eyebrows raise. 'I'm actually avoiding the kitchen fitters, so we need to be out of the house for a few hours. It's going to be a long walk!'

'Ooh, that sounds like some kind of awkward and personal situation. You must fill me in on every detail. Mind if I come along?'

I realise at this moment that Freddy and Ginger are at her feet on the end of their leads, both standing rigidly, staring at Harry. 'Oh, yes that would be great.'

'Righty-oh. Come along then, you two.'

At this point, Harry's highly evolved and sophisticated sense of smell finally notices that there are two other dogs nearby, and he turns towards them, and swishes his tail no fewer than three times. 'Harry, look, it's Freddy and Ginger, your friends.'

'Hello Harry,' Hannah says, on behalf of Freddy and Ginger. 'How have you been?'

He's been absolutely fine, as have Freddy and Ginger, so with the pleasantries out of the way, we start walking.

'So, sneaking out of Graham's place first thing in the morning, eh?' I ask her straight away, then regret it as she covers her mouth with her hand and looks away. 'Oh, God, sorry Hannah. I didn't mean to embarrass you.'

'Oh goodness me, no, you didn't, my lovely. I was giggling, actually. The thought of someone my age doing the walk of shame. In my comfy Dr. Scholl lace-ups and rain mac!'

A snort of laughter bursts out of me. 'That is quite an image.' Of course she's not wearing beige lace-ups or a rain mac, but is in her standard dog-walking coat and boots.

'I did stay at Graham's last night, in fact,' she says now, 'but I was in the spare room – '

'You don't have to explain.'

'No, I know, but I don't want you or anyone to think badly of Graham.'

'I wouldn't. You are both free to do whatever you want to do. Society is much more open-minded these days.'

She looks at me. 'I do know that, Stephanie. We may be over seventy but we're not completely oblivious.'

'No, no, I know. Sorry. That was…'

'Ageist?'

I flinch at her tone. But she's right. 'Yes, it was. I'm so sorry.'

She shrugs. 'Oh, it's all right. There is always prejudice, and most of the time people don't even know they're doing it.'

'Unconscious bias.'

She looks at me again. 'Oh, is that what they're calling it these days?'

I nod. 'Yes, it's quite a new expression that means… Wait. You know this don't you? You're teasing me?'

She laughs. 'I am. I'm so sorry, I couldn't help myself.'

I grin. 'You can be quite wicked sometimes, Mrs. – Oh, sorry, I've just realised that I don't know your surname.'

'It's Lewis.' She laughs out a huff of air. 'No one's called me Mrs. Lewis for a very long time.'

We walk on in silence for a moment, Harry loping slowly by my side while Freddy and Ginger scuttle along beside Hannah.

'So I do want to tell you about Graham and myself,' she says eventually. 'If you wanted to hear.'

'Oh I definitely want to hear.'

'Don't get excited, there's nothing much to tell. I really just wanted to say how grateful I am to you for introducing him to me.' She glances sidelong at me. 'We have so much in common, and exactly the same personality. It's honestly as if you conjured him up out of thin air, just for me.'

'You get on that well?'

'Oh yes. It's almost magical. Changed my life.'

'Oh, Hannah, I'm so happy for you!'

'Thank you.'

'So, when's the wedding?'

Abruptly, she stops walking. With that seventh sense that dogs have that connects them directly with their owners' brains, Freddy and Ginger stop instantly too. 'No wedding, Stephanie,' she says quietly. 'Not ever. I think you might have misunderstood.'

Harry and I stop a couple of steps in front and turn to face her. 'Oh. Sorry.'

She shakes her head. 'Shall we walk down the zig-zag path to the beach, let the dogs run for a bit, then get coffee at the Mermaid café? I'll explain what I mean then.'

The Mermaid café is in an absolute prime location, just four or five steps up from the promenade that runs along next to the beach. It has a large terrace filled with little white cast iron tables and chairs, and a thick Perspex screen to protect its customers from the salty sea spray. This part of the beach is called Mermaid Beach, to the delight of all children and many adults, me included. It's a shingle beach, but has been beautified recently by the hideous addition of several gigantic machines roaring up and down the stones for weeks like alien behemoths, doing something to the arrangement of the pebbles that is, seemingly, a complete secret. But eventually the beasts retreated and disappeared, leaving behind undulations in the shingle that look like stone tsunamis, and stop the actual waves from coming up too high and depositing ankle deep pebbles along the path, making it unpleasant for walkers and, more significantly, impossible for cyclists.

The beach does look lovely like this, but I preferred it without the infernal cyclists. It was worth picking my way slowly along a shingly path if it meant not being at risk from collision with speeding idiots in earphones.

That's the fifty-year old in me speaking.

Hannah treats us both to a delicious vanilla latte, and we sit at a table right at the edge of the terrace, adjacent to the screen. The tide is out, so there's very little salt spray to trouble us anyway, but the screen also deadens the noise a bit, making it easier to talk. Freddy and Ginger sit nicely by Hannah, while Harry lies down under my chair and puts his head on his paws.

'You know I was married a long time,' Hannah starts. 'My Ron. Love of my life.'

'He sounds wonderful.'

'Oh, he was. Loving, thoughtful, kind, funny.' She pauses. 'Jealous, moody, spiteful, unfaithful. He had plenty of flaws.'

'Well, everyone does.'

'Indeed.' She takes a sip of her drink, and at this point the proprietor – her name badge says 'Pat' – appears at our table with a bowl of water for the dogs. Harry ignores it, and her, but Freddy and Ginger lap at it enthusiastically for a few seconds. 'Thank you so much,' Hannah says to Pat. 'They needed that.'

'Aw, they're lovely little dogs,' Pat says, then notices Harry under my chair. 'Oh, and you have a lovely dog too. Look at him – strong silent type, is he?'

I nod. 'That pretty much sums him up.'

'Can they have a little treat?'

'I'm sure none of them would say no to that,' I tell her.

'Freddy and Ginger certainly wouldn't,' Hannah says, smiling.

'Aw what cute names!' Pat says, bending over. 'Here you go, guys. Little treat for you.' She holds out tiny bone-shaped biscuits towards Freddy and Ginger, and they seize and consume them instantly. 'There we are.' Pat bends further, reaching her hand out to Harry. 'Here we go then old fella, would you like one? Little treat for you?' After a few seconds she stands up again. 'I'll just give it to you and you can…'

'Thank you, that's really kind of you.' I reach to take the little bone and find three in my hand. 'Gosh, thanks.'

'Extra for him,' Pat says. 'Seems like he needs it.'

'Thank you.'

'You're very welcome, love.' Pat walks off back towards the serving area, collecting dirty cups and glasses as she goes.

'I love this place,' Hannah says. 'Sea view, dog friendly, lovely staff. Almost doesn't matter what the food is like.' She looks at me. 'Although it's very good anyway.'

I nod. 'It's silly not to be dog-friendly these days. There aren't many people who outright object to them, and you must attract so many more clients if you allow them.'

'Couldn't agree more.'

I take a sip of coffee. 'So – you were saying? About Ron?'

'Ah, yes. His flaws. And there were a lot. He once flew into a jealous rage and left me on my own in Tenerife.'

I blink. 'You're not serious?'

'Oh yes. We were out for dinner and the waiter was flirting with me.' She smiles. 'I was flirting back, I'll admit. It was very flattering. He must have been in his twenties, and I was about fifty…'

Speaking as someone of fifty, I feel pretty sure that this twenty-year-old waiter was flirting with his fifty-year-old client to improve his chances of a decent tip. I don't say this, though.

'I was quite a looker, you know,' Hannah says now, and I feel my face go hot. It's like she's overheard what I was thinking. 'In my younger days.'

'Oh, you still are.'

'Now come on, don't flatter me. I know I'm old now. No, don't. But I used to get looks right into my sixties. Never had children, you see. Kept my figure.'

'I can believe it. Having kids lays waste to every bit of female allure.'

She smiles, and I notice a man at a nearby table noticing her.

'So how did you get back to the hotel?' I ask her, going back to the Tenerife story.

'Oh, gosh, that wasn't hard. The waiter saw what happened and offered to drive me.' She puts a hand up. 'I refused, of course.'

'Of course.'

'But I did allow him to call a taxi for me.'

'And what happened when you got back? Did Ron apologise?'

She widens her eyes. 'Oh, no, Stephanie. He wasn't there.'

'Why not?'

'When I say he left me alone in Tenerife, I mean, he left me alone. In Tenerife.'

'You're saying...?'

'He checked out of the hotel and got a flight home.'

'Bloody hell!'

'Yes, that's what I said!'

'So – you had no room to go back to?'

'No. No room, no flight ticket, no money, no passport.'

My hand goes to my mouth. 'Oh my God! He'd taken your passport?!'

'Yes. I still had my suitcase – he'd left it standing behind the desk in reception – but that was it.'

'That's absolutely terrible.'

'It wasn't particularly fun.'

'How on earth did you get back?'

She smiles like the Mona Lisa and shakes her head. 'It's a long story. I didn't want to ask my parents so I had to get a job, and save up – '

'Oh my God, how long did it take?'

'It was a few weeks. But the point I wanted to make was about Ron. How he didn't always treat me well, or look after me, or have my best interests at heart.'

'You can say that again.'

She lays a hand flat on the table between us. 'No, you mustn't think badly of him. The point is that I loved him. Absolutely. There was no room for anything else.'

'I don't know how you could love someone who did that to you.'

She shrugs. 'I didn't choose to. You don't choose it, do you? It just happens. Something in your brain aligns itself with something in their brain.' She thinks for a moment. 'Or there's a chemical reaction – dopamine, serotonin, adrenaline, all those.' She looks at me with a half-smile. 'Makes it all sound a bit clinical, doesn't it?'

'It does a bit.'

'Either way, I loved him. For my entire life. Even now, and he's been gone six years.'

'Seriously?'

She nods. 'Seriously. I will never *not* love him. So. As lovely and loveable as Graham is, I'm never going to love him… in *that* way.' She meets my eyes frankly. 'How could I, when I'm in love with someone else?'

We both fall silent and sip coffee. Far out in the channel I can see silhouettes of some ships – fishing vessels or dredgers or… whatever they are. The spring sunshine is reflecting off the waves making them sparkle as they roll, and seagulls are everywhere, swooping and drifting and screeching and landing. One lands on the promenade below us and pecks at something unspeakable smeared on the path. I look away.

'I do get it,' I say to Hannah. 'I mean, I haven't felt that myself, but I get it.'

'Ah, I'm sorry for you.' She pauses. 'Although when he died it was the worst feeling I've ever known.'

I nod. 'Oh God, I bet it was.'

'And please don't say "better to have lost in love than never to have loved at all."'

She sips in silence and I watch the seagull tugging at the unspeakable mess on the path below. I'm seriously hoping it's the remains of someone's sandwich.

'So,' I ask after a few moments, 'are you saying that you'll never love again, because it was too painful when Ron died?'

She grins. 'Oh, you mean like when your dog dies and you vow you'll never have another pet?'

'Um…'

'Don't worry, I'm teasing. No, that's not it. What I'm saying is that actually I can't fall in love again because I'm still in love with Ron.'

I nod. 'Right. So Graham is...?'

'A wonderful companion.'

'I see.'

She leans towards me slightly. 'It's exactly the same for him, you know.'

'Is it?'

'Oh yes. He's told me about Barbara. She died fifteen years ago and he's been alone ever since.'

'No wonder he's grumpy.'

'But no one wants to be on their own, do they? That's the fear, I think, as we get older.'

'Yes I guess so. It certainly explains how people are making so much money out of dating websites.'

'Hmm, possibly. Although, of course, we oldies aren't really interested in dating. Or websites, come to that.'

'Can I get you anything else?' Pat says, appearing suddenly at the table.

Hannah and I look at each other, then turn back to Pat. 'No, thank you. That was lovely.'

'We'll come back for lunch one day.'

'We'd love to have you. And your gorgeous doggies.'

We decide to walk back to the Leas via the zig zag path. I resist the urge to ask Hannah if she's sure, and am glad I do as she glides up the steep slopes as gracefully and smoothly as a cruise ship, Freddy and Ginger trotting along either side of her like tugs.

When we get to the top, we walk back along the Leas towards the town, and pause for a breather when we reach the memorial arch at the end. The railings here are festooned in knitted and crocheted poppies all year round, in memory of the hundreds of thousands of soldiers who marched past this point during world war one, down the Road of Remembrance (then called Slope Road), to embark for France; many of whom never returned. Below us is Folkestone harbour and the harbour arm, recently restored and now littered with fabulous little cafes and eateries made from old railway carriages and buses. Greek food, Italian, Dutch, burgers, vegan, baked goods of all types; as well as any alcoholic or non-alcoholic drink you can think of. In the summer it's impossible to move along there, and there is often a live band in the evening and a wonderful party atmosphere.

At least, that's what I've heard, from my still-married Facebook friends. I myself only go there with Harry, during the day.

'There's a bench along here,' I tell Hannah, 'further up. You may have seen it. It's got a plaque on it that says something like "For my beloved wife Maureen, who loved to sit here..."'

'"The gardens are less beautiful without you, my darling,"' Hannah joins in, saying it with me. '"Until we meet again, your husband, Bernie."'

It's not "something like that". It is exactly that. We've both recited it word for word.

'That's how I feel about Ron,' Hannah whispers.

'Have you ever seen the man who sits there?'

She turns to me. 'Oh yes, I have. I know him. Bernie.'

'Bernie of the plaque? Of the beloved wife Maureen?'

She nods. 'He sits there a lot, thinking about her I presume.'

'Oh God, I wondered if that was him. How sad.'

She nods slowly. 'In the end, we all end up on our own, don't we? Married or single, companion or lover, one always has to die before the other one.'

'Like Romeo and Juliet.'

She bursts out laughing. 'Heavens, that's a bit dramatic.'

'Yes I suppose it is. But no less tragic.'

'Hmm.'

'Hannah, I've been formulating a plan. Kind of. Well, more of an idea than a plan, really. About somehow matching people up. Not for romance, like a website; but for companionship, like you and Graham.'

'Ooh, now there's an idea.'

'What do you think? I mean, I know there are already social clubs and coffee mornings and bingo and so on for people left alone, but maybe some people just want one person, one special person, to keep them company. To keep each other company.'

'Yes, I think I see …'

'You know, to watch telly with, or go to the theatre with, or have Christmas dinner with…'

'Or moan about the weather with…'

'…or go to Ikea with…'

'…or shop for a coat with…'

'…or just sit on a bench with.'

She hears my last one and stops. 'Yes. That's it. Or sit on a bench with.'

I watch her face. 'Do you think it's something? Is there a need for something like that? Do you think?'

She thinks, and nods, and looks, and thinks, and smiles. And eventually nods once, firmly. 'I do, Stephanie. Yes. I definitely do.' She touches my arm. 'And I can already think of some likely candidates.'

16
UNMARRIED MAN

Hannah comes home with me, which serves two purposes: firstly, to discuss how to put my idea into action; and secondly to eradicate the possibility of any awkwardness there might be between me and Ed.

'Fingers crossed Ralph is still here, too.'

'Who's Ralph?' Hannah whispers, as we come in.

'Assistant, I think.'

In the hallway, it's immediately obvious that Ed and Ralph have already finished for the day, even though it's barely 1 o'clock. What makes this obvious is the yellow tape that's been stuck across the kitchen doorway like a crime scene, and the sign saying 'KEEP OUT!!' that's attached to it.

'Gosh, my entire married life I dreamed that my husband would do that,' I say, smiling.

Hannah chuckles. 'You never did explain why you were avoiding them,' she says, eyeing the sign. 'Are they offensive in some way?'

'Um, no, not really.'

She swings round and narrows her eyes. 'Ah, I see I was right, it *is* awkward and personal. Do tell.'

I nod. It's an easy decision for me to decide to tell Hannah everything about what happened between Ed and me. She's probably the least judgemental person I've ever met. 'Let's have some more coffee, and I'll tell you everything.'

She taps her palms together lightly without making a clapping sound. 'Ooh, gossip and coffee, two of my favourite things!'

I make us drinks and give Freddy and Ginger one of Harry's chews each – Harry doesn't mind. He's gone straight to his armchair to clean up his undercarriage. He's also waiting for his chew to be brought to him by his human server. The two little ones settle down on the rug, and Hannah seats herself gracefully on the other armchair, and leans towards me. Quickly I fill her in on my not-quite relationship with Ed that's just ended.

'The worst thing is,' I tell her, 'I've also met Ed's dad.'

'His dad? So… his daughter works for you, and his dad is… who, exactly?'

'Oh it's so weird. I met this guy on the beach some time ago, and then later on it turns out he's Niamh's grandad. And what's worse, Niamh tried to set me up with him at her birthday party!'

'Oh no! That's awkward, isn't it? Being set up with the father, when you're already seeing the son!'

'Ah, well, no, that wasn't exactly what happened. I wasn't involved with Ed when Niamh tried to set me up with Jack.'

Hannah frowns. 'Oh. That's a bit confusing then. Why was it awkward?'

'Because he's a – ' I stop myself just in time before saying 'grandad.' After all, the only reason I was put off by that was because it makes him rather old; but Hannah is undoubtedly older. And, I admit to myself, wonderful company.

'Trekkie? Train-spotter? *Conservative?*'

I press my lips together. 'To be honest, I don't know about any of those things.'

'Ah.'

Jack's bewildered face comes into my head, fading into the melee of people at Teddy's funeral as I moved hastily to get away from him. I see him again on the beach – his kindness, giving me a ball for Harry; his humour, matching mine; his generous smile and sparkly eyes. Eyes that were definitely watching me leave. I turn back to Hannah and decide, once again, to be frank with her. 'He's a grandad.'

'Heavens no!' she says, covering her mouth. 'Run, Stephanie! Run, and don't look back.'

'Oh, I know, I know, it's silly. It just… put me off.'

'If you don't mind me asking, darling, how old are your children?'

'Josh is twenty-five, and Amy is nineteen… Ah, I see what you're getting at. Yes, I've thought the same thing. But if Josh and Chloe had a baby now, it would be a baby. And then a toddler, and then a small child – for years and years. It wouldn't be an adult, with a job, until…' I put my hands up. 'Well, I would be pretty old by the time it was twenty-one.'

'Yes, you'd be the very ancient and decrepit age of seventy-one. And doubtless a twisted and hideous old crone.'

I'm guessing from Hannah's response that she's probably around that age, and you could not find someone who was less like a twisted and hideous old crone than her. 'Well…'

'Did this grandad look like a twisted and hideous old codger?'

Jack's face again. The greying stubble. 'No. Definitely not.'

'Was he vile? You know, grumpy and unpleasant?'

I meet her eyes. 'No.'

'Pardon, darling? Sorry, my hearing's not so good these days.'

'I said, "No." No, he wasn't grumpy or unpleasant. The complete opposite of that, in fact.'

'Oh, well. Nice enough then, but still a grandad.' She takes a sip of coffee. 'Sounds like you had a lucky escape.'

We spend the next couple of hours chatting about my plan to assist people craving companionship. Hannah herself knows quite a few who would fall into that category already, Bernie of the Bench included.

'So, do you think people would need to record some personal information, and what sort of friendship they were looking for, somewhere?' I ask. 'So that they could be matched up?'

Hannah nods. 'Yes, I think that would be best. Otherwise you could get it completely wrong.'

'*I* could? Me? You're thinking that I would organise all this?'

'Well of course, darling girl. It was your idea, and you've already helped Graham and me find each other.' She pats my arm. 'You're obviously brilliant at it. And it could be a new venture for you.'

'Oh, I'm not charging. No way am I going to make money out of people's loneliness.'

She smiles long and deeply at me. 'I knew you would say that.'

We make an initial plan that we need some kind of event where anyone interested can attend, and they write a few details about themselves in a book by the door. I propose they email some information beforehand, but Hannah just raises her eyebrows at me, in a 'Really?' expression. I nod, rolling my eyes at myself. 'Yeah, ok, not email.'

'I could hold the event here,' I suggest. 'If it's a nice day, I'll do it in the garden. A garden party?'

'How about a barbecue?' she says. 'No need to go all pretentious and silly, is there?'

'Yes, you're right, that would be a bit ridiculous. Like trying to make out I'm the queen or something.'

'Well I suppose technically a barbecue is a kind of commoners' garden party, isn't it? I think it's a wonderful idea. And your garden is the perfect size to keep things intimate.'

'Small, you mean?'

She presses her lips together. 'Now Stephanie, you must stop thinking badly of your gorgeous home. When I said your garden is the perfect size, I meant that your garden is the perfect size.'

'OK.'

'See, you could have the barbecue on the patio, then a couple of tables set up on the grass, chairs all round, plenty of room for people to move about, get to know each other.' She looks at me and smiles warmly. 'It's absolutely perfect.'

I smile, picturing the old people sitting around, and a memory of my grandparents' anniversary party comes back to me. It gives me a surge of excitement. 'Oh my God, I could put on a little magic show!'

'It's far too small for that,' she says. 'Now, numbers. We'll only need about six or eight people at each one, no need to make things difficult.'

I stare at her. 'Each one?'

'Well, yes.' She stands up, and Freddy and Ginger immediately wake and get up too. 'There are more than six or eight lonely people in this town.'

'Yes, true...'

'And if they don't get on with their first match, they come back and you can pair them up with someone else'

'Oh, yes, good point.' And at this moment, I see my future swelling ahead of me down the months and years – the barbecues, dinners, and parties; helping people make connections with each other and, possibly, avoid the intense loneliness that so often comes with getting old. As I picture it, I feel a smile begin, and soon it fills my face.

Hannah is smiling too. 'I think this is going to be a marvellous thing, Stephanie. Such a wonderful thing for you to do for people.'

'I hope you're right.' I stand too. By now, Freddy and Ginger are running around the living room, always circling back to Hannah. Harry lifts his head and stares at them from the armchair. 'I'm just worried that people will think it's pointless. I mean, they've already got community centres and coffee mornings, and the W.I., and so many other things organised by various charities and groups.'

'Yes, those things do exist, but you know who didn't go to any of them?'

I shrug. 'No?'

Hannah inclines her head towards the wall I share with next door. 'Graham.'

'Really?'

'Nope. Not one. And you know why?'

'Because he's a grumpy old sod?'

She chuckles. 'You're laughing, but that's exactly why. He's an anti-social old so-and-so, who doesn't want to go along to any fusty, dusty, lavender-scented community centre and eat digestive biscuits with a load of boring old codgers.' She grins. 'His words, not mine.'

'He's quite poetic, isn't he? But I see what you mean. Polite conversation over a cuppa probably doesn't appeal to everyone.'

'No, it doesn't. And even if it did, it doesn't take away the loneliness.' We're at the front door now, and she pulls on her coat, then leans in and gives me a hug. 'People need a close connection. Someone that's there, just for them, who they can be completely themselves with. Someone they can ask for help without feeling like it's an imposition.'

'Someone to shop for a coat with.'

'Yes, darling Stephanie. Someone to shop for a coat with.'

Before she leaves, we set a date for the first event – May 14th, in three weeks' time. A Tuesday.

'Graham and I will come, and I will find four more people.'

'They don't have to be equal numbers of male and female, remember. This is not about romance, it's about connection and companionship, so gender is not important.'

She puts up one slender thumb. 'Roger.'

I close the door and stand there for a few moments. What am I getting myself into?

The following three days I spend mostly out of the house. With no available kitchen, I'm reduced either to getting salt-and-MSG-rich take-aways repeatedly for dinner, or eating things that have been bombarded with radioactivity. Fortunately Nina has me and Harry round for dinner on Wednesday and Friday after work, and on Thursday I get fish and chips and eat them on the beach. I stay there far too late, until it's dark, and quite cold, but not for any particular reason. Of course it would be so special to see Jack's beautiful Dalmatian again – Arnie, if I remember correctly – only because Harry showed a bit of an interest in him when we saw him here that time. Whenever it was, I can barely remember. Ed and Ralph will definitely have left my house by now, but I sit anyway and watch the tide go out, and start coming back in again. The sea is ice-smooth and nearly as still, so when the moon gets bright, everything shivers with silver. Gradually the number of dogs and their walkers diminishes and eventually dries up altogether, so I clip Harry's lead on and we head home.

Up on the Leas I spot Bernie the Bench in his usual spot, but it's nearly eight o'clock by now and he gets up and walks slowly away before I reach him. I wonder where he lives and consider following him for a moment, but then realise that would be creepy so I leave him to it. If my plan works, hopefully he won't have to sit here on his own for too much longer. It gives me a bubbly sensation inside.

My phone in my pocket dings with a text, and it's Josh reminding me of our annual dinner in a couple of weeks on Mum's birthday – the eighth of May. I text back, 'I don't need reminding, thank you,' but then delete it before I send it. I am to him what my dad is to me – getting older, not quite as sharp as I used to be, maybe a bit forgetful now and then. In many ways I can't wait for Josh to be fifty, so he can see how it feels, but then I will be 73 and everything that Josh thinks I am now, and am not. Fifty is quite enough to be going on with.

It's a family tradition that we all get together for a meal on each others' birthdays. We've always done it, and none of us felt like stopping Mum's birthday meal just because she doesn't come any more. Mum loved Mexican food, so we always go to *Consuela's* in the town, and we always have chicken fajitas, Mum's favourite. They have a table booked every year for the eighth of May for seven – me and Tim, Josh and Chloe, Amy and whoever her plus one happens to be that year, and Dad. Tim won't be joining us this year, of course.

When I get home, I write a better text to Josh saying that I'm looking forward to it, and would he mind picking his grandad up again. He replies with an eye-roll emoji and 'No of course I don't mind although I suspect he will. Xxx'

Ringing Dad to let him know Josh is collecting him will provide the perfect opportunity to ask how he's feeling about Julia's wedding.

'Oh, I'm not going to that,' he says when I ask.

'Oh Dad, come on. Why not?'

'Because I don't want to. Simple as that.'

'But you might – '

'Please don't tell me I might enjoy myself. And please don't tell me I *should* go, or I *ought* to go. I'm an old man and if I say I don't want to do something, then I'm not doing it.'

It's a default setting for him. I coaxed him away from it for a short time with the prospect of taking Audrey, but of course that bungee of misery pulls on him all the time. 'I'm not going to tell you that you should, or ought to. I'm disappointed, that's all. And Audrey will be too. She was looking forward to it.' I don't know for sure that this is true as I haven't spoken to Audrey since the funeral, but it could be, who's to say?

'Aagh,' Dad says, which means I've hit on something that makes him ever so slightly less comfortable with what he's said.

'You liked her, didn't you? When you met her?'

'Yes, yes, yes, a lovely person.'

'So just go for a couple of hours. Have a drink together, chat a bit. You don't have to stay late. If it makes you feel better, I'll drive you there, then go and get a coffee somewhere, and drive you home again.'

'Aagh.'

'Go on, if nothing else it will give you four different walls to stare at. Plus Marcus will be impressed when he sees you with Audrey.'

'All right, all right. As long as you're sure that Audrey definitely wants to go.'

'Of course I'm sure.' I'll call her immediately after this and ask her. 'She's looking forward to getting out and having something other than Teddy to think about.' Which must be true, even if she hasn't actually said it.

'All right then. But I don't need you to pick me up, I'm perfectly capable of driving there myself.'

'I know you are, Dad,' (he isn't) 'but this way you can both have a drink, can't you? Helps to break the ice.'

'Oh, fine.' Instant cave.

'Fabulous. You've got a week to get ready.'

'Of course I'll still go,' Audrey says when I ring her on Friday. 'Your father seems like a very pleasant gentleman. And I know I need to get out and do things.'

'Ah thanks Audrey. He needs to get out too, so you'll be doing him – and me – a huge favour.'

'Oh goodness, that's not how I see it at all, Doctor. It will be a very welcome distraction for me.'

I take the opportunity to let her know that Nina will be taking over her care from now on, as my patient list has suddenly become rather –

'Oh Doctor,' she interrupts, 'you don't have to make something up about your patient list. I have been thinking myself how inappropriate it could be for to continue as my GP, if your father and I are going to be friends.' She tuts. 'You really mustn't keep thinking of us oldies as being unable to comprehend things, you know.'

I bite my lip. 'I'm so sorry Audrey. You're right, I think I've been under-estimating older people for some time.'

The morning of the wedding arrives and I picture Julia waking up and smiling excitedly about the wonderful day to come, bounding out of bed and flinging open the curtains with joy at the prospect of being united forever with the one person she loves above all others. Cut to close-up of Julia's shrewish face, moaning about the late arrival of the hairdresser, and making unpleasant phone calls to the venue to give last minute instructions. 'Good God,' she'll be saying, 'I just want the eighty napkins folded into little swans. You're a hotel, aren't you? Is that beyond your capabilities?'

Dad and Audrey aren't going to the service, just the 'After Party', as Julia has dubbed it. I'm picking him up at half past four, then collecting Audrey at quarter to five. Julia's party is starting at five-thirty and finishing at nine-thirty, which is a huge relief for me. I can nip home and have dinner, then be back in plenty of time to pick them both up. I don't anticipate for one moment that they'll stay to the end.

My kitchen is starting to look more like a kitchen now. The cupboards are up and in, but have no doors on them yet; and the floor isn't done, but it's coming on. Ed's paused in the kitchen construction to paint the walls, and it looks good. I did always think he was good with his hands. I make a mental note to ask him to give me a quote to paint the rest of the house when he's finished.

'Morning Harry,' I say, as he strolls in from the living room. 'Sleep well?'

In response he sticks out his tongue, curls it back, then yawns with a creaky groan. He smacks his lips a couple of times, licks his nose, then looks up at me expectantly.

'OK, OK, it's coming.'

Once I've given him his meaty breakfast, I put the Nespresso machine on and scroll through my phone while I wait for it to heat up. A knock at the front door makes me raise my head and sniff the air with a low growl. I wonder if I've been spending too much time alone with Harry.

'No, it's ok, Harry,' I say to him, 'I'll go.' He doesn't even lift his head as I walk past. When I swing the door open, I nearly slam it again instantly.

It's Tim.

'Hi Steph,' he says, from a brown leather jacket and matching brown cargo trousers.

'Never saw you as an NSync fan.'

'Eh?'

I shake my head. 'How did you find me?'

He rolls his eyes. 'You do love drama, don't you? This isn't *Sleeping With the Enemy*,' he says. 'Can I come in?'

I don't want him in. This is my place, it's nothing to do with him. But if I say no, I'm positive I'll be the bad guy. I step to the side and pull the door wider. 'Of course.'

'Thanks.' He comes into the hallway, looking around him. I hate how he's looking around him. 'Hmm,' he says. 'Nice.'

'Fuck off,' I want to say. I don't, though. 'I'm just having coffee. Do you want some?'

'That would be lovely. Thank you.'

I eye him as I make the coffee. Why's he being so nice? I notice that he's not as smoothly shaved as he always used to be, and his hair is a bit longer and a little bit shaggy-looking. He looks like he's lost a fair bit of weight, too. His cheeks have that hollow look about them that you get when you're in a film about prison, and his eyes look a bit... sunken. Good God, is Tim *dying*?

'Renovating?' he asks, indicating the empty, doorless cupboards.

'No, I like it like this,' I want to say. I don't, though because, you know, might be dying. 'Yeah. It's nearly finished. Can't wait to get my kitchen back.'

He looks at me and grins, lifting his eyebrows. 'Seriously? You never used to like being in the kitchen.'

It's an implied criticism, and I rise, dying or not. 'Not wanting to cook every day doesn't mean I don't like cooking, Tim.'

He puts his hands up and widens his eyes. It's an expression I've come to loathe. 'Hey, don't bite my head off. Just making an observation.'

'And now you're gaslighting, just like always.'

'Pardon?'

I take a deep breath. 'Why are you here?'

He doesn't answer immediately. 'Can we sit down somewhere? Is that possible?'

'Yes, I did decide to buy a sofa in the end. It's through here.'

'No need to be sarcastic, is there? I was only asking.'

He's right, it wasn't an unreasonable question. But I'm not apologising. We go through to the living room where Harry has just installed himself on the armchair. 'Ah, Henry old boy,' Tim says, putting his hand on Harry's back, 'there you are.' He scratches his head a bit. 'How are you, boy? Eh? How are you?'

Harry doesn't react at all. Why would he? He barely reacts to people he knows.

'*Harry* is fine,' I answer for him.

Tim nods. 'Ah, that's good.' He tries to lower himself into the armchair next to Harry, but Harry, God love every molecule of him, doesn't budge even one centimetre, leaving Tim to perch right on the edge of the seat. Eventually he abandons that idea and moves across to the sofa. Harry is immobile. I put my hand over my mouth to hide the smile.

'So,' he says, and looks at me, pressing his lips together.

'So.'

'I'll cut to the chase.'

'Oh, I wish you would.'

'Ha ha. OK.' He closes his eyes briefly, takes a deep breath, looks across at me and says, 'I've made a mistake.'

I stand up instantly. 'For Christ's sake, Tim. Are you serious? Did you honestly think I'd want to hear this?'

'No, no, wait. Please hear me out. Come on, please?'

'This is unbelievable.' I sit anyway. 'I already thought you were a bit of a cliché. Now you're a double cliché.'

'Ouch,' he says, smiling.

I say nothing.

'OK, OK, I'll get to the point.' He thinks a moment. 'Thing is,' he says, 'I've done a lot of thinking the past five months. I've had time, and I'm pretty sure I made a very hasty decision…'

I'm already shaking my head. 'It wasn't your decision, was it? It was mine.'

He frowns. 'I think you'll find it was mine.' I start to respond but he puts his hands up. 'Hey, look, let's not argue about whose fault it was, or wasn't, or who made the decision or whatever. It's in the past, nothing we can do about it now.'

'Right. So what else is there to say?'

He looks at me frankly. 'It was a mistake and I'd like to reverse it.'

'*Reverse* it? Is that how you're phrasing it?'

'Well, yes…'

I stand up again. 'Look, Tim, I'll stop you there. You're right, I couldn't give two shits about whose decision it was to split up – it was mine – but the fact is, it was the best decision either of us – it was me – has ever made, so, honestly, you might as well…. What? What's that about?'

He's laughing. He's staring up at me from the sofa, hand over his mouth, shoulders shaking, eyes squeezed. 'Oh… my… God!' he eventually manages to splutter. 'Only a woman…!' And he convulses yet again into paroxysms of dry laughter.

I put my hands on my hips and narrow my eyes. He didn't laugh this much when we went to see Michael McIntyre. 'What ?'

He raises one hand towards me, the implication being that he can't speak for laughing, but it's so obviously wildly exaggerated and fake. I look away and stare dully out of the window, arms folded, while I wait for him to stop the charade. There's a lot of 'whoo'-ing, and 'oh my God'-ing, but when he realises I'm no longer watching, he stops.

'Sorry about that,' he says, wiping his eyes, letting a final couple of sniggers out. 'Ah, ha, it's just, ha, you actually thought I wanted to get back together. I mean...' He giggles again. 'It's just so bloody typical of women, isn't it? A man says he's made a mistake, and they *leap* to the immediate conclusion that he's talking about *them*!'

There's a pounding sensation behind my eyes that extends all the way down to my fists. 'Then what exactly are you talking about?'

He looks at me and huffs out one single laugh – probably the only genuine one – and says, 'The dog.'

'What?'

'You heard me. I want the dog back.'

I look at Harry, who is, as ever, motionless. Blissfully unaware of this threat to his existence. 'No!'

'Er, he's not your dog, remember? You can't just say no.'

'Yes he is, and yes I bloody can!'

Tim stands up and I take a step backwards. His lip curls. 'Oh fuck off Steph, stepping backwards. Don't pretend you feel threatened by me.'

'That is *exactly* how I feel and I'd like you to leave now.'

'Fine. That's absolutely fine. It's *exactly* what I want to do.' He turns to Harry. 'Come on, Harry.' At this point, he pulls a short red dog lead out of one of his many pockets and walks towards the armchair where Harry is lying. I can feel my heart beating in my throat and my breath is speeding up. I try to slow it down, breathe deeply, and curl and uncurl my hands.

'Get away from him,' I say in a low voice.

Tim turns to me, surprised. 'Now who's threatening?' He turns back to Harry who has finally opened his eyes. 'Come on boy, let's go.' He leans forward to clip the lead onto Harry's collar, but Harry raises his head and looks at me.

'It's OK Harry,' I tell him. 'Nothing to worry about.'

'She's right, Harry,' Tim says, adjusting the position of the lead in his hand. 'Nothing at all to worry about. You're coming home at last, isn't that great? You're coming home with me.'

In response Harry shuffles on his belly to the edge of the seat and kind of lets himself fall off it onto his feet. He walks over to where I'm standing and goes behind my legs, to stand peering around them at Tim.

'Come *here*,' Tim says now, gritting his teeth.

'Nope,' says Harry. Through me.

Tim apparently gives up on coaxing Harry to go with him, and looks at me. '*Give me* the dog.'

'Why do you want him, anyway? You just walked away from him last year, couldn't have given two shits about him. You've spent five months away from him without giving him a second's thought. Why so desperate for him now?'

'You don't know I haven't thought about him.'

'Oh come on. If he did flash through your mind for a moment, it didn't motivate you to want to see him, did it? Or even ask after him. What's this all about?'

'He's a great dog, he belongs to me, I want him back.'

'Yeah, and I smell bollocks.'

We both think about that for a second.

'I mean, bullshit. It's bollocks. Whatever. You're a habitual liar, Tim, and yet again you're proving it.'

He screws his face up as if he really can smell those bollocks, looks at Harry behind me again, then stuffs the lead back into his pocket. 'I'll be back,' he says. 'I'm taking this further. You've got my property and are refusing to return it to me. It's theft, whichever way you look at it.'

'OK,' I say, smiling. 'See you soon then.'

17
MAYBE NOT-SO-OLD MAN

I don't slam the door as he leaves because that would be childish. I go and punch the sofa cushions a few times instead. Whilst explaining to them very loudly which part of the male anatomy Tim most resembles.

My next course of action is to contact my best friend Zoe. She's a solicitor, although she never seems to be at work. I send her a text asking her to contact me urgently when she has a moment, and then stare at the phone until she replies.

'Soz, with a client, call you later xx,' is her reply. Which is surprising. I was expecting that she'd be ice-sculpting or bungee jumping.

I spend the day hugging Harry and telling him how much I love him and reassuring him that nothing bad will happen to him, as long as I'm alive. We have a lovely walk on the beach and I buy us both an ice cream.

'You shouldn't give him ice-cream,' someone says walking past.

'Oh fuck off,' I say. Quietly. After she's walked away.

I have a sense of Harry being on death row, enjoying his last few hours with me before the grotesque figure of Death, with his skeletal hand and hunched, wasted body – aka Tim – comes for him. His next treat is a burger, which he wolfs down without even chewing, then stares at me while I eat mine.

'Ah, regretting that a bit now are you?' I take a bite. 'Mmm, delicious.'

'That artificial food is bad for dogs,' someone says, so I smile and give Harry the rest of it.

I don't hear from Zoe all day. My phone is in and out of my pocket, but there's no message and no missed calls. At four o'clock I load Harry into the car and go to collect Dad.

'Why did you bring the dog?' he says as he gets into the car.

'I didn't want him to be at home on his own.'

'Oh. He's been on his own before, though, hasn't he?'

'Yes, but I just didn't want him to be left again. OK?'

'All right, no need to snap.'

'I'm *not* sn– ' I stop myself. Take a couple of breaths. 'No, you're right, sorry Dad.'

I don't want to tell him about Tim's demand. Somehow putting it into words will make it seem more likely. Or Dad will say something like, 'Well it's only a dog,' which won't help.

When we arrive at Audrey's bungalow, Dad gets out and knocks on her front door. My tummy is full of butterflies just watching them from the car, so God knows how they must be feeling. Audrey invites him in for a minute while she finishes getting ready, so I slip my phone out. Still nothing from Zoe. I click open Facebook to pass the time, but then decide to have a quick scroll through the *Butterflies* app, just for old time's sake. It's so easy to swipe left, left, left, giving each miserable face no more than half a second's consideration before moving onto the –

I stop.

One face, finally, is smiling. And it's a face I recognise. My index finger had actually started the left swipe movement before I realised, so I gingerly move it back to the central position and lift it from the glass. Yes, it's definitely him – that greying stubble, those twinkly eyes, that big infectious smile. The face of a – I can acknowledge to myself – pretty attractive grandad. I check the name, just to be sure, and he's called himself 'Harry', which makes me blink in surprise.

    Harry, 58.

        Single, house-trained, loyal and loving.

        Like running and walking, particularly on the

> beach. Will never stray. Happy just to snuggle on the sofa every night, but equally happy out on the town. Desperately seeking woman with tennis ball.

I smile as I read it, then I read it again. Then check out the photo again. That is most definitely Jack's face smiling back at me, yet he's called himself Harry, the name of my (yes, Tim, *my*) dog, which brings me to the conclusion that this message is aimed at me. At getting my attention. It is, isn't it? I take a breath and swipe right, and the word 'Pair!' flashes up, but then the car door is opening and Dad and Audrey are getting in, so I have to put my phone away.

'Thank you so much for picking me up,' Audrey says as she settles into the back seat. 'I do appreciate it.' She spots Harry, buckled into the seat next to her. 'Oh, hello again, Harry.'

'It's no problem at all Audrey. It's on the way anyway.'

'I'm almost positive that's not true.'

'No, it is,' Dad says as he gets his seatbelt on in the front. 'It's no trouble at all.'

'Well,' says Audrey.

I start driving, my mind a bit more on the pair I've made on *Butterflies* than it ought to be. I realise too late that I've begun looking for a parking space near the surgery, but luckily Dad and Audrey are engrossed in a conversation about Harry Potter and don't notice. I make a swift left turn, then another, and head back the way we've come.

'*Dragons,*' my dad scoffs, doing a Trump-face in the front seat that fortunately Audrey in the back can't see.

'Just try one,' she says. 'They're very exciting. And they get better and better.'

'Hm, well, maybe. I'm reading Michael Barrymore's autobiography at the moment. Have you read that? Very revealing.'

I drop them off at the venue ten minutes later, and they head towards the bar for a drink. 'Text me when you want picking up,' I call out of the passenger window. Dad turns round and waves, but undoubtedly has not heard what I said. I turn to face Harry behind me. 'What do you think, Harry? Shall we have another walk while we're waiting?' Harry doesn't object, so I nod. 'Walk it is.'

We're in Dover, which has its own beach, but I decide to drive back to Folkestone beach again. It's more secluded, and it's sandy which is more comfortable for Harry's feet, and Harry is familiar with it, and it's easy to park… I can actually hear myself in my own head over-justifying why I'm going back there again so soon, which is pointless because I already know why. It's because it has a higher percentage likelihood of a chance encounter with a nice grandad.

And Harry doesn't care that we were only here a couple of hours ago.

Yet again I don't have a ball with me, but Harry is not bothered. The ball that Jack gave me is lying on Harry's armchair where he put it, and I think he likes having it there – his little yellow companion. The tide is in now, although not all the way, so there aren't any other dogs or people here at the moment. We go down the steps and walk along the narrow strip of beach that's available, Harry following behind me and stopping now and then to sniff a more interesting piece of sand.

My thoughts return to Jack, and the match on *Butterflies*. The thought of him uploading that photo and that profile gives me a little excited feeling, and I look round repeatedly to see if he's here. I'm so distracted I realise eventually that luck has been on my side and the tide is on its way out, rather than in. If it had been coming in, Harry and I would probably have been swept out to sea by now. Well, I would. I'm pretty sure that Harry would have padded calmly up the steps to safety before his feet even got wet.

As the beach expands behind the falling tide, I spot one or two more dogs and their owners arriving each time I look round, all making the most of being able to be on here while they can. At the end of May dogs are banned until the end of September, a rule that feels grossly unfair. It's not dogs who leave plastic bottles and crisp packets and nappies and food wrappers. No, it's down to the few ghastly people who don't pick up their dogs' poo and ruin it for all dogs. And they're probably the same people who leave their picnic litter behind too, spoiling the beach for others while innocent dogs watch from the promenade, looking at each other and shaking their heads.

My phone rings and for a mad moment, because he's almost permanently at the forefront of my mind it seems, I imagine it's Jack. But he doesn't have my number of course, stupid me. It's Zoe, at last, and before she has a chance to change the subject I tell her quickly what Tim is trying to do.

'Is Harry Tim's dog?' is her reaction. Not what I was expecting.

'No! Well, Maybe. I don't know. He could be. He knows the original owner who didn't want him any more, so it was Tim who – '

'No, what I mean is, does Tim have any receipt, or paperwork of any kind specifying that Harry belongs to him?'

My blood goes cold. I'd assumed Zoe would just dismiss it and say that Tim was just trying to strongarm me into handing Harry over. But she hasn't. Tim could well have some agreement from his mate Aaron saying that he relinquishes Harry into Tim's care or whatever. Which would probably mean, legally anyway, that Harry is his property. I look over at Harry, standing at the shoreline watching a seagull floating on the waves, and my heart feels a tug. He's no one's property. He's a living creature, with his own opinions and preferences and ideas and thoughts. He deserves to be so much more than someone's property.

'Steph? You still there?'

'Oh, yes, sorry. I don't know, to be honest. He might have. I mean, it's unlikely, it was just some bloke who works with Tim who gave him to him.'

'Can you ask Tim?'

'Huh, no chance.'

'No, thought not. What about the colleague, the bloke who had him before? Can you get in touch with him?'

I think about that. I remember it was Aaron Sims who didn't want poor Harry any more. He was working with Tim at the William Harvey hospital in Ashford at the time, so that's a starting place.

'Zo, do you think you could do me a favour?'

'Yes, yes, I'll send him a letter at the hospital making it sound like it's a legal issue and asking if he has any paperwork…'

'Thanks, but won't he immediately tell Tim? They're mates, aren't they, they'll concoct paperwork and say it was exchanged in November.'

'Good point. What then?'

I hesitate. Harry is now following a feather that is blowing gently along the sand. His tail is swaying and his nose is down and he looks like he's finally living his best life. I'm asking a lot, but he's on death row, this is important. 'Could you ring him, maybe?'

Unlike me, Zoe does not hesitate. 'Yes, yes, of course I can. Or I can get my assistant to ring him. We'll tell him it's an ownership dispute. Which it is. I'll just not charge you.'

'Oh Zoe, you're such a good friend. Thank you so much. Can I take you out for dinner or something, to say thanks?'

'That would be absolutely lovely, thank you. Will have to wait for a couple of weeks though – I'm just about to release a bear.'

Harry and I walk up and down the expanding beach for another forty-five minutes, and while Harry is happy and diverted I take the opportunity to open up *Butterflies* again and try to compose a message to Jack. It feels very peculiar to be writing to him on this platform, where I've encountered such a wide variety of disappointment, and he almost starts to meld with all the others in my head. It feels like all men have had a meeting and chosen one giant self-absorbed, superior, inconsiderate man to represent them in the hunt for a girlfriend. I focus on the photo of Jack and remind myself how he's not like that in so many ways, and how he doesn't sound like the nasally, self-important, patronising voice I've got in my head that is the common voice of all these people. Jack has a mellow, caramel voice, a bit of rough biscuit at the bottom, and cream on top.

After several attempts that are all utterly dreadful and ingratiating, eventually I come up with, 'Hi Harry, how are you doing today? Eh? How are you doing? Are you doing OK? Oh you are, yes you are, you're doing OK, aren't you? Good boy.' I stare at it for about fifteen seconds before sending it, and then it's gone and it's too late to do anything about it.

Harry and I leave the beach not long after that, and I've trudged half way up the Road of Remembrance before I remember that I came in my car, and it's still parked down on the seafront. I turn and start walking back down again, but feel a yank on the lead and turn back. The man that had been walking down the hill towards me is holding Harry's collar.

'What are you...?'

He puts his hands up. 'Sorry, sorry, didn't mean to upset you. I'm Aaron, I work with your husband.' He pauses. '*Ex*- husband.'

I notice at this point that Harry has sat down but his tail is sweeping an arc across the pavement behind him, and his head is tilted backwards to stare up at Aaron's face. If dogs could grin, Harry would be doing it. 'Oh, Aaron? As in Aaron, Harry's previous owner?' I can't help myself and place a slight emphasis on 'previous.'

Aaron nods. 'Yeah. Harry was mine. Weren't you boy? Hey? You were mine.' Aaron looks up at me again. 'Well, I was his, really. You know what I mean?'

It makes me smile, and I nod. 'Harry belongs to no one.'

Aaron smiles too, but doesn't say anything. He pets Harry vigorously for a few moments, then stands straight again. 'Do you mind if I talk to you quickly?'

This fills me with fear and I pull Harry's lead gently towards me until he's forced to stand up and shuffle closer. He immediately sits down again. 'What about?'

'About Harry.'

'You're not having him.'

A car goes past us, travelling uphill, and comes within six inches of Harry's thigh. Aaron and I both see it and flinch, and I yank his lead and pull him as far away from the road as he will go, which is only about another inch due to the extreme narrowness of the pavement.

'Shall we just go down to one of the cafes and have a chat? Aaron says, quite reasonably, and I agree, just so I can get to the bottom of this hill and nearer to my car.

At the bottom, Aaron says, 'Where do you fancy? They do a nice coffee in Blooms round the corner, or we could get one from – '

'I don't want a coffee,' I say without looking at him. 'We are going back to my car and then to go and pick my dad up. You can walk with me if you want, but I don't have anything to say to you on the subject.'

I see in my peripherals that he's nodding, then he pushes his hands into his jacket pockets and strides along behind me. I keep Harry close to me and wind his lead around my hand.

'So,' Aaron starts. 'Difficult to know how to – '

'You can't have him back,' I say, head down, marching. I don't think Harry's ever moved so fast.

'I knew you were going to say that, but that's not – '

'Good. We're in agreement then.

'Yes, we are, except there is one – '

'Nope, forget it. Not even worth your breath to say any more.'

'No, it is… Look, can you please just stop a minute and let me say it?'

I stop and take a deep breath in, counting to three in my head. 'Right. You've got sixty seconds. Go.'

'Tim wants him back,' Aaron blurts out, then immediately looks away, as if he's just betrayed a confidence.

'Well I know that, for God's sake.'

'He's already spoken to you then?'

'He can't have him either.'

Aaron starts shaking his head. 'Oh, no, no, that's not why I wanted to speak to you.'

'Hang on.' I frown. 'Just how exactly did you know I was going to be walking down here today, at this time?'

He shrugs. 'I didn't.' He hesitates. 'Well, I kind of tracked you down…'

'What?'

'No, no, it's nothing sinister, honestly. It's just…' He releases a breath. 'OK. A few days ago Tim texted me and asked me to help him get Harry back.'

'Oh for God's sake.'

He's already shaking his head. 'No, please, let me finish. He told me he was going to speak to you today about it. He's taken a day off work. Anyway, I wanted to speak to you, to make sure…'

'No, no, hold on a minute. You tracked me down? What exactly does that mean?'

He looks at his feet. 'I got your address from Tim.'

'But I'm not at home.'

'Well, I…'

'You followed me! Didn't you?'

'No!'

'Liar!'

'OK, yes I did.'

I blink. 'Wow. You give up easily don't you?'

Aaron closes his eyes and breathes a couple of times. 'Look, I didn't set out to follow you. I mean, you know, from your home.' He puts his hands up as my eyes widen. 'No, no, I didn't do that. Yes, I admit I went there. I knocked. You weren't home. So I...'

'You what?'

'I asked your neighbour if he knew where you were. And he told me that you often walk your dog on the beach – '

'Oh my God.'

'So I came down and I saw Harry on the beach and I really wanted to see him, and I knew what Tim was going to do…' He stops and gazes down at Harry. 'I honestly, honestly, don't want to creep you out.'

'Right.'

'It doesn't matter if you don't believe me. I don't care. I just don't want...' Unexpectedly, his voice catches and his eyes mist over. He clears his throat and sniffs, looking away.

'What don't you want?'

Aaron passes a thumb under one eye, then looks back at me. 'I don't want Tim's shitty girlfriend to get her hands on Harry.'

We do end up having that coffee after all. I send Dad a quick text, knowing he's unlikely to look at his phone but hoping he will. He'll see my message when he takes his phone out to text me to come and pick them up. If he does.

So it turns out that my husband left his twenty-four year marriage and comfortable home to move in with an unpleasant, manipulative, controlling harridan. According to Aaron, she's put him on a strict low carb vegan diet, won't let him cut his hair, dictates what he wears, tells him how to stand, how to talk, what to talk about. She ridicules him in front of friends – or at least, in front of Aaron – and has now decided it's time to seal their relationship with a dog.

'She's absolutely vile,' Aaron says, blowing on his coffee. We got some from Blooms after all, and we're now walking along the bridge that crosses the harbour. The tide is right out, and all the little fishing vessels are stranded in the black, squelchy sand. I know it's squelchy because I went down there once with Harry and he sank in it up to his knees, then turned and looked at me to rescue him. 'Honestly, they've got a kennel for him in the garden, and a stake with a long lead attached to it. That will be his home if they get him.'

We both look down at the beautiful soul ambling along between us, and my heart squeezes. Trapped outside in a kennel in the garden, with very little human contact at all. He'll die.

'I've contacted a solicitor,' I tell him. 'Her main concern is whether or not Tim has paperwork from you saying that you're relinquishing any claim on Harry and handing him over to Tim.' I stop walking and turn to face Aaron full on. 'Please tell me you didn't give him anything like that?' I hold my breath.

Aaron nods, I panic, he spots it and quickly shakes his head. 'No, no, I mean, no, I didn't. We're friends, aren't we? I didn't think it was necessary.'

'Oh thank God.' We resume walking.

'I just handed him over. I knew that Tim would take care of him. I mean, he's a decent bloke – '

I start to interject, but decide to let it go. He probably is decent to his friends. In a shallow, meaningless kind of way.

' – so I had no qualms about it.' He looks down fondly again. 'It wasn't easy, you know. Letting him go. But I changed my job and it meant he was going to be on his own for more than ten hours most days. I couldn't do that to him. I was upset, but in the end I had to put Harry's needs first.' Harry looks round at the sound of his name, sees Aaron and swishes his tail a couple of times. Aaron reaches down and scratches his head. 'You've taken good care of him, I can see that. He looks great.'

'Thanks. He's a gorgeous dog, I love him to bits.'

Aaron smiles as Harry tilts his head back. 'Me too.'

We finish our coffees and I drive Aaron back to his car. We part on the agreed understanding that if Tim asks him to provide some kind of paperwork and pretend it was exchanged in November, Aaron will refuse.

'It might jeopardise my friendship with him,' he says, leaning back in through the passenger door, 'but he can look after himself.' He glances into the back seat at Harry. 'Harry can't.'

I pick Dad and Audrey up at eight o'clock and wait until after we've dropped Audrey home before asking him how it went.

He nods, pushing out his bottom lip. 'A very pleasant evening,' he says, then turns away to look out of the window.

'"Very pleasant"? Is that it?'

'Isn't that enough?'

I open my mouth to answer, but then think about that a bit. It was an evening out for them both, with a bit of companionship, some party food, and maybe a dance or two. What more was I hoping for? 'Well, yes, I guess it is.'

He turns back to face front. 'She's a very interesting woman, your Audrey.'

'She's not really *my* – '

'We're meeting up again tomorrow. For coffee.'

'Oh Dad…!'

'No, please don't say anything. I don't want it dissecting and gone into and talked about and analysed.'

'OK.'

'We're just friends, right? It's never going to be more.'

I nod and smile to myself. 'Believe me, Dad, I understand completely.'

18
CAVEMAN

When I wake up late a few days later, my phone doesn't recognise me. The little padlock at the top wiggles a bit but doesn't unlock. 'Enter passcode to unlock,' it says, 'and get an early night now and then.'

'Up yours,' I mumble to it from a dry yet paradoxically drooly mouth as I key in the pass code. To be completely fair to it, my tiny reflection is looking a bit squashed on one side this morning, my eyes are definitely puffier, and my lips much more skinned back. You can't really blame it for thinking a naked mole-rat has got hold of my phone and is trying to pass herself off as me. Hannah and I may have had a couple too many small Sherries last night when we were planning the barbecue, and I wonder if she feels as rough as I do this morning. Somehow I doubt it. I can picture her now, a serene smile on her face as she sleeps; her white hair spread out across a cream silk pillow, dappled sunlight streaming in, bluebirds pulling back the curtains and rabbits and raccoons making little chirruping noises outside the window.

It was a productive night though. We got a lot of things organised, most significant of which was a guest list. Bernie the Bench is coming; as are Eileen and Wendy, both friends of Hannah's; Hannah herself; Grumpy Graham; Audrey; Dad; and me. That's our eight for this one, although Graham has already told me about a couple of people he knows that would like to come along to a future event.

'They're not interested in that church hall, custard cream, uptight, so polite, powdery P's and Q's kind of club either,' he told me on the pavement a couple of days ago, and shuddered. I'd smiled, impressed with his poetry. 'We men don't want to be discussing lacy table cloths on our best behaviour, and how to get the best crust on a gypsy tart. We like to swear now and then, and talk freely about men's things.' Then he leaned in. 'But don't tell Hannah. Hmm?'

We also found a name for the events. I hesitate to call it a 'club' as that seems to have youthful connotations, and the Grahams of this world might be thinking it was a bit Enid Blyton. Hannah came up with *Silver Linings*, *Silver Belles*, and *Life Times*. My contribution was *Rainbows*, which we both rejected pretty much as soon as I'd said it.

'But it's a beautiful thing that comes after the rain,' I said.

'It's also where little girls go before they start Brownies.'

'Fair enough.'

We settled on *Life Times* in the end. *Silver Linings* seemed to imply that being chronically lonely had an upside; and *Silver Belles* was just too... tinkly.

'So you know my kitchen is finished,' I said, trying to emulate her by sipping delicately at my glass.

'Yes, I do know, you've told me several times,' Hannah said, and looking back now I notice that she wasn't holding her glass when she said it. Hers was still on the table, half-full.

'Yeah, I'm so pleased with it. Did you see it? It's just so beautiful.'

'Yes, I did, I saw it when I got here.'

'It's lovely, isn't it? Just perfect for making food in. Oh, I can't wait to start making food in it. It's going to be so lovely!'

'Yes, indeed.'

'I can do the food in it!'

'Yes you can...'

'The food for the barbecue! For *Life Times*. In fact, the barbecue can be a celebration of my gorgeous new kitchen!'

'A kitchen-warming then, if you will.'

'Ooh, yes, a kitchen-warming! What a fantastic idea. We can all warm up my kitchen together.'

'By cooking and eating our food in the garden.' She was smiling at me.

I blinked. Then smiled and nodded. 'What better way is there?' And that definitely needed drinking to.

Oh God, why did I do that? I'm rubbing my eyes now to try to get them to focus, as if rubbing them will remove the need for reading glasses. Surely half a bottle of pinot noir shouldn't make me feel as rough as this?

Then I remember I'm fifty, with the metabolism of a building.

Happily, the text I'm waiting for is there, and I smile as I read it. No arrogance, no self-absorption, no oblivious, relentless relating of facts. Jack is as interested in me as I am in him, and our conversations – by text and in person – are fun and mutually gratifying.

'Morning Steph,' it says, 'did you have a successful evening last night?'

He doesn't finish his messages with any 'x's; he doesn't say 'lol' instead of using a comma; he doesn't simply answer my questions without asking any. He's paid attention to what I've said and responded to it appropriately. It's like cool water on a scald.. There is one lingering issue with Jack, though, that is uncomfortable and awkward, and I am filled with nausea every time I think about broaching it with him.

'Great evening,' I reply. 'Bit worse for wear this morning, while Hannah is no doubt already up and gliding around Waitrose like the QE2. How was your evening?' I cringe as I type, but I have to ask. It's rude not to ask. Last night, my potential lovely new boyfriend was getting together with my recent ex-boyfriend, who is his son; and his adult granddaughter, who is also my receptionist. This is the thing I can't face, that's too awkward to deal with and will, I hope, simply go away all on its own if I just leave it alone and don't think about it. I absolutely do not want to think about it, or know about it, or think about Ed and Jack being related to each other, or in the same room as each other or both being men.

'You slept with the son, and now you want to try the dad out?' Nina said to me a few days ago. 'Does the father know about your sex with his precious boy?'

'Oh my God, Nina, no he doesn't! And don't call him that.'

'What?'

I swallowed a few times. 'Precious boy.' It came out as a whisper.

'Oh, sorry. But you know, Steph, you are going to have to choose.'

'What, between Jack and Ed? No I am not! It's not a choice, I don't just get to *choose*, any more than a man can simply – '

'No, no, no, just listen to me, stupid woman.'

I jerked back a little. 'Oh. Right.'

'OK. You have to choose if you can have a relationship with the father after doing the son. And you have to choose if you can tell them both. Because if you choose "yes" to the first one, you must choose "yes" to the second one.'

I stared at her and realised that she was right. If anything is going to progress with Jack, I have to tell him about Ed; and to mitigate against future awkward Christmases, I have to tell Ed about Jack. At this moment my stomach spasms and I slam my hand over my mouth as it floods with saliva. Maybe better not think about this right now. I can build up to it gradually.

I stand under the shower for fifteen minutes holding my head with one hand and my tummy with the other. It doesn't help, it just makes me feel hot and steamed up. I consider going back to bed for a few minutes or days, but as it's nearly her birthday my mum's voice comes into my head. 'That's a waste of a day, Steph,' she's saying. 'If you want to drink heavily and make yourself unwell, you have to do the penance the next day.'

'Why do I, Mum?'

But she's right, of course. Going back to bed feels juvenile, and like cheating. It's my own stupid fault so I have to deal with the consequences.

My phone dings but I'm pretty sure it will be Dad questioning the time of Mum's meal, or the venue, or the menu or some other detail that he doesn't really want to know at all, he just wants to prolong the contact with me today. I need to dry my hair, though, so I'll read it later.

'You can't read texts and dry your hair at the same time?' Amy's voice says in my head.

'No I can't,' I say out loud now. 'And I'm fifty, I don't have to.'

Harry and I head out to the Warren today. This is the much less attractive but so much more interesting eastern part of the beach, cut off from the Sunny Sands beach by a large rocky promontory that you can clamber across at low tide, if you were really, really stupid. The Warren is not smooth and pretty like the Sunny Sands. It's outside the sheltering embrace of the harbour arm, so the sea is choppy and hits the shore with a lot of noise. The beach is littered with huge, green boulders, and clumps of seaweed, and rock pools that turn bathwater-warm by the end of a long summer day. And, best of all, you can bring your dog down here all year round.

As you arrive at the beach, you can see to your right, stretching away to the far end, the row of massive concrete groynes that slope down steeply from the sea wall and divide the beach into sections. They are gigantic, ugly, concrete behemoths, ancient and crumbling, too dangerous to climb but a great way to leave the beach urgently when caught by a fast moving tide. From here, they look like fossilised Tyrannosaur skulls, from beasts that all perished together whilst, weirdly, standing in a line facing the sea.

On your left, to the east, is a vast expanse of ugly, old broken concrete that looks like nothing more than an abandoned car park, apart from the fact that it juts out into the sea. At the edge of it there is a sudden unnerving drop to the churny sea below, with not even a low fence to warn you that you're nearly there. Standing between the 'car park' and the beach, you can reach behind you and touch the actual white cliffs that were immortalised in the song about Dover. Sadly nothing rhymes with Folkestone.

I let Harry off the lead, then put my Airpods in and listen to a bit of The White Stripes while I watch him walk slowly ahead, nose to the ground. He stops at each rock and seaweed clump, lifting his head when a bird hops too near, but I let him take his time. We've got nowhere to be for hours and hours, and I let my mind stretch luxuriously at the thought. A little brown and black spaniel zooms past towards a low-flying gull, making Harry step back and stare, but he doesn't join in. I'm not sure whether he's disinterested, lazy, or knows he doesn't have a hope of catching it.

'Morning,' the spaniel's owner calls to me, and I wave and take out one Airpod.

'Morning. Blowy one, isn't it?'

'It is, isn't it? Thought we'd seen the last of it.'

There are some tents here today, up on the sea wall to get shelter from the wind under the cliff. Further east, between the scrub at the base of the cliff and the 'car park', there are very often semi-permanent encampments, with washing lines attached to blackberry bushes and little stamped-out fires. It's out of the way here and I guess homeless people come and set up for the summer because they're unlikely to be hassled or moved on. It makes me think about Nigel, and I hope he's doing OK. Now that winter is well and truly over, I can relax a little bit about him, and his fellow rough sleepers.

'Quite a few of them here now,' the spaniel's owner says to me, indicating the tents. 'Best steer clear.'

'Oh yes, we better had, hadn't we? I'm really terrified of people without the luxury of a roof over their heads.'

She widens her eyes. 'God, me too.' She glances nervously at the tents, and I bend over to pretend to tie my shoe lace.

'Seeya,' I call, as she lingers, apparently waiting for me. 'We are *not* friends,' I mutter to my shoe.

'Have a good one,' she says, and wanders away. Good.

When I look up, Harry is standing with all four feet in a rock pool, and is staring back the way we've just come. It makes me smile. 'You're a lovely boy, Harry,' I tell him, and scratch his head. His tail swishes but he doesn't look up at me. He seems transfixed by something in the distance. I put my Airpod back in, and pull my phone out of my pocket to read that text from Dad.

Except it's not from Dad. I stop walking and suddenly all the warmth is gone from the day. It's from Tim.

'I bet you think you're so bloody clever,' the message starts. 'You're not,' it finishes.

There's a creeping sensation up my back and, instinctively, I look behind me. Of course Tim isn't there. No one is. Not that I have anything to fear from him anyway – he's the father of my children, for God's sake. But this message feels vaguely threatening in some way. I read it again. Maybe it's just trying to be rude? Telling me how 'unclever' I am. Gosh, Tim, that really stings. I guess he's talking about his attempt to claim Harry, and it looks like he's done exactly as I predicted and asked Aaron for some backdated paperwork to demonstrate ownership. Only it's not my cleverness that's thwarted him. It's his choice of girlfriend. It's the vile machinations of Foul Fiona which led to Aaron's intense dislike of her. I look over at Harry. And Aaron's love for his dog, of course.

I close down the screen and slide the phone back into my pocket. It's childish more than anything. Tim has failed to manipulate me – for once! – and he can't take it. The only course of action left to him is to rubbish me with a text. The thought makes me smile.

Harry and I walk towards the rocky promontory which I have no intention of climbing over, so our arrival there signals the point where we have to turn back. Harry is never far from me, stopping to sniff some interesting clump of seaweed, then loping back to my side when he realises I've walked on. A crowd of seagulls lifts into the air in a grey mass as Harry trots towards them, and he stops and watches them flap away, before they all turn in the air as one and gradually alight fifty metres away. It seems they are having their AGM today. It's windy but a gorgeous spring day with more warmth in the sun that you'd expect for early May. Weirdly that text from Tim has lifted my spirits, knowing that he's feeling defeated, and I turn my face to the sun, smiling and feeling buoyant and joyful.

A sudden cry makes me look round, and the first thing I notice is no sign of Harry. It's a wide, empty, sandy beach with nowhere for him to hide or disappear to. Where could he have gone? I take out one of the earphones so that I can see better. 'Harry?' I call, looking around me, behind, in front, up on the wall, further along the beach. 'Harry? Come here, boy! Come on!' I start walking but I don't know where to, which direction. He was right here, standing here in this pool, staring at... Staring at what? I turn to face the way that Harry had been facing and there's a figure running, but it's running towards me, shouting something, waving its arms. '*Harry*?!' I call out, fixed to the spot, wanting to run, sprint, but with no idea where I need to go or what I need to do.

'Traveller took him!' the person running towards me is shouting. As she gets nearer I see that it's the spaniel's owner from earlier, and she's flushed and out of breath. In the background the spaniel is galloping optimistically towards a perched bird. The woman turns and points back up the beach, back towards the cliffs. 'Took him that way, just picked him up and, like, ran!'

'Sorry? I couldn't really hear… You said…a *traveller*?'

She nods. 'Yeah, one of those homeless. Just grabbed him and ran!' She flings her arms towards the 'car park'. 'That way! You know where they live? At the bottom of the slope, along past the bushes. Go on, quick, before they hit the road!'

A plunging sensation drops through me like a stone and my heart leaps into my throat. Suddenly I'm struggling to breathe properly. 'You're sure?' My fists clench and unclench and all my muscles tighten, ready to start fighting or fleeing. Or sprinting in furious rage after a dog-napper. Oh God, if it really was a traveller, there's a good chance Harry has been taken to sell on. He'll be moved quickly, passed from hand to hand, confused, frightened, depressed. A sob catches in my throat. I might never see him again. I start jogging back up the beach, not waiting for her answer.

'Yeah, definitely.' She trots with me. 'He's carrying a big dog, remember, he won't be going fast. You'll catch him easily.' She glances at my trainers. 'Plus he's got posh wellies on, so definitely won't be able to run fast.' She skips once and speeds up a little, jogging back up the beach towards the cliffs and the blackberry bushes. 'Come on, we'll get him! Come *on*!'

I speed up too, my mind an unfocussed blur, the only coherent thought being '*Hurry, hurry,*' which morphs pretty quickly into '*Harry, Harry,*' repeating in time to my pounding feet and laboured breathing. We head towards the track to the road where everyone parks, right back up at the top of the beach. I keep looking around me, behind, to the sides, back to the sea, certain I'll see him in a minute, trotting calmly towards me from between the groynes, or standing with his back to me, oblivious. 'Harry! Come on boy! *Harry!*'

Something about what she said doesn't sound right, but I can't pin it down. A traveller took him? "One of those homeless," she said. Is that really possible, or likely? I didn't know there were travellers living down here at the moment, I haven't heard or seen any evidence of it. And even if there are, who would be bold enough simply to grab a big dog like Harry in broad daylight? They would have no idea how soft he is.

'Wait!' I call to the woman ahead, and she stops and turns round. 'When you say traveller – how do you know?'

She shrugs. 'Who else would take a dog like that?'

I think wildly, and a slight prickle of possibility tickles in my mind. Would a traveller be wearing *posh wellies*? We carry on running, but it's hard work on the sand, and then further up the beach onto shingle. But we're making good progress because when we reach the bottom of the track to the road, right next to the edge of the apron, I look up the track and catch a glimpse of a figure trying to run, hunched back, head down, two furry paws sticking out either side, as it disappears round the corner.

'There he is!' Spaniel Lady shouts to me, then, '*Oi! That's not your dog!*'

The figure doesn't look back, only seems to speed up slightly, and I curse the woman for shouting. It would have been better if he thought he'd got away and slowed down a little.

But she's still shouting, and now I realise why. '*Dog thief!*' she's shouting, looking behind her at the other people on the beach, who are starting to take notice. '*Dog been stolen!*'

Around me, people look at each other, check to see their own dogs, then start moving up the beach towards Spaniel Lady and the track. I hear snatches of conversation – 'Did she say dog thief?' 'Which way…?' '…dog's been taken…' and like the seagulls they congregate into a crowd and move en masse towards the track. They're faster than me and before I even manage to reach the bottom, some of them are starting up the track. I hear shouting – '*Quick!*' '*This way!*' and '*I see him!*' – and I try to hurry my leaden legs just a few more steps. My breaths are coming fast now and waves of heat are pounding over me, but I keep going, and going, to the bottom of the track, then up it, and round the corner…

And there it is. Tim's car. Driver's door open, Tim in the front seat, Harry on his lap. Four or five people surrounding the car, two holding the door, more standing in front and behind. I stop to get my breath, bending over with my hands on my knees for a moment.

Then I straighten up, take my other Airpod out and drop them both in my pocket; clench my fists, take a couple more deep breaths, then march up to Tim's car like a Seven Nation Army.

'*Give. Him. Back.*'

'He's mine,' Tim replies. He says it so quietly, I have to lean in to hear him.

'No, he is not.' I straighten up and face the crowd. 'Thank you so, so much, everyone,' I tell them. 'That was absolutely fantastic.'

'You should call the police…'

'I'll fucking kill him…'

'Poor little doggy…'

'Oh, hello Doctor…'

I look around me at this wonderful group of humans, hot and panting, exerting themselves just for me, a complete stranger, and my heart expands. I want to hug each and every one of them, but right now I have a dog to take care of. And Harry.

'It's OK,' I tell them all, 'no need for the police. It's just my ex-husband.'

'Still needs the police, in my opinion…'

'Nah, no point, just a domestic…'

'Thought it was a traveller?'

'Travellers get married, you know…'

'Thank you,' I tell them again. They seem reluctant to disperse, still high on adrenalin and heroism, wanting to prolong the feeling. 'I'll sort it out. I honestly can't tell you how grateful I am.' A few of them glance at me, then back at Tim. 'I would have struggled to get him back,' I tell them. 'Just because he's my ex, doesn't mean I'm not relieved you stopped him.' I look a few of them in the eyes. 'He's a total – '

'Can't you people mind your own business?' Tim says from the car. All eyes turn on him instantly and he puts his hands up. 'Oh, whatever.' Harry takes the opportunity to get free and steps out of the car, then trots over to me, swishing his tail. When he reaches me, he astounds me by actually putting his front feet up on my thighs, and pressing his head against me. 'Oh Harry!' I bend forward and put my arms around him as tears flood my eyes and a cheer goes up in the crowd. Exultant Harry, loving the attention, puts his head back and barks as everyone claps and high-fives each other and the day feels like the best day that's ever happened to anyone.

Gradually people start to wander back down the track, arms round each other, chattering excitedly, recounting the event. Bending to stroke their dogs, reaching up for kisses. As they move away, I hear more than one person laughing. This unimaginable horror has given a lot of people a really good feeling today. I turn to the monster in the car.

'Get out of here.'

'It's my dog…'

'No *he* bloody well is not. You left him with me nearly six months ago. In what universe does that make him yours?'

He pushes out his bottom lip and looks down at his lap. 'I was the one who got him.'

'Yes. That's right. You did. You foisted a dog on me without asking me, without any kind of consultation, and then a month later you left him. You had a responsibility to him, you know. But you didn't care. And now suddenly you want him.' I look down at Harry who has his back to the car and is watching the crowd meandering back down the track. 'He's a living being. Not an object. You can't just come and claim him, like a CD. He lives with me and he will live with me until one of us dies.'

Tim looks up at me with vitriol. 'Don't think this is the end of it.' He pulls the driver's door shut and starts the ignition, then winds down the window. 'I *will* get him back.'

I bend so that my face is very close to his. 'If you ever try to take him again, I will tell Fiona Chapman about all the other little bimbos you've been shagging for the past five years.'

He's trying to pull away, but the car stalls with a lurch. 'Ha, what bimbos? You don't know what you're talking about.' But his face is white, and he tries to restart the engine with the windscreen wiper lever.

'Bye, Tim.' I turn to Harry 'Harry, say good bye to Tim.'

And Harry, in time-honoured tradition, lifts his leg and pees against Tim's driver door.

19
WOMAN

My mum loved food. I know, it's a stupid thing to say, because doesn't everyone?

Well, maybe not picky teenagers. But I know from experience they'll change their minds later.

But Mum really did. She used to spend ages in the kitchen creating meals like they were works of art. She didn't just cook food; she sculpted it. When I was a kid, she would sit us at the table and make us wait there for five whole minutes before she would bring out the meal. And it was presented as if we were in a restaurant. Szechuan chargrilled chicken strips on a bed of rocket, with a mango and pine nut salad. Seared salmon fillet on spicy mushroom and spinach cous cous. Home-made turkey burgers served in a brioche bun, with red pepper salsa, slices of Bavarian smoked cheese, and Caesar salad on the side. It wasn't until I went to secondary school and had frozen pizza at Annabelle Lewis's house that I stared to realise that my evening meal was quite extraordinary. And Mum wasn't terribly keen on eating out, because she took such pride and pleasure in what she was creating. Why get someone else to do what you could do just as well, or better, yourself? And for a fraction of the cost.

The exception was the Mexican restaurant, now called Consuela's. Mexican food was one of her favourites, and she adored putting a gigantic dish of enchiladas in front of us; or covering the table in bowl after bowl of toppings – cheese, refried beans, salsa, guacamole, fried chicken, pulled pork, garlic prawns – to pile onto crispy golden tostadas. But unlike almost every other dish she prepared, she enjoyed having Mexican food made for her. She used to say she enjoyed it more, could relax into the anticipation of it, if she hadn't prepared it. So when Marco's opened up in the town, that became her restaurant of choice for every birthday.

Twenty years on and we're still going there. We've watched it change hands and name, from Marco's, to El Cortador, Caza de Toros, and now Consuela's; but it's always been Mexican food. It's been Consuela's for about six years now, so they've started to recognise us, a disparate group of six or seven – depending on whether Amy brings someone or not – coming every year on the 8th of May. They don't remember the days when Mum used to come; they have no idea we are celebrating her birthday; they know nothing of her obsession with the perfect tostada; and that always makes me sad. The original owners – Marco and his team – knew Mum well, as we went for nine of Mum's birthdays, and countless other times in between, while they were running it. She used to quiz them about how they got their tostadas so golden and crispy without burning them or drying them out; and exactly what ingredients they put in their salsa – was it lemon juice or lime juice? But then Marco's wife died and he moved back to Spain. After that, El Cortador lasted about eighteen months; so it was Caza de Toros when Mum went for the final time. They didn't know, they didn't remember. She looked around her, taking in the surroundings – the silly hats, the miniature guitars, the paper mâché donkeys in bright reds and yellows and blues – as if she knew it was her final visit, as if she was trying to imprint an image of it onto her brain. She was already ill by then, and we had been told the treatment wasn't a guarantee. But of course we all believed she would recover. Dying was what other people's mums did, not mine.

When I wake up on her birthday, I have my customary little cry in bed, and go through some old family photos as I always do – Mum and Dad on their wedding day; Mum reading me a story when I was about seven; Mum and Dad playing with the kids in their garden. And one taken of all of us about a week before she died. She's got a smile on for the camera, but God knows what her mental state was like, knowing she was saying goodbye to everyone forever. My throat aches thinking about it, and I stroke her tiny, two-dimensional face. 'Mummy,' I whisper, tears dripping off my nose. 'Miss you.'

At this point, as usual, I start thinking about my own mortality, and what will happen to Amy and Josh when I've gone. It's Amy I worry about most – she still needs me so much. Who will read to her in the night when she can't sleep? Who will tell her how perfect and special and wonderful she is?

Right, no more wine or chocolate or late nights for me, ever again. I'm going to eat low fat, and exercise for thirty minutes every day, and practise meditation and yoga and maybe even start praying. I am determined to make it to 100, so that Amy and Josh will be old people themselves by then. And with any luck, they'll have children and grandchildren of their own to help them cope.

I take back the praying. No point in that.

Tonight it's a table for seven – no Tim for the first time, and Amy is bringing Mona. They've been on again off again for two years and my dad still hasn't quite grasped it. I just hope that he doesn't ask Amy if she's managed to find a boyfriend yet. I'm first, and order a bottle each of the house red and white, but don't pour any until the others arrive. Mum still has a place laid for her at the top of the table, but it doesn't make us feel maudlin. We don't talk to the empty seat, or pour wine into the glass; it's just there, a silent presence, as we eat and enjoy each other's company.

Amy and Mona arrive next, holding hands, which is a good sign. Amy does not do well when she's not with Mona, so it's great to see them together. Amy looks good and it takes me quite a while to realise that she's missing her customary thick black eyeliner. Also, she's wearing a dress. It's dark purple, but it's not black and that's a wonderful change.

'Hi Mum,' she says, coming straight over for a hug. Also a lovely change. I sink into it, closing my eyes and relishing the smell and feel of my baby.

'Hi love. You look wonderful. Hi Mona, how are you?'

'Hello Doctor Harkness. I'm very well, thanks.'

'You know, you can call me Steph. We're all adults here.'

'That's OK.'

They sit down and Amy tucks into the bread sticks. 'God, I'm starving.'

'You know that's my starter?'

She stops and looks down at the half-eaten bread stick in her hand. 'No it isn't.'

I try to stay dead pan but fail as usual, and start smiling. 'Never mind, I'll have some of yours when it arrives.'

She looks at me, then eyes the bread stick again. Then shoves the rest in her mouth. 'You're so mean.'

'Haha! Sucker.'

'Sake.' But she grins. 'You spoken to Josh lately?'

I nod. 'Yeah, a couple of weeks ago. You?'

She nods, mouth full. 'Mm yeah. This morning actually.'

'Oh, that's weird, when he knew he would see you tonight.'

She shrugs and doesn't meet my eye. 'Just a catch up, you know.'

'Oh. That's nice.' I watch her carefully. 'Everything OK with him?'

She continues avoiding eye contact. 'Yeah, all fine.' And she shoves in more desiccated, super-absorbent, wood-bread which sucks all the saliva out of her mouth making it impossible for her to say more.

Chloe and my dad appear soon after, and tell us that Josh is parking the car.

'Dreadful for parking round here,' Dad says, pulling out a chair next to Mum's. 'Makes it so awkward.'

'Only for Josh, though.' I lean over and give him a kiss. 'I mean, do you want to start going somewhere else each year? Somewhere with a car park, maybe?'

He glares at me. 'Don't be ridiculous.'

I look at Amy and we both hide fond smiles as I shake my head. Dad has to grumble, but the lack of parking, or cold food, or slow service, or overcooked veg, are never what he's really complaining about.

'Sorry, sorry,' Josh says, arriving. 'Have you ordered?'

The food is delicious, the waiter is cheerful, the wine flows and even Dad smiles a bit. He gets quite animated talking to Amy at one point, so I listen in.

'…not really appropriate,' he's saying. 'The woman has adult children, for God's sake. Grandchildren, even. Absolutely ridiculous to be in white.'

'I didn't think you were going to go, Grandad?'

'Hmph, well, no I wasn't. But I changed my mind at the last minute in the end. Decided I needed to get out more. You know, while I still can.'

'Haha! There's life in the old dog yet!'

'Well, I wouldn't go that far…'

'Did you enjoy it though?'

He nods. 'You know what, I really did. I didn't expect to, but it was a very lovely afternoon, all told.'

He's obviously talking about Julia's wedding, and although he doesn't mention Audrey specifically, I can see her there quite clearly in his face and words.

'Oh that's good,' Amy says. 'Sometimes the things we don't really fancy doing are the things that end up being the best times ever.'

Dad nods. 'That's very true, my girl. So speaking of fancying, what do you and your friend think of our handsome waiter then, eh?'

After the main courses, Josh tells us not to order dessert, as he's got something planned.

Dad turns to Chloe. 'Ooh, have you made a cake?'

'Good God, no, Grandad,' she says. 'Sadly this particular set of ovaries weren't given automatic cake-making ability when I was born.' She looks up at Josh. 'Josh is the one with all the culinary skills.'

'Hold that thought,' Josh says, and leaves the table.

'What's this all about?' I ask Chloe.

'You'll see.'

Josh returns, pushing a little dessert trolley draped with a white cloth, with a large silver dome on it – presumably covering a cake. It occurs to me at this point to glance at Chloe's left hand, but there's no ring there. Maybe she's having it resized? Ah, I like Chloe, I'm glad she's joining the family. I smile broadly, confident about what's coming.

'So, Chloe and I have a little announcement,' Josh says. He looks down at Chloe sitting next to him. 'Well, a massive announcement, in fact. An earth-shattering, life-changing – '

'Get on with it,' Chloe says, smiling.

He nods. 'Right. Yes.' He looks up and around the table, and puts his hand on the silver cloche. 'So, Mum, Grandad, Granny if you can hear me, Amy – here's our big news!' As he says it, he whips away the cloche, which was apparently attached to the white cloth as that is gone too; and as I start to say 'Congratulations!' I'm flummoxed by the sight of five or six pretty pink balloons lifting into the air from underneath the trolley where they had been hiding.

'*A girl!*' Amy gasps, and stands up to run round the table and fling her arms around Chloe, who is now looking a bit watery-eyed. I look from Chloe to Josh, to the balloons bouncing on the ceiling, to the glass of water in front of Chloe and realise she's had no wine all evening. And Josh's face, eyebrows up, staring at me, waiting for me to work it all out, is beaming. The very definition of paternal pride.

'Oh my God, Josh!' I stand up so quickly my chair falls over, and go to my huge little boy and hug him tightly. Then I half bend and try to include the seated Chloe in the hug and it all gets a bit uncomfortable and silly and we end up laughing.

'I'm going to be an aunt!' Amy says, hugging Mona. 'A little niece for me to adore and spoil and influence.' She catches Chloe's eye. 'You know, in a good way.'

'Of course.'

Josh, now sitting, takes hold of my hand. 'How do you feel?'

I gaze up at him, into those same baby blue eyes that first fixed on me twenty-five years ago. 'I'm blown away. What a surprise. And completely thrilled – for both of you, and for me, and for Amy, and…' My eyes get hot and my throat starts to ache. 'You know.'

'Thanks Mum.'

'A girl, then?'

He nods.

'How long have you known?'

'What, about the baby, or that it's a girl?'

'Either. Both. I don't know.'

'Well, Chloe is four months along, we had a scan the day before yesterday and found out then that it's a girl.

But we've known about the pregnancy for about eight weeks.'

'Gosh. Two months. You kept that very quiet.'

'We wanted to tell you straight away, but then once we'd decided to find out the sex, we thought it would be great to do it this way. All at once.'

'Oh, Josh, I'm not upset. Not at all. I am genuinely nothing but thrilled.'

(Just as long as Chloe's mum wasn't told first.)

'Thanks Mum. I thought you would be.'

'Hey Mum,' Amy calls from across the table. She's flushed and looks like she's been wetting the baby's ping-pong ball head already.

'Yes, my darling?'

'You know what this means, don't you?'

'What?'

'You're going to be a Grandmother!'

Dad turns to me and puts his hand on my arm. 'Did she say "ovaries"?'

'A grandmother, eh?' Jack says later, in bed.

Oh, no, no, sorry, nothing like that. He's on face time, on my iPad. I'm in my bed, he's in his. We're in different buildings. It's a bit too soon for any of that nonsense yet. I'm going to be sensible this time and not rush headlong and desperate into anything.

After I'd responded to his message on Butterflies, he sent me one more saying he really fancied a walk, and we arranged to meet up on the beach. It was surreal, seeing him walking towards me, a big grin on his face, knowing he was there just for me. It was a perfect spring morning - the sun was sparkling on the wave crests, seagulls were swooping and shrieking, and a silky sea breeze brought salty spray into our faces. Arnie the dalmatian was with him, and Harry and he gave each other a really good, long, intimate sniff when they met properly, which went on so long it verged on the awkward.

'I think they're falling in love,' Jack said softly. I felt my face flood with heat, and hoped he didn't notice. 'You look wonderful,' he said next, so either he didn't, or the redness enhanced my fifty-year-old allure. We held hands and walked around the beach while the two dogs did their thing – one prancing and dancing around; the other strolling and sniffing – and afterwards we sat in the sun on the harbour arm and ate chips. It was like the twenty-four years of marriage to Tim had never happened. Two nights ago, he leaned in suddenly and touched his lips onto mine, right in the precinct. I've never been kissed in the precinct before. We were standing under the streetlight by Phones 4 U, and the smell of fries from Burger King was filling the air. I felt like I was eighteen again and Joshua Aitken was kissing me outside the fish shop.

'Sorry,' Jack said, stepping back. 'I just – '
'Tripped?'
'Ha! No, that wasn't an accident.'
'Well if it was, you styled it out beautifully.'

He laughed, and we kept on walking.

'I'm glad you did it on purpose, though,' I told him. He took my hand then, and we walked closer together, our shoulders touching. It felt good. I am pretty optimistic that this one might one day get to stay for breakfast. At some point in the future. A long time in the future.

'Yeah, all right,' I tell him now, 'I'm a Granny. You can stop going on about it.'

'It's not a bad thing, you know? Being a grandparent.' He lifts his eyebrows. 'I love it.'

'No, I know. It's just the connotations, isn't it? Doilies, china dogs, beige sandals.' I shake my head. 'I'm not ready for beige sandals, Jack.'

He's laughing. 'You are funny.'

'But also deadly serious.'

'Just embrace it. You're this age anyway. Your son becoming a dad doesn't make you any older.'

'No, you're right, it doesn't. It just makes me feel older.'

'Nah, you've got it all wrong. When your baby has a baby, it takes you back. Makes you feel young again. It's like the first time you became a parent, all over again.'

'Is it? So am I going to feel like I'm twenty-four again?'

'Definitely.'

'Ooh, good. I liked being twenty-four.' I pull a wistful face, looking up at the ceiling. 'I had good legs then.'

'You have good legs now.' He looks away. 'Um, ahem, well. You know, from what I've seen.'

It makes me grin and I pull the tablet a little closer. 'No, Jack, actually I don't know. Maybe you'd better explain.'

He doesn't say anything, but instead of looking down at my image on his screen, he looks directly into the camera so his eyes meet mine. My heartbeat misses one or two. 'I'd love to do that. One day.'

'How about now?'

Yes, yes, all right, a woman can change her mind, can't she? Anyway, I'm fifty, I don't have to explain myself to anyone.

'On my way,' he says, and then all I can see is ceiling.

With a lurch, I sit up. Oh God. 'Jack!' I call. 'Come back!'

His face reappears, his hair tousled as if he's just pulled a jumper off. 'What's up? Changed your mind?'

I swallow. 'No. I definitely haven't. Not that way round, anyway.' He frowns, not understanding. 'Doesn't matter. The thing is, you might change your mind. When you know.'

He shuffles a bit, moving from the edge of the bed into a more comfortable position. 'Oh dear, this sounds ominous. When I know what?'

I swallow. 'OK. There's something I need to tell you.'

'Ah, that must be why you said "When you know."'

'Yes. It is.' He's staring intently down at my face on his screen and there are little creases between his eyebrows. He shuffles back again, leaning against the headboard, settling in for the night. I can see that in fact he has just pulled a jumper off, and he's now sitting in a plain white tee shirt. The contrast against his skin is incredibly alluring. 'The thing is, and please don't... Oh God, don't judge me, but I didn't really think about what I was doing.'

'Shit. Are you a detectorist?'

'A what?'

He shakes his head. 'No, sorry, ignore me. I'm being flippant and I can see that you're trying to get something off your chest.' He presses his lips together. 'Please, carry on.'

I stare at his face. His eyes are a bit too creased and twinkly and his lips are a bit too twitchy. 'Are you...*laughing*?'

A smile starts to appear, but he pushes it away. 'Laughing, no, of course I'm not laughing, whatever gave you that idea?'

'The fact that you're laughing.'

Now the smile won't be suppressed. Or he stops trying. 'Oh, I'm sorry, Steph. I'm trying not to, but it's just too funny. You confessing some huge wrongdoing in your past.' He looks into the camera again. 'I mean, you're a very highly respected G.P. You're classy, educated, sophisticated and clever.' His eyebrows go up and he looks sidelong at the camera. 'You're hardly going to tell me you once made a porno are you?'

'Jesus…!'

'See? See what I mean? The very idea! Or that you accidentally killed someone at uni? Or robbed a corner store with a fake gun? Or, I don't know, you've just got out after a ten stretch for fraud?'

'God, Jack, is that what you think of me?'

He tilts his head back. 'No! Steph! That's quite literally the opposite of what I think of you. What I'm saying is that your big confession that, in your opinion, might make me change my mind about falling for you – '

Breathe, Stephanie, just breathe.

' – is likely to be something like you cheated on your 'O' level cookery exam. Or you once walked past a homeless person without giving them a fiver. Or you cancelled a direct debit for a magazine subscription, without actually cancelling the – '

'I slept with your son.'

I slap my hand over my mouth and screw my eyes shut. When I open them again, he's looking at my face and not into the camera any more, so I can't really see the expression in his eyes. There's a protracted silence while he stares at me, and I stare at him.

'Sorry. I really didn't mean it to come out like that.'

He shakes his head. 'No, no, it's fine. I was wittering on, you had to grab your chance.'

'I wouldn't say wittering, exactly...'

'Well. Whatever it was. It was pretty endless. I just – ' He rubs his hand over his hair, tousling it up even more. 'I wanted to explain to you what a high opinion I have of you. Just so you knew that nothing you said would... change that. Nothing you could confess to would...' He tails off and looks away, and I feel my own energy draining away. I let my head flop back against the headboard.

'Except this, though. Right?'

He presses his lips together. 'Well... It's a very odd feeling, I can tell you that.'

'Yes, that's what I was expecting. That's why I had to tell you, before we...' I look away. 'You know.'

'In all honesty, I'm completely side-swiped. I'm blind-sided. I don't... I can't even think what to think.' He scratches his head, and it reminds me of Stanley Laurel. In fact, it actually looks like he's doing an impression of him. Then I blink and it's gone, and he looks into the camera again. 'Which son was it, exactly?'

I hadn't even thought about him having more than one. 'Oh God, of course. I didn't think about that.' I close my eyes. All I can do is hope his other son or sons are even younger than Ed, so when he hears Ed's name, he's relieved it wasn't twenty-three year old Gavin, or something. 'It was – '

'Wait!'

I stop. 'What? Don't you want to know? You'd rather never find out who it was?'

'No, no, that's not... No. Sorry, I just need to... pause you a moment. Because I need to tell you something first.'

'Oh Jack, really? Now?'

'Oh, yes, definitely now. Now is when it has to be. Now is absolutely the optimum, the most perfect, the topmost of the toppest moments to tell you.'

I peer at the screen, bringing the tablet nearer to my face. His eyes are all twinkly, and there's that suppressed smile again. What the hell?

'OK, go on. Tell me quickly, and then I'll tell you which son it was.'

Now he out and out grins. Oh God, he doesn't believe me. And that makes me feel worse, somehow. I definitely do not want to prove it to him with details only someone who's seen Ed naked would know.

'OK,' he says, leaning forward. 'Here it comes.' He props his tablet up against a fold in the bedding to free his hands so he can do a little drum roll with his index fingers. 'Here it is, gorgeous, complex, moral Stephanie.' He swallows. 'I....' (fingers drumming on the screen) '...don't have a son.'

I jerk back. 'Yes you do.'

He grins and looks into the camera again. 'No, no, I can honestly say that I'm not mistaken here.'

'Are you winding me up?'

'No! God, that would be cruel, wouldn't it? Of course I'm not.'

'Then... explain?'

He shakes his head. 'Explain what? I remember very clearly what children my ex-wife gave birth to that I'm responsible for.' He looks to the side. 'In fairness, she hasn't had any with anyone else, so there are only the two. And I changed enough of their nappies over the years to be very, *very* sure that they were both girls.'

'That makes no sense...'

'Maria and Polly.'

I'm shaking my head. 'But Niamh is your grand-daughter...'

'Yes, that's very true. But you don't have to have a son to have a grand-daughter.'

'No, but... Hold on.' I'm thinking back to the point where I found out that Ed's dad was Jack. 'He told me...'

Jack puts his hand up. 'OK, let's just go back to the beginning. Just exactly who was it that you slept with?'

'It was Niamh's dad.' I look at the camera now. 'Your son. Ed.'

Jack exaggeratedly rolls his eyes. 'Oh that little twerp. That's just typical of him, that is.'

'So you do know him?'

'Yeah, Stephanie, I know him. Of course I do, he's Niamh's dad.'

'Right.'

'My *daughter*, Polly, is Niamh's mum.'

It's so weird how things suddenly seem to come into focus. And it's ridiculously obvious to me now that of course Ed is not Jack's son. He couldn't possibly be. Jack is dark, with chocolate eyes and thick, black hair, albeit now heavily streaked with grey. He's refined and educated and so stylish, in his tight white tee-shirt and bare feet. Ed is…not. Lovely though he was, he had a penchant for slapping bottoms, calling women 'love', and referring to us all as 'girls'. How could I ever have thought they were related?

'But you were at Niamh's party, when I met Ed…'

He shrugs. 'I was invited, because it was her twenty-first, and it was a party. Apart from then, I hadn't seen Ed for, I don't know, fifteen years or something. The kids generally have two separate birthday celebrations – one with their mum and her family –' and he presses his palms against his chest, ' – and one with their dad and his family. I never see him, he's just someone I used to know.'

Relief surges through me like adrenaline, and I… No, wait. That *is* adrenaline. My heart is speeding up and I can definitely feel my pupils dilating. I slide down the bed a little more and half-close my eyes, then look directly into the camera.

'Haven't you left yet?' I ask him.

20
HUMAN

I've never noticed before how close the baby aisle is to the barbecue section. It's remarkably convenient. There's so much wonderful stuff here – tiny white sunhats and minuscule socks; bright plastic dolls and soft rubber rings; I feel like a kid in a sweet shop, surrounded by all of my favourite things. It's impossible to make a choice.

'Oh my God, there you are,' Nina says, coming around the corner. 'Have you been here all this time? I've been looking.'

I jump and move in front of the trolley. 'Nothing.'

Nina narrows her eyes. 'What is going on, Stephanie?'

She moves around me and peers into the trolley and we are both as surprised as each other to see a velvety pink unicorn with a shiny silver horn lying there at the bottom.

'I have no idea how that got there…'

'Oh don't be ridiculous. That is adorable. But we must get this food now, or we will run out of enough time.'

'Run out of time.'

'Yes, that's what I said.'

I didn't intend to make the barbecue Greek themed, but Nina offered to come with me to buy the food.

'You're going to help me prepare all this, right?' I ask her, as she tosses a couple of aubergines into the trolley. I have never used an aubergine for anything before.

'Yes, I will help you, yes,' Nina says, focussed on artichokes. 'We also need mint leaves. And cherry tomatoes. Oh, grab some cucumbers…'

An hour and half later, we unload everything out of the bags onto my kitchen sides.

'Your kitchen looks lovely,' Nina says, nodding slowly, running her hand along one of the edges. 'I like it very much. Who was that fittie?'

'Sorry? Which – ?' Ed pops into my head, standing on a ladder, his tee shirt riding up above his waistband…

'The fittie?' She indicates the kitchen around her. 'The one who did the kitchen.'

'My – ?' I've known Nina for over a decade but she still has the capacity to surprise me.

'Yes. Your kitchen fittie.'

Realisation erupts. 'Ohhh! You mean fitter. Kitchen *fitter.*'

'Yes, that's what I said.'

'I'll give you his number.'

I get my phone out to do that immediately before I forget, and find a text from Zoe. I'd forgotten until this morning that today is also her birthday, the birthday I've celebrated with her for the past thirty years, the birthday of my longest and best friend. How could I have so totally messed up? That's bad enough, but it's also her fiftieth, and I had been planning a day of fun surprises for her – a paddle-boarding lesson, a posh lunch, a theatre trip. But now it's all been postponed. Luckily it was only ever in my head so at least Zoe isn't disappointed. She's probably got some amazing thing planned for today anyway – I would have had to book her up weeks ago and I didn't. So instead I spent eight thousand pounds sending her some same day delivery flowers and champagne. I open the text.

'Thank you so much for my lovely booze and blooms,' she writes, poetic as always. 'What a lucky girl I am to have such an amazing thoughtful friend. XOXOXO'

Something seems a bit off. 'You're welcome Zo. Only the best for you. Xxxx'

'You so forgot didn't you?' She adds a 'crying with laughter face' at the end.

Which makes me feel instantly better. 'No?' I put the guilty eyes emoji on.

'Hahahaha don't worry about it I forgot I drove to work yesterday, got a lift home from a colleague, then simon had to drive me back to collect the car!'

'Omg what are we like?'

'Pair of forgetful dried up old hags!!'

'Might as well pack up our nighties and head to the nursing home now.'

'Hey not so fast, it's my birthday today! I'm going to enjoy it first.'

'Fair enough. See you there tomorrow then?'

'U have yourself a deal, lady. 😊 Now I'm off to paint the town beige!'

'Lucky girl. Have fun love you. Xxx'

'Love you too xxx'

I put Radio Two on, and Nina and I listen to Graham Norton solving people's awful family dramas while we put together a selection of delicious giant mezze platters using five big trays – pots of hummus, baba ganoush, muttabal, tabbouleh, and tzatziki; surrounded by toasted pitta bread triangles, olives of all colours and sizes, sliced spicy meats, boiled eggs, mounds of yellow and white cheeses, pink taramasalata, chopped cucumber, carrot batons, artichoke hearts, nuts, and bright red radishes and tomatoes. The food is colourful, heaped, and abundant, and looks deliciously decadent. I have lamb kebabs and spicy sausages lined up ready to go onto the barbecue when everyone gets here later, and two big bowls of green salad. I have no idea if anyone has any special dietary requirements, but I feel like I've covered it.

'I can't believe that woman thinks she has fallen in love with her daughter's husband,' Nina says, nodding towards the radio as she gets her coat on.

'I know, what a cow.'

She shrugs and turns at the door. 'You can't help who you fall in love with, though.'

'No, you can't, but that sounded like pure lust. They just need to walk away from each other forever.'

'I agree. But very tricky when he is her daughter's husband. She will see him at all the family occasions, won't she?'

'Yes that's true. They'll just have to control themselves, then, won't they?'

'I'd love to hear from them again in six months,' she says, smiling.

'Me too. I bet the family is broken apart.'

'Of course it will be.' She tuts and shakes her head. 'People are terrible.'

'They are.' I think about Jack. 'But not all.'

'No,' says Nina, reaching up to kiss my cheek goodbye, 'not all.'

'Won't you stay, Neen? After you've put so much work in?'

'Oh, thank you,' she says, taking off her coat again. 'I would love to.'

I blink. 'Oh, fantastic.'

'Is it OK to ask Georgio to come?' She goes back into the kitchen. 'Where's the wine?'

I put a hand up. 'Hold on one second – who's Georgio?'

She pauses in the process of unscrewing a bottle of rose, and beams at me. 'Oh Georgio is the wonderful man I'm going to spend the rest of my life with.' She presses her hand to her bosom as she speaks.

'What? I thought you were with someone called… What was it, Colin? Cyril?'

'Oh you mean Lucian? That silly boy who lived next door to Audrey's stepson?'

I have a quick think. Audrey's stepson, Audrey's stepson… Oh, yes, Teddy's secret son. Charlie. 'Um, yes, I think that was it…'

'Well that wasn't it. No way. Not him, that infant.' She beams over to the window. 'Georgio is a proper adult.'

'Right. And how long have you known Georgio?'

She swings round and narrows her eyes at me. 'It does not matter. When you love someone, the length of time is not material.'

'Yes, that's what you said last time.'

At four o'clock, the door goes and it's Happy Hannah and Bernie the Bench, looking a bit anxious. Hannah of course is smiling and serene, and gives me the most perfect hug and cheek kiss I've ever experienced, with no awkwardness or bad timing. We go in, we embrace, there's a kiss, we come out again.

Smooth. Bernie comes next, and he goes for a handshake while I'm moving in for a cheek press, and we fumble it badly, all hands and arms coming and going. We try again, with awkward fake laugh sounds, and this time only end up bumping heads. We pull back, both of us apologising and rubbing our bumps. Except Bernie is also trying to see if my head is OK, and is in the process of physically pulling my fingers away from my temple to inspect the damage.

'No, honestly Bernie, I'm absolutely fine...'

'Let me just have look though, need to make sure it's not swelling, head injuries nasty things...'

'For Heaven's sake, Bernie,' Hannah says gently, taking his hand, 'Stephanie is a doctor. I'm sure she can take care of herself.'

I show them into the kitchen and get them both a drink – white wine for her, orange juice on the rocks for him – then they wander out into the garden where Nina is sitting. I watch her get up to hug them both, before I'm called to the door again.

A woman is standing there, leaning across the little fence towards Graham's front door, apparently trying to peer into his window. She's a vision in salmon, apart from a pair of white sandals. As the door opens, she turns back to face me. 'Oh, hello. Is this the right place? For the *Life and Times* garden party?'

'It's more of a barbecue really...'

She turns back towards Graham's door. 'Wendy, it's all right, this is the place.'

A head pops out from around the far side of Graham's house. 'What did you say?' it says.

'It's here,' I tell them both. 'Come on in.'

'Ah.' The head moves forward, bringing with it a navy blue polo neck jumper and burgundy A-line skirt. 'Mrs. Wendy Forrester,' she says, as she walks across Graham's flowering beds. She arrives on the path next to me and holds out a hand.

'Stephanie Harkness.' I give her mine and she squeezes my fingers together as she forces it up and down a couple of times.

'Good to meet you, good to meet you.' She looks over my shoulder into the hallway. 'Now. Where do we go?'

'I'm Eileen,' says the woman in salmon, stepping forward at last. 'Eileen Cash.' She smiles. 'Like – '

'Like Johnny,' Wendy says at the same time, then flings her head back and laughs like a horse.

Eileen meets my eye and a moment of understanding passes between us. 'Yes,' she says. 'Like Johnny. Thank you, Wendy.'

'She always says that,' Wendy says to me, as if Eileen wasn't there. 'Makes that same joke every bloody time.'

I smile. 'It's an unusual name, Eileen. You're lucky to share it with someone so awesome.'

Eileen nearly faints with joy. 'Yes, yes, exactly, that's what I always think.'

'Oh good God,' says Wendy.

I point through the hallway towards the kitchen and garden. 'Right ladies, if you'd like to walk the line straight through to the kitchen, and my friend Nina will get you both a drink.'

Eileen sniggers as they both go through. I'm just closing the door when I hear a voice from outside. 'Are they gone?'

I pull it open again, and there stands Graham, glancing around. I give him a big smile. 'Good afternoon, Graham. How are you?'

'Never mind that. Have those two busy-bodies gone?'

'I don't know about any busy-bodies. What did they look like?'

He tuts. 'Bloody hell, course you do. They came this way. Peering in through my windows, tramping all over my begonias. I had to hide under the table.'

'Oh, you're talking about Wendy and Eileen – Hannah's two friends.' I incline my head towards the interior of the house. 'They're through there.'

'Hannah's friends?'

'Oh come on Graham,' I say, stepping back to let him come in, 'come and be friendly.' He hesitates, his eyes flicking back to his own door. 'Hannah's already here.'

'Oh, she is?' He steps forward. 'I hear you have a new kitchen?'

Out in the garden, Nina is apparently describing something very interesting, with the other four people standing in a u-shape around her on the lawn, watching intently. Their drinks are stationary in their hands as they stare, while Nina waves her arms and entire body around, almost dancing as she explains. Graham peers through the kitchen window at this strange tableau, then frowns and turns to me. 'Who's that?'

'That's my friend, Nina.'

There's an explosion of laughter outside, as Nina apparently reaches the climax of her story.

'She Greek?' says Graham.

I blink. 'Wow. Yes, she is. How did you work that out, Sherlock?'

Graham shrugs. 'Elementary, my dear Stephanie. This food,' he says, pointing at the mezze platters. 'I'm guessing she helped you prepare it. Her name, of course. And now she's dancing out her story to an audience. Typical Greek.'

'No, there's no such thing as a – '

'I brought some beers,' he says, lifting up a carrier bag that I hadn't noticed. 'Shall I stick them in the fridge?'

'Oh, that's kind of you, thank you. Yes please.'

He pulls three bottles of beer out of the bag, puts two into the fridge, and keeps one in his hand. I guess these aren't for general consumption then.

'Bottle opener?'

'Oh, yes, of course.' I get it from a drawer and give it to him, and after levering the cap off, he goes out into the garden and walks over to where Hannah and Bernie are sitting.

A few minutes later, Josh turns up with Dad and Audrey, and that's our eight people. Well, nine now, with Nina.

'Thanks for bringing them,' I tell Josh, giving him a hug in the kitchen. 'How's Chloe doing?'

'She's fine, Mum. Same as she was when you saw her a few days ago.' He picks up an olive from the mezze tray nearest to him. 'This food is amazing. Did you do it yourself?'

'With a lot of help from Nina. Oi, get your mitts off.'

'It looks absolutely fantastic.' He looks out of the window into the garden. 'They all seem to be bonding quite nicely, don't they?'

'Thanks. I thought eight would be about right – enough for everyone to find someone to chat with. Not so many that it's overwhelming.'

'But you've got nine.'

'Oh, yes, well, I asked Nina to stay at the last minute. Seeing as she helped with the food.'

He eyes the five giant platters. 'You know you've got far too much food here for nine people.'

'Oh, do you think?'

'God, yes, definitely. This would feed fifteen people at least. Especially if you've got barbie stuff too.' He pauses, as if he's waiting for something.

'What?'

'What?'

'Josh. I can tell you're thinking something. Out with it.'

He grins. 'Well, I was just thinking, we haven't got anything organised for dinner yet today. You have nine people, enough food for fifteen, and Chloe's eating for six at the moment, so…'

Panic fills me. Of course I'd love Josh and Chloe to be here, stay for the afternoon, even have the spare room overnight. I'd like nothing more. But this is supposed to be a *Life Times* event, people are supposed to be in a small, comfortable group, chatting, getting to know each other, and, with any luck, forming a meaningful connection with another person. In my head I've been picturing a scene from a film where elegantly dressed people are sitting around a table, talking quietly, while candlelight glints on the cutlery. This is already quite a long way away from my imagining, and two more will take the group up to eleven, more than Hannah and I decided. If it gets any bigger, people will find it difficult to enjoy themselves. I glance out of the window and spot Bernie apparently using Nina as a ventriloquist's dummy, while Eileen and Hannah are holding their tummies laughing. Oh. OK.

'I mean, I didn't expect you to have to deliberate for quite as long as that…'

'No, no, I'm sorry, Josh, I was just thinking about numbers. But please stay. I'd love that.'

'Great! I'll text Chlo.'

'Got any burgers?' Dad says at this point, eyeing the platters.

When Chloe turns up twenty minutes later, she's got Amy and Mona with her. There's a lot of noise and bustle as they come in, hugging Dad, talking, interrupting, shoving each other, throwing casual insults. In the garden they go from person to person, shaking hands, chatting a little to each one, making them smile. I watch from the window and feel a surge of love for everyone there, even Wendy, who is currently inspecting the underside of one of my 'fake boulder' solar lights. But it doesn't matter because everyone is smiling and relaxed, the sun is shining, and we have got enough Greek food to feed a Trojan horse.

Either Amy or Chloe has brought Twister, and they set it up on the lawn. Nina jumps up – 'Let me go first!' – and Josh brings my kitchen chairs outside so everyone can sit and watch. Chloe comes and stands by me with a glass of sparkling elderflower presse, and I feel closer to her than I ever have, knowing that she has my little grand-daughter Stephanette curled up in there.

'You OK?' I ask her.

She nods. 'I'm absolutely fine, Steph. Blood pressure is fine, blood sugar is fine, no proteins in the urine, baby's heart rate is good...'

'That's good to know, but not really what I meant.' She looks at me. 'I'm not asking as a doctor. I'm asking as your mother-in-law. As the baby's grandmother.' I squeeze her arm. 'As someone who loves you.'

'I knew that.' We both grin. 'So, yeah, I'm fine. I mean, I'm not really getting that blooming feeling everyone talks about in the second trimester, and I'm tired, and my feet ache.'

'Oh no.'

She shrugs. 'Doesn't matter. It's worth it, isn't it?'

I look over at Amy and Josh, balanced on their hands and feet, Amy half twisted onto her side, Josh making an arch with his body over the top of Nina, and nod. 'Oh yes. Every second.'

The game is very tense, with Josh, Amy, Mona and Nina all trying to fit on and eventually when Amy spins a hand on a blue dot, she has to reach just a bit too far to get there and the whole human pyramid collapses into a hysterical pile of arms and legs. The door goes again and I drag myself away to let in a dark haired, dark eyed man who kisses me on both cheeks and puts a huge silver platter stacked with delicate pastry baklavas into my hands.

'I am Georgio,' he announces.

'Good to meet you, Georgio. I am Stephanie.' I have no idea why I'm announcing myself like that too. 'Come on through.'

'Ah, Stephanie, I hear about you. You are good friend to Nina. Very good friend.' And he wraps his arms around me again, almost making me drop the baklavas. He steps back. 'And so good friend to me, too.'

'Oh, good, that's lovely then.'

'I am going to marry her,' he says conversationally, as we walk through the kitchen. 'She is love of my life.'

'Well, that's great, but you've only known her a few – '

'We have been betrothed since we are children,' he says.

'What?'

'This food is excellent, Stephanie. I think maybe Nina helped you with this?'

'No, no, go back a bit. You're... *betrothed*?'

He waves a hand. 'Oh, it's not so old-fashioned. We are not forced to marry. But if we want, we can do it.' He turns and grins at me, showing beautiful white teeth and heart-stopping dark eyes. 'I want to. I have wanted to for thirty years.' He shrugs. 'Nina wanted to try out some others first I think. But now...' He turns to look at Nina, lying on her back on the grass, laughing. 'Now she is ready, yes?'

I don't know whether to be elated for her, or bloody livid that she had gorgeous Greek Georgio up her sleeve this entire time without telling me. Introducing me to the *Butterflies* app. Listening to my horror stories. Advising me to keep going anyway. And I did, in spite of my misgivings, because she was so adamant it was the way to meet people at our age. Georgio is striding across the grass towards her now, and as she sees him her face beams like a floodlight, lighting up the lawn. She gets to her feet instantly, smoothing down her hair and dress, locking eyes with him, melting into his embrace when he reaches her.

The cow.

The seated guests seem to think this is the happy ending to some love story and burst into spontaneous applause. Someone has brought a speaker out into the garden and at this point *Jump Around* by House of Pain starts playing. Amy and Mona start, well, jumping around, and then Bernie the Bench gets up off his seat and joins in, waving his arms in the air and hopping from foot to foot. Amy and Mona laugh, and the three of them throw themselves into it, each one completely un-self-conscious, enjoying the moment absolutely.

'Is Bernie drunk?' Dad asks me, as we watch the man cavort.

'Nope, he's been on orange juice since he got here.'

'What's wrong with him, then?'

'Dad! Nothing's wrong with him. He's just feeling happy, I suppose.'

Dad stares at Bernie in silence for a while. 'Odd.'

'Why odd? Amy and Mona are dancing too.'

'Well, yes, I know that. It's just... A man of Bernie's age. Behaving like that. A widower.'

'Why shouldn't he? He's feeling happy now, in this moment. Maybe later he won't be, but right now, he's not a sad widower who has been levelled by his wife's death. Right now he's just a man, enjoying the feeling of dancing to music, with friends.' I turn to face Dad. 'There's nothing wrong with that.'

Dad doesn't say anything, but I can see him thinking about what I've said. Eventually he nods slowly, gets up and walks to where Audrey is sitting. He takes her hand and pulls her up and they move together onto the lawn, Audrey looking back at us over her shoulder. And then, right there on the lawn, in front of his daughter and his grandchildren, and a whole host of other people he doesn't know, my dad starts dancing to *Shake it Off*, by Taylor Swift.

My phone vibrates in my pocket and when I look at it I've got a text from Jack.

'I heard there's a party going on.'

'Where did you hear that?'

'It's pretty obvious from out here.'

'Out where?' I stand up and go back in through the double doors, making my way slowly through the house. The grey speech bubble is there telling me that Jack is replying, and after a few seconds his message appears.

'Out here at your front door. You gonna let me in or what?'

He's not alone. 'I didn't think you'd mind if I brought them,' he says, lightly touching my hand as he comes in. 'The more the merrier, right?'

'Hi Steph,' Niamh and Steve say simultaneously, leaning in together and each kissing one of my cheeks.

'Hi you two. Thanks for coming.'

'Thanks for having us.' They move as one, hand in hand, out into the garden, and add two more people to the crowd out there. By now I've lost count of how many people are here, but I realise it doesn't matter. There are people in their eighties, and people in their fifties, and people in their twenties, all dancing around together, all feeling the same age in their heads. Enjoying the moment, loving life, even just for this short period. My phone buzzes again in my hand and when I look, it's a message from Zoe.

'U wanna press charges against Tim for attempted theft?'

I blink in surprise, as the words shoot into my expanding euphoria balloon like a dart. It hadn't even occurred to me that Tim could be prosecuted for making off with Harry, and immediately I type, 'Can I?' Harry was only with me because Tim left him, so would it be theft if Tim had simply come to get him?

'We cd have a go,' she writes. 'If he was reclaiming his own property, he wd just have asked u surely? The fact he snatched H while u weren't looking is clear indication that he didn't truly believe H was his property.'

'Good point.'

'Might not run, but we could make him think it was gonna.'

'Put the frighteners on him, you mean?'

'Lol yeah!'

I think about it for a tenth of a nanosecond, then type 'Hell yes let's make the bastard pay.' But before I click 'send', I stare at the words a few moments, my thumb stroking the button. I look up at the garden, to the bright colours flashing and the faces grinning and the joy bursting out of everyone, and my initial savage lust for revenge trickles away. What would be the point? There would be stuff I'd have to do, taking up my time; and things between Tim and me would descend yet further into acrimony. The one positive would be Tim suffering, even a tiny bit, but Josh and Amy would suffer too, and I will give up my life before I knowingly let that happen.

There's a low bark from the garden, and I start a little, worried someone's had a fall or is choking or having some kind of episode. I quickly scan all the knees and hips, but thankfully find nothing out of order; and then I realise that it's just Harry, waving his tail and bouncing a bit among the dancers. My face stretches with a grin and my euphoria bubble inflates again. Harry isn't property, anyway. He's family.

I delete the message and instead type 'Nah, he's not worth the effort. Thanks for the offer though.'

'Thought you'd say that!'

I'm very glad Zoe has such a great view of me. I seem to have successfully duped her for over thirty years.

'Wanna come round?' I type, on impulse. 'It seems I'm having a little party, would love to see you on your birthday. Bring Simon.' It's definitely a party now, anyway, and I know she will enjoy the dancing. 'Make up for the shit present.' The grey bubble appears on my phone screen, so I wait for her reply.

'Come and dance with me,' Jack says, putting his hand out.

I look up and smile. 'Two minutes, then I'll be there.'

'OK, but I may have to start without you…'

I giggle. 'Now that I would love to see.'

I walk out to the patio and feel the warmth of the spring evening on my skin. The music is still playing but it's something I don't recognise. It doesn't matter though because now Eileen is dancing with Bernie, and they're doing some kind of old fashioned jive, Eileen's salmon skirt flaring out around her, showing off her rather fabulous legs. I worry about injuries, but we can cross that bridge when – and if – we come to it. Bernie is flushed and shiny, but his feet in his black patent shoes are almost a blur, twisting and kicking as he picks Eileen up and puts her down again. Everyone else has paused in their own activity to watch, and all around me I can see faces lit with delight. Everyone looks so happy and full of life, and I feel privileged to have been able to bring this about.

Finally my phone buzzes in my hand and I look down at the message to see if my wonderful friend Zoe will be joining us, on the day she's lucky enough, after fifty years, to have reached this most magical age of all.

'I'd love to hun,' it says, 'but I'm afraid I'm busy right now. Simon's just about to take me up the Shard.'

THE END

ABOUT THE AUTHOR

Beth has been writing since she was child, and has had four previous novels published. Check out her other works, also available on Amazon:

CARRY YOU
HIS OTHER LIFE

She has also written two books in her own name of Debbie Carbin:

THANKS FOR NOTHING NICK MAXWELL
THREE MEN AND A MAYBE

Printed in Great Britain
by Amazon